Cassandra's Web

Sometimes a storm in your life is what will blow you to the place you are longing to be.

Beth Moore

Contents

CHAPTER 1. BEHIND CLOSED DOORS - Cassandra 6

CHAPTER 2. TAINTED LOVE - Cassandra 9

CHAPTER 3. PRESERVING THE SCENE - Cassandra 15

CHAPTER 4. PRIVATE INVESTIGATIONS - Cassandra 21

CHAPTER 5. THIS INTERVIEW IS BEING TAPE RECORDED - Cassandra 27

CHAPTER 6. CHEERS TONY. - Cassandra 37

CHAPTER 7. THE PUPPET MASTER – Paul Melville Grainger 43

CHAPTER 8. SECONDS AWAY - Cassandra................................ 48

CHAPTER 9. PASSAGE OF TIME – Cassandra Weaver - 1992 55

CHAPTER 10. WHO AM I NOW? – Tracy Brown 1995 65

CHAPTER 11. MINARD ROAD – Tansy Alexander 2004 73

CHAPTER 12. ALL TRUST BETRAYED – Tansy................................ 84

CHAPTER 13. THE BOTTOM – Tansy 92

CHAPTER 14. SINK OR SWIM – Cassandra................................ 101

CHAPTER 15. THE SHOEBOX – Siobhan Williams 115

CHAPTER 16. UNFOLDING MY LIFE – Siobhan 122

CHAPTER 17. AMONGST THE DUST – Siobhan............................ 126

CHAPTER 18. A MATTER OF DISCLOSURE - Siobhan....................... 134

CHAPTER 19. THE SISTERHOOD 143

CHAPTER 20. BUGS AND LOW LIFE 152

CHAPTER 21. OBSERVATIONS REQUESTED – Bruce Wayne............... 164

CHAPTER 22. THE TRAIN TAKES THE STRAIN – Tansy 172

CHAPTER 23. DADDY – Siobhan 179

CHAPTER 24. PAYBACK – Peter Balfour 189

CHAPTER 25. THE NARK – Peter Balfour 198

CHAPTER 26.	DINNER FOR TWO	208
CHAPTER 27.	UNIT 42	216
CHAPTER 28.	OPERATION RAGWORT.	226
CHAPTER 29.	JULIA GRAINGER	234
CHAPTER 30.	POLICE, POLICE, POLICE!	241
CHAPTER 31.	ONCE MORE UNTO THE BREACH	248
CHAPTER 32.	CAST ADRIFT- Tansy	259
CHAPTER 33.	CLIENT CONFIDENTIALITY – Ray Williams	265
CHAPTER 34.	THE RAIN IN SPAIN – Paul Melville Grainger	273
CHAPTER 35.	PLUNGED INTO DARKNESS – Tansy	279
CHAPTER 36.	RETRIBUTION – Lenny Smith	293
CHAPTER 37.	SPANISH FLY	301
CHAPTER 38.	HELP AND RESCUE - Tansy	310
CHAPTER 39.	STRANGERS IN THE NIGHT - Tansy	321
CHAPTER 40.	SPANISH INQUISITION	330
CHAPTER 41.	AN APARTMENT TO DIE FOR	337
CHAPTER 42.	THE DEATH OF HECTOR PARRAL	344
CHAPTER 43.	A GREAT DISAPPOINTMENT	358
CHAPTER 44.	AN UNEXEPECTED PACKAGE - Cassandra	366
CHAPTER 45.	GOTCHA	377
CHAPTER 46.	NOT STRICTLY LEGIT – Ray Williams	385
CHAPTER 47.	WE CAN BE HEROES -Sarah James	391
CHAPTER 48.	IT'S ALL IN THE NEWS – Bruce Wayne	397
CHAPTER 49.	FOR OLD TIMES SAKE – Bruce Wayne	402
CHAPTER 50.	THE BREAKFAST SHOW	412
CHAPTER 51.	QUITE FRANKLY - Tansy	420

CHAPTER 52. OPTIONS – Tansy 427

CHAPTER 53. ASHES TO ASHES 436

CHAPTER 54. AND NOTHING BUT THE TRUTH 442

CHAPTER 55. DREAM CATCHER - Tansy 448

CHAPTER 56. EVERYTHING COMES TO THOSE WHO WAIT 454

GLOSSARY OF ABBREVIATIONS 458

ACKNOWLEDGEMENTS 459

COPYRIGHT 460

OTHER WORKS BY THE AUTHOR 461

1992

CHAPTER 1. BEHIND CLOSED DOORS - Cassandra

Bristol 1992

Sandra Weaver's hands shook as she leaned on the kitchen counter. If things carried on, then one of them was going to die; she was damned if it was going to be her, not today anyway.

As she turned, her voice was became a whisper, 'No Tony, No. I will not live like this anymore.' The words hissed between her cracked and bleeding lips, hissed with all the venom she could muster.

She was wedged in the corner of the cupboards, her back against the bespoke wooden worktop. Her usually immaculate highlighted blonde hair fell in unwashed, greasy strands from its scrunchie, while mascara streamed down her tired face. Snot and blood ran from her bruised nose. Her left eye was swelling rapidly; in a few minutes, she would not be able to see out of it. She felt slightly sick as she wiped her hands down the thighs of her Levi's, noticing her bare feet and the broken glass strewn over the floor.

'You will live how I fucking well say! You will do as I fucking tell you.'

His huge hand grabbed her hair, pulling her forward onto the waiting fist which punched the wind from her fashionably thin body. Sandra sank slowly to the floor, her knees crumbling as her breath was forced from her body.

'Now clean this fucking mess up. Look at the state of this place, it's worse than a fucking pigsty.'

'No self-respecting pig would live here.' Fear kept the words silent As he turned and walked away from her previously unspoken words she slipped from her lips.

'Fuck you, clean it up yourself, you fucking, sadistic bastard.'

Dragging herself to her feet, she reached behind her. Finding the stone pestle and mortar within reach, she grabbed the edge of the mortar just as he began to turn back towards her. His face was no longer glowing with rage, it was pallid grey with fury.

Tony's entire body was shaking, his eyes were bloodshot, and the pupils dilated. All reason had left him, but Sandra was damned if her life would end like this.

She launched the mortar at Tony's head, her arm strengthened by pure adrenaline and regular gym. The heavy stone bowl fell slightly short, glancing off Tony's huge shoulder, and falling with a crash onto the floor, cracking another of the expensive slate slabs. The blow did not stop his advance. In panic, she reached behind her again, this time finding the wooden block containing Tony's precious chefs' knives – professional kitchen knives, sharp enough to cut a falling sheet of paper.

The boning knife was first to hand. Sandra wrapped her fingers around the handle and held it with both hands in front of her, the point shaking visibly as her husband of four years bore down on her.

Sandra would tell the Police later that, at that moment she had believed she would die, that she had felt a genuine fear for her life. She thrust the knife upwards, and felt it penetrate Tony's slim-fit designer label T-shirt, before slicing through his skin. Just like stabbing a joint of pork she thought, at first. Then the point pierced the skin. Then there was blood, at first just an ooze from where the handle of the knife stuck out, of his abdomen just below his ribs.

Then, there was a lot of blood. It ran around his hand where he clutched at the black wooden handle. Tony's eyes opened wide with surprise as he fell forward, his right hand still reaching out for his wife's neck. His sixteen stone frame of carefully built muscle wilted onto the glass and crockery-strewn floor.

She sat cradling her husband's dark head in her lap as he bled out on the floor in front of her, that peculiar but unmistakeable smell beginning to trouble her senses. It was not until she reached for her mobile phone from the wooden countertop of the island unit that she realised that four small eyes, two brown and two blue, were watching her.

'Oh my god, my babies, what will happen to my babies?' The words hung silent on her lips. The thought unspoken.

The call connected in three rings.

'You have dialled 999. Which emergency service do you need?'

The operator recited the opening script as Sandra waited patiently before answering.

'Police please.'

The operator was heard connecting the call,

'Police? I am connecting a call from a mobile number 07682 587692. Caller you are through to the Police.'

A second voice was then heard on the line,

'Police, what is your emergency caller?'

'I think I've killed my husband.'

'What is your address caller?' The dispatcher's voice sounded ice cool

She heard herself give her address before hearing a further dispatcher click onto the line advising the first that an *'ambulance is enroute.'* This last piece of information was an aside to the main dispatcher, a signal not only that the Ambulance service had the call but that a third person was listening in.

She gave her name, and her date of birth, then provided the code for the big, electric security gates. She advised them that the back door would be open and, when prompted, she confirmed that there was no dog at the address. Then she sat and waited for them all to arrive.

While waiting, Sandra poured herself a large measure from Tony's bottle of 12-year-old Malt Whisky, using one of the last unbroken Edinburgh Crystal glasses. She slowly sipped the liquor, letting the potent amber liquid trickle down her throat.

With a small, sad smile on her face, she raised the glass in the air, thinking, *'Cheers Tony'*. The toast was a silent one, but the hidden camera fitted in the LED spotlight over the kitchen door caught it all.

From their hiding place in the cupboard under the island unit, the place they loved to use as a house for their dolls and teddies, Amy and Charlotte crawled over to their mother, knowing that *'Mummy needs us, Mummy sad again.'*

CHAPTER 2. TAINTED LOVE - Cassandra

'Cassandra Weaver, I am arresting you on suspicion of the murder of Anthony Weaver. You do not have to say anything, but it may harm your defence if you do not mention anything now which may be used in your defence and anything you do say may be given in evidence.'

Police Constable Phillip Hayes was very young in service, he stuttered over the words, obviously nervous at the magnitude of what he was about to do. The caution was an invitation to speak, to give some form of explanation, but where would she ever start.

As the crime scene officers set about preserving any evidence which might be on her body, she was searched, roughly. The hatchet-faced female officer Detective Constable Erica White took little care for her privacy.

'I am going to search you. Do you have anything on you which could harm either yourself or others, including us? If you do, be assured, I will find it.' The threat was veiled, but it was there.

Sandra said nothing. She took one look at the searching officer. '*Butch cow,*' she thought. '*Bet she wears comfortable shoes,*' but she surrendered to the search without fuss. Sandra said nothing. She knew that she would surrender all her jewellery, her watch, her wedding and engagement rings, her dignity, and her sanity before too long.

Hands and feet wrapped in plastic bags, she was restrained in handcuffs behind her back and unceremoniously escorted to the waiting police van. She knew the score, there would be no comfort in the back of a plain car for her. The hard plastic washable seat of the cage hit the back of her calf muscle and a rough pressure on her shoulder forced her to sit. The metal door slammed shut and she heard the crackle of a radio going live. P.C. Hayes spoke.

'Foxtrot Bravo One One, enroute with one violent female in custody on suspicion of murder.'

'Roger Foxtrot Bravo One One.' The radio controller repeated his callsign.

Then the message passed on, 'Whiskey Lima to Central. Foxtrot Bravo unit enroute, one drunk and violent female suspicion of murder.' Violent! Drunk! The words echoed in her mind, she was neither of those things, but if that what they expected, that's what they would get.

Already she felt dehumanised, reduced from a person to an animal. The tiny confines of the cage started to close in on her, becoming more and more claustrophobic. Sense said she could not fight it. Her wrists burned with pain, the arresting officer had forgotten to double lock the handcuffs, a training school mistake. An error from him, a painful experience for her. The bracelets of the rigid cuffs tightened as her arms instinctively pulled to get free of them.

Pain shot up her elbows and through her shoulders. She screamed. No one listened. They were used to prisoners screaming. It was all part of the process. The van took a corner slightly too fast. The momentum threw her from her seat. With no hands to break her fall she hit her head on the door and landed on the filthy floor of the transport van. For her own safety she wriggled herself into the space under the seat and wedged herself in, all the time listening to the conversation being had in the front.

Sandra knew both the driver and his colleague. She had worked with them, socialised with them, counted them at one time as friends. But then so had Tony. She could expect no favours from any of the 'boys' network'. Wrapping one leg round the metal stanchion supporting the seat, she tried to rest her head on her own shoulder, a vain attempt to find some comfort for the half hour journey to Central Bridewell.

It was a journey she had driven herself many times, but under far different circumstances. In her mind's eye she knew every traffic light, every roundabout, every speed bump and every pothole. As the driver made unnecessary changes up and down the gearbox and overzealously applied the brakes, she felt every twist and every turn, as if she was in a washing machine without the benefit of the water. Every jolt was designed to hurt.

Then they stopped. The driver's window opened, and she could envisage the huge, barbed wire topped gates to the walled yard opening at the buzz of a button. Like a stunt driver from a low-budget cops and robbers movie, the driver reversed up to the reinforced and double locked steel door which was under an illuminated sign announcing **CUSTODY OFFICE**.

The vehicle stopped allowing just enough room to open the rear doors, forming a neat pen between the doors and the wall of the building. She heard the driver buzzing the back door and waiting for a response. She heard the muffled words, '*drunk, violent*' repeated and knew that there would be a reception committee. She knew what was about to happen. She had seen it done often enough, but to recalcitrant drunks who would feel nothing through the haze of alcohol. Sandra had drunk precisely one large glass of whisky. She was not in her view drunk, though a custody officer might view it differently and probably would.

The inner cage door of the van flew open and two large sets of hands belonging to two large male police officers seized her by the shoulders and the legs and, despite her struggles, carried her bodily face down into the passage. The familiar sight of the pale blue heavy duty linoleum flooring and the mushroom-coloured walls flashed before her eyes and the accompanying smell of microwaved food, unwashed bodies and stale urine filled her nostrils. Instinctively her feet paddled in the air, her shoulders burned with pain and her wrists felt as though they would snap. She wished that they would, that might be less painful. She pleaded that they were hurting her, but no one took a blind bit of notice. Sandra Weaver was now a statistic, just another body to be processed.

They finally stood her on her feet in front of a desk which was at the level of her chest. Sergeant Mike Harris, the custody sergeant, looked at her in a pitying manner. He had been her Sergeant when she had joined the job all of ten years ago. She thought that he should really have retired by now, but here he was, still in command of his desk. He looked sternly at the officers restraining her.

'Arresting officer?'

Police Constable Phillip Hayes stepped proudly forward. This was to be his moment of glory.

'Circumstances?'

Hayes related the facts as he had been told to. Now he had a real live arrest for murder under his belt. Something to tell the lads on his next probationer training course. But why him? He was pleased to have the collar, pleased to be involved in a big case, but not sure why they had allowed him to make the arrest, under the circumstances.

'Okay Cassandra, Mrs Weaver, do you have anything to say?' Sergeant Harris spoke. He used her full name, not its more friendly abbreviation.

Sandra enquired reasonably 'My girls, who has my girls?'

'Don't worry, luv, they will be better off without you!' some wag passing through commented, a spectator eager for a snippet of gossip to take back to the canteen. There was always someone eager to gloat about a colleague's downfall.

This had the desired effect. Already totally overwrought, Sandra lost all control.

'What are they doing with my fucking kids, sarge?' She struggled to get free, kicking out at the officers holding her arms, her head went backwards as she hawked up a mouthful of phlegm. Before she could aim it at any of her captors, her arms were pulled back, she was bent at the waist and once more placed face down. She heard a voice, an instruction shouted only inches from her ear.

'Cell 13 and strip her. Bag her clothing.'

They did not give her a chance to undress herself. She was not asked to cooperate. She was not given a chance. Within seconds a number of detention officers had arrived and she was pinned on the rock-hard floor of the cell, her clothing and jewellery removed, her hands and feet swabbed for evidence, of what she was not sure, and she was left, naked, on the blue sparkly cell flooring, with only a plastic covered mattress, a rip proof blanket and what she used to call a suicide suit - a thick two piece padded garment with no seams, no waistband, and no shape. And the bastards had taken a box cutter to her favourite jeans. Was nothing fucking sacred. Suicide suits were supposed to be cleaned between uses, but Sandra knew that they weren't always, and this one had probably been taken from the pile of dirty ones waiting for the laundry. She dreaded to think whose flakes of dead skin were embedded in its seams.

There had been a time when she and her colleagues had joked that they would never ever dress in one of those. Well, she still would not, she wrapped herself in the blanket and sat on the mattress which she laid on the floor behind the cell door out of sight of the surveillance camera. The adrenaline was wearing off, she was getting cold.

After about half an hour she had calmed down sufficiently to think of pressing the intercom buzzer and asking for some clothing. She was not suicidal. She should be allowed clothing. She knew that there was a stock of cheap sweatpants and T shirts kept for that purpose. She remembered the days before such things were kept as stock, when she had loaned a lady in exactly her circumstances her personal tracksuit so that she could appear decent in front of the magistrate in the morning. Those days were gone. '*Bing, Bong*' the intercom sounded but no one answered, '*Bing Bong*' it went again, still no one came. Well, if they weren't going to come and see her then at least they could cancel the alarm. She pressed the buzzer again.

It seemed like hours later, after she had worked out that the intercom sounded just like the tune by the band 'Soft Cell', the one called 'Tainted Love', the riff was just the same. Ironic that. A different Custody Sergeant came to the hatch. The advice was terse.

'Calm down and try and get some kip or its going to be a very long night for both of us. Don't buzz again. Room service is cancelled until the morning.'

Then he stumped off back to his desk leaving the lights in her cell on the brightest setting and failing to cancel the intercom. Sandra watched through the gap in the hatch as his fat arse and huge gut wobbled up the cell corridor. '*Fat bastard*', she thought. She suppressed the tears which started to well up. No self-pity Sandra. Suck it up girl, you are better than this, her inner voice told her.

Sandra curled up naked under her rip proof blanket, she knew she was in a camera cell, well she hoped that the perverted bastards had gotten a good eyeful. Time ticked by slowly and Sandra saw every second of it. Her eye was swollen shut, her body was bruised and aching all over. At least, she told herself, 'I am still alive.'

Bing Bong – Tainted love. *Bing Bong* - Tainted Love. Touch me... please............

CHAPTER 3. PRESERVING THE SCENE - Cassandra

By early afternoon the whole police circus had arrived at The Laurels. The large electric gates were permanently open to admit search teams, crime scene investigators and detectives. The pantechnicon which housed equipment from ball point pens and paper suits to thermal imaging cameras was reversed neatly onto the block paved driveway. The house was now unoccupied, the two little girls had been taken by social services. Their father was dead and their mother locked up in a police cell.

In the cul-de-sac outside, curtains twitched as the stay-at-home mums with children at school were distracted from their tedium by the rumble of the cavalcade of law and order making camp outside the Weavers' house.

Detective Chief Superintendent David Holly was the appointed Senior Investigating Officer. He had hoped to wind down his career in the comfort of his oak panelled office in the upper floor of the police station, but another detection was another notch on his truncheon. Literally, he had kept his old hardwood truncheon with its lathe turned handgrip and leather strap, the one he had been issued with well over thirty years ago. He had been issued with a newfangled extending telescopic beating stick, as he called it, at his last fitness refresher. Senior officers were not exempt from one day of torture a year. Holly had kept his old wooden truncheon and engraved a name on the item in question for every murder his team had detected. There was always room for one more. Holly was long in service and experience and short on protocol. Tie the loose ends up quickly and neatly. Tuck in the corners, cut a few if you can. He loved a shortcut. His briefing with Detective Inspector Ron Ashton and Detective Sergeant Terry Larkin had been exactly that. Brief.

'She's admitted it, let's not make a meal of it, I aim to be done in a week, disgrace to the job, make sure she gets what she deserves.'

Holly had brooked no argument and Ashton knew from previous encounters it was pointless to argue. He would do what needed to be done. In his bones he knew this case had the potential to bite him in the proverbial. It could also embarrass the force in years to come. Red faces all round, huge headlines in the gutter press. Another IPCC enquiry. But by then Holly would be sipping his G & T on his Spanish veranda, shorts and sandals on, feet up and laughing at the mess he had left behind. The sun would be over the yard arm, it must be six o'clock somewhere! Detective Chief Superintendent Holly had a cupboard full of skeletons, all waiting for their day of resurrection. Ashton did not intend to be part of the fallout.

The nondescript small blue van pulled up to the rear of the house. Two men wearing blue jeans and sweatshirts climbed out and the passenger opened the rear doors. The driver reached in and pulled out a black and yellow toolbox. An unremarkable looking man, you would never spot Detective Constable Mark Jones in a crowd, he was a grey man. Early forties, mid brown hair, average height, average build, he wore cheap clothes, a la High Street, a New York Yankees baseball cap pulled down over his eyebrows. His partner Detective Constable Ian Rogers was a similarly nondescript.

'In and out quick then, Ian.' Jones turned and headed for the back door of The Laurels.

'If SOCO find our kit we're fucked. Best clear it out while we can, salvage something at least.'

Ian pulled an empty canvas holdall from the van. Both men then climbed into the standard issue white suits and bootees. Hoods up and hands encased in blue latex protective gloves, business like they breezed past the uniformed officer protecting the scene and went about their work.

Both men had intimate knowledge of The Laurels. They had been there before. They knew the lay out of every room, every hidden nook and cranny. It took them all of half an hour to retrieve most of what they had come for. Wires were pulled through ducting and stowed away. Cameras and microphones were disconnected and if they could not be retrieved with ease, wires were cut and they were disabled and abandoned, never to be found, unless the building was demolished, or the odd wall knocked down. They made their exit via the front door, nodding in a nonchalant manner to P.C. Amanda Thomas who guarded the door in the manner of a recumbent bulldog.

'We are done.' Ian winked at the bulldog and waved an ID card at her, as they departed. They left too quickly for her to log their names, not to worry, she hadn't logged them in either. That would have been too much of an effort. She had recognised them as being that species of policeman who were invisible by their nature, from a department those on her pay grade had no knowledge of. There was nothing left to suggest that they had ever been on the premises. No prints, no mess, no DNA. No awkward evidence.

Sarah James was bored with the standard briefing about health and safety at work, she'd heard it all before, after all, many times. She stood on the metal steps to the mobile office at the rear of the pantechnicon. She had recognised the blue van as it pulled onto the plot. She didn't recognise the occupants, but she knew what they did. She said nothing but filed the information away. It may be useful, later. Pound to a pinch of it they would have had to leave something behind. Her office was next to the one occupied by their boss. She had heard the budgetary tantrums over lost equipment, expensive kit abandoned possibly to be found and resurrected by others, betraying the secrets of their dark world. It was an occupational hazard, but not one Detective Inspector Wayne swallowed easily. It didn't salve his temper much when his team flippantly called him Batman. What the fuck had his mother been thinking of or was it his father who was to blame for christening him Bruce? Whatever, it was he who had to put up with the jibes about Gotham city. *'Caped Crusader, my arse'*, she heard him muttering to himself through the wall. Well, thought Sarah, it was a good thing he had a sense of humour.

Maybe this was something that could help her old friend in a crisis. Sarah James never forgot a friend, and Sandra Weaver had been more than a friend to her on occasion. Over her shoulder she heard Ron Ashton bring his briefing to a close and swallowing the last dregs of her cold, machine produced coffee, she snapped out of her reverie and returned to business.

'Sarah James! Sarah, your team have the kitchen, get on it.' Ron's voice of command prodded her into action.

The Weavers' kitchen was unlike any kitchen Sarah had ever seen before. Outrageously high spec, all granite tops, slate floors, the doors were solid wood finished with some high sheen substance. No Formica here. No expense spared. *How on earth did Tony Weaver afford all this*? She raised a cynical eyebrow and started work.

The contents of the cupboards painted a picture of a high-end lifestyle. The crockery was Villeroy and Bosch, stylish, tasteful white with just a hint of colour. There was another set for the kids she hoped, cheaper, probably sourced from home bargains or a similar discount store. More resilient against accidental damage.

The glasses in the display cabinets were Dartington or Edinburgh, the few that were left were the Thistle pattern. Sarah recognised it, she had coveted those glasses and had drunk many a post work glass of wine from them, in another house, in another time. Now all but four were in a million shards of glass on the floor.

She opened a cupboard, curious as to the contents. The groceries, tins, and packets behind the sleek solid wood doors were arranged in alphabetical order. The health foods and gym supplements in separate cupboards all similarly indexed. The chicken nuggets and fish fingers which occupied the freezer were all in careful order, not shoved in the trays in haphazard fashion, like most busy couples would do. Weird.

'Photograph all of it! No, I want a video walk through. Show the contents of the cupboards, this is all very, *'Sleeping with the Enemy.'* Sarah hated that film; it creeped her out in a big way.

As her team worked their way around the kitchen, methodically marking, swabbing, and collecting, she logged the neatly bagged exhibits into the exhibits book, all the time scanning the room for a sign of what she was looking for.

It came just as the evening began to fall. Having difficulty seeing clearly to write in the fading light, she sat up and stretched herself on the stool she had set up to the central island unit. An ideal spot to use as a desk. She was facing the entrance door.

'Is that switch all done with?' the question directed at the white clad form of Cyril Williams senior man on the team.

'Certainly, is, we are just about done here.' came the reply.

'Knock the lights on then, it's like the black hole here, I can't see to pick my own nose!' she jested, badly.

'Better go to Spec Savers.' was the predictable reply as the light switch was pressed and the spotlights mounted into the ceiling bathed the room in bright white light.

'Dim them down a bit Cyril, I don't need a suntan.' she grumbled.

As Cyril dimmed the lights slightly, Sarah noticed a flicker in one of the bulbs. Just a microsecond behind the rest.

'Do that again mate, would you, please.' She alighted from her perch and still looking upwards stood under the offending light.

Cyril turned the dimmer switch. There it was again. There was something not quite kosher with that bulb.

'Get me a set steps and a bag, Cyril.' She reached up towards the light knowing full well she would be several feet short of the ceiling.

'And can someone see if the van carries a bug detector?'

Several miles away a finger pressed *'stop'* on a recording device, a video cassette was removed from a machine, a copy made. All done in a suitably sterile manner. New tape, no fingerprints, no DNA. The one tape was placed in a safe and the door locked behind it, the other was deposited by an anonymous youth at the front desk of the Central

Bridewell. For the Attention of Ron Ashton. It would give Sandra Weaver something extra to worry about.

In the kitchen of The Laurels, Sarah James stepped off the step ladder, turned the lightbulb around in her fingers.

'Neat bit of kit.' she commented. 'Wireless. There must be a recorder somewhere, or at least a monitor.' she murmured to herself.

'Scan the rest of the house, it can't be the only one in here.'

It was nearly midnight before they were through, the radio frequency scan had found nothing, but a minute examination of sockets, switches and light bulbs had revealed a whole network of similar cameras, all of the same specifications. The home life of the Weavers was being watched, by someone. It was nearly two o'clock in the morning when after much deliberation Sarah telephoned Ron Ashton

A sleepy voice growled at her through her work mobile phone.

'Ashton here.'

'Sir, it's Sarah James, sorry to disturb you but I think you should know about this before the morning.'

CHAPTER 4. PRIVATE INVESTIGATIONS - Cassandra

Ron Ashton's wife Sylvia turned over in bed, reached across her husband's sleeping form and hit the snooze button on the alarm clock. Then she took hold of his raised left shoulder and shook gently.

'Its six o'clock, love.'

'Hmm what, shit, yes, ten minutes, ay.' Ron turned onto his back and breathed deeply.

'Who was that on the phone last night?' his wife asked. 'Did they really need to wake you up at that time?' Policemen's wives never quite trusted their husbands.

'Only Sarah, you know SOCO Sarah, you've met her, stuff she thought I needed to know, she was right to call.'

Ron yawned and slid his legs out from under the quilt, the alarm sounded again. He rubbed his eyes and headed for the en-suite and a brisk power shower.

Sylvia pulled a large pink sweatshirt on over her pyjamas and headed downstairs to the kitchen. Coffee was essential and hopefully her espoused would choose muesli over a bacon sandwich this morning. She knew he would probably get a bacon butty when he got to the office anyway. An examination of the contents of the fridge settled that discussion. Despite his slim frame her husband still ate like a small horse - hollow legs, she called it. Built like a racing snake he might be, but his blood pressure was still the stuff of raised eyebrows from his doctor. This in mind, she put the kettle on to boil, coffee in the cafetière and his blood pressure tablets next to his favourite mug.

Twenty minutes later, Ron meandered into the kitchen, casual jacket, trousers, crisp clean shirt with the tie hanging loose around his neck, he would tie that later. He was combing his still luxuriant but greying hair which was still damp from the shower.

'Got much on today, Sylv?'

'Two classes at college this morning, and I need to take hay down to the yard, and I must do a food shop. Any chance I can use your car, Ron?'

Sylvia volunteered as an equitation coach with Riding for the Disabled, she also rode horses herself and helped out at a local stable. It filled most of her spare time since her retirement and their daughter leaving home.

'Carry on, I can take yours then use a job car.' Ron didn't mind, but he didn't relish the drive into the centre of Bristol in his wife's mini. He much preferred the comfort of his top of the range Volvo estate, the mini, affectionately named Gilbert, due to its vile green colour, didn't even have a radio.

Detecting no smell of bacon, Ron poured milk on the offered muesli and after a munching couple of spoonful's he picked the keys to the Mini off the hooks by the kitchen door, grabbed his briefcase and his reefer coat from the stand in the hall.

'I'd best be off if I have to take Gilbert. No danger of speeding this morning!' he quipped, hoping that Terry Larkin was hot on the trail of fried slices of pig encased in white crusty, and anointed with brown sauce. Muesli was best fed to hamsters. Maybe he ought to buy Sylvia something on those lines. It was her birthday soon. Cheaper than the second-hand Range Rover she was fancying. He chuckled to himself.

Ron loved to amuse himself with little flights of fancy. The Range Rover was already reserved. It had been taken off the dealer's forecourt, much to Sylvia's distress. The seed of an idea sown, he felt a visit to the pet shop coming on. He could always donate the wee beastie to the primary school. Ron was still chuckling at his own private thoughts when he parked Gilbert between the brand-new Audi driven by D.I. Wayne and the older but very high spec BMW driven by David Holly.

'Shit is about to hit the fan, then.' he mused to himself.

Ron tapped in the entry code to the back door and began the climb up three flights of stairs to the incident room. As he approached the door to the main office, on his right, he passed the small kitchen. There, on his left, true to form, there was a brown paper bag bearing tell-tale signs of its contents sitting on a small plate, alongside the makings of an instant coffee in a mug bearing the name **RON** in capital letters.

'Morning boss.' Terry Larkin crossed the passage from the gents, adjusting his flies as he entered the kitchen and pressed the switch on the rear of the kettle.

'Where are they then?' Ron pointed to the two boss's cars in the yard below.

'In the secure intel unit, the handler's office, with the door locked.' Terry was matter of fact about it. 'Whatever happens, we'll be the last to know. How do you want to play it this morning? I've been downstairs. Custody say she had a rough night. She's understandably not very happy, but she's calmed down and sobered up a lot. Should be ready for us mid-morning.'

'Let's start by getting some background, antecedents if you like, we won't touch on yesterday's events too much. There's time for that later.' Ron poured boiling water into his mug and unwrapped his sandwich.

'Let's see what we've got to run with so far.'

As Terry pulled up a chair to the D.I.'s desk, the timid face of the front desk clerk appeared round the door.

'This came for you sir. It was just left on the desk.' She handed the brown padded envelope to Ron, then hastily beetled back down the stairs to her office by the front doors.

'Blueys on speed dial is it boss?' Terry felt the package and detected a video cassette.

Ron pulled out the cassette. 'Do we even have a video player these days?'

'I'll get one of the boys to go to T.S.U. for you, they'll have one of those cube things, you know TV and video player in one.' Terry rose to get one of his detectives on the errand.

'Great, we can watch it after we've got an interview into Cassandra. Give her brief a ring. Tell him we'll be ready to rock and roll at about 11:30 hours.'

Ron picked up the lengthy overnight progress report on his desk and pulled his notebook from the drawer. By the time he had finished reading he had made two pages of notes.

'Terry, get HR to pull the personal files on both the Weavers, oh, and any intelligence on either of them, calls to the house, signs of domestic unrest. And I want chapter and verse on what case Tony Weaver was working. Rattle a few cages with our friends in the drugs squad. Don't take no for an answer. Send Richard Miles, he doesn't suffer fools and he has a healthy disrespect for authority.'

'Right, you are boss, I'll put the action into the room right away, then give me five minutes to catch up.' Terry liked to be well prepared for an interview. He didn't like to go in cold.

'Read that, it's interesting, especially the SOCO report. I'll sort the room actions.'

Ron went next door into the incident room to speak to the room manager, the officer in charge of generating and keeping track of the myriad of things to be done, and the entering of them, along with the results, into the HOLMES computer. The only thing HOLMES didn't do was make tea.

Detective Sergeant Martin Cleveland did not look up from the pile of computer printed forms in front of him. Sensing someone standing at his shoulder he raised his right hand in dismissal, 'The answer is no!' He punctuated the hand signal with the terse announcement.

'I need some actions generated, Martin, and I need them as soon as,' Ron coughed before he made the request and completed it with a rather sarcastic, 'if it's not too much trouble, please, Martin.'

'Ah... be with you now, boss, what can we do for you?' Martin realised his faux pas. 'Can't do enough for a good boss.'

Ron presented him with a list and watched as the harassed officer input them into the system and sent them for allocation. Then he returned to his office at the end of the corridor to await the phone call from custody to say that Simon Hastings had arrived and was awaiting a briefing.

The green plastic telephone on his desk chirped. Ron lifted the receiver and placed it to his ear. 'Ashton.' he answered.

'It's really kicking off down here boss.' A hushed female voice whispered down the line.

'Sarah is that you?' He was curious.

'Who else would it be? It's been pistols at dawn down here. Mr Holly arrived at eight sharp, demanded to see Batman, like now. Then he demanded to know, *'whose fucking equipment we had recovered, and what the fuck was it doing in that fucking house in the first place.'*

'And?' Ron prompted as Sarah paused for breath.

'He must have shown him the kit I recovered, because there was a bit of a pause, then Batman denied it was our kit, too advanced he said, not what we would use. Then old Holly told him to, *'stop lying and tell him what the fuck was going on.'* Sarah came up for air again.

Then Batman, who usually knows his stuff when it comes to equipment said he'd, *'make a few enquiries.'* He called in two of his team and had a 'closed doors' with them. Then he assured Holly that anything we had found was not ours. That suggests to me that we had our own stuff in there anyway.'

'Why?' Ron was even more curious.

'I've no idea, but two of his boys were at the scene on a mission while we were there. Yesterday. I saw them. Maybe they were removing the evidence. Then Holly asked Batman a question, well it was more of a statement. *'There are no recordings are there, this was monitor only, wasn't it?'* Batman was silent and Holly went off on another one, insisting that there were no tapes, nothing that could affect his case, for or against.'

'Sarah, has he brought your exhibits back?' Ron sounded genuinely concerned, missing exhibits was a ball-acher if there was an audit later.

'He left them with Batman. When Holly leaves the building I'll get them back. I don't suppose he signed for them. But it begs a question sir. Why were the Weavers living in a house wired up like a nineteen seventies horror film?'

'It does indeed. Thank you, Sarah.' Ron replaced the receiver to have it immediately chirp at him.

'Custody here. Brief is ready for you now.' The custody officer was to the point.

'Down in five.' Ashton repaid the brevity. 'Come on Terry, lets rock and roll'

The interviewing team of Ashton and Larkin collected their notes and cleared their minds for the job in hand and made their way down the stairs to the cells.

The briefing with Simon Hastings was concise. This initial interview would be all about establishing a rapport with the prisoner, not a problem her brief had said. She intends to talk, and I have not advised her otherwise. All her cards will be on the table.

CHAPTER 5. THIS INTERVIEW IS BEING TAPE RECORDED - Cassandra

This interview is being tape recorded.
I am Detective Inspector Ronald Ashton.
Also present is my colleague Detective Sergeant Terry Larkin,
And Simon Hastings, legal representative.
The interview is being conducted at Central Police Station.
The time is 11:35 hrs, the date is Monday 6th April 1992.
I am interviewing.

Please give your full name and date of birth.

Cassandra Anne Weaver. Born 6th April 1962. I am 30 years old. She anticipated the question.

The D.I. smiled. Sandra saw his eyebrow raise as he thought about wishing her happy birthday. Professional to the core, he did not.

The rest of the formalities were completed, Simon Hastings explained his role as Sandra's legal representative. The Detective Sergeant explained what would happen to both copies of the tape.

The D.I. explained that the interview was also being monitored remotely and that he and his colleague were wearing an earpiece so that they could hear any instructions from outside the room.

The Detective Sergeant explained that they could take breaks as and when needed.

Ron Ashton took a deep breath in and let it out, loosened his tie, asked if anyone needed a glass of water. Then we will begin.

'Cassandra, may I call you Sandra? You have been arrested on suspicion of murdering your husband, Anthony Weaver. When you were arrested and cautioned you made no reply is that correct.'

'Yes, you may, and yes, it is.'

Sandra was informed that she was under caution and the caution formally read to her from the laminated card securely taped to the table. Then Ron Aston continued.

'Later at the custody desk you asked where your girls were.'

'Yes, I did, I still haven't been told where they are.'

'Rest assured, they are safe.'

'If anything happens to my girls....'

'They are in the care of social services. Unless you have a family member they can go to, that is where they will stay.'

'That is what I am afraid of.' Sandra looked at her hands and picked at one of her fingernails, her expensive manicure had been ruined.

'Sandra,' The DI looked at her with a very direct blue gaze. 'do you understand how serious this is?'

Sandra did not answer immediately.

'Murder is pretty serious, isn't it, sir.' She could not resist the smart remark. Ashton ignored it.

'I see that you have an injury to your left eye, it looks very swollen and black. How did that happen?'

'I'd like to say that the bullies who brought me in yesterday did it. They did these.' She held out her wrists to show angry red marks, swelling and bruising from her wrists to a point halfway up her forearms.

'That Patsy they got to arrest me didn't put the locks on the cuffs. I want that noted.'

Simon Hastings noted the injuries on his legal pad. 'D.I. will these injuries be photographed, that is an elementary error, most unprofessional of the officer.'

'They will, Mr Hastings. Now Sandra, who gave you the black eye?'

'Tony, that's Anthony. My husband.'

'Right Sandra, let's not talk about yesterday just yet, tell me a little about you and Tony. Start at the beginning. How did you meet?'

Sandra sat back in her seat. She looked briefly for reassurance at Simon Hastings who imperceptibly nodded his head.

'Okay,' Sandra started. 'Tony and I met in work about six years ago, we were both working the same shift. We were both uniformed police officers. I was senior to him, he had just finished his probation. He arrived with a bit of a rep. He was put with me for me to show him round the patch, and to straighten him out.'

'What do you mean by a rep.'

'He had already applied for CID with only two years' service, when he didn't get it, he played the card.'

'What do you mean, Sandra, stop talking in riddles.'

'Okay, the relief he came from. His Inspector, he sent a report to our Inspector, that Weaver had a big black chip on his shoulder, expected to run before he could walk.'

'And how exactly could you 'sort this out'?'

'Well sir, us women get the shitty end of the stick too, we have to prove ourselves before we are accepted. Yes, it stinks, but it's life. He could vent to me, and I would know how he felt.'

'And did it work, this 'sorting out'?'

'The bosses set us up to fail, they wanted rid of him, and they wanted rid of me. Instead, I found out that Tony was actually very good at the job, he was knowledgeable. Given his background he could talk to people, and he knew everyone, every scrote on the patch. With my technical know-how and bit if practical experience, we made a pretty good team.'

'So, I heard. Carry-on.'

'Well, it started with a drink after work, and over a few months it progressed. He was a good-looking guy, I scrub up quite well, he made me laugh, and we had a lot in common.'

'Elaborate.' Ashton let her talk, and Sandra did.

'Tony grew up in care, he never knew his parents, had no brothers or sisters, he was left in a telephone box outside the railway station of all places. He was set up with an apprenticeship when he left care. He trained as a car mechanic, but the firm went bust, so no job for Tony. He packed his bags and worked his way around Europe, then he came back home. He was 20yrs old with no job, no home but a good head on his shoulders and a qualification. He was fit and trained regularly, he didn't fancy the army, so he applied for the police. At least that's what he told me.'

'Carry on, Sandra.' Ashton encouraged.

'By the time he arrived with me he was 23yrs old, he was living in digs behind the nick, one room and a landlady on site, you know the type. I was 24yrs old. I had 6yrs in, I was treading water, I had passed my exams but was passed over for promotion each and every time. I was thinking of jacking it all in. The bosses said I had an attitude problem, but maybe it was because I didn't climb into bed with them at the first opportunity. I had a mortgage I could only just afford, and an elderly mother in a care home which cost more than she could fund. Tony moved in with me, as a lodger to start. He paid rent, and no, he didn't have permission and, no, I didn't put a bloody form in. But that didn't last long, we became a couple and six months later I was up the duff. Pregnant.'

'I know what 'up the duff' means.' Ashton smiled.

'Tony wanted to get married. He said he would have asked me anyway in a few months. He wanted a family, even if it was only me and my old Mam, and a baby. Mam loved him, so did I.'

'All was roses round the door then.' Terry Larkin chipped in.

'Yes, it was, if that is ever possible. I worked until I had to stop, the boys on my relief laughed at me, they teased me about giving birth in work, that if it was a boy, it would be called Bobby or Nick.' She laughed at the memory. Tony put in the overtime, we had it all sussed. I would take maternity leave and when the money dropped to statutory pay, then I would go back to work, part time if I could. There were always part time posts available.' She adjusted her position in the chair, stretched her legs and her back.

D.S. Larkin cut in. 'Tape is nearly cooked, guv.'

They took a break while the 45-minute tape was removed and sealed and a new one started. D.S. Larkin returned with three paper cups of machine coffee and some sachets of sugar but no spoon. Ron Ashton added two sachets to his cup and stirred it with the blunt end of his pen.

'Now where were we?'

Sandra took a mouthful of coffee and grimaced.

'Some things don't change,' she quipped. 'still tastes like burnt toenails. Where were we? Our daughter Charlotte was born. Charlotte, she's the blonde one. When she came out with blonde hair and blue eyes Tony didn't bat an eyelid, she looks like me, after all. He doted on her, nothing was too good for daddy's princess. Then he applied for the drug squad, the surveillance team in particular. Given all the busts we had made in uniform and the nature of the drug dealers in our area, they had little choice but to give him the job. They needed someone of a certain appearance and Tony fitted the bill. He loved it, like a duck to water. He worked all the hours god sent, but when he was off duty he always had time for me, and Charlotte. Things were good, so good that within three months I fell pregnant again. My girls are what they call Irish twins. Born on the same day within a year of each other. My pregnancy with Amy was complicated, I never went back to work, I was placed on protracted sick leave. Then, after Amy was born, she's the dark one, I arranged to transfer to a civilian role, part time, in the intelligence unit. It was Tony's boss who put me forward for the role. Thought I would be an asset to the team, and I was.' She took a big breath in before continuing.

'What with two adults and two young children it was very cramped for space in my two-bedroom link house. It was Tony who suggested we find something larger, he said. He had saved loads for a deposit and with both our incomes it would be easy. He sorted the mortgage. The house was to be in his name, made a change he said, for him to wear the trousers. That's when he started to change, after we moved into that house.'

'The house on Lock keepers Lane, your current home.'

'Yes.'

'How did he change?'

'He started being impatient with the girls, they were only babies, babies make a mess. All of a sudden he couldn't stand to change a nappy. He started wearing designer stuff, he didn't want mess on his clothes, and the bling, you know, the big gold chains, the ear piercing. He was turning into everything I despised. When I challenged him about it he snapped at me, it was part of his job, he said. A persona, nothing to worry about. I pushed him further and he stormed out of the house, one night he didn't come home. I suppose that was our first proper domestic argument.'

'Was he violent towards you?'

'No, he wasn't. He came home just after breakfast. He was sorry. We made up, it was his day off and we took to girls out together, but even then, we were in the café in the park, and he got stuck in conversation with this guy, another big black guy, all muscles and bling, swish Mercedes sport with tinted windows. Heavy duty yeah.'

'And?' Ashton prompted.

'I said nothing, but next time I went in to work, I ran some checks, I found out who it was. Tony was batting well out of his depth. I spoke to him about it, I was very angry. Whoever was planning the job he was on, was out of order, expecting Tony to involve me and the girls. No matter how distant we were, he had endangered us. You don't take your kids anywhere near a job.'

Ron Ashton took a mouthful of cold coffee and nodded.

'That night Tony arrived home late, he was as high as a kite, coke I think. I had suspected he was sampling the wares but loads of the squad do, don't they. It goes with the turf.'

'Do they?', interjected D.S. Larkin.

'That night Tony went ballistic. He accused me of interfering in his work, he threw me bodily across the bedroom, he pinned me to the bed, he tried to strangle me. I knee'd him in the balls to get him off me, then I put the girls in the car, and I went for a drive. When I got home, he had locked the gates, we spent the night in the car, me, and the kids. In the morning, he was sorry, so, so sorry. He promised he would get a grip on things. He did for a while.'

The beep which signalled the end of the tape sounded.

'Thank you, Sandra,' Ron Ashton closed the tape, 'shall we have a break for some food? When we resume you can tell me about yesterday.'

Sandra signed the seals which sealed the tapes and Simon Hastings asked for a consultation room. Better than eating a microwaved meal in her cell she thought.

'Right,' said Simon, that was easy, all very good background, some things they can verify, some they can't, some mitigation building. Now think carefully about what you want to tell them about yesterday. I wouldn't advise, 'no comment', because you've been happy to talk up to now. What do you want to do?'

'Well, Simon, they are bound to have a copy of the 999 tape. I told them then, that I thought I had killed him. That's as good an admission as you can get. But it was self-defence. He was so angry, I'd never seen him like it, I really thought I was going to die.'

Sandra's façade cracked, her face crumpled, tears streamed down her naked face, no make-up today, she wiped her nose like a child on the sleeve of her grey sweatshirt, supplied by the police to replace her own clothes. She had no one to fetch her clothing from her house. She was now a leper to her colleagues. The circumstances did not matter, she was a copper who had sinned against the system, no-one out there would give her a hand up, and she knew that while she was down, all those in what had once been her support network would kick her as well.

'I loved him, I really loved him, but he was so changed. Why did no one else notice? I found out, I found out about him, he had sold us all out.' The words came tumbling out.

Sergeant Harris knocked the door and offered a meal. 'Curry, or lasagne?' He tried to be cheerful about it. He felt a little sorry for Sandra. Now was hard, but there would be worse to come, he was sure of that.

'Nothing for me, sarge, thanks, but a tidy coffee would be great. I know you have your own out the back, in a mug would be nice, but I understand if you can't manage the best china.'

'I'll see what I can do.' His vast frame left the room.
Coffee was forthcoming, a large hot steaming coffee, not in a mug, but at least in a tall, waxed cardboard cup.

'Sarge, you are an angel.'

The next tap on the door signalled a return to business. Resuming their seats and completing the tape loading formalities, Sandra confirmed that nothing had changed since the break.

Ron Ashton spoke first.

'So, Sandra, what happened yesterday?'

Sandra began slowly. 'Tony said he was a day off, we had made plans to go out for the day, spend some time with the girls. Tony was a late shift the day before. He said to let him sleep until about eleven and then, once he was awake, we could go down the coast for a run in the car, walk on the beach, get an ice cream with the girls. They were excited, looking forward to it, time with their daddy.'

Ashton didn't ask another question, he let her talk, sitting back slightly in his chair. Sandra knew what he was doing. He was waiting for her to trap herself.

'Well, Ronald Ashton, the truth is the truth, and that's what you are getting, tell the truth and shame the devil!' The thought stuck in her mind as she took a breath, then it finished itself. 'And then reap the whirlwind.' She continued.

'I had given the girls their breakfast, I was still in my scruffy joggers and about to clean up in the kitchen. I nipped upstairs to get my phone and pull on my jeans. I had left my phone on the bedside table. When I got to the bedroom Tony was awake. He was leaning over the basin in the en-suite with two lines of coke neatly cut on the vanity unit. I begged him not to do it, but he snorted them both anyway. He looked at me like a huge, black, mutinous child who intended to get his own way by throwing a tantrum. I laughed at him, it wasn't a funny laugh. I expect it told him exactly what I felt for him in that moment. Scorn.'

'*Not in my house*,' I screamed at him, '*not in front of the girl*s!' He yelled back at me. '*It's not your fucking house, darling!*'

I screamed at him, '*Our fucking house, then, you know damn well what I fucking mean.*'

He stopped for a second then very slowly and deliberately, clearly, he told me, '*It isn't even our house, you stupid bitch.*' Then he stormed out of the house.

Ashton didn't interrupt with a question, he sensed there was more to come. He was not sure he believed it all, but he was willing to listen.

'Why did he say that? I knew that he was tired. He had been late back from the job last night. I had felt him fall into bed at about 4am, and he had reeked of cheap perfume, tobacco smoke and booze. Booze on his clothes, not on his breath. I searched his office. He was meticulous with paperwork, I had taught him to be that way. He knew I was a bit paranoid about being homeless, that having a home was a 'thing' with me, just as it was for him. I had seen the papers for the lovely detached new build house we lived in, four bedrooms, three en-suite, bespoke kitchen, the whole nine yards, I had signed the mortgage agreement alongside him, hadn't I? Had I been so happy I didn't read it properly? Well, D.I., I went to the drawer and got out the file marked, '*house*' and I read.

My house doesn't belong to me, or to Tony Weaver, the property known as The Laurels, Lock keepers Lane is owned lock stock and barrel by one Paul Melville Grainger. Tony has been working for him. I didn't have to run that name through the computer, I had seen it often enough. He was the main player in the job Tony was on. The man Tony had met on our, '*Day Out.*'

I had been reading intelligence logs from a C.H.I.S for weeks all saying that Grainger is clean. Nothing more than a successful businessman. I put two and two together just as Tony came back. I had the papers spread over the desk reading them. He pulled me out of the chair by my hair, the first punch winded me, the second blacked my eye. Then I heard Charlotte shouting, '*Mummy*' and a crash in the kitchen. Tony relaxed his grip on me, and I managed to make it as far as the kitchen to find that Charlotte and Amy had pulled all my glassware out of its cupboard to play at, 'Dollie's tea party.' The crash was my crystal wine glasses smashing on the kitchen floor. I shouted at them, and they started to cry. It was then that they must have gone and hid.

Tony was behind me, he grabbed me again, he shouted at me to clean up after the girls, I shouted back. At that point, Detective Inspector, I knew if he turned around, one of us would die, and it wasn't going to be me. I had caught him in his lies. He knew I wouldn't go along with them. He was very, very angry.'

Sandra proceeded to walk the interviewing officer through what had happened next right up to the arrival of the Police.

'Sandra, when you were booked into custody, the sergeant marked your record that you were drunk. When did you have a drink? In fact, your custody record says that you were drunk right up until 10am this morning.' Ashton was curious

'D.I., far be it from me to comment. I drank a large glass of whisky while I was waiting for the cavalry to arrive. I'm sure you will find the glass and the bottle in the kitchen.'

'Thank you, Sandra, you have given us a lot of information. Unless there is anything anyone would like to add, I am concluding this interview. We will probably want to interview you again later to clear up minor points. Sergeant Larkin, any questions?'

'Sandra, just to clarify, did you stab Tony Weaver?'

'Yes, I did.'

'Sandra, did you intend to him to die?'

'I intended to save my own life.'

'A ten-inch professional boning knife would do a lot of damage wouldn't it?'

'Sergeant, I only knew I had a knife in my hand, I wasn't fussy which one.'

Sandra heard Simon Hastings suck in his breath. Then she added,

'He would have killed me, I could see it in his face. I needed to live, for my girls. Where are my girls, sergeant?'

D.I. Ashton switched off the tapes.

Simon Hastings escorted Sandra back to their little consultation room, they needed to talk.

CHAPTER 6. CHEERS TONY. - Cassandra

'Looks like manslaughter, boss.' Terry Larkin dropped his notebook on the desk in Ron Ashton's office and sat down in his boss's chair, pushing it back on its casters and stretching his legs.

'How can we say just yet? We know she killed him, and we know all wasn't well in the Weaver household. We are still in a very grey area.' Ashton ran his fingers through his hair. He was looking out of the window down into the central yard. He could see the SIO David Holly opening the door to his BMW, the long door of the Beamer bumping gently against the green paint of Gilbert, his wife's old faithful Mini, the narrow gap hardly allowing enough room for the man's big frame. Ashton snorted as he watched the door dink against the battered paintwork. Another chip amongst the assorted damage to the Mini wouldn't harm, but he did resent the fact that Holly really couldn't give a fuck. He rested his hands on the windowsill.

'Holly is up to something, I don't know quite what, but he's up to something, I'm sure of it.'

Turning back to his desk he remembered the package which now lay in his **IN** basket.

'Where's that video cube they promised me? Get on it, Terry, and get your fat hairy arse out of my chair while you are about it.' Ron reached for the padded envelope. An unquiet voice in his head told him to preserve it. A feeling in the pit of his stomach told him it might need to go to the lab. Instead of ripping it open like a kiddie playing pass the parcel, he carefully picked open the flap. Then, donning a set of blue latex gloves, he removed the contents, setting the envelope to one side. One VHS cassette. Now all he needed was the means to play it.

Downstairs in the custody suite, Sandra Weaver sat in the lawyers' consultation room. It was a small, spartan room. The walls were painted a delicate shade of police pale blue, grey contract carpet, window high up above eye level. No chance to see out, but the sky she could see seemed to coordinate its colour perfectly with the flooring. There was a table about four feet square, standard issue from Bristol Office Furniture, perched on black metal legs and securely bolted to the floor, two dark blue plastic chairs. The door was self-closing and heavy with a vertical viewing pane in reinforced glass inserted at its outer edge. She knew that the outside bore a sliding sign which declared the room occupied. Looking around her, she took in the graffiti on the walls. Even in these rooms some little oik had managed to sign his name in biro. The desk was similarly adorned. Funny how lawyers allowed their clients access to writing tools and left them alone while they visited the coffee machine. These interview rooms could be locked but rarely were.

The whole passage was secured, the occupants having to press the big green buzzer at the main door to get out. Sandra was processing all these minor thoughts when Simon Hastings let himself into the room.

'Prepare yourself for more, Sandra, they've been easy on you so far.' He placed his briefcase on the table, opened it and pulled out a legal pad, and a pen. 'It is self-defence you know. A jury would go for that. Is there anything you haven't told me that I ought to know?'

'Simon, I've told you everything, I killed my husband, I can expect to go down for a long time. I need you to make sure my girls are okay. I have no family they can go to, no friends who would take them in. They need to stay together, wherever they end up.' Sandra would not sit down. She paced up and down the room like a caged tiger, arms wrapped around herself.

'Sit down, you are wearing a hole in the carpet. I will contact social services before I leave you. I expect they are in temporary foster care. If things run true to form, that's where they will stay until we know what is happening to you. Then the court may, and I say may, try and make an order regarding their future. But that is a long way down the line.'

Sandra kept pacing, 'So they could try and take my kids off me?'

'In short, if they feel that's in their best interests, then yes.' was the brutally honest reply. 'If you are convicted, you will face a life behind bars. How can you care for them?'

Sandra slumped into the vacant chair. Her head rested on her arms which were folded on the table. The noise which came from her was that of a wounded animal. She banged her fists on the table. 'Fuck you, Tony Weaver. I hope you fucking rot for what you have done.'

'Composure, Sandra, you need composure, how about I see what I can find out. You will have to go back to your cell for a while, but I can make a few calls, see what they will tell me over the phone.'

Simon closed the briefcase and buzzed them out of the briefing room and back into the brightly lit, stark world of the cell block. He booked her back in with the desk sergeant and saw her back to cell thirteen.

'I'll be back in an hour or so, I expect they'll want to speak to you again by then.' Then he left.

Upstairs in Ashton's office, Terry Larkin plugged in the fourteen-inch video cube he had managed to purloin from the Technical Support Unit.

'We only use DVD players these days.' the stressed D.C. who was on duty complained. 'VHS went out with the ark.'

He inserted the new batteries in the remote control and switched it on. The screen fizzed into life and the cassette carriage popped in and out expectantly.

'Are we sitting comfortably?' Ron slid the cassette into the machine. He flicked the office blinds to closed and sitting down in his chair, he pressed play.

'Is there popcorn and Kia Ora in the interval?' enquired Terry.

As the tape began to play, Martin Cleveland's head craned round the door. 'Is this a private viewing boss or can anyone watch. I've got that background stuff you wanted. It's just been logged in. Interesting reading.' He dropped a full manila folder on the desk.

'Most of our Tony's work was level two, cross border crime. His team were doing a job on Paul Melville Grainger, a long-term surveillance job; with a U.C. element.'

Ron paused the video. 'Pull up a pew, I have no idea what's on this, it may or may not be relevant. It was left for me this morning.'

Malcolm perched on the corner of the desk.

'This will do me, I've been sitting down all morning.' He stretched his legs to ease the tension in his calf muscles and restore the circulation to his posterior. A wiggle of his hips scratched the itch which had been plaguing him all morning, rubbing it away against the corner of the boss's desk. There was no feeling better.

Ron pressed play and the tape began to roll and hiss.

The screen cleared of interference and a slightly distorted image appeared. Viewed from above and down the narrow view of a camera lens, the rear view of a man appeared. The scene which played out was viewed from behind wide shoulders clad in a fitted white T shirt.

As the audience of three watched, stunned initially that this footage even existed, the man moved and Sandra Weaver came into view, her face bruised, her expression one of rage and determination. This woman did not look like a terrified housewife. Yes, the man's hands were reaching towards her, but his face was not visible. There was no sound. The viewer would have to add their own commentary to the scene playing out before them in glorious technicolour. In his subconscious, Ron added what Sandra had told them in interview. Did the words fit with the actions which played out on screen?

An object was thrown. Heavy, you could tell by the effort it took. It hit the man a glancing blow on the shoulder. It did not halt his progress. He advanced on the woman, relentless, towering over her. Intimidating. She reached behind her, eyes fixed on the man, one hand groping. There was the knife. It's eight-inch blade gleaming in the light cast by the ceiling mounted spots. She held the knife securely in two hands and as the male figure closed in on her she thrust it forward and upwards. Only once. A fatal wound. Both fell to the floor and were still for a minute, a whole minute. Then the woman stood and reached for an item on the counter. Her phone. A call was made. Then, in full view of the camera, Sandra Weaver poured herself a large drink from the distinctive bottle of Dufftown Whisky which stood on the counter. The deep amber coloured liquid poured to half fill one of the heavy glass tumblers which stood on the tray beside the bottle. She sat on the floor cradling the head of the man in her lap, and in full view of the camera she could not have known was there, raised the glass in a toast. The silent words easily lip read.

'Cheers Tony.'

'That could be the difference.' Martin Cleveland spoke first. 'She doesn't look very out of control, she doesn't look terrified, she looks angry, very angry, and to drink his health afterwards, well.'

'That's a very cynical view, Sergeant,' Ron Ashton entered the verbal fray. 'but I agree, it could sway a charging decision, she needs to account for it, let's see what she says. And let's see what she really knows about what her husband was up to. Motive. We may find motive. Is Sandra just playing the abused woman or is there more?'

'I'll ring downstairs, and make sure her brief is in the building.'

Half an hour later, Simon Hastings was made aware that CCTV of his client had been seized and entered into evidence. He was not shown the footage. Some cards were best kept close. Ron wanted to see for himself Sandra's reaction to the tape. He wanted to see whether she was indeed playing the saint. Or was she really the sinner?

Ron and Terry started to read the intelligence package which related to Paul Grainger. They also read the undercover debrief files on Tony Weaver. The combined picture was enough to raise eyebrows from both men.

Ron wondered to himself how a department could fail to realise the way Tony's UC handler had failed to communicate with anyone running the show. Were they too close, too tied up in the narrative? Sure, Tony had been adamant he was in control, remaining sufficiently detached from the target to be effective, not becoming too involved. Was the handler blind!? You didn't need Specsavers to see what was going on. Ron kept his counsel.

Terry finished reading the intelligence logs, the redacted versions. Not even a murder enquiry would see the identity of the source of the intelligence. That would take a court order. The source must be protected. Was there even a source? Terry's mind was adding things up. He hoped his two and two wasn't making too much. He handed the bundle to Ron, and they swapped packages.

'I smell fish.', Terry announced as he finished reading. 'I smell very rotten fish.'

'Maybe the lady downstairs is going to tell us just how rotten. It won't help her case, but from what I've heard of her and what her file says, she will tell us. She won't keep schtum about any of it.'

Ron picked up his notes and his notebook. 'Let's go and find out, shall we?'

CHAPTER 7. THE PUPPET MASTER – Paul Melville Grainger

Paul Melville Grainger was worried. Justifiably so. He had carefully constructed his empire, recruiting only the most reliable and useful henchmen. Carefully cultivating contacts in all the right places, he had fingers in many pies, so many, his already dark skin was tinted the colour of gravy browning.

Councillors, Magistrates, Police Officers both high ranking and lowly, several Judges and a very odd Member of Parliament. If Paul Grainger needed a friend in a high place or a low one, there was a number on one of his mobile phones to suit.

He was a careful man, always keeping himself well out of the line of fire. His shadier business affairs were carefully wrapped in layer upon layer of subterfuge, designed so that he would never get his collar felt. Maybe he had stretched the envelope too far this time.

Tony Weaver had been easy meat. The man was completely gullible. He had been played like the salmon Paul loved to fish for on his weekends at that lodge on the Tay. The lure of money and a certain lifestyle had appealed to the financially overstretched and overworked copper. A few easy jobs, nothing incriminating, a bit of a heads up in the way of information here and there. Who was in the spotlight, who was under investigation? Who were the narcs talking about? A bit of counterintelligence here and there, all high grade of course. Reliable. Not to be disputed. Tony Weaver had proven useful until he started to believe his own publicity. Over inflated ego had brought many a man down. Tony Weaver was no exception.

Then there was that wife of his. She was a different kettle of fish. Paul had misjudged her. He had thought she would immerse herself in domesticity. Enjoy the fruits of Tony's labours and hang up her uniform. Instead, she had been recruited even closer to his nerve centre. He knew incorruptible when he saw it. Sandra Weaver was incorruptible. As with all his employees he had taken certain steps, made sure that none of them knew each other unless they had to. Everything was on a need-to-know basis. Paul had just sat back and held the reins, the puppet master. Now the strings were starting to break. *Damn Tony Weaver and most of all damn his wife.*

It was time to shut up shop for a while, scale down certain parts of the business, maybe cultivate shoots growing in a different direction, something just as lucrative as the transport of recreational chemicals, something less obtrusive. He had the contacts. Now he just needed to clear the pitch.

He pressed a button on his mobile phone and waited for an answer. The ring tones ended and the line cleared and he was put through to a voicemail service. 'David Holly is not able to take your call. Leave a message and he will get back to you.'

Paul Grainger disconnected and waited for the call back. None of his acolytes ever failed to return the call, and this one had more reasons to return it than most.

He did not have to wait long. Within five minutes the display on his smart phone lit up. Holly's private number identified the caller.

'Good morning, Paul.' The greeting was civil. 'What can I do for you this fine morning?'

'Cut the crap, how much does the wife know? This is all very inconvenient. She needs to be muzzled. If you can't do it, I will.'

'Calm down, can't you. I can't talk now.' Grainger heard the click of a door and the decrease of background conversation as Holly stepped outside to take his call. I'm in overall charge of the case, but it's Ashton who is investigating. He will be the one compiling the evidence. He's been told to keep it tidy. But I'll have another word. That's all I can do. He's very thorough, I'll say that for him. If there is evidence there, he will use it. I'll call you if there is a hitch.' Holly ended the call, leaving a gobsmacked Grainger staring at the screen of his handset. Grainger placed two more calls in the next half hour. He liked an insurance policy.

Andrew Toller had a habit which needed feeding. It had developed whilst he was at The University of Bristol reading Law. He found it helped him stay awake through the long nights of study. Nights punctuated with wild parties at the flat he shared with four other students on the Cromwell Road. He had qualified with a second-class degree. Had he partied less, he might have attained a first, but he was inherently lazy and enjoyed easy money, and a good time. He had seen the job with the Crown Prosecution Service as a stop gap, and a stepping stone. He came from a well-heeled family, his parents were elderly, his father had contacts. Eventually he would inherit enough money to buy into a private practice. Until then he had other ways of subsidising his baser habits.

His desk was awash with half completed files. Minor cases, mostly deferred bail with long dates. This was the CPS. Nothing ever ran to schedule. The police would have to wait. The police would always wait. The defendants were usually relieved to put off the inevitable, happy in the delusion that the longer the CPS considered the matter, the more likely they were to get off. He relished the chance of getting his teeth into a major case, and the Weaver murder had legs. He had been assured that it was his. From two sources, it would be a while coming through for a decision. He'd better get some of his other cases done or eyebrows would be raised.

Toller pulled out a domestic burglary from the pile and started to read. He knew there would be insufficient evidence to charge before he started, but he would read it anyway. While he read, he considered. He really should be getting a bigger slice of the pie. He knew his supervisor was extremely well recompensed for his flexibility on certain matters. Maybe he should ask for more. Visions of Oliver Twist and his bowl of gruel filled his mind. That request hadn't worked out well, had it?

The telephone on his desk rang. He lifted the receiver. 'Andrew Toller, CPS.'

'Andrew is that you?' the tremulous female voice on the phone was familiar.

'Christine, you've been told not to keep phoning me at work. This has to stop.' Andrew's voice was a harsh whisper, head low over his work, behind the soundproof barriers which separated his desk from that of his colleague.

'Andrew, I'm pregnant!' The air froze around him. Life went into slow motion. Another problem to add to the pile.

'How....?' He began.

'If you don't know that, I'm not about to tell you.' She was flippant, but he could hear her lower lip trembling.

'Christine, I really can't discuss this with you now, is it even mine?'

'You bloody well know it is!' He heard her façade crack, and she broke into sobs.

'I'll meet you in town at lunchtime, I'll call you later, goodbye Christine.' He hung up.

His colleague from over the barrier raised her head and smiled at him, her blonde graduated bob falling prettily around her chin. She picked up her overloaded briefcase, and her handbag, and pointed at the filing box on her desk.

'Before you sort out your love life, Andrew, be a darling and put that lot in the lift for me. I have Court in half an hour.'

Penelope Major had the sort of voice which gave him a hard on. He knew she was completely out of his league. Senior lawyers and above for her; weekends in country houses with the Barbour brigade, Glyndebourne, the opera, Ladies' Day at Ascot.

'For you, Penny, anything. Fancy dinner tonight?' He picked up the heavy box and headed for the lift.

'I'd rather remove my eyes with a sharpened spoon.' was the anticipated reply.

He watched as she closed the lift doors behind her. She had it all, the looks, the ability, the attitude. Penny Major loved to prosecute. She loved to see the bad guys punished, or at least a fair and just result for the victim. He watched the top of the lift disappear down the glass shaft and wondered where he had gone so wrong. He felt the world closing in around him. He felt like what he was, trapped. Was the Weaver case to be his salvation, or was it a poisoned chalice, like everything else he seemed to drink from these days. He had no choice but to take the case. His paymaster had called. It was all arranged.

CHAPTER 8. SECONDS AWAY - Cassandra

Terry Larkin carried the video cube in his arms and his papers wedged under his left arm. Ron Ashton carried only his notes and his 'blue book.' They had briefed Simon Hastings that there was video evidence, they had not elaborated.

Simon Hastings had broached the subject with his client. The response had been explosive.

'How the fuck can there be fucking video? It's a family house for fuck's sake. Whose f'ing video? What else has some bastard got on film? My kids! Is some evil perverted bastard getting his rocks off over my children in the bath!?'

'Calm down Sandra, they haven't said more than that they have video evidence. I don't know the content. I haven't seen it. My advice is, be calm, think before you speak. My hunch is that they want a reaction from you. Don't give them what they want.'

'Simon, there is never just one camera, if someone has bothered to wire up inside my house it's not to watch me strutting my cordon bleu stuff in the kitchen, is it. Is it?'

'I can't say, can I. Because I'm as in the dark as you. Just be calm about this. Think before you speak. Remember that.', Simon advised.

'Amy and Charlotte are together. They are with an emergency foster home out in Winford. That's all I could find out for the present. They are okay. You need to think of you for now. The best outcome for them is a good outcome for their mother. Are you ready?'

'Ready as I'll ever be, let's do it.'

Sandra and her legal representative walked into the interview room and sat in their chairs. Sandra noted that there was a video cube just like the one in her daughter's bedroom on the table. It made her smile. She held that thought and composed herself. She doubted that they were about to watch a Disney film.

Sandra was just adjusting herself for another forty-five minutes on the hard plastic chair when the interview team arrived. It was then she realised that round one had been a blur, she hadn't really taken it all in. Reality started to kick in. She suddenly felt rather sick. Too late to change anything now, what was said was said. The truth was the truth. *'Have faith in the system, you have to trust honesty, tell the truth, and shame the devil.'*, she told herself again.

The interview opened with the usual formalities. The interviewing officers introduced themselves. They cautioned her, they unwrapped the tapes in her presence and loaded the recorder.

She introduced herself. Simon Hastings explained his role in interview. Yes, they had had sufficient consultation time. Yes, they would say if they needed a break. Then Ron Ashton loosened his tie and took a deep breath and began.

'Sandra, this video has been entered into evidence. I'd like you to watch it, then I will be asking you about its content. Don't say anything until you have seen it all.'

Terry Larkin pressed play on the remote control which he held under his hand, on the corner of the table.

Sandra watched. She saw instantly what they had seen. But she said nothing. In her mind she was taken back to her kitchen. She was confronted by sixteen stone of drug fuelled anger, all directed at her. Her reaction after ten years of training was not what 'normal women did.' She had not screamed. She had not been hysterical. She had defended herself, hadn't she? But not like these men would expect. She had seen younger female colleagues coached out of, 'hitting like a pansy' on self-defence courses. She had been put forward as an example of how to, 'hit it like you mean it.' hadn't she. She had reverted to type. The result did not look favourable. But though the camera might show the look of grim determination on her face, it could never show the feeling of abject terror in her mind.

The video stopped.

'Well?' Ron raised an eyebrow.

'Well, what?' she replied. She felt Simon Hastings foot press down on hers in warning.

'What did you see?' Ron expanded.

'You tell me.' Sandra ignored Simon Hastings' warning.

'Okay, Mrs. Weaver.' Terry Larkin took over. Closed questions requiring only one-word answers. 'Firstly, is that room your kitchen?'

'Yes.' She mumbled.

'Is that kitchen in the house called the Laurels?'

'Yes.'

'Is the female person you?'

'Yes.'

'Is the male person your husband, Tony Weaver?'

She lost her cool, as he knew she would. 'Yes, it fucking is, and you know it, and yes that's a fucking knife in my hand!'

Simon Hastings foot pressed down on hers. 'And you can stop playing bloody footsie with me.'

Then her façade cracked, she began to cry. Through tears and great big hiccoughing sobs, punctuated by snot tinged with blood from her healing broken nose, she screamed at him.

'Yes, I killed my husband. Yes, I stabbed the bastard. It was me in the fucking kitchen with the boning knife!'

Ron Ashton took over, his mellow voice calming, soothing even, lulling her into a certain sense of security. 'We need more, Sandra, what were you thinking, what did you feel. Why did you do it?'

'I was angry, in fact I was livid. He had betrayed everything I thought we meant to each other.'

'So, you wanted him dead then?'

'No, I did not want him dead, I wanted him back. I wanted my Tony back.'

Ron fixed her with a very direct gaze, as if willing her to say the right things, a look which saw through the hard shell this woman wore daily, now the shell of a bitter, angry woman.

'Explain.' One word, an open question, 'Tell me.'

Sandra took a breath in. She sniffed and Simon passed her his handkerchief. She wiped her face and her nose and began.

'Firstly,' she said, 'the police service made me what I am. It taught me how to fight, it took a shy young recruit and taught her how to defend herself, how to react in a confrontation, how not to show my feelings to others.'

'Go on.' Ron nodded his head,

'I told you what happened before I reached the kitchen. I told you what I did. You can see what I did. At the moment when I picked up that knife, I knew I was in danger, I was shitting myself with fear. Tony was mad, he was high on coke. I thought he was going to kill me.'

'Tell me more about Tony Weaver, you said you wanted him back.' Ron continued.

'I did, he was no longer the man I married.'

'How so?'

'The kind, caring, intelligent Tony had been seduced by his work.'

'In what way?'

'The lifestyle, the bling, the gold chains, the flash cars, the late nights.'

'He was in character then, for his job, undercover.'

'He was living it, it became him, the character was wearing him. He couldn't take it off. It corrupted him.'

'How long had you known?'

'I read stuff, in my job, I read the incoming logs, all graded as reliable, but all false, all saying that Grainger is clean. The informant details redacted. All of it a smoke screen. The telltale signs, most of it led back to my husband. He was painting a false picture. He was working for the man.'

'You mean for Grainger?'

'Yes, for Grainger. My suspicions were confirmed when he took me and the girls out to the park. He met Grainger in the café. I saw what went on. I saw him hand Tony a package. I also saw the log Tony fed into the system afterwards. I saw his colleagues on the plot. He had to put some information in. So, he faked some. Then I started looking.'

'Did that make you hate him?' Terry asked.

'No, I didn't know the ins and outs of the operation. It made me suspicious, and he was sampling the merchandise. He was nearly always high. That, I did hate. But he was the father of my girls, I still loved him.'

'I think it made you despise him, Sandra, so much so that you wanted him dead.' Terry pushed her.

'You can think what you like, but that was the last thing I wanted. I wanted him to clean up his act and be a father again, not the coke snorting, pseudo-gangster he seemed to have turned into.'

'What else did you find out?' Ron took the lead.

'I found that every piece of intelligence he was faking was painting his target as whiter than white. Squeaky clean. A legitimate businessman. But I know different. Read it all yourselves, it's there in black and white.'

'Now back to the video.' Terry took over.

'Yes, the video, where did it come from anyway? What else was recorded in my home? With all due respect, is it even admissible if you don't know its origins?' Sandra's tendency to argue the toss was taking over. Simon Hastings cleared his throat loudly.

'I think Sandra has a point, can you document who made the recording, and on what device? Should the matter be raised at trial, we would ask to have it made inadmissible as evidence if it is not properly introduced.'

Ron Ashton raised an eyebrow, 'I can assure you enquiries are ongoing to provenance this exhibit. Will that suffice for now Mr Hastings?'

'In that case my client has said all she wishes to say regarding its content, Mr Ashton.'

Ron continued. 'Sandra, do you have anything else you would like to add before I conclude this interview?'

Sandra took in a deep breath. 'Mr Ashton, yesterday I thought that the man I loved, the father of my children was going to kill me. He was raging on cocaine and very, very angry, I defended myself, I did not intend to kill him, I intended to stop him from killing me. Just because I have been trained over the years to hide my fear does not mean I was not terrified. I have also just found out that mine and my family's lives were being filmed. Until I am told why, I have no more to say.'

Terry Larkin concluded the interview and sealed the tapes.

The interview room emptied, Terry and Ron upstairs to the office, Sandra to her cell and Simon Hastings back to his own sanctum in a nearby side street.

Ron and Terry knew they had enough to ask the Crown Prosecution Service for a decision. They also knew that they would have to involve the SIO David Holly. He would want his four penn'orth, no doubt about that. Looking out of the office window Terry could see a space where Holly's car had been.

'He's buggered off for the day, always has had his own agenda. You'll have to ring his mobile, just hope he's not on the golf course.'

'If he is, it's the nineteenth hole! He hasn't swung a club in anger for years.' Ron began to dial his boss's mobile number.

The call was answered, and the clink of glasses and noise of background chatter confirmed Ron Ashton's suspicions. He heard a door open and close as Holly found a more private spot for a conversation.

'I'm at Coombe Park, meet me in the car park, we can talk there, hmm, my car is my office these days.' Holly had obviously been socialising.

'You need to see the tape, sir, it may make all the difference.' Ashton was firm.

'I leave it up to your judgement Ron, you don't really need my views, do you, a man of your experience?' Holly was evasive.

'But...' Ron began.

'I've already primed the CPS, they are waiting for the call. You sort it, Ron, you really don't need me.' The phone went dead.

David Holly returned to the gentleman's bar and his waiting gin and tonic, announcing to all who would listen, 'Bloody incompetents, no one has the balls to make a decision these days.'

Ron looked at the mobile phone in disgust. 'Looks like we are going to the CPS alone then, Terry, he's not interested. Apparently they are expecting us.'

'Can you smell it, Ron?' Terry raised an eyebrow and sniffed the air in a speculative manner. 'This whole thing is starting to stink like a well-rotted dung heap.'

It took them an hour to complete the necessary forms. Then, with little time to spare, they walked the short distance across the city to meet with the appointed lawyer.

In a small room off the main open plan office, Andrew Toller prepared for action. He had been well briefed by his paymasters. His decision was already made.

CHAPTER 9. PASSAGE OF TIME – Cassandra Weaver - 1992

Time had become blurred, minutes blurred into hours, into days. I was a person who was used to living by a clock. Time had now become unimportant, it just passed. I had travelled through the whole gamut of emotions. I had done angry, upset, and plain pissed off with life. I had felt sorry for myself and then settled into a mode of resignation. I was powerless to control my own destiny. I had been swallowed by the system and would in time be digested by it. What was left would then be dumped unceremoniously on the shit heap of life, to propagate new seeds or sink in the mire.

Certain words stuck in my drug fogged brain. Did I forget to mention the anti-depressants. The chemical cosh I had been prescribed by the visiting medical officer to level out my mood. To help me cope with my predicament. I had swung between bouts of extreme anger, fear, and paranoia in turn. Much as I detested the thought of chemical assistance, I was confronted at every request for alternative help by reports which stated that, 'Mrs Weaver has been offered but refuses to take any form of medication to alleviate her symptoms.' So eventually I had succumbed.

Murder - that was the first word. No alternative charge. Just Murder.

Cassandra Weaver you are being charged, that on Sunday 5th April 1992 you did murder Anthony Weaver contrary to common law.

I knew that there would be an application to remand me in custody. Bail had been refused, as I knew it would. In the chaos, which was my former home, no one had found my passport. The house had been searched by professionals. I could only imagine that every piece of relevant paper, and much that was not had been bagged as evidence. But my passport was not there. I had been questioned about it. As far as I knew it was in the small grey filing cabinet in the corner of the study. As with everything else, its absence had been twisted. I was classified as a flight risk. I had no alternative place to live. If allowed my freedom I was sure to attempt to retrieve my children and flee the country. I won't say the thought hadn't crossed my mind. Life on the sunny Costas had its appeal. But as a single mum with two young children and no job it was only a thought. And then there was my mum. I hoped she was too far removed from reality to know what was going on.

The journey, in the back of an enclosed van, sitting in a three-foot square cubicle with no window to see out of, I was sick, the smell of my own vomit adding to the smells of every other imaginable bodily function, mixed with stale air and a chemical air freshener whose 'perfume' bore no resemblance to any substance in the natural world.

I had been in these places before, only then I knew that the doors which locked behind me would unlock on my request. I knew that there was no permanence attached to the turn of the key. I had been, *'just visiting'*, usually to glean information from one of the inmates' carefully cultivated for the purpose. I knew this would not be easy. I had not realised just how hard it would be.

Time on remand passed. I was allowed my own clothes, a few home comforts. My only visitor was Simon Hastings, but he brought no good news. My daughters had seemingly disappeared into a parallel universe. He said he had enquired and been met with a wall of silence and prevarication. On one hand he was assured that they were safe. On the other they could or would not tell him where they were. It was, as one hatchet faced social worker in cheap brogues had said, 'in the interests of the children and their welfare' not to divulge their whereabouts.

After several months of my incarceration being repeatedly renewed a date was set for trial at Cardiff Crown Court, Monday 13th December 1993. My case had been transferred at the request of the prosecution. Too much local interest so they said, in Bristol. Cardiff was nicely out of the way. Out of sight, out of mind.

Simon Hastings had done his best. He had been dispatched with permission from and accompanied by Ron Ashton to collect some clothes for me from my home, along with a selection of utilitarian underwear, jeans, t- shirts and joggers. He had managed to find my formal suit. More used to appearing for the prosecution, it was a well-tailored charcoal grey skirt suit. Pencil skirt fitted box jacket worn with low heeled shoes and with my hair tied up in a loose bun, and my face made up, I looked like what I had been. More detective than defendant, out of place and slightly swamped by the massive old furniture of courtroom no 1.

My Barrister Robert Eaves took charge. He was young, inexperienced, but clever, maybe a little too clever for his own good. No one likes a smart Alec, elderly crown court judges in particular. He did not endear himself to anyone.

There was legal discussion which I was not party to. I was not to be included in my own destiny. If I had views, they were immaterial. There was more legal discussion behind closed doors, a flock of black gowned and bewigged carrion crows dissecting my life in my absence. A plea to manslaughter was offered by my defence. No deal. The Crown wanted murder only, they were happy to roll the dice. If Robert Eaves couldn't smell it, then I could. The rank smell of corruption.

I knew the system well. If the Crown could get a plea which resulted in a long sentence they would take it. I could get such a sentence for manslaughter. I sensed there were other factors at work. Interests being protected. Examples to be made. The trial was listed for four days, the prosecuting Barrister an eminent lawyer with years of experience declared it a simple matter. The defendant had admitted her guilt. There was CCTV footage of the crime. A security firm had been traced. They had installed the camera at the request of Anthony Weaver the deceased, as a security measure. There was further legal argument. The jury was sent out, the judge, Justice ap Meredith QC ruled it admissible. Little credence was given to my explanations in interview, much was made of my demeanour on video and my cynical toast, a glass raised to the man I had once loved, who had betrayed and abused me once too often.

Slainte Tony.

Next key word.

Guilty.

The Judge adjourned for sentencing and social reports. More blur, more fog. More consultations with faceless grey social workers, a mental health team. I was on the criminal justice treadmill, it was accelerating, and I could not jump off. I would be carried along on its never-ending journey until someone or something pressed stop. Stop the world. I need to get off!

The sentence.

Cassandra Weaver, you have been found guilty of murder. I have considered all the evidence put before me. I have listened to the arguments of learned council both for the prosecution and the defence. You were a person in a position of trust. A person sworn to protect life. Yet you took a life, the life of the father of your children. You knew the possible consequences of your action. You will go to prison for life, and in your case, life should be at least twenty years.

I am mindful that your daughters are only three and four years old. In view of this, the nature of your conviction, and the length of sentence I have seen fit to impose, an order will be made removing your rights as a parent, and in the absence of any suitable family member, the children Amy Weaver and Charlotte Weaver will be taken into the protection of the state with a view to them being adopted.

Even the spectators in the public gallery sucked in a breath on hearing the length of the sentence and the order regarding my girls.

I think I screamed. I know I fainted. I came to lying in a grey painted, featureless medical room with a pale faced ineffectual nurse fussing over me. I had hit my head on the furniture in my fall and bruised the side of my head. A medical officer declared it superficial, and I was left sitting in my holding cell. It was five o clock when the next stage of my journey began. I remember hearing the clock at the top of the city hall tower tolling the hour as the van pulled out of the archway from the underground cells. Next stop would be my home for the next two decades.

HMP. Stafford.

I surrendered my clothing and was issued with the standard dehumanising prison uniform. Shapeless was the only word which described it. No other word seemed to fit as well as it fitted badly. It was Thursday 16th December 1993. Only nine days until Christmas. I choked back the tears which welled at the thought of two small girls. Girls without their mother. Christmas alone.

Through seemingly endless locked doors I was escorted to a cell, where I would meet my cell mate. Dawn Crole. No one had mentioned my history, the elephant in the room, but everyone in the establishment would know by now. There would be a reception committee. I had no doubt of that. What form it would take would depend largely on circumstance.

Having nothing better to do until Dawn returned from her job in the laundry, I lay on the bottom bunk and counted the slats above my head until the sleep of exhaustion took over. I was only disturbed by the sound of the key turning in the door and the entrance of Dawn.

Dawn was not at all what I expected. She was older than me for starters, short cropped white hair, highlighted with a streak of yellow down one side, her face wrinkled from hard living and poverty. Booze and drugs looked to have also left their mark and her cheeks sunken in from a lack of teeth and from almost constant smoking. But her eyes were alive with humour, olive dark splashes in her sallow lined skin. I rejudged her age. She was probably a lot younger than she looked.

The warder left the door ajar, I knew she wouldn't be far away, monitoring this first contact. How would a disgraced copper be received? Especially one with kiddies on the outside.

Dawn looked me up and down with distaste and grunted, 'I did have a nice single berth, now my life smells of pig shit.'

'I'm Sandra, I don't like it much either.' I countered. 'Pleased to meet you, too.'

'At least you ain't taken my bunk, I'd have been right pissed off if you 'ad.' Her accent was so strongly Bristolian it was hard to understand, but she put out a hand for me to shake. Her grip was like a vice. 'I'm Dawn, I hope you don't snore like one.'

'No, I don't,' I replied, 'but my table manners are awful.'

At this, her face cracked into a toothless grin. She started to laugh. Vaulting easily up onto the top bunk, she lay on her back and continued to laugh for several minutes.

'Cassandra Weaver, I think us shall get on fine! Now what have you got in the way of scran. I'm starving and there's an hour before we get fed.'

I surrendered the slightly squashed unwrapped Mars bar from my small pile of belongings. I had been allowed to keep it. I hadn't eaten anything since breakfast. I broke it in two and handed her the bigger piece.

Dawn spoke again. 'They've given you an old dog for protection, you won't get it easy for a few weeks. I won't be around all the time. There's a few who would like to see you scarred. Word is, there is someone on the outside who would dearly like you dead. What you did upset a good many apple carts, Cassandra. You will need eyes in your back, there is always someone who will do dirty work for money. Those who have nothing left to lose.'

I must have swallowed hard because the laughter started again.

'Don't worry Cassandra, I'll point them out. Stick with me kid, you'll survive.'

'Do me a favour, Dawn. Less of the 'Cassandra', you're not my f'ing mother. And spread the word, a twenty-year tariff and an adoption order on my kids may just give me not a lot left to lose either.'

'Fighting talk like that will get you right into hot water, boiling hot water. Suck it up for now, suss them out, bide your time, you've plenty of it, Cassandra. Oh, and be good to me, I'm the nearest thing you have to a mother or a family right now.'

Dawn took a toothless bite out of my Mars bar and half chewing, half sucking on it noisily, my cell mate closed her eyes.

I managed to raise a smile and from my bottom bunk, I poked her in the backside through the wooden slats. 'Fancy a night out later?', I jested. 'I could murder a pint.'

'You've done enough murdering from what we've heard, now get your head down for an hour. It's been a long day, there will be another long one tomorrow.'

I closed my eyes and pictured Amy and Charlotte wherever they were. I needed to feel that they were still together, for now anyway. I could not bear to think of them, apart. Simon Hastings had said he could fight the adoption order, if only there was someone who could be appointed to care for them in loco parentis. That was the problem. There was no one.

The next thing I heard was the shrill bell which summoned us to the canteen, followed by the turning of keys in locks and the movement of many bodies. A wing full of women of all shapes and sizes, stretching, belching, farting then filing out into the passage for the highlight of the evening. Evening meal. It was a noise I would grow used to three times daily for a very long time.

If anyone ever made a joke about school dinners, they could make a fortune writing them about prison food. It is beige. Varying shades of beige. I'm sure that technically and chemically it provides for all your nutritional needs. I expect there is a law which says it has to. There is also a custom and practice which boils the colour out of everything and highlights that lack of colour with the charring effect of an extra ten minutes on 'Regulo-9'. I sat with Dawn and kept my head down. I ate what I could. Pudding looked passable, but that was neatly removed from my tray by a large woman with long arms and tattoos. She was sitting four places to my left.

Its removal was punctuated by a chorus of farmyard noises which honed itself to a chorus of OINK. Not, I thought, a compliment to the chef, more a social comment about Gaynor Jones the pudding thief's table manners. The chorus was augmented by the rhythmic percussion of mugs and cutlery on stained Formica tabletops. Sandra Weaver was being drummed into their world, a world where I would be viewed with suspicion, derision, scorn, and outright hatred. Pigs don't do well in prison. Pigs are kept in pigsties not cells.

The second movement of the canteen symphony was interrupted by one of the older female screws unleashing her best ex-army parade ground voice.

'Hush the fuck up, you tribe of bitches.' Miss Wellington, aka the Old Boot made herself heard above the din. Miss Wellington, I was told, had the power to cancel this evening's television and recreation hour, the daily opportunity to watch someone else's choice of viewing on the very wobbly picture which displayed itself on the ancient Bush Television set. The noise died down, but I could feel the visual daggers probing between my shoulder blades, and I could see the venomous looks from the inmates across the table.

I stayed in that first night! Nothing like an early night with a good book. The night was early, the book was boring - the prison codes of practice. The rules and regulations. Every sensible inmate had one, I suspected few had ever bothered to read the small print.

Lock up was at nine pm. The Old Boot and her accomplice walked the landing turning keys in doors and wishing us all a cheery good night. I buried my head in the single thin foam pillow and cried myself to sleep.

That week passed in a flurry of legal visits. Simon had tried his hardest to find my girls, but without success. He had been met with a social services wall of silence. He had no alternative to offer as a home for two very young children. My only living relative was my elderly mother and she was two steps to the wrong side of sanity. Simon was also trying to separate my affairs from the tangle that was Tony's life. Would I have anything left when I was released. I did after all have some assets and a pension which I had worked for, and which had not been taken from me. Yet.

Simon was of the opinion that my crime was not injurious enough to public confidence in the Police for the service to take this action against me. I no longer had confidence in a system which could treat me as it had. If I was ever released back to society, I would face a grim and lonely future, denied access to everything I had ever loved and all that I had worked for.

2007

CHAPTER 10. WHO AM I NOW? – Tracy Brown 1995

I remember that I was four. Miss Turner the social worker had dressed me up in my school coat and my school uniform skirt complete with woolly tights and shoes. My curly hair was teased into two pigtails, just like for school but with a pair of bright red ribbons. Something was up. My four-year-old senses felt it. Today was different.

Breakfast at Oakbrook, the children's home where I lived with my sister Charlotte, had been the usual scrummage, the bigger boys and girls getting to the cereals first, the milk being tipped, and the sugar being spread everywhere. Mrs Willis, the lovely kindly lady in the kitchen winked at me as I ran past with my empty bowl.

'Never mind Amy, have these my dear.' Her smooth Jamaican lilt a calming raft in a sea of noise. The small box of Ricicles she gave me from the Variety pack in her special cupboard was the only breakfast I would get. Charlotte was a year older than me and fared better in the scrummage that was life in care.

Now the other kids were going out into the garden to play or waiting for the staff to turn a blind eye to their going missing for a few hours, but I was being dressed up for school. It was Saturday, there was no school. I wasn't so stupid as not to know the days of the week. Something was up!

Miss Turner knelt in front of me and straightened my collar and smoothed down the burgundy fabric of my nicely tailored coat. A coat which had belonged to my sister, my twin sister, Charlotte.

We had been teased about being twins, the older girls had pulled my hair and danced around me, pushing, and shoving me, singing bad songs about us. How could we be twins when we were so different, when I was so very dark, and she was so very fair? Irish Twins they called us. Born on the same day exactly a year apart.

'Amy, child, today is a special day for you. Today you get a new mummy and daddy. Today you are going to stay with Mr. and Mrs. Brown and if you all get along together, that is where you will live. It will be your home.' Miss Turner spoke softly and kindly, but she did not fool me.

'I want Charlie, I want my sister.' I set my bottom lip and stared at her.

'She can always visit.' Miss Turner lied. 'It's not far.'

'I want to stay with Charlie.' my mind was made up. 'I am staying with Charlie.'

An ordinary looking light brown car pulled up to the door and a couple got out, Mr and Mrs Brown I assumed. He was small and thin, with a wispy beard and collar length hair, he was dressed in old brown corduroy trousers with brown slip-on shoes and wore a multi coloured jumper with no sleeves. The whole impression he gave was nondescript. She was large, very large, a big round woman, dressed from head to toe in a construction of turquoise and orange floral material, topped with a turquoise and orange turban, and she was black, like me. She looked friendly. He just looked beige.

Mr and Mrs Brown were to be my foster parents, they would take me into their home and look after me, not here in the children's home with Charlie. They would take me away to their home.

My mind went into rebellion. 'No, I won't go without Charlie!' I threw myself on the floor of Miss Turners office, kicking like a toddler and screaming. 'I want to see my sister, NOW!' Miss Turner stood me back on my feet and slapped me on the legs. The blow stung. I kicked her, right in the left shin, and remembering some of the words had first heard a lifetime of a year ago, I screamed at her again.

'Fuck off you bitch!' I didn't know what the words meant but I knew they were bad and that I had heard them somewhere, somewhere before here. Mrs Brown glided into the room, taking charge of the situation. She sat down on the floor with me, occupying most of the small office with her huge presence and outlandish robes.

'What's all this then?' She sounded just like Mrs Willis. She spoke with a rich deep voice, 'Are we as bad as all that? Hush that crying now.

How about we go and get a MacDonalds, then we can go home, and, if you don't like us, you can always come back. I promise darling.'

My bottom lip trembled. 'Will you tell my sister where I am, she will miss me.'

Mrs Brown laughed. 'Of course we will.' That was not the last lie she told me. At least it seemed to be a lie because I never saw my sister again.

I liked Mrs Brown or mama Alice as I would call her. I walked quietly to the car, holding Alice Brown's hand tightly, Stephen Brown carrying my small bag of belongings, walking two strides behind. That was fourteen years ago.

I stayed with the Browns until I was twelve. I came to love Alice Brown, she was everything a mother should be, kind, caring, strict when needed, sympathetic and wise. She included me in everything. The Brown's house was chaotic. Alice and Stephen had no children of their own, but they fostered, only one child at a time, but there was a constant stream of boys and girls visiting mama Alice, those she had fostered in the past, all of whom seemed to gravitate towards the wave of joy she created.

Alice Brown loved to sing, the house was always full of music. She also loved her church, she sang in the choir, the gospel choir and from the very first she took me with her. I soon found that I could sing too. Singing took me out of myself and I threw myself into it. On my twelfth birthday Alice proudly gave me her old guitar. *'I will never play it again, girl, these old fingers be too stiff with arthritis now, you have it, learn to play it. If you can cook and play guitar you will never be alone.'* Alice taught me the basics and with help from a dog-eared copy of Bert Weedon's book, I soon mastered a few tunes. I had a natural ear and could play most things after hearing them only once. I would practice for hours in my little bedroom at the back of the house, singing and strumming along to the radio. The chaos of the Browns' house made me forget Oakbrook and, most of all, made memories of my sister fade and become more dim with every passing week.

I was twelve when I met Julia Grainger. She was new in school, and with her new uniform, complete with blazer, her shiny leather satchel and her regulation shoes, she looked like she was fresh out of a box and like me, she was black. Her mother was tall and thin and very beautiful and walked her in through the gates on that first day like a supermodel down the runway at fashion week. Julia was collected at half past three sharp in her huge black Range Rover with tinted privacy windows.

By lunchtime of the second day, her shoes were scuffed, her blazer was muddy, and her satchel was full of wet toilet paper. She had been initiated into life at a Bristol Comprehensive School. I found her crying her heart out in the girls' toilets, frantically trying to straighten her clothing and dry out her sodden school books. I shared my lunch with her. One of the older girls had tipped out Julia's lunch box onto the floor and stamped all over her neat triangular sandwiches, her yogurt, and her apple.

'My mum told me to tell a teacher if anyone picked on me, Tracy, but I don't want to. They said it would be worse for me if I did. My dad will be really mad about it.'

'No,' I told her, 'that will make it worse. You'll learn. You need to stand up to them.'

Julia and I became inseparable. We found our safe space, a corner behind the shed where the games equipment was kept. We sat next to each other when we could and I invited her home to Mama Brown's for tea. Julia's mother insisted she drive us there that day, she wanted to see where Julia was going. I understood that. But I told Julia, 'Next time, we both catch the bus.'

Mama Brown had reservations about Julia, I could tell. I heard her talking to Stephen about her. 'I am worried, don't you know who that child's father is? And you know where our Tracy came from, it is trouble, for sure.'

And Stephen Brown's reply, 'All you can do is keep an eye out, Alice. Julia is her closest friend. She seems a nice girl, don't tar her with her father's brush.'

Alice Brown made a grunting noise of dissatisfaction in her throat, then came back to the kitchen where Julia and I were tucking in to our fishfingers, beans and chips.

The return visit to Julia's was an education. Julia lived in leafy Clifton. The Grainger house was a three storey Edwardian villa with views out onto the downs. It was a palace compared with mama Brown's inner city terrace. Everything was new and modern or subtly renovated in keeping with the style of the house. Julia Grainger's home was truly lovely, but her mother was not a patch on Alice Brown when it came to cooking for children. Julia's mother went to endless trouble producing home-made lasagne which she served with garlic bread dripping in real butter. She sat us at the big dining room table and insisted that we eat with a knife and fork and not just with our fingers. All we really wanted was fish fingers and beans in front of the TV and then to go out and play. High point of going to Julia's for tea was getting to play on the downs, acres of grass where we could run free, as long as we were home before dark. Then I would catch the bus back down Black Boy Hill into the city, and home. Yes, I loved my life with the Browns.

A few days before my fourteenth birthday my life changed forever. I came home from school, hopping off the bus at the corner of Gloucester Road to find a police car outside the house along with a big black estate car with tinted windows. I ran in through the front door and was headed for the kitchen, running smack into the front of PC Green the neighbourhood Bobby. He took me firmly by the shoulders and turned me around and diverted me into the little used best room at the front of the house. Stephen Brown was sitting on one the very upright formal chairs arranged around the dining table which occupied the centre of the room. He lifted his head from his hands and sniffed, and visibly straightened his shoulders. I could see that he had been crying.

'Mama Brown is dead, child. She is gone.' It was a bald statement, not wrapped in pleasantries or softened in any respect. 'Her heart gave out, I am sorry, Tracy, but you will have to go back to the homes. I cannot look after you by myself, that's just how it is, I am so, so sorry.'

'We can get by, I can look after you, I can do everything.', I pleaded.

'It doesn't work like that child. The law says you have to go back, it may not be so bad, you can still visit like all the others do.' His voice was resigned.

'Is my sister still there?' I asked him hopefully.

'No, my dear, she is not. She is with another family. I think she may even be in Scotland. I heard that woman Miss Turner mention Glasgow, but I didn't tell you that. Me and Alice were not even supposed to know,'

I ran upstairs to my bedroom and slammed the door, I shut myself in and threw myself on the bed and I cried. Sometime during the afternoon, I heard the front door close, and the car reverse off the driveway. Stephen had gone out. I crept downstairs and into the study where I knew Mama Brown had kept all her paperwork.

Every child Mama Brown had looked after had a file. I knew that. When you moved on the file was supposed to go with you. I was never much bothered with mine, until now. Had Mama Brown written down anything about Charlotte? I did not have to look far. My file was out on the desk. Stephen was collecting together things which would need to go back to Oakbrook with me. I had no idea how long he would be out. I read quickly, thumbing through mundane details of inoculations, medical records, dental appointments kept and missed, school reports. Then at the back, written in pencil, erased but still visible in the indentations left in the thicker paper of the cover was a brief note. It read, *"Both together possibly",* Marcia and Adam Alexander, 4 Minard Road, Glasgow. G412DL. Then I saw that there was a line struck through the word 'both'. There was a line written underneath in what I recognised as Miss Turner's neat hand. It read: *C only and short term*. I did not read any further. I scribbled the address on the palm of my hand and scuttled back upstairs just in time to hear Stephen Brown close the front door behind him.

'Tracy.' He called up the stairs to me. 'Come down, please, I've got fish and chips, your favourite, and I may have some news for you.'

I was not interested. I pushed my bed in front of my bedroom door and barricaded myself in. I was not going to be dissuaded from my course of action. It was all happening too quickly. I felt as though Stephen just wanted to get rid of me. I had no time to digest what had happened. I was told that Mama Brown had had a massive heart attack. Her big kind heart could no longer support the massive bulk around it. Her husband had found her dead in the kitchen. It was sudden. Mama Brown had not been to see the doctor for years. She had never taken the tablets that she had been prescribed on the last visit. She had believed that her faith in God would heal her if she had a problem. Mama Brown had had great faith in the power of prayer. Prayer was no cure for COPD or furred up coronary arteries. It was pure luck that PC Green had stopped me from getting into that room. Another minute and I would have seen her, lying on the scrubbed lino floor. Lifeless. Gone. If Stephen Brown had not come home early from work, then I would have found her. Lovely, kind-hearted, Mama Alice.

That night I decided. Stuffing a change of clothes into my school bag stealing what cash there was in the housekeeping jar in the kitchen cupboard and emptying my piggy bank, I ran away. I would never go back to the homes again. I was fourteen years old. I would be fine. I would find Charlotte and we would be fine together. The only other possession I thought to take with me was Mama Alice's old guitar in its soft case. I slung it over my shoulder.

That morning Stephen Brown waved me off to school thinking that I might be late home after a guitar lesson. He would never see me again. I had liked, even grown to love the Browns, but there was no way that I would ever go back to the homes.

I made my way to the railway station at Temple Meads. I was getting very good at reading timetables and was well used to using public transport around Bristol, so seeing that the next train to Glasgow was not until the late afternoon, I hid out of sight until it was time to get on board, then I hid In a luggage car between the carriages of the sleeper train and prayed that this diesel-powered magic carpet would whisk me into the arms of my sister.

I did not know how it was going to get there, neither did I care. I made myself small and curled behind the baggage and went to sleep. Glasgow. I had to get to Glasgow and find Charlotte.

I was woken up by a kindly looking man in a uniform, but he was not the Police. He spoke with a very strange accent.

'Are ye okay, dearie?'

I yawned and sat up. 'Yes, I'm fine.' I rubbed my eyes and felt for my schoolbag.

'Did ye miss yer stop, lassie, only yer in Glasgae, I din'nae recognise yon school badge, but I ken it's from Bristol, am I right, lass?'

'I'm visiting my gran, I'm here for the holidays.' I started to make a move for the exit.

'Well, here in bonnie Scotland the holidays din'nae start for another three weeks. I fancy yer a bit early, but if ye tell me where yer grannie lives, I can ask yon PC Macdonald tae take you there, make sure ye are safe like.'

I ran. I barged past him, bags flying, guitar case banging against the floor and legs pumping, out of the station, into the fresh air and onto the streets of Glasgow.

How I came to be living with Marcia Alexander was another twist in the tale.

CHAPTER 11. MINARD ROAD – Tansy Alexander 2004

I was fourteen years old, dressed in a school uniform which stated on the badge which adorned my burgundy blazer, that I was plainly not attending any school in the local area. I had stuffed only a pair of jeans and some clean underwear and a sweatshirt into my school backpack. I had the contents of the housekeeping jar and my piggy bank and Mama Alice Brown's guitar, and that was it. I did not even have a warm coat. Maybe this was not such a good idea after all.

I had not eaten since breakfast time and my stomach was starting to rumble. There was a Mucky D's almost directly outside the central railway station. I pushed my way through the door with as much confidence as I could muster, I ordered myself a 99p happy meal and sat down to collect my thoughts, trying to look as inconspicuous as possible, blending in with the furniture.

I had an address. I had no idea where it was apart from that it was in Glasgow. I had no idea how to get there. I had no idea what I would find when I did. I had nowhere to stay and very little money. It was also getting dark. I finished my burger and my drink and asked the girl on the counter if she knew the way to Minard Road. She had raised her eyebrows and made a noise which suggested that she thought it too well to do a street for the likes of me. Then she looked me up and down and established in one scan of eyes too knowing for her age, the likely possibilities. She had noticed that I had been into the toilets and changed from my alien school uniform into jeans, Converse tennis shoes and a hoodie. Standard uniform for off duty school kids in England, but this was Scotland. I really should have brought my Parka coat, but that would have raised suspicion. I never ever wore my Parka to school. Stephen would have smelled a rat. I wrote down the directions she gave me on the back of a napkin, slowly my ear was becoming tuned to the thick accent. Apparently Minard Road was not that far. It was about two and a half miles away on the other side of the river. If I crossed the Clyde by the Gorbals Street bridge and kept to the right until I reached the athletics stadium at Darnley Road, then turned left, I wouldn't go far wrong. I shouldered my bag and my guitar, gave her a made-up story about having an aunty that lived in the aforementioned street and set off for the bridge over the Clyde. I did not hang about, nice though she seemed, the girl on the checkout at MacDonald's plainly knew a teenage runaway when she saw one. She did, however, give good directions.

I turned left off the main road and into Minard Road. Four-storey blocks of refurbished flats stretched along both sides of the road, built of red sandstone, each with a large front door out onto the pavement. I was looking for number four. I arrived outside the block at just after 7pm. The large slate plaque beside the door announced that the whole block was number 4. An entry phone with a number of different buttons named the occupants of the individual flats. The names were faded with age, and several were missing. I pressed the central button used by delivery persons and visitors and trying not to sound like the child I was, I asked boldly for Mrs Alexander. To my amazement a voice came through the speaker.

'Come in dearie, its flat B.'

I pushed the huge black wooden door inwards and instinctively wiped my feet on the coconut mat inset into the tiled and polished floor. I looked around and there in the back corner was a burgundy door bearing the identifier 4B.

I walked cautiously up to the door and knocked. I heard footsteps on the other side, a high-pitched bark and the patter of dog's claws on hard flooring, a female voice telling the dog to stay and then the door opened before me and there she was. A woman who I assumed was Marcia Alexander. I looked at her hopefully. Maybe she would tell me what I needed to know without the need for twenty questions, but no.

'What can I do fer ye, lass.' she asked.

'Are you Mrs Alexander?' I queried.

'I am that. Now who are you and what on earth has brought you here?' Her voice was friendly at least.

'Is Charlotte here?' I couldn't help myself. 'My sister, Charlotte.'

Mrs Alexander looked puzzled. 'Charlotte? Why no, my dear, I have never had any Charlotte stay here.'

'But……….'

'Come in lass, you look freezing and about to fall over, where on earth have you come from. Are you run away?'

I did not answer. She looked me up and down, forming her own opinion, perfectly correctly, that I was. She took my arm and ushered me into a spacious and comfortable room, homely, lived in, cluttered with books and papers. A small tan coloured dachshund dog perched on the back of the settee, tail wagging and ears pricked in a friendly manner, looking at me from its vantage point with one brown and one blue eye.

'This is Piccadilly.' She introduced the dog. 'Now who are you? I want the truth mind, the way I see it, ye are plainly English, I can tell by yer accent. Ye plainly had my address from somewhere and if ye have run this far, if I were to make a phone call then ye would probably run again. Am I right?'

She was so right. I nodded my head. She turned and walked through into her kitchen, and I heard her fill the kettle and the sound of an electric kettle starting to heat. Then the thud of two mugs being placed on a work surface.

'Tea, coffee or chocolate?' she asked, 'Oh, and call me Marcia.'

'Chocolate, please.' I replied.

'Thought so, you look like a chocolate kind of a girl, now who exactly are you?'

I started at the beginning, I told her about the Browns and then about my sister. She looked at me in amazement.

'My dear Tracy or would you rather be Amy, or you could pick another name. I don't mind at all. One is as good as another to me.'

I looked out of the window and pointed at a patch of yellow flowers growing like weeds in the terrace outside her lounge window.

'What flower is that?' I asked.

'That my dear is ragwort, I don't suppose you want to be called ragwort. But it's also known as Tansy.' She smiled.

'Tansy then, call me Tansy.' I took a sip of my hot chocolate.

'Tansy,' she began, 'Tansy, yes I like that, it suits you.' She rolled the name around her vocal cords then after a few minutes lost in thought she continued.

'Many years ago, I had plans to adopt children, I was married then, my husband and I could not have children of our own, so we applied to adopt.' She took a photograph from the mantel shelf.

'This was my husband.' She pointed out a big man with dreadlocked hair and a huge smile. 'Adam, his name was, unfortunately my Adam did not live to see us adopt. He was taken very ill very suddenly.' She stopped and wiped her eye with a finger. 'It was not long afterwards that I received a letter offering two girls who were in need of a home. I could'na take two girls at that time no matter how much I wanted to. I could only just look after myself. I said I might foster one of you on a temporary basis, but not permanent and not both. They turned down my offer. It was a Miss Turner, I think. Yes, that was her name. She said she wanted you to stay together. So, your sister Charlotte, if that was your sister, never came to me. That was many years ago, Tansy. I never heard a thing more. I'm sorry.'

'So where is my sister?' I asked her again.

'Your guess is as good as mine.' was her reply. 'Now I suppose you will have to stay here for the night, and we can start to sort the rest out in the morning. I still have a few contacts, young lady, I shall have to tell someone in authority where you are, but with a little persuasion, they may let you stay, if you want to. You'd have to go to school mind, and I'd expect you not to be on yer toes at the first sign of a disagreement.'

I looked around Marcia's flat, it was homely, lived in. For tonight at least I had a bed for the night. Marcia seemed nice, she was down to earth and practical, I could live here. I smiled at her, giving her my best *'I'd like that'* smile. She smiled back and, without being asked, Piccadilly came and sat on my lap, burying her head into my armpit, as if she was getting to know a new friend.

'Pic likes you! You can stay!' Marcia was laughing. 'She doesn't do that to everyone, you know.'

Marcia left me sitting on her comfy but saggy sofa.

'I'd best make you up a bed, then.' She disappeared across the hallway and I could hear her busying herself in another room. 'It's a long time since I had a house guest.' She proceeded to give me a running commentary on her progress, first finding the bed under a pile of books, then making sure the sheets were clean, turning back the quilt and pulling the curtains closed. Eventually she called me to inspect her work. 'It will do for tonight. You can help me shift the rest of the clutter tomorrow. Now do you want to watch TV with me hen, or have an early night?'

A bed had never looked so inviting, I chose the early night. I had a good feeling about Marcia. If I had chosen to sleep in the flat of an axe murderer, to be decapitated in my sleep it would still be better than being sent back to Oakbrook.

While I slept, Marcia must have searched my backpack, for I awoke to hear her talking to someone on the phone. From the half of the conversation, I could hear it was Stephen Brown.

'She's found her way to Glasgow, ye ken.'

'Yes, she's safe here,'

'No, ye di' nae need tae come and get her, she can stay wi' me as long as she wants.'

'She says she will na go back to that children's home, and she is looking for her sister.'

'Can ye no' let her stay wi' you, Stephen…….. I see….. okay…. And this number will get me through to Irene Turner herself then?'

I heard Marcia fumbling for the notepad by the phone and writing with the receiver wedged between shoulder and ear.

'Yes, I've got that…. It's early yet, I'll ring her a bit later. You take care Stephen, I understand completely… if it works out ye can send it up by post. I used to foster as well, years ago, but I'm still on the books as it were, they just din'nae use me. I suppose they think I'm a bit long in the tooth fer teenagers and they think wee bairns would be too much work and too emotional fer me! …… I'll get her tae call ye this evening when we know a bit more, ay!'

Marcia replaced the receiver.

I felt a warm glow of happiness start in my mind. I hugged my knees to my chin as I sat in the cluttered bedroom. 'I think I'm going to like it here.' I told myself. I reached down beside the bed and pulled my guitar from its case. As I tuned the strings and thought of a song to play,

I heard Marcia singing to herself in the kitchen. Recognising the song despite her tuneless efforts I quietly picked out the chords. In my mind I heard the words and changed them slightly 'How many roads must a girl walk down ………then I joined in with the chorus. 'The answer my friend, it is blowing in the wind, the answer is blowing in the wind.'

From across the hallway, I could smell the smells of breakfast, fresh toast, and bacon. I could hear the sound of the kettle as it came to the boil to the strains of Marcia's singing. I had a good feeling about today. I pulled on my jeans and hoodie and finding a huge old pair of sheepskin slippers under the bed, I shuffled across the passage.

'Bacon, egg and a little bit of toast.' Marcia greeted me, she sang the last few words.

'Yes please.' I answered, taking the offered seat at her table. Marcia looked down at my feet, her face clouded for an instant. 'I hav'nae seen those since my Adam went!' She sniffed slightly. 'I'm sure I threw them in the bin, but if they're back, you're welcome to use them. It must be a sign.' Marcia saw signs in lots of things, in fact she lived by them.

Marcia spent most of that day on the telephone, to make sure she was still as she put it 'on the books' in Scotland as a foster carer. She was assured that she was, they updated her personal details, and she told them what she was proposing to do. Then she phoned Oakbrook. Armed with a contact number to give them for her 'line manager in Glasgow,' Marcia went into battle.

'Ten years ago,' she said, 'you were happy for me tae take in both sisters, with a view tae adoption, but unfortunately my husband was taken from me, and I had to say no.'

I heard the silence on the phone. Marcia continued.

'Now one of the wee lasses has turned up on ma' doorstep, she can'nae find her sister, I presume her sister has found a family, aye' ……

'Well, I ken it's a wee bit unorthodox, but I can offer her a home, she does'nae want tae come back to Bristol, surely it would be better for her to have a stable life here, rather than be running away constantly, for she will nae stay there. She got here under her own steam, do ye think she'll stay put if she is'nae happy?'

I could almost hear the tumbleweed drifting across the barren wasteland of Irene Turner's mind. What would she do? She had the power to give me an emergency placement even on a temporary basis. Marcia waited.

'Three months then, as a temporary measure, in the meantime you'll review her case, and let me know. Thank you, Irene.' The call was ended.

'Well?' I asked.

'Well, indeed, you've been listening, haven't you? You get to stay for three months. I have to apply to make it a permanent thing. You have to show everyone that you want to stay. That means school, no bunking off. That means no running away. You get the idea?'

I flung my arms around Marcia's neck and breathed in the floral smell of her perfume, mixed with the slight whiff of Piccadilly the dog, and patchouli oil.

'Marcia, you have no idea how good I can be.'

'Tansy Alexander, I shall hold you to that. Now let's get ourselves together, we've things to do. Stephen is going to send your things up by parcel post. But you are still going to need clothes, you can't exist in what you stand in.'

Marcia took me shopping, strictly high street. She couldn't stretch to designer gear, not that I had ever worn anything that was not 'Primani' or Peacocks, or counterfeit knock offs from Eastville market. We had fun. We even stopped for a MuckyD by the train station. The girl on the counter was the same one as yesterday.

'Found yer aunty then, hen!' She winked at me - I winked back. We spent the whole day in town, Marcia showing me round the bustling slightly grubby city of a Glasgow which I would make my home and would grow to love. We walked along the Clyde. She pointed out where the great ships had been built, until the decline of the shipyards. She showed me the upmarket cafes where the up-and-coming professionals socialised, the modern flats being built where the old warehouses once stood. It was not unlike Bristol in some respects, only it seemed far bigger, far busier. Would I stay here forever? I heard Marcia start to hum to herself, 'How many roads......'

I was fourteen years old. I had travelled the length the country alone in search of a sister. I had not found Charlotte, but I had found a home of sorts. Had things been different, it may have been a home for both of us. I determined to make the best of this opportunity. Marcia had acquired a daughter and I had found a home. 'How many roads indeed.' I thought. 'The answer is blowing in the wind.'

My three-month emergency placement was soon extended to six. I was enrolled in the local high school, a report from my school in Bristol had pronounced me a capable student and after an interview with the head teacher and the completion of a myriad of forms, I was accepted as a bursary student. Marcia was over the moon with this, she still worked part time, to subsidise her widow's pension, but she was by no means wealthy. The flat had been paid for on her husband's death and his pension just about paid the bills.

Settling in at the new school was hard, I was an outsider and was treated as such. My physical appearance raised eyebrows. I was very tall for a fourteen-year-old, my hair an uncontrollable mop of curls which are not quite afro in their nature, and, to go with my dark skin I have blue eyes. *Unusual* was how one of the teachers put it.

Marcia encouraged me to keep up with my guitar lessons and I found that this was the one thing that built bridges between me and the other students. I could sing and I could play. I soon found out that their reticence in speaking to me was that they found my west country accent as difficult to understand as I found their Glaswegian. As the language barrier fell, I began to make friends.

Amongst these was Joey Callahan. Joey and I were fellow bursary students. He was three years older than me, he was smart, and he was good looking in a surfer dude sort of way. He lived with his father in a different area of the city. He didn't talk much about his home life, but from the little he did say, I understood that he would be glad to finish school and leave home. He had plans to go into business for himself. What business he didn't say, but he said he had contacts and that with a bit of luck he would make the big time. Joey and I became inseparable.

I studied hard and I did well, my life became filled with all the things teenaged girls enjoy. With Marcia I had a stable home and a mother figure. Marcia filled the flat with music and her slightly unorthodox attitude to life. She encouraged all things creative, she painted herself watercolours of the local area, urban landscapes in and around the city. When she was not the doctors' receptionist, she could be found with her easel and paints sitting alongside the Clyde sketching the great cranes and the industrial remains of the shipyards. Sometimes a painting would sell and there would be extra money in the pot and treats all round.

It was too good to last. It was not long before my sixteenth birthday that things changed forever. Joey had left school. He had completed the sixth form but had not sat his exams. He had dropped out and disappeared. There were rumours that he was, '*In with a wrong crowd,*' even that he had probably been sent to prison for some misdemeanour. I caught the bus across town and went to his father's house in search of him. The place he had described to me was unoccupied, there were no signs of life. The scruffy looking red brick semi-detached house had the remains of an old Ford Cortina rusting in the front garden. There was an old settee under the boarded-up front window, its upholstery stained with a myriad of unidentifiable substances.

The neighbour's house was in a slightly better state of repair and seeing the door open, I knocked and waited for an answer.

'Who is it?' an angry male voice answered. 'If yer the rent man I hav'nae got yer money.'

'I'm looking for Mr Callahan or his son, Joey.' I called in through the open front door, my nostrils assaulted by the pungent smell of cats, stale chip fat and unwashed clothing.

'Come in, hen.' the voice invited. I stepped inside as far as the door to the living room where I could see a large man with a huge belly clad only in saggy jeans and a string vest sitting in a recliner chair whose arms were decorated with an intricate pattern of cigarette burns.

'Din'nae be afraid, I din'nae bite, aye.' I could smell a strange cloying smell and hear the regular hiss of a small machine in the corner connected to two small tubes which were pointed up the wearer's nostrils. This man was not well. His breath was short and sounded like the gurgle of congested drains.

'Have you seen Joey, Mr….?' I began.

'I'm Dougie, Dougie McCann, Theres been no one livin' in that there shit hole fer months, lassie. Hamish Callahan is deid. More than a year ago, the drink took him, he'd been on his last legs fer years. That boy of his did nothing but rob him. I've not seen that wee bastard since the day of his old man's funeral, and good riddance.' He gasped for breath and turned up the flow on the nebuliser.

'Did he leave any message?' It was a stupid question 'Have you any idea where he is?'

'If yer in the family way, lassie, I tell ye, ye won't get a brass farthing from Joey Callahan. Forget him lass, he is nothing but trouble.'

'No, I'm not! I'm a friend that's all. If ye see him….' I started.

'If I see him before the Polis, I shall tell them, if they hav'nae caught him first. If ye know what's good fer ye, ye'll stay in school and make something of yersel', forget you ever met him. Now off with you……'

'Tansy…… Tell him Tansy was looking for him, Tansy Alexander.'
I stepped back out onto the weed infested front path. The sun was low in the sky, but it was still fairly warm.
'Leave the door open, lass.' Dougie McCann shouted as she left, and he reached for another can of Tennent's lager.

I caught the bus back across town to Minard Road to find that my guitar tutor Alan Gorman was at the flat. I had not missed a lesson. What was he doing here? He was sitting on the settee in the lounge and was making himself very much at home.

'Ah, Tansy,' He greeted me. 'ye will 'na mind if I take Marcia out fer a bevvy this evening.'

The noise of heels on the tiled hall floor made me turn and I saw Marcia sweeping towards me from her bedroom, not dressed in her usual jeans and sloppy T shirt. Hair freshly washed and newly cut in long layers and wearing a brightly coloured tunic top over black jeans and high heeled boots, she looked quite stunning.

'Don't scrub up bad, do I?' She must have seen the look of amazement which adorned my face. 'Alan is taking me for a few bevvies and then to a music gig. I won't be too late, hen, don't wait up for me.

This was the first time in nearly three years that Marcia had left me to my own devices to go out with a man. I could not begrudge her a life outside of looking after me.

'You enjoy yourself, Marcia, you deserve it,' I told her, then addressing Alan, 'and you look after her.'

He laughed. They gathered their belongings, and I settled down to an evening of television and homework. Today I had seen the other side of my good friend Joey and of my foster mother Marcia. Life threw you a curved ball sometimes.

I switched the TV off, put my books away. I put my headphones on and turned on some music. I drifted off to sleep to the hypnotic sounds of Pink Floyd's, 'Comfortably Numb'. I dreamed that night of a great gig in the sky.

I vaguely heard Alan and Marcia stagger in through the front door just after midnight and fall in through the door of Marcia's bedroom, landing heavily on the bed. I turned the music up and pulled the quilt over my ears to drown out the grunts and groans from the room across the hall. Marcia and Alan were now an item.

CHAPTER 12. ALL TRUST BETRAYED – Tansy

At first it was like a breath of fresh air. Alan Gorman and Marcia were an item, they had been seeing each other regularly for well over six months. Alan was still my guitar tutor, he still taught my regular lesson at school, and he still came to the flat to teach my extra lesson on a Wednesday evening. He was nothing if not professional. He never called me by anything other than my proper name Miss Alexander, in school that is. When he came to the flat, he did drop the formality and called me Tansy. He always left the door to the living room open. He was never on his own with me without Marcia being within easy reach in the kitchen. He was a teacher. He had been my teacher for three years. In some ways he had become a bit of a father figure or a hero. I looked up to Mr Gorman the guitar tutor with his long, glossy, dark red hair and his scruffy, short, trimmed beard.

I was not the only teenager in the school who would admit to having had a bit of a girly crush on Mr Gorman. He was younger than most of the other male teachers, he was single, some of the sixth form lads thought that he might well be gay. He was certainly in touch with his feminine side. He played guitar like a dream, both acoustic and electric. He still had contacts in the music industry and if any of us had read his resumé we would have seen that he had been a very busy session musician before he fell into teaching. Now here he was sitting in Marcia's living room giving lessons to a sixteen-year-old. He remained professionally attentive and considerate right up to the time that he moved his belongings into our small flat.

The flat at Minard Road had only two bedrooms, the third was used as a study and as Marcia's studio. This hardly mattered as Alan had no intention of sleeping in a separate bed, he and Marcia were together after all. He gradually moved most of his belongings in, filling the hallway with amplifiers and speakers. His guitar collection invaded the cupboard in the hallway forcing Marcia to take the double doors off to accommodate the expensive instruments which needed a highly regulated environment. It was no longer permissible to allow the steam to flood out of the bathroom or the kitchen into the flat, heaven forbid the neck of his Fender should warp or some other moisture issue take hold of his electric acoustic. I was not impressed. Mama Alice's old 'flat top' had survived everything that was thrown at it including a night on the express train from Bristol. Mr Gorman was going down in my estimation. He was a control freak. Everything had to be done his way, or it didn't happen.

He complained constantly about female lingerie hanging to dry from the airing rack which hung from the kitchen ceiling. He insisted that I wear a dressing gown over my pyjamas. He began to question whether I was doing my homework and who I was seeing when I went out with my friends. To make matters worse, he started to catch the same bus as me to school, even when he wasn't teaching.

Subtly, over the course of several weeks or even months, guitar lessons became more intimate. A hand over my shoulder to adjust my finger position. A hand on my thigh to adjust the position of the instrument. A finger brushing my neck to push my hair from my face when it escaped from its hair tie. A feeling that he was invading my personal space.

It was a Thursday night. Marcia and Alan had gone out for the evening, a local band was playing one of the larger music venues in the city. The drummer was a friend of Alan's or so he said. They went out early and did not come back until the early hours of the morning. Marcia was very drunk, so drunk that Alan had had to wake me to open the door and help him to get her into bed. I had opened the door in my short pyjamas and vest. My hair was loose. I did not have time to put on my dressing gown, Alan had been making enough noise to wake the whole block in his efforts to get into the flat.

Between us we put Marcia to sleep on the couch, I offered to sit with her in case she vomited, but he said that he would look after her. I made us both a hot drink, hot chocolate for me and a black coffee for him. I left him sitting with her, his bare feet resting on the coffee table. He had switched the TV on and was flicking through the channels dipping in and out of the music programmes without selecting anything. I took myself back to bed and plugged myself in to Pink Floyd

I never locked my bedroom door, there had never been a need to. I think I had been asleep for about an hour when I heard the door handle twist and the door to my bedroom pushed open.

'Tansy, are ye awake?' It was Alan.

'Is there a problem? Marcia, is she okay?' I was half awake. My eyes bleary with sleep.

Then he started to pull back my bedclothes and climb into the single bed with me. I could see in the light of the early dawn that he had taken off his jeans and was wearing only his T shirt and boxer shorts. I felt his penis hard against my leg through the thin cotton underwear. Then his right hand went over my mouth and his hand began to grope down my body. I was by now fully awake, and as I tried to scream he pressed harder with his hand, half stopping my breathing. I tried to bite him. His heavy body dipped the mattress and squashed me against the wall, his long fine fingers with their guitarist's nails forcing themselves inside me, the stale beer on his breath in my face. He prised my legs apart and he raped me, in my own bed, in the only place I had truly called home, he raped me. The brief fight as he forced my legs apart, he was all over me, too strong to resist. Sharp pain as his prick pushed inside me, the grunting pushing, desperate thrusts of his body, then the slack, slimy smear of him wiping himself on the quilt and creeping back to the couch where Marcia lay sleeping. The things he said to me while he pushed himself into me and spilled himself inside my body would stay with me forever. Yet I would say nothing.

'Come on you little slut, you know you want it, all darkies do. Take it, bitch, you'll beg me for it next time.' Then, when at last it was all over,

'One word, tell anyone and you die, do you hear me!?'

I did not go to school that day, something drew me across town to Joey's house, maybe a feeling of kinship. We were both soiled goods, the unwanted. I did not know what I expected to find there. But as I approached, I could see that both houses were now apparently empty.

Dougie McCann was gone. His house too was boarded up. I heard the metallic creak of the metal grille which covered the back door.

I heard footsteps on the path. Standing in front of me was Joey Callahan. I flew up the path and flung my arms around his neck.

'Joey, I've missed you so, so much.' I cried into his chest breathing in the comforting smell of tobacco smoke, patchouli and weed. He held me close to him, like the big brother I had never had. He hugged away the pain.

'Come on in, hen, I've got just the thing to make it all go away.'

I don't know quite what I expected as I allowed myself to be ushered into what was now Joey's home. It was dark, there were no lights, it was damp, the wind blew through the metal shutters on the glass-less windows. It stank of piss and filth. Takeaway cartons littered the floor, empty drink cans of all denominations adorned every surface, cigarette ends left to burn out on the arms of a settee ingrained with the stains of unwashed humanity, and so damp it would never catch fire.

I perched on the edge of a cushion, like a rabbit caught in headlights, unable to take flight. Yet I felt safe. Joey was my friend. He would never hurt me. Joey was unwanted, just like me. My mind swam with voices, I seemed to hear Dougie McCann from the empty house next door. *'Keep away from Joey Callahan, he's nothing but trouble.'* But his warning fell on deaf ears.

'I came looking for you, Joey.' I whispered, as I watched Joey warm the brown powder on the square of cheap aluminium foil, the foil already showing the charred residue of previous use.

'Dougie did mention it, hen, before he left. I knew you'd no' stay away.' The white vapour was starting to spiral upwards. Joey handed me the cardboard tube; he showed me how to place it between my lips. 'Now breathe in through yer mouth, slowly, that's it,'

I began to cough violently, I felt slightly sick, he rubbed my back 'and again, breathe it all in Tans, it will make everything go away.'

My head began to spin, life slowed down, I was weightless, floating on some sort of cloud, nothing seemed to matter, my whole body glowed, I was warm. Nothing mattered, not Alan Gorman, not Marcia, not school, all that mattered was this moment. I felt Joey pick me up and lie me on a bed of dreams. Dreams which took me to a different place, I was back in my cosy room at Marcia's, but this time I did not fight, I was naked, my limbs heavy with sleep, a warm feeling all around me and Joey. Joey made everything right.

'Come back Tans,' his voice was urgent. 'shit… don't nod on me hen.'

I felt him tapping my cheek with his hand, not slapping, just tapping, hard enough for me to open my eyes. The room spun, I started to retch, he held my head while I tried to throw up. There was nothing inside me to eject. 'Wake up Tan, wake up.'

I groaned and turned on my side, and I slept. I must have slept for the whole day. When I came to, it was already dark. The room was lit only by the stubs of candles and cheap tea lights. They cast a false romantic light over the degradation which was now my life. For I could not go home. Home for me was here.

This became the pattern of life for at least a month. Joey kept me. In return I looked after the house, I tried my best to tidy up the mess, to keep some sort of order. But I was not his only lodger, the place was home to any number of transient teenagers, some were runaways, some just kids with nothing better to do with their lives than sink into the mire created by Joey Callahan. I was different, I thought. Joey would look after me. Joey liked me. He was my friend.

'There's no more freebies, ye ken I have tae pay fer the gear.' Joey was looking at me pityingly. 'I'm sorry Tans, but if ye want it, yer goin tae have tae pay fer it.'

'I've no money Joe, you know that, and ye know I've been reported missin'' it had come as a shock to see my face all over a milk carton, and on the wall in the local shop. But no one seemed to be looking very hard. The police hadn't been overzealous in looking for me.

'Well, your goin tae have tae earn some, somehow, it's life Tansy, we all get tae pay, no more freebies.' I was seeing the true nature of Joey Callahan. All the kindness was gone from his eyes.

'Ye may not be able tae get a job, but ye can earn, like all the other wee sluts that come by here.'

I shouted at him, 'That I will never do, Joey Callahan, do you think you're my pimp, that you control my life, well you can fuck off, I will never sink that low.'

'Aye, ye will! And ye'll do it this afternoon, get yourself cleaned up, ye have money to earn.'

He knew that in a few hours the craving would start, the dragon would call me, and I would do just about anything to feel her kiss again. That afternoon behind the public toilets in a nearby park, I sank to my knees in front of my first paying customer. I gagged as he forced the foul-tasting scab encrusted crusty length of his penis further down my throat, and then I vomited, narrowly missing the crotch of his expensive gaberdine slacks. He may be well dressed but the bastard wasn't well washed. I took the two crumpled fivers which he stuffed into my hand. One for me, one for Joey.

'Easy, wasn't it?' The smug bastard was laughing. 'Now ye can start tae pay me back.'

He took me to the tea stand and bought me a steaming hot mug of hot tea with two sugars, arm around my shoulder like we were boyfriend and girlfriend. Life with Joey was like that. One minute all smiles and kindness, next all harsh words and anger. But he never touched me, and he never sampled any of his own merchandise, he never laid a hand on me unless I asked him. And I never did

Over the months that followed, I lived in the squalor of Joey's old house. It became a rat's nest of youngsters, some who had run away from home, some who had no homes to run from, most unwanted by their parents but wanted by the police. Joey was a hero figure to them, a cross between Fagin, The Child Catcher, and the Pied Piper. He lured them in with promises, then, once they were hooked, he put them to work. Every one of Joey's gang were expected to pay their way. Some shoplifted, some burgled, some just begged from the doorways, working as teams, one of their number always on the lookout. Feral children, living on their wits. No one seemed to care.

I never knew exactly what had happened to Marcia. The newspaper article was brief. About a month after I left, the police had been called to her flat. Marcia was dead. Alan Gorman had been arrested and charged with her murder. In this case, justice had been swift. Life imprisonment. Had she found out why I left? Had she called him out over it? Had my slightly bohemian, beautiful Marcia challenged him and been strangled for caring? Was it my fault? I had made her a promise not to run away. For three years I had kept my word. My breaking trust with her would have broken her heart. I packed this little piece of guilt away. I hid it in a corner of my soul from where I thought it would never escape.

Joey had rules. Especially regarding the house. We lived with the screens closed, no one was to see us coming and going. If it all went to smash then we were on our own. We had rigged up lights using a system of car batteries. Joey said not to divert the supply from next door. No attention was to be drawn to the McCann house.

I knew that at least the water to that house was connected. The outside toilet in the garden still flushed. I had bought a padlock and used the small brick built privy with its asbestos roof as my own personal space. Dougie McCann's family plainly weren't interested in his home or its contents, if indeed he had a family in the first place.

The council checked the houses once a month. Joey seemed to know what day they would come, and, on that day, we must be gone. The man from housing would check the screens and make sure everything was locked up. Then he would leave. His report would say that everything was in order. After all, the whole street was due for demolition and redevelopment in eighteen months. Another pane of broken glass was neither here nor there.

Joey moved on. If we wanted his services then we had to call him or find him. He had developed a code of numbers and emojis to denote how much and where. He turned up at the house once a month after the council had been. He made sure all his little soldiers as he called them had paid their dues. I noticed that he looked smarter, his hair was cut professionally by a barber, not the usual home haircut with the clippers that he gave himself. His clothes were better quality and he had started shaving on a regular basis. Joey was on the up. On his way up he had forgotten all about his friend Tansy Alexander. He had lured me into his web, he had turned me into a junkie and put me on the game. If I never saw him again it would be too soon. To Joey, everyone was either a customer or a commodity, and he could sell sand to the Arabs.

CHAPTER 13. THE BOTTOM – Tansy

Glasgow 2007

The wind whistled in through the metal security screens on the windows. The glass panes in the frames were smashed, leaving only jagged triangles wedged in dried out putty. The screens rattled against their frames making it almost impossible to sleep. Security installed by the council was to stop the likes of her from moving in, but there was always a way in if you knew how to open the shutters without setting off the alarms or if you could climb in through the attics from one of the adjoining houses.

There were still a few residents who hadn't bricked up the dividing wall between the properties. The man from the council had been the day before and she had made herself scarce while Joey got his dues paid by his lodgers. She had wandered the streets for half the day, she was tired and wet and cold, and she needed a fix. He had left her gear when she had texted him. She had left him money in return, all exchanged wrapped in clingfilm and stashed in the cistern of Dougie McCann's outside toilet, neatly padlocked after every visit. She hadn't seen Joey in person for weeks.

Tansy pulled the stained quilt over her shoulders. It stank, it was damp, but then everything was damp, and life stank. She was used to the damp. She was still fully dressed, tracky bottoms and a hoody over a stained T shirt. She had taken her trainers off. They were under the cushion she used as a pillow, no one could steal them from there unless she was completely out of it. Yes, she could feel them, a knobbly rubber and canvas lump under her left ear. Nothing was bloody safe here. Life itself was not guaranteed to last further than her next fix. Her backpack of clothing was wedged behind her knees and her phone was well hidden.

She was starting to sweat already, cold, clammy sweat, and her stomach was starting to cramp, she felt sick as the craving for oblivion crept over her. She needed to see Joey, but first she had to get up. She had made her money last night, a quick fumble with some old geezer in the alley behind the snooker hall. She could still taste the filthy old bastard, but a tenner was a tenner, a fiver might get her through the morning, and after that, well that would come later.

Sometimes she contemplated expanding her offerings to include 'The Full Monty' but that would be losing control of the last bastion of her body. She would not do that, even if it had the advantage of not looking at the object of disgust and not having to taste it either.

She rolled over and swung her long legs off the greasy faded brown corduroy settee. Pulling her trainers on over her size seven feet, she hopped on one leg to avoid contact with the needle and glass strewn concrete floor. She had no socks. They had been stolen months ago. Socks were not on her priority list.

 Out of habit she rolled up the quilt and the cushion and stashed them behind the settee. She may find them still there later. The standard of low life who occupied this squat was too stupid to look behind the furniture. She closed her eyes and hoped that when she opened them again the view would be better. It wasn't. She told herself today would be different. This was only temporary. It had been temporary for nearly a year now.

She swallowed hard to repel the urge to vomit, took a drink from the dust encrusted glass bottle which was on the floor beside the bed. The label said Lucozade. Well, it aids recovery, doesn't it! The contents passed her lips and she swallowed. The foul tasting liquid rebounded from her stomach. Dirty stinking rotten fucking bastards, some evil prick had drunk her breakfast and pissed in the bottle for good measure. Fuck it! Fuck life! Fuck everything! She pulled her phone out of its hiding place in her knickers and texted Joey. The text was simple, just a figure and a question mark.

'**5**?'

The answer was simple a tree emoji and a figure.

'**10**.'

The park then in ten minutes.

Tansy Alexander, missing person, climbed the aluminium loft ladder into the attic of the rundown grey council property, crawled through the loft and lowered herself into the derelict house next door. She squeezed out through the swollen back door, into the rear lane. The stench from the McCann house was nearly unbearable. It was a good thing there were no neighbours around to complain.

She pulled up her hood, picked up the backpack which contained the rest of her belongings and, head bowed to hide her face from watching eyes, she headed for her next fix. Life on the streets of Glasgow was not being kind to Tansy, sometimes she wished she could go home. She knew Marcia, the woman she had last called mother, had reported her missing, her face was plastered all over a milk bottle for goodness's sake, and a distinctive face it was. But now Marcia was dead.

Tansy Alexander was a tall girl, in that aspect she followed her father. She was broad shouldered, slim hipped and had legs like a gazelle. Her skin, when it wasn't ravaged by the pimples which betrayed her addiction, was a dark honey colour. Her hair was dense, black, and curly, not quite tight Afro curls, but wild enough to nearly have a life of its own. Uncut or self-cut for the last four years, it rampaged around her face, highlighting with its darkness, the most stunning feature of all. Above the wide smile and the firm chin, and the long straight nose, Tansy Alexander sported eyes best described as electric in their blueness.

It was drizzling fine misty rain which coated everything in a layer of wet. Grey clouds hung low in the sky, promising heavier rain for the rest of the day. Another day in which to survive.

As she walked, Tansy was deep in thought. There must be more than this, more than shoplifting as a means to live, stealing Lynx deodorant and razor blades from the shops which didn't keep them locked away, lifting bacon and ham joints from supermarkets and selling them at knock off prices in the seedier pubs of the area, nights of turning tricks in back alleys to survive. She wasn't stupid, she'd bothered to go to school, she was bright, she came top at things, she had qualifications.

Marcia had been so proud of her. But then HE had moved in. Tansy remembered the night she had run away, the night after he had stolen into her bedroom. In her nightmares she still remembered him pulling back her cosy bed clothes, just before she dropped off to sleep, dreaming the normal dreams of a teenager. Now my dreams took her back to that night. *'Come on you little slut, you know you want it, all darkies do,'* his hand over her mouth to stop her screaming *'Take it bitch, you'll beg me for it next time' 'One word, tell anyone and you die, do you hear me.'* No, she could never go back there.

Now she was a heroin addicted runaway, another statistic, another lost soul to be swept under life's carpet. Alan Gorman was in Barlinnie. Two months after Tansy had left, he had strangled Marcia. Tansy had seen it on the news and read about it in a newspaper she had found in the bin behind the toilets in the park. She crossed that very park and made for the public toilets and the burger van. Joey would be waiting for her.

Joey Callahan, a small wiry ferret of a being, Joey considered himself a bit of an entrepreneur. He prided himself on staying clean, he never sampled the goods, chemical or human. He was a supplier and everything and everybody else just a commodity. One day he would make it, then he would live the dream. Tansy could see him now, his slouch woolly hat pulled over his ears, the collar of his multi coloured surfer jacket turned up, shuffling from one foot to the other, his hands warming around a beaker of tea, steam rising to blend with the Glasgow mist. This morning, he was not alone.

'Shit!' thought Tansy, 'I can't take a customer now, no way, pal, not now.'

'Hi Tans, can I get ye a brew.' Joey smiled at her. He reached out his hand, the small wrap of brown powder changed hands. She slid him her money.

'No mate, I'll buy it.' He pocketed the fiver and bought her tea anyway.

'Three sugars, hen? Ye look as though ye need it.' He laughed at her and pulled his friend out of the shadows. 'I've a job for ye, if ye've a mind tae make a bit o' cash.'

'Cut the crap, Joey. I need to split, I'm clucking for the Gorbals, man.' She shivered visibly and bent over double. Joey could see the cold sweat appearing on her forehead.

'Ach yer a mess, Tans but can ye' no' wait and hear this man out, it could be a break, for both of us, ye ken.'

'Why me, why not another of yer bitches, Joe?' She stammered and shivered her words out, taking a mouth full of the warming sweet liquid in front of her.

The other man spoke. He was in his early thirties, he was handsome in a rough sort of way, and he looked expensive. As he drew closer her heightened sense of smell told her that he also smelled expensive.

'Joey tells me ye've no got a record.' His accent was broad.

'I've not sung anything in years, are ye offerin me' a deal or something?'

'Not that sort of record, ye chimp!' Joey was laughing. 'A Police record.'

Tansy laughed, despite herself and began to give them a lilting rendition of 'Roxanne, you don't have tae put on the red light. Appropriate, no?' She shot back at him. 'Not even a fuckin' caution, mate, but my face is all over the milk bottles, I'm a well-publicised missing person the Old Bill should be looking for me.'

'Joey also says he trusts you, that you aren't enough of a smack head to start cheating him, in fact he thinks you'd clean up pretty well.' He continued.

'So, what's in it for me?' She mumbled into her tea. 'It better be good, I'm suffering here.'

'I need a courier, no, not drugs. Papers and things, things that the authorities need not see, most of it is legit, but there are some things I'd rather were kept under cover.' He stopped.

'What do I get.' Tansy asked, desperate to be away.

'Ye get tae leave this shit hole a couple o' times a week, £100 a trip, cash, clear of expenses.' The offer hung in the air.

'Trips where?' She asked, brightening slightly. A vision of foreign travel flashed in her brain.

'By train, down south, at first.' He was cagey.

'If I say yes, what then?' She was curious.

'You stay with the man here for a few weeks, you get clean, then we talk again.' He turned to go.

'No strings? I can say no. If I want, I can walk away, right?'

'Right,' came the reply. By the time she looked up he had disappeared around the azalea bushes and only Joey was left, leaning on the tea van, two Kit-Kats in his hand. She heard the click of an expensive car door closing and the purr of an equally expensive engine starting. Two minutes later and the shiny rear end of the low slung, dark green Audi sports car left the car park.

'Tans, this is a legit chance, I've been looking out for you for ages. Looking for this. Where have ye bin, gel. You've been right off the grid fer weeks. You fit what he needs down to a tee, you can carry this off.' Joey was excited.

'If you are pimping me out, Joey Callahan, I'll gut you like a herring, then I'll smoke you all the way past Arbroath.

'Would I do a thing like that, hen? We've always been mates you and me, haven't we?'

It was true she had known Joey since school, he was only two years older than she was, but he had changed since then, the streets changed people. Was he still her friend?

'Do ye ken who that was, hen, that was Peter Balfour, he owns half o' the city and the rest isn't worth having.'

Swept along on the wave of weakness, need and Joey's enthusiasm, she went along with him, back to his flat. He had taken away the wrap of brown powder, comically he had refunded her five-pound note, run her first hot bath for weeks and reassured her.

'I'll see you through it, Tansy, stick with me, ay.'

As she sweated and shivered her way through the next few days, her body cramping in pain, every muscle aching as though she had run a marathon, she felt like running again, only she didn't have the energy. She dosed herself with Flu-plus and that certain brand of cough mixture which took the edge off things. There was nothing like cold turkey to focus the mind.

After a week, Tansy was feeling a lot better. After ten days she actually felt like a human being. She was not stupid enough to think that the heroin demon would never call her again, but for now, she was content that her size six jeans no longer fell off her hips. Many of the other girls she knew wore a child's size. 'Cheaper', they joked. They never paid for anything. Tansy's legs were too long for that. The extra holes were nearly all the way along the thick leather belt she wore to hold body and soul together.

Joey's flat was nice, it was simply furnished, very masculine, no frills, but nice, nevertheless. It had only one bedroom with an ensuite bathroom and a lounge with a lovely view out over the city. Tansy had been sleeping on a bed settee on the mezzanine level, a raised area designed to be a study or work area for the usual up and coming professionals expected to occupy the apartment. During the week she had spent staggering from bed to the toilet and back, she had grown to love the sights of the city and Glasgow Harbour after dark, the twinkling lights of the nighttime lighting up the dark waters of the Clyde.

The display of her phone told her that it was 19th June 2008 It was still dark. Joey never bothered to draw curtains. He slept in a bedroom with no windows, his box as he called it. Tansy lay staring at the view as the dawn broke over the city. In two days', time she would be eighteen years old. Would her they stop searching for her then?

'Wakey, wakey, Tans, it's time to go shopping.' Joey shook her shoulder and waved a cup of hot sweet tea under her nose.

'I've been awake for hours, I'm not going thieving for you. If you want me to do this big job for your mate, I can'nae risk thieving,' she protested.

'No, stupid, you need to get kitted out, the man himself has given me his card to use, you need to look the part. Businesslike, smart, you know. Think Pretty Woman. Today, Tansy Alexander, you get to spend money like Julia Roberts.' Joey was high on life.

'Joey, tell me honestly, and tell me now, what is Pete Balfour into? Do you even know?' Tansy was still not convinced that she should ride this gift horse out of Glasgow. Right now, she was looking it straight down the gullet.

'Peter Balfour is a property developer, I met him in a bar. I'll not say he doesn't have other interests. He hasn't told me his whole life story, Tans, but he's done good by me over the years.'

'This flat his then?' Tansy looked about her.

'Yes,' was the reply. 'I could never afford it, it's part of my wages.'

'And what does Joey do to make Joey's money then?' Tansy was cutting.

'I run errands for him, I find people for him, I carry his bags.' Joey shrugged.

'And for a few errands you get all this?' She was smelling a rat.

'Tansy, I am not a fool, I know that eventually there may be a time I have to pay it back to him, but for the moment I will ride my luck and his. I'm just asking you to join me on the wave.'

'Come on then, Joey boy,' she started to get out of bed, 'it's time to hit the shops.'

Later that evening, a suited and booted Tansy Alexander and Joey Callahan were sipping drinks in the Ben Nevis bar with Peter Balfour. When they left, Tansy was carrying a leather laptop case, complete with Apple MacBook laptop and a first-class return ticket from Glasgow to London's Euston Station. She was to travel by cab to Brown's Hotel in Mayfair and leave the laptop. It was to be put in the safe at reception for Mr. P.M. Grainger.

The journey there would be about 6 hours, then she should not hang around before making the return trip. She was also given a brand-new iPhone which she was told she could use as her own but under no circumstances was she to use it to contact any of her old associates. That included Joey. There was a number listed under I.C.E 1, which she could use in an emergency. He left it to her to decide what exactly constituted an emergency. There was also a money card loaded with £500 which should cover any London expenses. This card, he stressed, would be topped up monthly. She would be paid in cash on her return. For the time being she would continue to live with Joey.

'You cannot be seen to be too affluent too soon, Tansy. Slowly does it.' Peter Balfour looked directly into her ice blue eyes and for a moment he was lost. Tansy Alexander was the most beautiful woman he had ever seen. It was a shame he was about to jeopardise her whole existence. But business was business after all.

CHAPTER 14. SINK OR SWIM – Cassandra

HMP Stafford 2004

Life is a bitch. Her Majesty's Prisons are jam packed with them. One year on and I know exactly who the bitches are, who to avoid at all costs, who bears a grudge, who is just plain '*nasty*' and who may have been paid on the outside to ensure my journey on the inside was as hard as possible.

I have been hospitalised twice, once with scalds from boiling water, accidentally tipped down a stairwell, the next time from a freak accident in the gymnasium involving the leg press machine and an eighteen stone dyke called Mandy. One had resulted in a nasty red scar down the back of my left shoulder, the second had resulted in orthopaedic surgery to my right knee. I now walk with a slight limp, and I will never run a half marathon again. The holder of the kettle was never identified. Mandy was hailed a hero for saving my life from the two hundred kilos which had descended, nearly crushing my spine and twisting my leg to an impossible angle. Protesting the fact that it was Mandy who had pulled the safety peg out of the machine in the first place would cut no ice.

Mandy was just a pawn in the game. I didn't blame her, though I didn't like her much. She was easily led, and her services had been bought and paid for by one who was much higher up the food chain, someone who was paid from the outside. As Dawn never failed to point out, I must have upset some pretty powerful people.

When I returned to the wing on crutches I was given a job, not the kitchen, too much hot water, too many knives, not the laundry, again too much water and steam. That only left the library, peaceful, tranquil, hardly visited and an opportunity.

Working the library was easy enough. It was neither big nor particularly well stocked. There were all sorts of restriction placed on the nature of the reading matter which was allowed to grace its shelves. No books on terrorism, no instruction manuals for bomb makers. Shame that, I was rather into Stephen Leather novels. There was a large section devoted to books on the law and the legal system. There were reference books on the benefit system and social services. These books were rarely booked out. As far as novels were concerned there was a selection of dog-eared trashy romances, some thrillers and mystery, plenty of crime thrillers.

    Every morning, I went through my list of requests and loaded up the trolley. My job was a bit like the hospital in that way. The women selected a book from the catalogue I carried, I put their request in on a first come first served basis and then delivered their choice when it was available. If I didn't have the book and there were enough requests for it, I could try and requisition a copy, a daunting process which involved forms in triplicate to the governor, and a précis of the book in question to ensure it was not a manual on how to build a glider from scrap wood and bed sheets. This process was so arduous that few new books ever arrived. Stock was usually refreshed from the boxes of donations made by the screws and various charities. Sorting and cataloguing these was my biggest job.

    I was trusted with a laptop. I had access to the internet, though it was severely restricted as were all my portals to the outside world. Everything was strictly monitored, any breach of the rules punished by a loss of privileges or in the worst cases, extra time added.

    I had also started a reading clinic and a book club once a week, the former for those who wanted to learn to read, it had surprised me how many of my new acquaintances could not, the latter for those who wanted to discuss what they were reading, who read for more than just a good story. These ladies were mostly the white-collar criminals, educated women who had been tempted to the dark side by money, or love. It was always one or the other. They were an interesting bunch, businesswomen, lawyers, and tax inspectors, mostly on short sentences, short sharp shocks. University educated, intelligent, not at all what I had expected.

The internal phone which sat on the crowded central desk rang, its loud clamour reverberating around the bookshelves. Was I supposed to answer it? It had never rung in my presence before. The silence shattering noise continued. To put my ears out of their misery I lifted the receiver.

'Library, 12063 Weaver.' I thought that sounded official enough.

'Ah, yes, Weaver.' It was the governor's office. 'Weaver, you have a legal visit.' This was unexpected, visits from Simon Hastings my brief, were now few and far between and I always knew well in advance. He would only visit if he had news. His only instruction on my behalf now being the ongoing search for my girls. I was rendered speechless.

'Well Weaver?' The voice on the phone demanded a response. It was Mrs Wellington.

'Yes, ma'am.' was all I could say. In the next minute, a sad looking young screw with a spotty face and a dirty grey uniform appeared bearing the regulation orange tabard. She was to escort me to visiting. Thoughts were racing through my head. Had he found them, what news was there? As I approached the door, my hands were shaking. When I was ushered into the room Simon was sitting at the table. Perched uncomfortably on the hard chair which was, like the table, bolted to the floor, he looked thoughtful. I sat down opposite him.

'Well?' I asked. Anticipation hung in the air.

'Sandra, I have come with a proposition for you.', he started, almost nervously.

'You've found them then?' My voice trembled with pent up emotion.

'No Sandra, I haven't, I have employed researcher after researcher and, nothing. It is as if they dropped off the planet. The last place they definitely were, was Oakbrook children's home. That place is closed, in fact it's been demolished. Their records were sent to some central underground bunker, one of those post war things which the

Government rent out for storage. There was a flood several years ago, or was it a fire, no one was sure. Nothing has been found.' He stopped for breath

'My boss has told me that I will have to start charging if I continue to work for you. As you know I was doing it for free, pro bono, but I have a new partner, and new brooms…well he wants the firm to be financially viable which at the moment it is not. By that he means I am not.'

He looked at the legal pad in front of him and then at the clock which was on the wall behind me. 'We don't have long. I shall cut to the chase.' Simon was now all business. 'I understand you haven't had an easy time of it.'

'I didn't expect to.' I replied.

'Word outside in some low places is that there is still a lucrative contract on you.' He was matter of fact.

'Why does that not surprise me?' It didn't. Dawn had told me only last week to watch out for any newbies who tried to get close. Another few months of watching my back in the shower and in the canteen.

'I have been approached by an individual who says that, that particular contract can be removed' Simon started gingerly, 'if you agree to certain things.'

'Go bent you mean, never. Is that fucker Grainger behind this?' I shook my head in disbelief.

'Get real Sandra, that life is over for you, you need to make the best of this one, hear me out, and don't shoot the messenger.' He looked at me with his pleading face. 'What's in it for you?', I thought.

'Go on then, what do they want?' I wasn't really listening.

'Simple,' he continued. 'you keep your ears and eyes open in here, anything which involves any of these people.' He tapped a folded list of names he had in front of him. 'You tell me, I pass the info back to them.'

'Grass for the opposition?' My eyebrows were disappearing into my hairline.

'In effect yes.' came the reply.

'And in return?'

'And in return, you get an easy ride, no fear of a shiv to your throat in the shower.'

'And what about those I inform on, they aren't going to be too chuffed. No, I think I'm safer with the status quo.'

'You don't understand Sandra. This is not really a request. If you don't, you won't survive the next month.'

'What do you get out of it?' Simon blushed to the roots of his hair, more orange than the tabard I was forced to wear, the one with HMP on the back. My thoughts whirled. Simon remained silent.

'You tell your masters,' I fixed Simon with my best glare. 'I will do what they ask, but I want the same deal as you.' He winced visibly. 'And,' I continued, 'tell them I want a guarantee on early release, I know they can swing it, after all they swung it for me the other way. Then they can tell me what the bastards did with my kids.'

'Sandra, there are limits.'

'Simon, there were no limits to what they did to me. I was put here to shut me up, I know that now. You tell them, I haven't quite lost my voice, but if I get out in one piece with a bit of a bonus as it were, I will nark for them. You tell them they won't find a better one.'

The bell rang signalling five minutes to the end of the visit. Simon stacked up his papers. He winked at me and smiled. 'Why do you think they asked, I will pass your proposal back to them, in the meantime watch out for this lady.' He placed a piece of paper with a name on the table. 'I'll book in for same time next week.'

I stared in horror at the name on the note. 'Treacherous bitch,' I thought, or was Dawn Crole just playing a very canny game.
I dawdled back to our cell, chivvied along by Wellington herself.

'Had news, have you Weaver?' she fished for information. As the cell door closed behind me, I sensed Dawn watching me from her bunk. I smiled at her broadly. She smiled back and winked. So, Dawn was on a payroll as well, but whose?

I did not need to excuse myself to anyone in this place, but my increased legal visits were neatly framed as being about my daughters, or about considering an appeal. This was not all fiction. I had to formally apply for a reduction in my sentence. I was assured that the tariff could be massaged down to fifteen years - a substantial reduction. In the end the final figure was eighteen. Not too many eyebrows would be raised at that, there was a light at the end of the tunnel. That light would be switched on in 2010. In the meantime, I would provide my paymasters with information on certain individuals. Dawn would put her claws away and I could sleep easy in my bunk.

Over the next few months, I saw a pattern build. The women who I was watching were usually smart looking girls, they called themselves businesswomen. Most of them were high class escorts. They were university educated trying to fund their education. They all had short sentences, six to twelve months. They spoke little. Few of them said anything about their crimes, or their life on the outside other than that they were only trying to make a living, turn a few extra quid. Having had several meetings with Simon and telling him that I had nothing to tell our paymaster, he didn't seem unhappy.

Then the penny dropped, how stupid was I? The point was they were keeping their traps shut! They were not mouthing off about things they should not, things which could implicate those on the outside. I had no doubt I was not the only nark on the wing, so I kept my nose clean. If some little bird started to sing too much, I told Simon. This would usually result in some minor act of retribution. A dinner would be spat in, a cell would be searched, and contraband planted and found. Privileges would be withdrawn as a result. A year could soon extend to eighteen months. A message would be sent. On the outside the puppet master pulled the strings, and on the inside, we danced to his tune.

I slept better in my bunk. Some nights I dreamed of a small cottage by the sea, or in the mountains somewhere well away from people and life, a cosy little home where I would be visited in my dotage by my two daughters, and maybe grandkids, roses round the door, a big hairy dog lying by the fire. Sometimes there was a man involved, a tall man with curly blonde hair and a body to die for, but mostly I was happy to live my dream alone, until the wake-up call came in the morning with its chorus of belching, farting, stretching women, and Dawn's racking cough from the bunk above me.

And so, life continued on the inside, endless in its monotony but at least I had some form of end date. If Simon was to be believed, I had not lost my pension, but I would have to wait to claim it.

I managed to glean from my girls at book club and in my reading classes that most of the names on my list were couriers of some sort. Most of them felt that they had been set up. They had not been couriers for drugs. If drugs had been involved then none had been found on them or inside them or anything that they carried. The ones who were willing to say anything at all maintained that all they were required to do was to transport an item, the item varied but was usually a tablet or a laptop or sometimes documents by rail, or sometimes by executive car. For this they were paid and paid well. They deposited their cargo at a pre-arranged destination and left it with a named person. Then they made the return journey at their leisure. Most of them had no earthly clue what they had been couriers of. They had been swept up, they thought, in some form of smuggling conspiracy. The girls who were more savvy remained tight lipped. All of them said that they had been very well paid.

In return, Simon continued to do his research and provide his services pro-bono. At least, I wasn't paying him. Someone else may have been. Simon was getting older. He wanted the quiet life and eventually he told me that he was retiring to his cottage in Cornwall with his family, to learn to surf and drink far too much local cider. Before he hung up his wig and gown he introduced me to Andrea, his replacement.

Andrea Atkins was my sort of woman. She did not take no for an answer. She had a background in family law and was quite au-fait with the devious ways of social services when it came to the care of children.

She also had contacts everywhere. It was 2004. I had been on the inside for nearly ten years. I was still alive with an end nearly in sight. Andrea continued to dig for a while and the results were still the same. Then she managed to glean from one of her many contacts that my daughter Amy had been fostered by a couple called Brown. A mixed-race couple from Bristol. She had stayed there for several years until unexpectedly Mrs Alice Brown had died of a massive heart attack. Her husband, being left on his own, did not think it appropriate to keep on with fostering a teenaged girl.

Amy, who had been renamed Tracy by the Browns, was due to return to the homes. She had never arrived at Oakbrook home for children. Amy had gone missing. She was still on the missing list. No body had been found, but there had been no sightings of her either as Amy Weaver or Tracy Brown or any combination of the two. Andrea also found a letter from a Mrs Taylor written when the girls were still very small. She had adopted Charlotte and wanted to adopt Charlotte's sister. She was told that Amy was already with a family. That must be the Browns.

So, what did I know? My girls had been separated by the time they were five. One, my darling Charlotte, had been adopted by a white couple. There was no indication of where the Taylors lived or who they were. Amy had been fostered by a mixed-race couple in Bristol and when this had fallen apart, rather than return to the homes, she had run away. There was some hope I might find Charlotte. But where was Amy?

The years crawled by. My cell mate Dawn was released and managed to stay out of the clutches of the law for all of eighteen months. Then, after a short spell in a mental institution, she returned. She was still the same. By hook or was it crook she managed to get back in the same cell as me. She still had no teeth and she still coughed loudly enough to wake the whole landing.

Screws came and went. The Boot retired, no one was upset to see the back of her, until she had actually gone. Then we realised that it was she who actually prevented complete anarchy on the wing. Her replacements were far too soft, young, naïve girls with no experience of dealing with human beings. To them we were just inmates, heads to be counted.

I continued to work the library. I had gradually increased the stock of books and my reading class had blossomed into a literacy and numeracy class. The prison did benefit from formal access to education services, but most of my ladies did not want to admit their failings and often they came to me to brush up their skills before going to any form of formal education. By the time I was approaching release my resume was glowing.

By my reckoning and by the arrangements I had made with Simon all those years ago, I would be released in July 2010. I was wary. To those on the outside I was still a threat. Would they still buy my silence or would they seek to silence me in a cheaper manner?

Several months before I was due for release I was introduced to my probation officer. He was a short bulldog of a man, ex-military, clad almost exclusively in combat gear and hiking boots. I could tell that he spent most of his time out of doors. His name was Paul Carruthers. It was his job to prepare me for the outside world. He guided me through the myriad of forms I had to fill in registering for this and that. I would have no choice but to spend my first six months in a hostel. Initially I would have to wear a tag. He winked at me and advised. 'Play ball for six months and it will be removed. After six months you will also have a job and once you show the system that you are contributing, you will earn a degree more flexibility.'

Paul Carruthers assisted me in opening a bank account. Online banking had not been a thing when I was first incarcerated. I don't know whose payroll Paul Carruthers was on, but when I was eventually released through those huge iron gates topped with their coils of razor wire, Paul was there to meet me, driving a neat grey Mercedes saloon, less than a year old, quite high spec but nothing too flash. He was seated in the driver's seat wearing a chauffeur's cap and leather gloves and with no small degree of ceremony deposited my plastic bag of belongings into the boot.

The passenger in the rear seat was a large black man in his late forties, very expensively dressed, his hair in dreadlocks and smelling like a cross between an accident in a Chanel laboratory and a coconut grove. This was the first time I had been up close and personal with Paul Melville Grainger. I had of course seen his mugshot plastered all over the Police Daily Bulletin and had seen him at a distance on that fateful day that Tony had taken his whole family to a meet. He had been younger then, ten years younger. I had to hand it to him he was still breathtakingly handsome. The man had a certain presence. He also had an unmistakeable air of danger about him. Another bad boy made good. I got into the front seat alongside the driver.

Paul drove around the corner to the next layby and Grainger called me to sit in the back alongside him. It was only then that I realised just how bloody large the man was. His voice was like the hum of a swarm of bees, bees that were just dripping in honey. He reawakened hairs on the back of my neck which had not been active for 18yrs. He spoke first.

'Cassandra, welcome, it must be good to be out.' My name rolled over his tongue like toffee.

'Mr Grainger, it is indeed a pleasure to meet you in person.' I replied rather formally.

'Call me Mel, short for Melville, only the judge and my mother use Paul. From what my spies tell me you have kept your part of our little arrangement.'

'I have.' I replied, not in too friendly a fashion, 'I hope that you will keep to your part of the bargain.'

'My dear Cassandra, I shall call you Cassandra, it has far more of a ring to it than Sandra. Sandra is rather common, not suitable for one of your talents. I feel that Cassandra rolls off the tongue, it flows, don't you think?'

'Whatever you choose Melville. It makes no difference to me.' He was building up to something, I was not at all sure what.

'If I were to tell you that Simon Hastings is dead, what would you say?'

'I would ask you, "How?"'

'As I recall, you asked for the same deal as his, did you not Cassandra?' He was emphasising the double 'S' in my name like some sort of huge snake. I felt my stomach knot with fear. Then I felt something hard prod me in my ribcage, about four inches below my right arm. Grainger's arms were folded almost casually, and I began to realise that in his right hand he held a gun.

'Let this be a warning, Cassandra. I will honour what you requested, what you believed that worm of a solicitor was getting you for his work. But when you continue to work for me, for you will, I can assure you, if you choose to negotiate, which you may, always find out what the bottom line will be before you accept the deal. Arright?'

He opened the central arm rest of the rear seats and placed the hand gun into a purpose built safe. Before he locked the safe he handed me a top of the range iPhone. 'This is yours. It is already set up for you. You may change the security passcodes as you wish. I have no reason to spy on you in that way. Check your mobile banking. You will see that I have more than compensated you for your troubles.'

As if money could ever replace what I had lost. I thought, but I said nothing.

'Here are the keys to your new abode. You asked for something rural and remote, perhaps near the coast. I hope this fits the bill.' He handed me a set of keys. I started to speak.

'No,' he laughed, 'there are no hidden cameras, it is just a cottage, a very nice cottage, mind you. I may visit someday, it is only a short walk from the beach, well off the radar of the revenue as well. Those cameras, they were for your husband's benefit. You think I did not know what was going on? He was a very stupid man. You saved me a job, Cassandra. Call all this payment for that debt.'

'You bastard, you really would have……'

'I never wanted you to suffer like you did, that was down to another man. But you knew, and you still know too much. This time I will buy your silence with kindness, if you let me.'

'And the other matter. My girls?' I asked, 'Don't they deserve some kindness too?'

'Alas, Cassandra I do not know where they have gone. That order, it was not supposed to happen, that too was …….'

'David Holly.' I finished the sentence for him. 'If I could get my hands on that bastard.'

Paul Melville Grainger did not answer, but I knew I was right. Once he had seen me check my bank balance and heard me voice my happiness at his generosity, he made a further phone call and another Mercedes pulled into the layby behind us. This one was low slung and sporty with black windows. It was driven by a young lady dressed in black leather sporting a fine array of solid gold bling. My master and benefactor slipped his huge frame into the driver's seat and within seconds had disappeared in a cloud of road dust.

Paul Carruthers looked at my baffled face in the rear-view mirror.

'West Wales it is then.' He put the car into gear.

'No tag, no hostel, just this?' I asked

'Your carriage awaits, milady.' he joked. 'I'm sure you know that there are still strings attached.'

Half a mile in front of us Paul Grainger headed north. He would not stop until he reached the border with Scotland. He had things to do and people to see. And he was late.

Pen y Banc has been my home now for seven years. I have my job. I work part time for a local solicitors' office. I take statements and write reports. It pays the bills. My home is a long, low, grey stone cottage, it is on the hillside above Carmarthen Bay with a grand view of the Milford

Haven. It is only a short walk to the beach. Grainger has not visited in the whole seven years, I doubt he ever will, unless he needs a place to hide. Then I will be expected to provide one. But until that happens I remain relieved and grateful.

There is still a hole in my heart where my girls should be. By now they will be twenty-eight and twenty-seven, respectively. I could have passed them in the street and not known. Sometimes when the wind is whistling around the chimney pots of Pen y Banc I think I can hear them calling me. In my mind I call them back.

It is 2017 I am fifty-five years old. I am a widow with my own home and a truck full of baggage, but at least I am alive, and I am free.

2017

CHAPTER 15. THE SHOEBOX – Siobhan Williams

Bristol 2017

I don't think I was always called Siobhan, sometimes when I was asleep, as a child and on the point of waking, I could hear a woman's voice calling Charlotte. Then I wake, and the voice is gone.

Williams is my married name. My husband Raymond Williams married Siobhan Taylor, that's what it says on my marriage certificate, and on my birth certificate, the one my mother kept in her box full of the family papers. So, it must be true, mustn't it? My mother would never lie to me, would she?

I am Siobhan Williams, I am 28 years old, I am happily married to Raymond. I am a working mum, with a job I love, yet there has always been something missing. Raymond says I am a restless soul, never wanting to stay put and settle down, like a captive animal always looking out of its cage for freedom, or a horse seeking the greener grass over the fence.

My parents are dead. My father passed away following a long illness ten years ago, long before I married. My mother died only a few months ago, leaving me with the unenviable task of putting her affairs to rest. That was when I found the envelope, an official looking brown manila envelope. It was addressed to my parents Alan and Lydia Taylor. It had been opened and the contents read, and then it had been filed in the bottom of the shoebox where my father kept their wills, and the deeds to the house.

I had a great life with Alan and Lydia, a childhood filled with dogs and horses and my little brother Malcolm. Home was a slightly run-down rambling farmhouse with a few acres of land just on the edge of the Vale of Glamorgan. I attended the local primary school, then the county comprehensive school. I was not an academic, I loved the outdoors and all things practical. Aged 19, I joined the Police Service. It was there I met my future husband and found a niche in life. Now here I am sitting at the kitchen table in my parents' house, my brother Malcolm sitting opposite me as we go through what remains of our parents' lives.

The old shoebox, a green Clark's box which once contained a pair of the Daisy sandals I wore to school, is empty except for that envelope. I hated those sandals, but mum said that they were the best for my feet. As always, she was right. Whilst I was teased about them through my teenage years, I have pretty much indestructible feet. No claw toes or embryonic bunions for me.

I open the flap and take out the dog-eared sheaf of papers. Clipped to the outside is a velum envelope, with my name written in my mother's very neat writing on the front. In it is a letter that will change my life. I open the seal.

My dear Siobhan,

I have battled long and hard in my mind over what is best to do. Your father would have known exactly what course was best, but he is no longer here, so it falls to me. My better judgement, which knows you quite well, tells me that you should know about the contents of this envelope, for doesn't everyone have a right to know about everything these days. But then sometimes ignorance is bliss, isn't it.

When you read this, I will be with my beloved Alan. You have long since gone through the stage of searching my cupboards and drawers as you did as a child. You were always looking for something, weren't you. Whatever the outcome, please remember that we loved you and forgive us if we failed you on this one occasion.

My own mistakes as a teenager meant that I was told that I could not have children of my own. Malcolm was a complete surprise. You were a gift and so, so precious to us, you needed so much love and most of all you needed protection. Maybe that need to protect you blinded me to your need to know the truth.

For some reason, the social workers kept your birth certificate and they insisted that they would deal with the formalities of changing your name. There was some form of court order in place, they said. Your name had to be changed and you were not to be adopted in the area where you were born. We were never told why, but I expect that it had something to do with the court case. We were just happy to be able to give you a loving home. So, I can tell you little about your birth parents apart from the press cutting which I received in an anonymous envelope eleven years after we adopted you. It was then that I further enquired after the girl who I believe may be your sister. If the article is correct then your father is dead, and your mother will have spent some time in prison. They would tell me nothing of your sister.

I know in my heart that after I am gone you will search for your roots and your birth family. I hope you will find some peace in your search, my little restless spirit.
Your ever-loving mum
Lydia

My hands shook as I pulled out the contents of the envelope. First there was a newspaper cutting, yellow with age, lurid headlines speaking of a murder, 'Cop on Cop Behind Closed Doors', emblazoned in large type on the front page. Why did I need to know about Tony Weaver being brutally stabbed by his wife. I scan read it and put it to one side. My detective's brain took over. Read it properly, my inner voice told me. I read it again.

Murder was what it was. Sandra Weaver had stabbed her husband with the kitchen knife, in the kitchen. Very 'Cluedo.'

The accompanying photographs, obviously from the scene, showed a female officer in uniform carrying a small child on one arm and holding another firmly by the hand, getting to the open rear door of a plain car: Sandra and Tony's children.

I felt slightly sick, my world stopped. It was started again by Malcolm shaking me by my shoulder. 'Shonnie, what's wrong, Siobhan, speak to me.'

The next document was a letter from a social worker, brief and to the point. The re-registration of my life was complete, there was no mention of my previous name, no mention of another date of birth. There was, however, another line at the bottom.

As regards your enquiry about the other child, I am able to inform you only that this child was placed with another family.

The date on the letter was a few days after my fifth birthday.

There were several hand-written notes which were so faded I could not read their contents and finally another short note on plain paper, it was unsigned.

Mrs. Taylor, it said, this is all I can tell you. We hold no file on your daughter's sibling but, searching my own files from the time, I found this. It is all I can give you.

I inferred from this that the note had accompanied the press cutting. I pushed the papers towards Malcolm, and elbows on the table, I held my head in my hands. 'Read that Mal, then please tell me it's not true.'

Malcolm read, a wry smile spread across his face, my junior by four years, I was the big sister he idolised and hated in alternate breaths and on alternate days.

'I remember mum opening that note, it arrived just before your sixteenth birthday. Mum had so many big plans, it was not one of your finer moments, Shonnie.' He used the pet name he had given me when he couldn't say Siobhan. 'Mum had planned a nice, civilised party with a cake and candles and you in a nice dress. As I remember you and your school mates caught the bus to Cardiff and you all came home drunk. You threw up all over the bathroom. Mum put you to bed and sat with you all night.'

'We did not,' I bridled at him. 'I would never have.'

'I remember mum and dad clearing the table, mum crying and dad comforting her, telling her that you would come round, maybe we could do cake and candles in a few days.' He paused, 'So that's what we did. You were a witch at sixteen, Shonnie. This would have sent you away on a broomstick. She was right not to tell you.'

I continued for him. 'Then dad was diagnosed, and that took over everything.' I remembered the endless rounds of chemo, the trips to Velindre hospital and my big, solid father's slow surrender to the brain tumour he fought against so bravely. My voice cracked and caught in my throat and my eyes glazed with tears at the memory.

'Surely Mal, when I got married, surely, then, she could have told me herself.'

'I remember your wedding, too. Mum was so proud. She was truly happy for the first time in ages. I was proud to walk you down the aisle, it was a great day. Your Raymond's mob outnumbered us by about four to one, it really was a great day.'

My husband's family is huge, he has four brothers, a tribe of nieces and nephews and cousins - don't mention all those cousins. It was one of the reasons I loved his family, they were like a huge wriggly comfort blanket. Not all of them were always comforting, but in a crisis, there was always a Williams with a shoulder and a cup of tea, or a pint of beer and a glass of whisky, whichever you preferred. If there was more than one Williams in a room, a mundane gathering became a celebration.

What would Raymond think of this, then? I would not have to wait long to ask him. He was picking me up at four o clock and it was quarter to, already. I stuffed the envelope and its contents into my shoulder bag.

'Let's put all this away for today, Mal. We have weeks to wait for probate to come through, we don't need to beat ourselves up with it.'

We cleared the table, keeping the neat piles of paper carefully in order, slotted them into neatly marked folders and replaced them in father's filing cabinet. Mum had no conception of filing. Her address book had me listed under D for daughter and Malcolm under B for boy. The closing of the filing cabinet was heralded by the crunch of tyres on the gravel outside. Raymond had arrived.

I locked Mum's house and we left in convoy, Malcolm's old Land Rover bouncing through the potholes in front of Raymond's sporty Audi. It no longer felt like home, and I did not know if I could ever go back. Raymond had safely negotiated the craggy driveway. He had mastered the art of not grounding his low-slung sports car on the high central ridge of the lane. He changed gear as we pulled out onto the smooth tarmac of the A48 and headed for the M4. As he accelerated away from the slip road and into the main carriageway, he turned down the radio.

'Penny for them?' he asked.

'Not until we get home.' I replied, 'I need a drink, a large one. Maybe I need several. I just found out that Mum was not my mum, and Dad was not my dad.'

He drove the rest of the fifty miles to our home in silence. He drove onto the driveway of our neat, semi-detached home. He parked the gleaming Audi alongside my battered old Ford Fiesta with its fine external coating of farmyard mud and internal smell of horse manure.

Before I could put the keys in the front door, he put his arm around my shoulder, turned me to face him, and, looking down at me with his clear green eyes and a big smile on his face, he kissed me slowly.

'What difference will it make, you are still my Shonnie. Pub?'
He guided me up the street to the Red Lion and ordered two large whiskies. I found a seat at one of the old worn tables in a quiet corner of the bar. He joined me two minutes later

'Now what's all this about?'

Seated on a creaky chair, my elbows rested on a table with wrought iron legs which once supported an old Singer sewing machine. My foot rested on the remains of the treadle, a dusty ray of sunshine fought its way through the small Georgian panes of the pub's front window. I nursed my double Penderyn with a splash of water and I told him.

'Why wasn't I told?' I finished. 'They should have told me.'

'I'm with Malcolm on this.' he replied. 'I know you, Shonnie. You would not have taken it well, and what with your dad and everything. Your mother, well, it wasn't a good time for her, was it.'

'There was never going to be a good time, but she should have told me.'

'Well, you know now,' he took my hands in his and held me with his most engaging gaze. 'and knowing you, you are about to start on a journey. I love you Shonnie and I'm with you every step of the way.'

CHAPTER 16. UNFOLDING MY LIFE – Siobhan

When mum died, I had taken what compassionate leave I was due, enough to get me through the funeral and out the other side. I had also taken any hours which I was owed, mainly for the purpose of sorting mum's affairs. Sergeant Shonnie Williams would not be in work for a while. Mum had had dementia. She had insisted that she was fine and had managed to pass the simple tests set her by the visiting social worker with ease. But she was quite a confidence trickster, and, as soon as the medical professional and the social worker had left, her façade of coping would fall away, and her life would descend into chaos. Over the years, I had taken the step of stopping her from driving. I had borrowed her car. It was still on our drive several years later. Mum had eventually stopped asking after it.

Between her failing eyesight and hearing and the fact that she could not find her way to the shops anymore, and if she did she could not find her way home, she had become a liability on wheels. She refused point blank to consider residential care or to have any carers across her doorstep. The massive stroke which had ended her life had not come as a surprise, her blood pressure was the stuff of legend at her GP practice, and she had suffered several TIA's in the last few years. We both missed her terribly, she was our mother, but we were thankful that she had not lain for weeks in a hospital bed waiting to die.

Malcolm and I were finding it hard to make sense of her affairs. Amongst the clutter which had become her life at the age of ninety-two, there was all manner of collectibles, bits of china, jewellery, paintings, furniture. Mal and I had taken what small items we wanted. The formalities of probate were rolling on. Nothing could be done to dispose of anything before her affairs had been settled.

The old house had been valued and we were making headway through the sea of paperwork mum had stored. Every piece of paper had to be read, Mal had already skipped over a folder containing several hundred pounds worth of premium bonds, nearly consigning them to the shredder. Not only had there been documents relating to her family and our father's family but whole cupboards of history relating to every relative since Methuselah. My enthusiasm for tracing the family history had been shattered by the revelation in the contents of one small shoebox. None of this treasure trove of documents had anything to do with my bloodlines. Malcolm's yes, he knew where he came from, but my previous life was now a mystery. Jewellery bought by dad for mum for anniversaries and milestone birthdays was now mixed in with costume pieces from Marks and Spencer and local craft shops. It all had to be sorted.

It was some weeks later that I finally took my manila envelope from where I had placed it in the big white kitchen jug on the Welsh dresser. It was a Wednesday morning. It was half past eleven, I sat down at my dining room table with a large mug of instant coffee and started to read again. I did not have the whole of the newspaper article, only the headlines and the photographs. The local newspaper which had run the story had closed down years ago, lost along with its mother paper whose demise came amongst a scandal over phone hacking and corrupt practices that had made national news. There was not even an indication of what part of the country I came from. I had seen those, *'who do you think you are'* programs on the television. Didn't those individuals who resorted to allowing their stories to be broadcast always start out with a file of some sort. If they did, then where was mine? What did I know about the real me, how was I connected to a murder in 1992? Was that voice in my head which called me Charlotte more than a figment of my childhood imagination? I certainly had not heard it for many years.

I dragged my laptop out from under my desk, opened a packet of custard creams, my biscuit of choice, made another coffee and while windows started itself up and the old Toshiba connected itself to the internet, I prepared myself for a journey down a thirty-one-year-old rabbit hole. I felt a chill raise the hairs on the back of my neck and a thrill of excitement form a knot in the pit of my stomach.

Google is my friend. The first hurdle was simple, I should apply to the general records office for a copy of my original birth certificate. Start at the very beginning. A very good place to start. The government website gave clear instructions, I created an account, filled in what details I knew, those being my current name and my date of birth. I paid the fee using my credit card and hit the send button. One confirmation email later and my journey had started.

Not satisfied with having nothing to show for my morning's endeavours, I googled a name: Anthony Weaver. I found nothing. Try Tony Weaver: nothing which fitted the profile of who I was looking for. I tried another: Sandra Weaver. Again, the search engine produced nothing. Whoever these people were and whatever had happened in 1992, there was no digital footprint. The headline sprang out at me next, COP ON COP, but this was thirty years ago, and I did not know where they had been stationed, not even the Police Force they had worked for.

I was still deep in thought when Raymond came home. I had searched social media, I had trawled the internet and I had found nothing. I heard his motorcycle purr onto the drive and the whir of the motor which raised the garage door. He parked his favourite mode of transport and let himself in through the side door. He always looked like some form of superhero in his one-piece black leathers and boots. He placed his full-face helmet on the table alongside my laptop and, pulling the office chair on which I was sitting backwards he spun it to face away from the screen.

'Enough, have a break, I bet you haven't stopped all day.'

He was right. My eyes ached with looking and my fingers were sore from typing.

'Good day at the office, dear?' I rose from the chair and slid my arms around his waist. I buried my head in his chest breathing in the smell of traffic, leather, and Spice Bomb aftershave.

'Not particularly,' he replied. 'been at the cop shop all day, my turn for duty dog. Right load of idiots they've had in, but it pays the bills.' Raymond worked for a firm of Solicitors. He was not quite a junior partner, he was next on the list to be recruited, just waiting for one of the senior lawyers to hang up his suit. Then, maybe, he would get his name on the wall under the other names at the front door of Messrs. Lloyd, Roberts, and Ingram, Solicitors at Law. Until then he always seemed to fall for the call out to the Police Cells. That was where we had met, twelve years ago, when I had been an ambitious young constable, and he was the newly qualified lawyer who had visibly made female jaws drop when he adorned the custody office with his presence.

Raymond Williams was mine, all six feet four inches of him in his stocking feet, the Lawyer in Leather as the custody officers called him.

'What's for tea?' he mumbled through my hair as I undid the zip which held the top and bottom, of his leathers together.

'Me, if you're lucky.' I slid my hands under his T Shirt and felt the muscles either side of his spine hard under my fingers.

He lifted me from the chair and carried me up the stairs. 'I knew my luck was about to change for the better.' He dropped me on our king size bed and continued to undo zips. He raised a dark eyebrow at me as he shed the last of his leather skin and lowered himself onto the bed beside me.

As I lay wide awake, curled up next to Ray, my head nestled under his shoulder, my mind was still a whirl with thoughts. I needed to return to work. I had taken enough time off. In the morning, I would make the phone call. Detective Sergeant Siobhan Williams was returning to duty.

CHAPTER 17. AMONGST THE DUST – Siobhan

It seemed like ages since I had been at work, it was time to get some normality back in my life. Stop dwelling on what I could do nothing about and think of the future. I arrived back to find all in a state of turmoil.

In my absence I had acquired a new boss. Detective Inspector James Perry. He and I had met before. He was a misogynistic dinosaur. To him women were a subservient species. In his mind, women made the tea, looked after stray children and dogs, and held everyone's coats when the men were fighting.

I did not join the police service to hump boxes, did I? Does humping boxes and emptying cupboards fall into the category of jobs called *'in the exigency of duty'*? My aching back and arms and my sore legs were testament that carrying the contents of an office up three flights of stairs would probably improve my fitness but would not improve my humour. The local intelligence office was moving, and I was in charge of the move.

Along with my three colleagues, I have been tasked with spiriting our place of work to the top floor, where we will be suitably locked away behind a keypad access door, in a larger office with our own kitchen and sufficient storage for our needs. Surely in this day and age there was an easier way than brute force and ignorance. There was a conversation to be had with my Detective Inspector, not known for his tact and diplomacy and well known to live by his budget.

'Will the powers that be fund a removal company to move our numerous filing cabinets and their contents?'

'No, they won't. It's only up the stairs after all.' came the blunt reply.

'Is the dumb waiter lift working? That would help a great deal.'

'No, it's not.' D.I. Perry showed signs of irritation. In fact, I was well aware that the facility in question hadn't worked since some wag on a night shift decided to dare an overweight probationer to ride it up to the top floor while he himself ran up the stairs. No names, no pack drill. The officer concerned has been suitably reprimanded, the probationer had since resigned. Fitness test failed. The dumb waiter remains inactive. It never talked much anyway. If it could I'm sure it would have a few similar pranks to tell of. There had, over the years, been rumours of items of highly personal property being found trapped in its mechanism. The dumb waiter remained silent. This was a conversation I had had at length with our boss. To no avail.

    It had taken the best part of two days to complete our mission but now we have completed the ascent to the fourth floor. The ascent of Everest would have been less traumatic, the north face of the Eiger less of a challenge to two fairly robust female officers, one male well into his fiftieth year and a stranger to physical exercise, and a fourth whose slipped intra-vertebral disc was legendary. But we had made it with much puffing and panting up the three flights of stairs to our new home. Job done.

    I have the keys to our new abode. As well as the keypad, most of the office doors are also locked, double locked with a mortice and a dead lock, a hint at the nature of the former occupants who have been re-housed in a nice new offsite building. Nothing too good for them it seems. In the meantime, we, the local intelligence unit, must make do. The top floor is not really ideal for the passing trade we sometimes get from those inquisitive officers who actually use our services, but it is sufficiently quiet to allow us to function without being disturbed or having our security breached. Heaven forbid some useful snippet of information should leak from these pale blue, slightly damp walls. The bucket strategically placed in the stairwell reminds me that this nineteen seventies monstrosity of a building leaks like a sieve and if the planners have their way it will be demolished before the end of the decade. This part of the city does not need a Police Station, but it does need more social housing and another car park to encourage footfall into the already dying shops.

Having moved our belongings into the larger of the offices and allocated each of us a desk, being the *'keeper of the keys'* I made my way to the far end of the corridor and started to unlock doors.

The first office at the far end of the long corridor is an impressive wood panelled affair, resonant of its former occupant in days gone by. This had once been the inner sanctum of a Chief Superintendent. There is a door leading into a smaller typist's office, which is still equipped with its utilitarian desk. Three drawers one side, room for a desk top computer and in and out trays, and not much else. The main office is empty, except for a top quality carpet in dark blue, slightly faded with age and sporting the force crest woven into its thick pile. The carpet continues into the typist's office. No expense spared at this level.

The main office is bare of furniture, the telltale indentations left by the large and heavy desk appropriate to the occupant's large and heavy rank and the marks left by the accompanying chair give testimony to what once occupied the space. I open the window slightly to allow the musty smell of dust covered Venetian blinds to vacate the building and note that the window is coated with that film which renders it opaque from the outside. Why? We are on the fourth floor for goodness's sake. Is there danger from peeping toms in low flying helicopters!? I smile to myself wondering how many terrified constables had stood before the huge desk, swaying with unsure footing on the unfamiliar soft pile to face the Superintendent's wrath for some small misdemeanour. On the carpet indeed. I had been there once or twice myself - in my younger years, of course.

I stifled a giggle of a memory and moved back into the corridor with its grey contract cord covering, complete with cigarette burns, coffee stains and other as yet unidentified black sticky marks. The carpet in the main office is not much cleaner. The desks have evidence of cigarettes being allowed to burn out with the ash falling over the edge onto the carpet and leaving a telltale half-moon shaped mark on the varnished surface. There is chewing gum trodden into the floor together with what could be the remains of a mouldy pasty or a sandwich. The previous occupants were plainly not houseproud.

The next office is similarly locked and slightly smaller. The remains of a Perspex sign on the outside of the door declares it the former home of the Chief Inspector. No plush carpet. A larger desk than the typist, with two sets of drawers – the desk, that is. Window suitably opaque. No chair. Well, someone probably half inched that long ago, before the days of health and safety briefings and comfort in the working environment. The Chief Inspector's probably leather padded chair would have disappeared within an hour of him vacating the office. I open the window to air out the smell of dust, cobwebs and inactivity and move on.

The offices at the front of the building look out onto the street below, those on the other side of the passage have a view down into the rear yard. I unlock the door of the small office opposite the large open plan room where my colleagues have made their home. The carpet is the standard grey, but at least it is clean. The desk is a typist's desk, but there is an additional set of lockable drawers. And there it is. A big leather chair on castors. Possession is nine tenths of the law. And this will be my office after all. I dump my handbag in the chair and my cardboard box of 'stuff' on the desk. Sergeant Siobhan Williams has landed.

I continue to unlock doors and open windows, finding that we have a small kitchen area but no kettle, and very little water pressure, two toilets, male and female, and opposite the Chief Super's Office a private bathroom complete with shower and a small sauna. This truly was the senior officer's corridor back in the day. Ah! The Superintendent's sauna. How many of us were left who could still recall the number of officers caught 'inflagranté' whilst making use of this facility on a night shift. I knew several whose careers and marriages had gone into a tailspin as a result of such dalliances along this very corridor. That was back in the misogynistic old days, before the dawning of the age of equality and all that went with it, days which were not so very far behind us.

I have one key left untested on the bunch in my hand. Where are you, Cinders? I look for the door which it might fit. There it is at the far end of the corridor, set into the wall, a cupboard, right next to the fire extinguisher, double doors, and besides being locked with a dead lock, it is also padlocked. I have no key to the padlock. I call my colleague, Mark Fish.

'Have you got the jemmy, Mark?'

Mark has custody of the small tool bag we keep for operational use and emergencies. Hammer, screwdrivers, adjustable spanner, sharp knife, pliers, a small crowbar, glass cutter, toffee hammer and a set of bolt croppers. There is also small tin of black treacle and some brown paper at the bottom, its use, in conjunction with the toffee hammer very effective on single panes of glass, all but redundant in these days of double glazing. With a bit of persuasion and a minimum of damage the padlock is removed, and the cupboard opened.

'Bollocks and buggeration!' I exclaim, an odd phrase for me. I had expected the cupboard to be empty. But no, it contained two large filing cabinets and a hanging rail which still supports a suit bag containing the owners No1 uniform, another containing a dark grey suit with a clean shirt and a discreet maroon tie with a golf club crest and a fine blue diagonal stripe. I remove the suit carriers. The uniform has the officer's collar number 479 embroidered into the lining, obviously issued when the Tailors Department was what it said on the tin and not just a uniform stores. The pockets of the suit are empty save for a business card with the force crest announcing the bearer as David Holly, a man who retired some years ago and moved to Spain to live out his retirement in the sunshine, an officer I had never heard a good word said about, universally referred to in his absence as, *'a complete bastard of a man.'* Something made me take photographs of both items and replace them where I had found them. *'Complete bastards'* had a knack of returning to bite the unprepared on the backside. *'Complete bastards'* also tended to have friends in very high places to do the biting for them.

Mark had opened the filing cabinets with his specially designed bent spoon. The bent spoon or fork is a must for any proficient police station burglar. Once it is bent to the required angle, no standard filing cabinet lock is safe.

I pull the top drawer of one open. It creaks slightly on its runners. It has not been opened for years. The contents are neatly filed in manila folders, each labelled and suspended in alphabetical order in green hangers, each folder labelled with a name. Surname first in capitals, then underneath the offence code and the offence. This should not be here. This should have been sent to central filing years ago for assessment and proper disposal. These cases are ages old, many dating back over twenty years. I feel the hair on my neck bristle. I hear Mark cough and mutter, 'Can of bloody worms, Sarg.'

We look at each other and simultaneously close the cabinet and the cupboard.

'Later, Mark. We will have to go through it later, but not now. Let's move in properly first.'

'Aye, aye, skipper.'

He reverts to ex-naval type and marches smartly away from the cupboard and into the kitchen where someone has had the presence of mind to find us a kettle and some makings. They have also located the mains water and immersion heater. The cold water tap coughs and splutters and after half a minute of light brown discharge, a liquid resembling fresh water resumes its service to the top floor. Good.

One look from me to Mark tells him not to mention the contents of the cupboard over coffee and chocolate hob nobs, at least not just yet. Mark replaces the padlock with one to which only he and I have the key. We will have to raise the subject with D.I. Perry at some point but let's not encourage his presence until we have at least moved in. I expect he will want the Super's office. Plenty of room for his ego and for the width of his backside.

We four musketeers spend an afternoon unpacking boxes and arranging desks, locating data ports and electric sockets in preparation for the IT department to issue and plumb in our nice new laptop computers. Every officer must have one. We are amongst the last to benefit. Nothing unusual there.

The clock on the wall has been issued with a new battery and its hands are now indicating that it is nearly 6pm and well past clocking-off time.

'Pub?' suggested Mark. 'My throat is drier than a witches left mammary gland.'

'Just say, 'tit' Mark, subtlety does not become you. I'll come for one, but I'd better clock in first. Ray thinks I'm made of cotton wool since Mum passed.' I did not tell Mark the real reason for my husband's concern. Ray was half expecting the call.

'Stay and have a few if you like,' he suggested. 'you haven't been out for ages. I'll pick you up. Leave the car where it is.'

Mark and I made our way across town to, 'The Fleece.' By the time Raymond collected me three hours later, I had told Mark everything. It felt good to have an independent audience. Mark is that sort of calm and level-headed person who manages to never generate a drama out of a crisis.

'If you want to look, I'll help you.' he announced. 'If it's any comfort, I'm adopted myself. Sure, it's nice to know where you came from, but it doesn't change the person you are, and it doesn't change where you are going to. It's just a stop along the way.' That was his personal view. The wisdom of Fish.

Ray helped me in through our front door and suggested I go straight to bed and have a lie in in the morning. He had a late start. He would sort the kids and we could pick my car up from the nick later, maybe catch some lunch in town, chat about things. It had been good to let off steam, vent my feelings away from home, as it were. Good as his word, Ray whisked me back into the city on the rear of his motorcycle. We ate a very satisfying but early lunch at Gino's restaurant and I collected my car from the back yard of the nick where it had spent the night.

We discussed my search for my roots, what should be my next move, the possibility that I may discover things which I did not like or that would upset me further. I agreed not to do anything until we had sorted out Mum's estate, not to take on too much at one time. Sound advice as usual, but the contents of that shoebox weighed heavy on my mind. I felt that I needed answers.

CHAPTER 18. A MATTER OF DISCLOSURE - Siobhan

When I was a probationary police constable in 2009, a wise old head told me to consider the disclosure of evidence in a court case as a game of trumps between two players. Each has in their hand a range of cards if played in the best order will enable them to win. The evidence in a criminal case can often be simplified in this way.

The prosecution gathers their evidence aiming to convict the guilty party. However, during this gathering, they may encounter evidence which at best aids the defence case, or worse, actively undermines the prosecution case. It is the role of the Police to gather their evidence in a fair manner and to record not only evidence which is in their favour but to also record that which is not. This is in the interests of justice. The prosecution is required to disclose these things to the defence. This is done in stages.

The defence will naturally conduct their enquiries in a more blinkered manner. The accused is not under any requirement to tell the truth or to disclose anything they do not wish known. An accused person will lie if it saves their skin. In the case of a not guilty plea, the case for the defence is guided largely by how the person in the dock has instructed his legal team and what advice has been given. This advice is, of right, confidential.

Round 1. The defendant enters their plea of *Not guilty*.

Round 2. The prosecution may then be ordered by the court to disclose the evidence they intend to present to the court to support their case, and before the next court hearing. This is where the strengths and weaknesses of each side are teased and ferreted out.

In response to the disclosure made by the prosecution, the defence will be required to issue a defence statement which outlines the basis of the defence the accused will offer.

Round 3. The defence asks for disclosure of any evidence which the prosecution holds which may assist their case. This may include witnesses, exhibits, forensics.

Round 4. The defence may ask if the prosecution holds any evidence which actively undermines the prosecution case. This may include unreliability of witnesses, including police officers concerned. The dirt.

Once all these cards have been played, there is a degree of legal argument amongst the parties. Many letters are sent between the Crown and the defence and the Crown and the police. Many cases are decided outside the courtroom. Charges are amended, pleas are changed, cases are dropped, deals are done.

The innocent are sometimes convicted due to lack of proper disclosure and many a guilty party has walked free due to the weakness of the prosecution case. Such is the British Criminal Justice system. Appeals against the results are often won on matters of disclosure, withholding of evidence and disposal of the same. Proper disclosure is a can of worms. There are also some things which are never disclosed without an order from the Judge. There are laws designed to protect those perceived as at risk should their identities be discovered. These legal cupboards are the last hiding places for the skeletons hidden by the corrupt and the dishonest.

To try and eliminate these legal hiding places, in 1996 the Criminal Investigations and Procedure Act was passed. This formalised the process of disclosure of evidence which up until that date had been largely governed by what the investigating officer saw fit to tell the defence, which was usually as little as humanly possible. By the time I became an officer of the law, all was computerised and in major cases a whole team of officers was devoted to making sure that the disclosure of evidence complied with the law.

It took until the end of a week for us to install ourselves fully on the fourth floor. During that time, we still had to provide a service to our *'customers'*. The needs of operational policing could not stop while we unpacked our boxes. Eventually the time came to tackle the contents of *'the cupboard.'* I had hoped that, for once, our lily-livered boss D.I. Perry would make a decision and send the contents of the cupboard to the Central Records Unit and let them examine it. It would be their job after all to correctly dispose of it or retain it, depending on its relevance. That was not a decision D.I. Perry felt he could make.

We, as in myself and the trusty Mark, would wade through it. We would assess what of it was legally required to be kept, extract any intelligence, dispose of what was now irrelevant and then send the results to the CRU. The CRU would, I knew, repeat this very process. They were the experts on what needed to be retained. In my book it was their decision to make, not ours, or ultimately mine. For, if the crap ever hit the fan, Perry would make sure it was me sweeping it all up. After all, shit only ever rolls one way.

On the Monday morning at eleven o'clock after morning briefing and armed with large mugs of coffee and a box of donuts from Gregg's bakery across the road, Mark and I began. Utilising the sack truck with which we had manoeuvred our belongings up the stairs, we wheeled the two four drawer filing cabinets into my office and began with cabinet, No 1.

The top drawer: the neat, suspended files were in alphabetical order, the Manila folders contained therein held schedules of disclosure for cases all before 1996 when the Criminal Procedure and Investigations Act had come into force. Some of the defendants were almost certainly dead by now. We started to wade through the quagmire.

'Okay, Mark, shall we start by checking who of the defendants is still alive. Let's deal with the dead first. If the defendant is deceased, we send it to CRU, they can dispose of it.' First decision of the day was made.

'Are we making a spreadsheet of what goes where, Sarge?' Mark had spreadsheets for everything. His bed was probably covered with a quilt with an XL spreadsheet for a pattern, with filters at the head end. That interesting thought made me smile, smirk even, just a bit.

'Yes, Mark, I think it will be useful, even if only to record what we have here before we box it all up.' I could feel Mark tapping on his keyboard as I spoke. He knows I am probably as obsessed with spreadsheets as he is.

By the end of the morning, we had sorted the living from the dead. Three filing boxes of folders were stacked in the corner of my office. We were left with a dozen who were still alive, some still incarcerated, some who had served their time and were now back in society. The curious thing was that of those left, most were the older cases, from a time before the hands of the detectives were more effectively tied, when the Detective Chief Superintendent was only slightly lower than God himself.

Mark entered the name of each defendant on a new tab, laboriously deciphered the handwritten lists of evidence, some things marked with ticks some with crosses, some with annotations in the margin, notes in a different hand as to the destination of an item. In certain cases, a picture was developing. These folders contained details of what was not to be disclosed, under any circumstances. The top drawer was the index.

On opening the second drawer we found that it was arranged in a similar fashion. Suspension files filled with folders, all in alphabetical order, but these contained the documents referred to in the index. By the time we had finished removing the dead, our pile of boxes had increased one box for each of the deceased.

Now the real reading started. Some of the cases had been high profile. They had made the national news. David Holly had been a bit of a legend in his time. There were press cuttings filed along with statements from witnesses and evidential reports. All were cases which had been contentious, some of the outcomes unexpected, cases where there had been speculation over whether justice had really been done. It drew both of us in with a sense of morbid fascination as we read forensic reports which would cast doubt on a defendant's involvement. All suppressed by one man. Hidden from sight for decades. Evidence which on occasion had indirectly led to the wrong person spending years behind bars. But why had none of them appealed? Some had protested their innocence until the day they had been released. But none had sought to clear their names. Why?

A little further digging showed that most of the cases had been gang related killings, some involved notable underworld figures, men and sometimes women involved in organised and lucrative criminality. How many palms had been greased? How many had been paid for their silence, a token protest over the years, a token headline announcing an appeal refused, lies fed to the press when no appeal was ever lodged? Oh yes, David Holly had been good at more than one job, too good to have left a trail of evidence this wide. Was this his insurance policy? Would what we were about to find incriminate others further up the food chain? What was his ace card? Or did he feel sufficiently safe in his sun kissed retirement to keep his aces up his sleeve? We read on.
By Wednesday we had reached the third drawer and had opened the second cabinet.

The second cabinet was full of sealed padded envelopes. Each envelope was again labelled, this time with a surname. In feeling the contents, they felt like cassette tapes, the hard plastic cassettes, some in boxes, some not, could be felt through the padding. Initial exploration with a latex clad hand detected that some were video cassettes, and some were smaller, possibly those from a hand-held camcorder or a Dictaphone. Some of the sealed envelopes were marked with surnames, initials, and numbers. G. WILLIAMS 10000. C.ap. MEREDITH 5000. I heard Mark muttering, '*Fucking hell.*' Several times under his breath, then very loudly, '*Bloody fucking hell.*' This alerted the whole office.

'What's occurring, Mark?', Sarah chipped in from across the corridor in her best pseudo-Welsh accent.

'It's all going fatties' leg!', Mark added. He loves the film, 'Twin Town', it seems to have a reference for everything in everyday life. 'This is a dog job that's gone wrong.' he continued.

'Okay, let's take a break.' I straightened up in my big leather chair, it wasn't as comfortable as it looked. Maybe I'd trade it for another one, someone on the ground floor would have a home for it, maybe in exchange for one of those lovely skeleton chairs which actually supported your spine instead of encouraging you to slump into that well-padded journey to severe, untreatable lumbago.

On cue, Sarah appeared with three mugs of coffee and two donuts on a plate, with a custard slice for me, proof positive that she intended to get in on the action. 'If you need help deciphering the forensic bits, don't hesitate to ask.', she hinted. 'I have several years of experience in that direction.'

Indeed, she had. Sarah had been a scenes of crime officer before health issues had forced her to take a more office-based role. Now only a few months from retirement she was a font of knowledge. She placed the tray on my desk. I could tell she was reading the file which was open.

'Don't forget, I worked with 479 David Holly.

David Holly's uniform, David Holly's suit. Were these all-David Holly's cases? Mark, who had wandered across the office, stretching his legs and leaning on the window ledge, looking down into the rear yard where the aforementioned David Holly had once had his own parking bay, suddenly returned to the cabinet whose bottom drawer was still open. Something had caught his eye. He squatted in front of the drawer and thrust his arm to the back of the cavity, taking hold of what looked like a piece of old duster. He pulled out a wooden object encased in a slim cloth bag. From the bag he unsheathed a length of turned wood, some eighteen inches long and just under an inch and a half in diameter, tapering at one end with a turned ridged hand grip and a leather wrist strap. It was smooth and polished and somewhat worn with age, and horizontally all along its length like trophies were engraved names, each name accompanied by a number, the last of which was WEAVER, against which no following number appeared.

'I heard about this,' Mark placed it on the desk in front of me. 'but I never thought it existed.'

'Oh, yes, it existed.', Sarah added. 'The bastard added the names personally after every trial. I'm surprised he left it behind, though he did go in a bit of a hurry.'

'Tell us more.' Marks curiosity was pricked.

'Well, it was after his last case. Once the result was in, he left. Just packed his personal stuff, sold up and left. We all knew he was due to retire, he was well over his thirty years. Even before the trial started, he'd put his house on the market. He handed in his notice, told his wife of forty years to fuck off and was on the first flight out of Dodge. The official story was that he couldn't handle any more stress, didn't want to be persuaded to take on another case. He shook hands with the chief, got his certificate of service and, hey presto! He was gone. To all the federated ranks it stank! But then the higher up you are the less you smell the bullshit.' Sarah took a long gulp of coffee.

'I suppose he just forgot to take it. I doubt he had developed a conscience. Or maybe he thought it might incriminate him, to be basking in the misfortune of others as it were. Shall I leave you to it, Sarge? If you need me, I'm only across the way.' Sarah left, leaving more unanswered questions. We finished our coffee and got back to work.

'Let's get to the end of it, then assess what we've got. Then I have a feeling we may need to involve the boss. He's not going to like it.', I encouraged Mark.

'Theres a storm coming, Shonnie, I hope we aren't stuck in the middle of it. You know what they do to the messengers.' Mark looked at me like Eeyore the donkey, his slightly jowly face all hang dog with concern. It was not often he called me anything other than Sarge.

We beavered away, reading documents, assessing them, listing them, and developing a picture. What was the common factor? What was obvious was that it was all about David Holly. But who were his paymasters? He was the puppet, now who was the puppet master?

Finally, we came to the end of the paper files. The videos were another matter. Sarah had been sent to try and scrounge a VHS player, hopefully one which could convert the tapes to DVD if needed, but primarily one which could play them. I placed the last file in front of me. Last alphabetically but was it Holly's last case. 'Sarah!' I called across the corridor, have you got a moment?'

'Certainly, I have.' came the reply.

'What was his last case? Do you remember?'

'How could anyone ever forget, it was the Weaver case, and all that went with it. A right bucket of shit that was, poor woman.'
I handed Sarah the file.

'Then you can pick the bones out of that! Did you find a video player by the way?'

'It's older than the ark, the screen isn't very big, but it's working, and Danny says it will copy to DVD as well. He also provided me with these.' She produced a set of leads with multi coloured end plugs. 'You can connect it to your swanky new laptop to get a better picture. He's all kindness is my friend Danny.'

'Sarah James, you are a gem. You get stuck into that file, Mark and I will start on the tapes. By the end of the week, we should have a report at least for that……' My flow was interrupted by D.I. Perry walking in unannounced.

'Haven't you lot finished yet? It's only a few files for god's sake. Too much talking and coffee, I knew it was a mistake to allow you lot anywhere near the kitchen.' I could feel Mark mimicking him behind his back. I restrained the urge to giggle.

'End of the week, boss.' I kept my reply short.

'Make it so!' he replied, his attempt at humour failing miserably. Turning on his heel he left us to it.

'Make it so! My fucking arse, I'll make this so fucking smelly, he'll need a big bunch of roses for the Chief before he's through.' Mark echoed my thoughts exactly.

The can was being opened, the worms were escaping, the skeletons were dancing in the cupboard, the fan was turning, the shit was on trajectory and the storm was about to break.

CHAPTER 19. THE SISTERHOOD

From the moment she saw the name on the front of the file, she knew that she knew more about this case than was probably good for her. But what the heck, she thought. She had only another three months left before she could retire completely.

Sarah had served out her thirty years as an officer. She had completed four years as a civilian employee. She had told no one that she had been recently diagnosed with the Big C. A small but inoperable brain tumour, small now but likely to grow, a ticking timebomb inside her skull. She might just make it as far as retirement, but not much longer. Her children were grown up, they had left home. She would tell her partner soon, as soon as she plucked up enough courage to break his heart.

She opened the Weaver file and started to read. As she read, the past flooded back to her, memories of a woman who had been her friend. Should she feel shame at what had happened to her, should she feel guilt that, like many of her colleagues, she had turned a blind eye to her friend's predicament. Should she have broken ranks and told her what she knew. Where was Cassandra Weaver now? Was she still in prison or had she been released? Was it too late to try and help her? In the folder marked Weaver was a copy of the whole file, statements from the attending officers, Sarah's own statement as a scenes of crime officer. For a murder file it was remarkably slim. It also included statements from social services regarding the two little girls, Charlotte, and Amy. What had happened to them?

The hidden camera. Why would Tony of all people want a camera installed in his kitchen? That did not ring true. She added it to her list of enquiries. The other sophisticated surveillance equipment - whose was it? The surveillance team were definitely involved in something, she had seen them. She had told Ron Ashton what she knew. But had she done enough?

Sarah read carefully as she always did. Dates, dates were always important. Officers signed and dated things on auto pilot, sometimes there were discrepancies. Signs of a decision made ahead of its time, a jump to a conclusion, a mistake. On a sheet of paper, she started a timeline. If there was a fuck-up to be found, Sarah James would find it. She would pick at the scabs of the case until one bled. If David Holly was involved, then there would definitely be pustules and corruption, but it would be well hidden under a layer of legal wallpaper, the cracks sealed with the filler of greed - money. That was what it all came down to in the end.

Ron Ashton had been fair. All his case notes, the doodling in the margins, all pointed to a good case for manslaughter. The defence would run self-defence or an action in a moment when all control had been lost - a moment of madness. Yet Holly had pushed for murder from the outset.

Sandra had not helped herself. Sarah was sure she had been truthful. It was not in Sandra's nature to lie. But had she told them everything? Sarah read on.

Siobhan broke open the first envelope marked Weaver and pushed the cassette into the video player. She pressed play and after about ten seconds of screen wobbling static, a picture emerged on her laptop. There in glorious technicolour was the impressive figure of Tony Weaver, seen from the rear but obviously Tony Weaver.

The garage of The Laurels was huge, there was ample room for two cars, there was a dormer room in loft above with its own en-suite wet room. The garage had been designed with a view to easy conversion into a grannie annexe or a separate flat. The architect had been inventive with the plans.

Tony Weaver was busy. As Siobhan and Mark watched, he could be seen carefully removing the contents of a suitcase and packing each cellophane wrapped square parcel into the space behind the wooden panelling in the eaves of the loft. This camera was carefully positioned with a view of the neatly concealed void. Had this void been searched at the time? Either it had not, or it was empty. The recording was date stamped several weeks before Tony's death. As she watched, she saw Tony take the last package from the case. This he placed to one side. Tony did not know about this camera, then, did he.

The puzzle was not hard to figure out. If this footage was recorded by the surveillance team, then they would most certainly have acted upon it. Tony was part of a bigger picture. He might, if necessary, have been arrested. It would have complicated matters, but some form of operation would have happened. No, this camera was placed by someone else. This camera was keeping an eye on the merchandise, and it was keeping an eye on Tony Weaver. If this was the same equipment as that installed in the kitchen, then that statement from the security company was a fiction. Ashton had been pacified, he had been provided with his chain of evidence, but by who?

She would need to confirm a few points, it was not good to assume anything. On the note pad in front of her she wrote – Batman, ring Batman. Where was Bruce Wayne now? He had retired several years ago. There had been no news of his death in the retired officers' newsletter, maybe the retired officers' association would know where he was. She wrote NARPO next to his name.

The next video was mundane. Tony Weaver cooking for the kiddies. The tape showed a father dressed in a pink frilly pinafore apron, preparing food, two small children standing on chairs pulled up to the worktop alongside him, the backs of the chairs safely against the cupboards to prevent them toppling over, two little girls watching intently while daddy sliced carrots into sticks and cut potatoes into real 'daddy chips' for their tea. Where had those words sprung from, there was no sound on the video? Yet the words, 'daddy chips' repeated themselves in her head, over and over again. She pressed pause.

'How's it going in there, Jamesey?' She called across the passage.

'Slowly.' Came the reply. 'Someone wanted our Sandra gone, that's certain.'

'Let's take a break, then round up what we have, I need the loo.'

Siobhan walked down the passage and let herself into the privacy of the former Superintendent's private facilities. She wanted complete privacy, her head was swimming, her mind was confused, she had never met Tony Weaver, yet she felt she knew him. She had never been to that house, but she knew it. She had never seen that child before, or had she? Reaching into the depths of her handbag, Siobhan Williams felt for the blister pack of Valium. Turning on the cold tap, she let the water run until it was clear, disregarding the warning sign *'not drinking water'*. She ducked her head over the basin and swilled her face, grateful that she wore no makeup and took a mouthful, just enough to wash down two of, 'mother's little helpers'. She hoped they would give her the assistance she needed. She leant her forehead against the cool of the mirror and breathed out, her breath clouding the glass. Then with her right index finger she wrote in the misted patch one word, 'FUCK.'

On her return to the office, she found that Sarah had made herself at home in the big leather chair. Mark was sitting balanced on its arm next to her, and they were re watching the second video. Someone had made coffee. In the far corner of the main office, she could hear Alfie Lewis moaning about the pile of work he was doing alone, complaining about his bad back and giving notice that he would probably be on the sick next week. That figured. She had promised the D.I. that they would be finished by the end of the week. Alfie had been holding the fort, dealing with all the current workload. Alfie was big mates with the DI. They lived in the same street. They drank in the same pub. Alfie felt he was owed a break, so, he would take one. Alfie still believed that he was entitled to at least ten sick days a year. She couldn't be bothered to argue with him today, her head was aching, she could feel the slight euphoria of the tablets kicking in.

She closed the lid of the laptop. The video disappeared from view.

'Okay, team, what have we got so far?'

She heard the click and whirr of the video player as the tape carriage spat out the tape. She did not see Sarah place the tape back in its envelope and secrete it under her pile of papers.

Sarah began to talk, conversationally. 'Let me tell you a little of what I know of Cassandra Weaver.' She sat back in the big leather chair.

'Is this going to be book at bedtime or Jackanory?' muttered Mark.

'From what I heard she was a liability, a bit unstable, and she did admit she killed him.'

Sarah bit, instantly. 'The propaganda department certainly did its job on you, Mark Fish. Sandra would have been long gone before you were a twinkle in the Chief Constable's eye. Don't judge her if you didn't ever know her. Just shut the fuck up and listen.'

Mark looked into his coffee mug, ashamed and suitably rebuked. Sarah continued.

'I joined the job alongside Sandra. She was Sandra Davies then. We were recruits together two women in an intake with twenty-eight men. She was my friend. In those days there was no such thing as equality. There was one female officer per relief. You were expected to do more and do it better and not receive any recognition for even existing. To rise above being told to make the tea you needed to shit miracles. Sandra and I cut our teeth in the days when having your backside felt by a male colleague was considered a compliment. Comments on the size of your boobs was an honour. It wasn't what you knew, it was who you knew. Certain of our sisterhood had reputations. So and so only does Chief Inspectors or above. Those were the bad old days. In those bad old days, you needed friends, and Sandra and I were friends we had each other's backs - until she got with Tony Weaver.

Sandra never had a problem with authority as such, but she stood up for herself. She didn't suffer fools. Back in the day that wasn't good for one's career. The bosses put her and Tony to work together to try and get them to hang each other. They wanted both of them gone. He was a bad boy, and they considered her a ticking time bomb. She was a good officer but too honest for her own good. Cassandra Davies could not be bought.' Sarah put her hands to her head and massaged her temples.

'Headache?' Mark asked.

'It will pass.' Sarah had gone very pale, she breathed in and out deeply and pressed on the soft spot just above her eyes. Then she shook her head and spoke again.

'Before Tony came on the scene, she was seeing Bruce. They were an item. Then with the advent of big, bad Tony, Bruce was sidelined, but Bruce always carried a torch for Sandra. He was very protective of her. When she dumped him, he was heartbroken. I knew he wanted her back, but she was swept up in bad boy romance. She thought she could tame Tony, change him. When they first got together it was Sandra who wore the trousers.'

'How did she know Bruce?' Siobhan asked.

'He was about the only civilised lad on our intake, well the only one with a brain. A degree in History and English all wrapped up in six feet three of curly blonde, blue eyed loveliness.' Sarah rolled her eyes.

'We both fancied Bruce, two of the guys did too!' she joked. 'But I digress. Bottom line is, Sandra was as honest as the day is long, she couldn't lie, she always said that she had a flashing red light which lit up if she lied! So, she just didn't. Tell the truth, shame the devil, was her motto. It got her into trouble many times. But she was a good officer, a great colleague and most of all a loyal friend. The job treated her badly. It chewed her up and spat her out.

'Before…… ' Sarah stopped hastily. 'It may be too late, but I intend to help her, if it's the last thing do.'

'Where is she now?' Siobhan asked. Even as she spoke, she could hear Mark's fingers tapping keys. Then he spoke.

'She was released in 2010. On paper she has a life licence, but she seems to have dropped right off the radar. She's been out for seven years. She could be anywhere.'

It was Siobhan who spoke next. 'Then find her, Mark. If anyone can find her, you can.' Siobhan went to the window and flicked the blinds closed again.

'Now let's get stuck into these tapes.'

Having watched most of the tapes it became evident that the Weaver house was being watched. There was a camera in every room, two in some rooms. This, and Sarah's knowledge of the van she had seen at the scene all those years ago, showed that there were two sets of eyes doing the watching. Were either of them official? Siobhan suspected not. Another jotting on her pad, 'authorities.' If there had ever been an authority, for how long was it kept? In those days before RIPA, was one even needed!

The other set of eyes, well Sandra had found out who actually owned the Laurels, who had built the whole site. The Land Registry searches which were in the file showed that Anthony Weaver was the owner of the plot and all that stood on it, but he himself had said otherwise, if you believed what Sandra had said in interview. It all began to tie in. In a nutshell, Tony Weaver was bent. He had sold out to the very criminals he was deployed to catch. The watcher was being watched, he had become one of them, but he was not quite trusted. His wife had not signed up for the deal. She had fought back. She was willing to risk everything to get her man back and keep her family together. That accounted for one set. But who was behind the second set of eyes?

Sarah lifted her head from her reading and, taking a plastic card from her wallet dialled the number on the back. A male voice answered the phone. The enquiry was short. The result was a dubious, 'I'll see if I can reach him, I'll ask him to call you back, but no guarantees, can I tell him why?' Sarah answered in the negative. She had sown the seed. All she could do is see if it produced a result.

By now they had managed to organise the video tapes into two batches and put each batch in chronological order. Mark had started to log the contents of each, documenting significant events with a date stamp, describing each in detail. He could, with time, splice the two sets into one piece of captioned viewing, but that was for later. D.I. Perry expected his result in two days' time. In two days', time it was expected that the filing cabinets and their contents would disappear, never to be seen again.

The worms however continued to turn, the lid of the can became less secure, and the skeletons had all but found the key to the door. One thing had become very clear from all that they had seen and read. Cassandra Weaver was not guilty of murder. Had the jury seen half of what they had found, then maybe manslaughter, if not an acquittal, on the basis of self-defence.

Mark typed into his timeline for the hour before Tony Weaver's death.
Frame 1: Black male identified as Anthony Weaver can be seen in the en-suite bathroom preparing two lines of white powder on the vanity unit in front of the mirror. He bends with a rolled-up tube in his hand and ingests the white powder into his nose and sniffs. In the mirror the reflection of a woman identified as Cassandra Weaver can be seen watching.
Frame 2: An argument takes place. The male is seen lunging towards the female and throwing her onto the bed. He starts to place his hands around her throat. She kicks him in the genitals. He releases his grip and leaves the room. He leaves the house via the front door.
Frame 3: The Kitchen: Cassandra Weaver can be seen preparing breakfast for two small children. She leaves the kitchen and is next seen in an office or study.
Frame 4: The Office: Cassandra Weaver can be seen taking documents from a filing cabinet and spreading them on the desk. As she is examining them Anthony Weaver returns and grabs her by the back of the neck, he picks her bodily off the floor and throws her at the wall. She stands back up. He slaps her face, visibly making her nose bleed. She runs from the room towards the kitchen.
Next frame: The Kitchen

'The rest is history.' Mark murmured to himself hitting the save button with the mouse. He set the document up to print and scratched his head. This was beyond his comprehension. Had he not seen it for himself then he would not have believed that this existed. D.I. Perry was going to have to escalate this. But would he? Mark would pay good money to be a fly on the wall when the report his the D.I.'s desk.

CHAPTER 20. BUGS AND LOW LIFE

Bristol

It was half past five on Thursday, Sarah looked at the clock displayed on the front of her iPhone. She stuffed the video tape into her shoulder bag and shut down her laptop. It was time to go home, home to her lonely existence. Who was she kidding? Dean her partner of twenty-five years would be out with his new squeeze. She still loved him dearly, but the passion had long since worn off and they had come to a certain arrangement. They lived separate lives in the same house. The rule was that each was free to see other people if they chose, but not to bring them home, not to do anything which would lead to the embarrassment of the other. Dean was suitably discreet in his relationships. She knew it would hurt him if he did not know of her diagnosis, yet she felt at the bottom of her heart that he had long ago given up the right to know the ins and outs of her life. They were not married. They had two grown up sons together.

They shared a host of monetary commitments acquired through the course of a relationship which meant it was financially impossible for either to survive alone. She sighed deeply. She had hoped for so much more from her life. When had it all seemed to go wrong? It had all started to fall apart after the Weaver case.

After the Weaver case she had remained on Scenes of Crime for several more years, but sidelined, shunted into the siding which dealt with endless photographs of injuries, examinations of stolen cars and property. All those expensive courses she had been sent on were wasted. All she was told was that her experience was needed in those areas and to let the youngsters get called out of bed on the small hours. So, she dusted endless ignition cowlings with aluminium dust, examined random pieces of plastic with superglue and on one occasion even sent a shoe ingrained with dog shit for comparison with that found in an old lady's back yard.

That request had more or less ended her career on Scenes of Crime even though it had been successful. The burglar whose shoe it was had pleaded guilty. The officer in the case had denied it was down to the forensics, but Sarah knew differently. But the week after that case had been concluded she had been unceremoniously advised to take leave. She must be under stress, in need of some time off. She had decided on retirement and had enjoyed the feeling of doing nothing for six months. Then the boredom had kicked in. So, she had applied to return. Intelligence as a civilian. Part time. She had not regretted it so far.

She checked her purse, it was the end of the month, her card was nearly maxed out, she had just enough in her purse to afford a bottle of red to go with the television for the evening. She was just closing the flap of her shoulder bag when her mobile vibrated. The display sprang into life to the strains of her ring tone, 'I want to dance with somebody.' An unidentified number. She tapped the green icon and answered the phone with a bald, 'Hello.'

The answering greeting was equally terse. 'Who is this?'

Sarah half recognised the voice, more gravelly with the addition of years, slightly deeper but just as seductive. 'Bruce, is that you?'

'Sarah James is that you?' The reply echoed hers.

'Now that we have established that neither of us are perverts or axe murderers and I am not after the password to your pension can we talk?' Sarah was laughing as she spoke.

'I'm sorry Sarah, the NARPO secretary is getting a bit old, he only gave me a number and said that you were a Sarah. He didn't say Sarah who. Where are you?'

Sarah told him. She was about to say more when he stopped her. 'I've been expecting, if not hoping for this call for years, I'll pick you up from Frogmore Street in ten minutes if that's okay.'

Sarah looked at her low-heeled brogue shoes, not her most comfortable purchase. She could make Frogmore Street but not that quickly. 'Make it fifteen.'

'Fifteen is fine, make sure you are wearing a pink carnation. I'll be the one wearing the blue tights and the face mask.' Bruce was always a jester. He hung up without another word.

Slinging her shoulder bag onto her back and forgetting all thought of her bottle of Rioja, Sarah headed for Frogmore Street, the traffic was heavy, crossing the roads would be a nightmare. Flexing her feet in her slightly tight shoes she stepped out across town.

She was just passing the junction with Orchard Avenue when the low-slung black Toyota sports car pulled up alongside her. The electric window was lowered, and a familiar voice ordered her to 'Hop in.' 'Hop in?' That was a joke. Hopping in was a complicated process of lowering oneself, posterior first, off the pavement to a position no more than six inches above the tarmac. Manoeuvring complete, Sarah stretched her legs into the footwell and sat back into the low-slung passenger seat, shoulder bag resting on her lap. The driver depressed the accelerator, and she was for a few seconds pressed back into the soft leather interior.

'Relax and enjoy the ride, it wasn't safe to talk on the phone. Let's go somewhere a bit more conducive to conversation.' Bruce was always a smooth talker.

'But I am expected home.' Sarah lied unconvincingly.

'Pants on fire!' Bruce laughed at her, 'You haven't been expected home since 1996. I haven't been dead for the last four years you know. I still have my sources.'

They drove out of town until they reached the small village of Wellton, and the pub called the Fox and Goose. Bruce pulled into the car park and parked the Toyota in the space behind the building marked 'reserved.' Opening the back door, he ushered Sarah inside. 'Welcome to Chez Bruce.' Sarah looked perplexed.

'Yes, this is my retirement project. I have been the landlord here since six months after I left. Nice, isn't it?'

'Lovely!' She peered around the olde-worlde fixtures and fittings, the open fires and generally cosy atmosphere. It was indeed the epitome of a small country pub.

He indicated a table in the corner by the fireplace and sat down opposite her. 'Red wine?' he suggested.

'Please.' she replied. He rose and disappeared through a door alongside the bar. It was early, there were only two customers in and the barmaid was looking professionally bored.

'Two glasses, please Sharon, there's a good girl.' The teenager who looked only just old enough to work behind a bar, raised an eyebrow and reached onto a shelf and produced two large and sparklingly clean wine glasses. Bottle in hand, a returning Bruce lifted them off the counter and brought them over to the table. Sarah noted that he still looked the part. He had not gained weight and his tall frame was still in shape. Long legged, broad shoulders, not easy to hide on a surveillance job. His only concession to age was his receding hairline. To combat the "comb over" look, he wore it short all over. His eyes were still sparkly blue. He was still Bruce. She wished she had aged as well.

'Still looking good, Bruce.' she winked at him.

'Still single as well, for the third time.' he answered.

'Bruce Wayne are you chatting me up?' she bridled.

'No, most certainly not, I thought we all got past that in 1983. God, that was so long ago. Now what do you want to talk to me about, I've a feeling I am not going to like it much, and I've a feeling I know what it is.'

'Do you remember Cassandra Weaver?' Sarah leaned across the table as the name dropped heavy as an elephant into the room.

'Remember her? How could I ever forget her? You know how it was. Cut the crap Sarah, what is this really all about?' He had ceased joking.

'This.' Sarah placed the video cassette on the table. 'Do you still have a VHS player? If you don't, I have a copy on DVD in the office.'

Bruce went visibly ashen. 'Keep your voice down, Sarah, all this is still very dangerous. There are still some very big players interested.' He looked around at the customers seated around the lounge bar. No heads had turned, all was well.

Sarah replaced the cassette in her bag. 'Let's talk equipment, I was there, I saw two of your boys removing stuff from my crime scene. It seems that now, only 25yrs later, we are seeing the product.'

'Sarah, Sarah, my hands were tied.' He whispered.

'How much did they fucking pay you?' she hissed. Bruce went quiet and she saw that he was visibly upset.

'That's the thing. Holly came to see me, all of a tizzy about the camera you found. That camera wasn't one of ours, but he came armed with knowledge that my boys had been seen at the premises. I managed to fob him off. Until he spoke to Ashton. Ashton was trying to get that bloody tape served as evidence. He wanted it validated. Holly initially brought it to us. I told him straight that I could not do what he wanted. Should anyone bother to check, they would see that the camera was far too hi-tec for one of ours. That camera was only just in use by MI5 for heaven's sake. No way would I put my name to it.'

'So how much did they pay you?' she persisted.

'It wasn't only putting pen to paper. Holly knew about me and Sandra, he knew that I still carried a flame for her. He offered me money then, money to find someone to validate the video. Then he would go easy on Sandra. I was a fool, I believed him. I went to a security firm I knew, one with jobs in some very high places. I paid one of their operatives for one sheet of paper saying that a dead man had wanted one camera installed. It would be untraceable. There was a receipt produced which was suitably dated. It was inferred that Tony thought she was cheating on him. Holly lied. In return for believing his lies I was paid enough to buy my share of this place. I have been a sleeping partner here for years, but it's in my ex-wife's name. My first ex-wife that is.'

'You stupid bastard! You stupid, stupid bastard!' Sarah took a large swallow of the very smooth Rioja which Bruce had poured into her glass.

'I still love her, Sarah, wherever she is and whatever she's done, I will always love that woman. I suppose you want to know the rest.' The big man's eyes were filling with tears.

'Shoot.' Sarah drained her glass and waited.

'My team realised that Tony Weaver had gone bad, they told me, they told me that she was suspicious of him, one of them had been ordered to key stroke her computer. The anti-corruption unit was actually looking at her, not at Tony. Young Danny Fraser could see that Sandra was viewing all the logs relating to the man who was then our target. She was taking too much of an interest, but she could justify it, it was part of her work and for a policing purpose. Young Danny told me.

We all knew that Tony was heavily into the merchandise and that he had the potential to be violent. I had my boys wire the house, I wanted to protect her in some way. Motion activated cameras, in most of the rooms, including the bedroom and the bathroom. While they were being installed the boys came across other stuff. Stuff already in place. Better kit than ours. They left it there. What else could they do? I don't know how Holly got hold of our footage. I was the only person with access to the results. No one else needed to know. But if Holly has a contact in anti-corruption, they can remotely access anything they like, if the computer is linked to the web.'

'You complete bastard, what you recorded could have saved her.' Sarah was getting louder.

'It could also have gotten her killed. Listen Sarah, it was a setup, from Holly, to the CPS, and the judge, they even had a plant on the jury, or so I was told. If she had been released and lived to tell what she knows about certain individuals, they would spend the rest of their lives inside, together with half the senior officers on the force and members of the judiciary.' He leant his head in his hands and then motioned to Sharon who fetched another bottled from the cellar.

'Sharon is my granddaughter, she is safe.', he added. 'The only one they couldn't get to was Ashton, so they tied his hands, took the decisions away from him'

'It's not too late to help her, you know.' Sarah was slurring. 'She was released seven years ago, one of our team is trying to trace her. She had two daughters. No one knows what the fuck happened to them. His lordship seems to have 'disappeared' them as well.'

'Sarah I am retired, I have commitments, I really can't get involved.'

'I should have seen through your crap at the time!' Sarah erupted 'If you really loved her, you would have helped her, we all failed her, the job hung her out to dry and we all helped. Grow a pair of balls, Bruce!'

'Sarah, you don't understand, they are influential and dangerous people, they are still out there. I don't know what I can do.' Bruce patronised her.

'I understand completely. I can't see why they called you Batman. You are no superhero, grow a fucking spine can't you. If it's any consolation, Holly isn't safe. We found his insurance policy. If you value your own safety, you'll help us before the shit really hits the fan.' She countered.

'David Holly is tucked up on the Costas in sunny Spain, they'll have a bugger of a job getting him back. From what I hear he isn't a well man. Heart disease, too much easy living, too many long lunches. Who else do you intend to go after, the fucking scarlet pimpernel?' Bruce was back to bad jokes.

'Yes, if necessary.' Sarah was angry. 'Does your beloved pub do bed and breakfast? I can't afford a cab from here.'

'Sharon! Service room five. On account.' He raised a glass to Sarah 'It's the one at the top of the stairs. It has an ensuite, best room in the house. Now chill out and let's finish this bottle, I'll have a think about what I can do. Let's change the subject and talk about old times.'

Sarah did chill. Bruce had always been good company. He had a wicked sense of humour, self-deprecating in one breath and cuttingly witty in the next. She learned that Bruce had been tracing his family tree. He had managed to find several criminals but no royalty so far. This was a common interest. In her hours of solitude Sarah had done the same, sorting through all the old photos from her parents' home, the old documents she had come across. She found it fascinating, though she had failed to get further than her second great grandparents. Bruce offered to help. She said she would think about it. They talked about everything and nothing for hours.

The pub closed, Bruce saw the last of the customers out and locked the doors. He handed her the keys to room 5. 'Until the morning then.' He showed her to the room and disappeared along the landing to the door marked Private at the opposite end of the building. Sarah was sure she heard Sharon disappear in the same direction.

'Granddaughter, my arse!' was her last thought before she slept. Sarah was woken at half past six by a loud knock on the door, 'Rise and shine, Jamesey!'

Oh shit, it was a work day. Whatever had possessed her to spend a night in a strange bed and breakfast, run by a man she hadn't seen for years. What had possessed her to drink nearly two bottles of very nice red wine. Who was she kidding, she would have drunk more than a bottle if she had spent the night at home with the telly. Would anyone miss her? Probably not. She showered in the very swish but compact ensuite using the toiletries provided, then dried her hair with the hair drier which was neatly wired to the wall alongside the mirror. She dressed in yesterday's clothing she made her way down to where she could smell the delicious aroma of bacon cooking. She was summoned into the kitchen where Bruce sat at a large table presiding over two plates of, 'full English.'

'Will that set you up for the day?' He greeted Sarah cheerfully.

'Thank you, and sorry for kicking off last night.' She replied.

'No trouble, I deserved it. I've been thinking.' He started.

'Don't, it's dangerous.' Sarah quipped.

'Are you looking for her, seriously, if you are, anything I can do I will.

'I am not scared of the likes of David Holly. Get that down you and I'll give you a lift into town.'

They were half way back into Bristol City Centre, the sporty Toyota growling ominously under Bruces right foot. Stopping at traffic lights by the Tobacco Dock, Bruce adjusted his rear-view mirror, an unnecessary adjustment, but done with a practiced hand and a minimum of movement.

'We are being followed.', he announced, turning right down a side street without indication. They drove with an excessive degree of normality across town using the side streets instead of the main thoroughfares. Bruce pulled the Toyota into the disabled bay at the front of the Bridewell.

'Follow my lead, he whispered.' His eyes focussed on his reflection in the wing mirror. He saw the unremarkable blue ford escort pull into the bay behind them. Then he leaned close to her across the passenger seat and kissed her pushing her down into the footwell below the level of the dashboard. He felt her squirm and struggle under his lips and held her shoulders tightly preventing her from escape.

The bullet hit the rear screen of the car. The glass shattered with a dull thud but did not break. Had the glass not been reinforced, the bullet would have penetrated the headrest of the driver's seat.

'That was a fucking warning.' Bruce's hands were shaking on the steering wheel. 'Now do you believe me?'

From the window on the fourth floor, Alfie Lewis saw the whole thing, and for once in his life managed to write down the registration number of the Ford Escort as it drove off in a cloud of tyre smoke up Maudlin Street. Sarah emerged from her position beneath both Bruce and the dashboard

'I believe you, oh, God, I'm late!' She was flustered. Her lips were glowing for the first time in years.

'You have my number. Don't ring me from yours, it's your phone they are watching. Buy yourself a PAYG. Use cash. Try and use a false name. Make it harder for them at least. Send me the number but send the last six in reverse order. It may work. It looks like someone is treading on toes again.'

Sarah climbed out of the vehicle and ran in through the front door, just in time to see several operational officers emerging from the shelter of the rear yard intent on speaking to the driver of the Toyota.

Too late. The Toyota was already several hundred yards away and accelerating towards the M32 and a circuitous route into the countryside.

There was no lift to the fourth floor, Sarah's legs barely carried her up the stairs. By the time she tapped in the code to open the locked door her head was pounding with hangover and the onset of shock. She stumbled into the kitchen and was violently sick in the appropriately coloured green plastic bowl in the sink.

'What the fuck was all that about?' shouted Alfie from the main office. 'I got the number if it's any use.'

'That, Alfie is some sort of warning. Where are they then?' Sarah spoke from the office door.

'In with the boss, since 8am, I don't think it's going well.' Alfie replied.

'Check out that number for me, Alf. It's probably stolen or made up, but we have to show willing.'

'Already done, Jamesey: BA51TRD: No trace PNC.'

'Show me that again,' Sarah couldn't help but smile 'Bit of a bastard that, isn't it, Alfie.'

'It's probably stolen on false plates.' came the reply.

'No, it's not, it's some fucker having a laugh at our expense, put a report in. That number is going to turn up again.'

As Bruce was driving, his mobile rang. He saw the number on the display and took the call

'Batman?' He was given a name and an address. He took the next right onto the Brislington Road and headed back into the city.

Sarah walked quietly and casually down the passage and loitered outside the door to D.I. Perry's office. She could hear the hushed tones of sensible conversation punctuated by the D.I. expressing disbelief and Siobhan firmly making a point.

'You think you will have enough to go to the top with this?'

'I do. We can prove that evidence has been withheld. We can show that this case at least was a miscarriage of justice. Who knows how many others may come out of the woodwork. D.I. we can have Holly's retired arse on a plate.'

'What makes you think that anyone actually wants Detective Chief Superintendent Holly's retired arse, as you put it, on any form of plate? He was a decorated officer, a pillar of the community, a legend in his own lunchtime.

'Sir, he was a legend built on clay foundations. All his cases were fit ups. We have the proof. And Sandra Weaver……', she started.

'Stop! Stop right there! Sandra Weaver has never appealed her conviction. She murdered a police officer in cold blood. She received a fitting sentence, one to which she never objected.' Perry was incandescent.

'She never appealed because she knew there was no point, she was tucked up like a kipper!' Siobhan was shouting back.

'Spoken to her, have you?'

'No, but I intend to.'

'You do any prison visits without my written authority, and I will have your stripes faster than you can eat breakfast.'

'She's out.'

'What do you mean she's out?'

'Just that. And it is fuck all to do with you, sir, if I choose to visit a member of the public and an old friend in my own time.'

'You be very careful, Siobhan Williams. The Sandra Weaver case will not die until she does.'

The phone on the desk started to ring. Perry answered. 'D.I. Perry. Intel. What, are you sure, the Toyota, Bruce Wayne, are you sure? Thank You.' He replaced the receiver.

'It may interest you, D.S. Williams, that there has just been a shooting in the layby outside. Some wag in a blue Ford Escort has pumped a .22 calibre round into the rear of a black Toyota parked unlawfully in the disabled bay.'

'That's a bit harsh, sir.' Siobhan was flippant, the witticism passing swiftly over her boss's head and fortunately not registering in his grey matter enroute.

Mark Fish, who had remained silent through the whole encounter, bit his bottom lip and resisted the temptation to laugh.

'The Toyota is owned and was driven by retired Detective Inspector Bruce Wayne. You might find he was heavily involved in the Weaver case. Be careful what you wish for, Detective Sergeant, you might find you have bitten off more than you can chew.' Perry seemed to be ending the interview. Siobhan turned and headed for the door. As she was leaving the D.I. spoke again.

'We can't be having that, not in the centre of the city, in fact not anywhere. Your team seem to have opened a lot of old wounds. Carry on. You have my backing, all three of you. Let's see how much blood we can spill on the carpet, shall we? But be careful. These are not tuppeny ha'penny gas meter bandits you are dealing with. Good Luck D.S. Williams, D.C Fish.'

Siobhan barrelled out of the office, colliding heavily with Sarah James.

'Where the fuck have you been?'

'You really do not want to know. I take it he gave us the green light.'

'After a fashion and grudgingly. What-the-fuck was Batman doing outside the nick?' Siobhan looked directly at Sarah.

'Dropping me off. No offence there, is there?' Sarah shot back.

'Let's cool this down shall we, get our heads together and see what else we have in those envelopes.' Mark calmed the situation. 'I have a feeling there is more and better on the audio cassettes.'

CHAPTER 21. OBSERVATIONS REQUESTED – Bruce Wayne

Central control to all units. Observations are requested for a Dark blue Ford Escort. Vehicle has dark tinted windows and displays the registration BA51TRD. Registration is no trace PNC.

Driver is male IC3, early 20's short, dreadlocked hair and slight beard, wearing black Harrington style jacket and dark jeans. Responsible for firearms incident Bristol City Centre at 0920hrs today, shot fired. Last seen heading Maudlin Street at high speed. Sightings only, do not stop. Occupant believed to be armed.

On waste ground near the railway arches of Bedminster, Lenny Barrington Smith, Barrington to *'da gang!'*, Little Lenny to his mother, sprinkled four-star leaded petrol liberally around the half leather interior of his souped-up Ford Escort XR3i. He had removed the expensive sound system the previous night, no need to waste everything. The cavernous, insulated space beneath the back seats had once held the massive bass speaker which blasted out while he cruised the neighbourhood. He had removed those stupid plates and thrown them into the boot along with that plastic toy gun he had been given.

'Fuck', he thought. His hands were shaking as he struck the match and threw it into interior. He stood back as the *"whoooff"* of heat hit him and watched the flames take hold. Once he heard the bang and guttural rumble of the fuel tank exploding, he turned away from his teenage pride and joy, his first set of wheels. He couldn't bear to look.

Okay, so it no longer passed an MOT, and he was a stranger to insurance, but it had been a bit of a babe magnet. He had fond memories of cruising the streets of St Paul's with his homie, Redvers, in da front and a bevy of hot pussy in da back! Barrington spoke like a gangsta-rap track unless his mother was listening. Then Little Lennie spoke the Queen's good English, and less of that ridiculous jive talk! He could hear his mother's constant reprimands as he pulled his headphones over his ears and his hood over his head, zipped up the Harrington jacket and walked towards the tunnels.

In the distance he heard the telltale wailing of the fire engine sirens, different from that of the diesel Peugeots driven by the local Babylon. He broke into a jog, best not run, and draw attention to himself.

He was heading for Victoria Park, and then to his basement flat at Kensal Road. He hoped to find a thickly stuffed envelope on the mat, enough to fund a nice new ride, some decent threads, and a whole lot of Ganja.

'Fuck!' he thought again. 'Fuck, that was no fucking toy, fuck, and double fuck again. Why had it been loaded? Scare the flash old dude, was what he had been told. That old dude had clocked him at the tobacco dock. The man could certainly handle a set of wheels, he could see that.

That fucking gun. Fuck! He wasn't supposed to fire it. 'Oh fuck!' Just point it at the guy, that was all he was supposed to do. It was a plastic toy for fuck's sake, it wasn't supposed to be dangerous. The realisation of what he had just done was starting to hit home. Maybe the offer of ten grand in his back pocket wasn't quite so great after all.

Lennie jogged up Raymend Road and down the slope into Kensal. He skipped down the steps and let himself into number 3a. His key turned easily in the door. He pushed it inwards and then pushed aside the heavy velvet curtain which his mother had said would keep out the draught. The flat was dark anyway, but it dawned on Lennie that the curtains were closed. He was certain he had opened them when he left this morning. Yes, of course he did, he had pulled the curtains back to flick the top vents of the windows open, to air the heavy fog of Ganja smoke out before he had visitors. It would not do for his probation officer to smell the stale weed of the night before. There was no cool draught that he could feel, the slats were closed.

He reached for the light switch and the single energy saving bulb spluttered into life. He had a visitor. Sitting in his only serviceable armchair, was a man, a tall blonde man with very short cropped curly hair. The man's long legs were stretched out in front of him and crossed at the ankle in a leisurely manner.

'Fuck!' It was the old dude. 'Oh, Jeeezus!'

'Barrington Smith, or is it Little Lenny?' The old dude's words were laced with sarcasm. Lennie began to stammer, his words were failing him, as quickly as his bladder and his anal sphincter. The dude had a pistol in his right hand, the black steel barrel resting on a pair of well-worn Levi jeans. In his left hand was an envelope, ripped open, its contents visible, nice, crisp £20 notes, ten thousand pounds of used £20 notes.

'What's it to be, Lenny, a nice chat and some information or a nice charge of attempted murder?' Bruce Wayne raised the barrel of the pistol speculatively.

'Please, man, I was only supposed to scare you.' Lenny stammered.

'You? Scare me? You just shot the arse end of my car, in Broadmead, and in broad daylight, in front of the biggest nick in Bristol? You should be scared of yourself. Now, who sent you?'

Bruce began to rise from the chair. He slid the envelope into the inside pocket of his black biker jacket and zipped up the front, gripping Lenny by the front of his jacket with one hand and reversing him through the living room into the already open bathroom. He neatly flipped the scrawny legs upwards and Lenny folded backside first into the avocado-coloured bathtub.

'Try again, Lenny, or do you respond better to Barrington.' The hammer clicked back on the pistol as the action primed.

'Some dude paid me. I don't know who for certain, he came on to me in the Hatchet. He pointed out your car, nice wheels, you had just picked up that woman. He asked me to follow you, he already knew where you lived, asked me if I wanted to earn some dough, enough for a new ride. Gave me the plates, and a toy gun. It wasn't supposed to be fucking loaded. I wasn't supposed to pull the fucking trigger, they told me it was a toy, man, a fucking toy. I was just having a laugh with a toy, man!'

Bruce was curious. 'Tell me more about the gun.' Lenny was staring up at him from the bath, eyes round with fright, looking straight up the barrel of Bruce's handgun which was definitely not a toy.

'It wasn't like that mother fucker.' Lenny pointed a trembling finger at the black metal barrel. 'It was all black, and plastic, all of it was plastic, I've never touched a gun before, man. It looked like a plastic pellet gun to me.'

'Where is it now?' Bruce saw the wet patch spreading on the front of Lenny's jeans.

'Fuck, you da Babylon or what, man?' Lenny's voice was pleading. He was reverting to kit. 'It's in da car, man, I burn it with da plates, it's melted down, man!'

'I think you'd better run, Lenny Smith. You are in well over your head. Your next visitors won't give you options.' Bruce pulled the trigger and the hammer fell harmlessly on an empty chamber, the smell it produced was pungent and nauseating.

Bruce opened the kitchen door of the tiny flat, vaulted over two garden fences and walked the few yards down the alley onto Raymend Road where his motorcycle was blending in with the parked cars along the pavement. He donned his full-face helmet, stowed the pistol in the rear pannier, kicked started the engine and headed out of town. As he turned left onto St John's Lane, he saw the tail end of a blacked-out Mercedes turn up the hill heading for Kensal Road. Lenny was about to have more visitors.

The second interrogation was conducted to the tunes of Bob Marley. The interrogators' fists were not interested in hearing explanations. The gun they used was not plastic. The last thing Lenny heard was Bob, Rita, and the Wailers. Little Lenny would never have to worry about a thing again. Bruce rode out of town, opening the throttle down the A roads out towards the airport. When he reached Avonmouth, he stopped at the services and made a phone call from the pay phone near the old police box.

A male voice answered the phone. 'Robinson speaking, who is it?'

'Your old friend Bruce.' Wayne pumped more change into the phone.

'What can I do for you?', the voice enquired politely, sounding mildly surprised, taken aback.

'Gordano café, I'm already here, usual spot. Tea is on me.' Wayne was brisk, he was running out of credit.

'Give me half an hour.' The arrangement was made.

The melamine topped, tea-stained table was situated in a booth in the front window with a clear view of the truck stop and the petrol station. Truckers avoided the café. It was outrageously expensive. But the showers were at least clean and functional, and the car park big enough. Bruce had used it as a rendezvous point for years. It was impersonal, crowded with families heading up or down the M5, a place you could be just another face in the crowd.

Over the years it had also been a handover point, until the police post was closed. Bruce bought a large cappuccino and a mug of tea, picked up a fist full of sugar sachets. The last time he had made this meet, Robinson had taken at least four. The man had a very sweet tooth. Bruce was just stirring the froth off the top of his coffee with the long wooden spatula which passed for a spoon, when an impossibly lanky man lurched around the corner and into view. Gaunt as a ghost and thin as a skeleton, grey hair slightly too long plastered across his forehead, horn rimmed spectacles hanging from a random piece of green gardening twine around his neck, his tweed trousers hung from a set of green braces worn over a blue shirt with a worn collar and covered by a hand knitted multi coloured tank top. His blue Peter Storm windbreaker dangled from one finger and was slung over his shoulder. He saw Bruce, and without smiling, slid into the bench seat opposite him. Seizing the utilitarian white China mug gratefully in both hands, he spoke, just one word. 'Biscuits?' Robinson was hopeful.

Bruce rose and crossed to the checkout, swiftly removing two three packs, one of bourbons and one of custard creams. He dropped two, one-pound coins on the cash register.

'Keep the change.' The stressed checkout girl put the change in the charity box which lived alongside the biscuits. Bruce returned to his seat, dropped the biscuits in front of Robinson. 'Take your pick.' Robinson took the custard creams.

Richard Robinson worked for forensic science services. Though he, like Bruce had retired several years ago, he still padded out his government pension by doing agency work. His speciality was firearms and ballistics. What Dick Robinson didn't know about guns could be written on the back of a stamp. He was a highly intelligent and slightly eccentric individual. Paranoid about security, with a fear of being followed and obsessive about cleanliness, he had probably washed his hands at least twice on his short journey from what he believed was a secret location in Avonmouth to the meeting in Gordano Services. Bruce began. 'What can you tell me about plastic guns?'

Robertson raised one grey eyebrow and placed his spectacles on his face, giving him an owlish look.

'In what way plastic, and in what way a gun?'

Bruce explained to him what had happened earlier that day.

'Sounds like 3D printing.' Robinson sucked his lower teeth.

'Amazing what they can do these days, frightening really.' He went on to describe how a plastic extruder, connected to a computer programme and a sophisticated, specially made printer could build more or less anything. His grandchildren, he said were learning the skill in school, they were only eleven years of age. Last Christmas they had made 3D snowflakes and Christmas decorations.

'Given the right software and the right materials they can make just about anything, the components for a firearm included. The tricky bit is getting them to fit together well enough to withstand firing a projectile.

Oh, and some of the parts need to be metal, plastic just won't stand the forces involved.'

'Well, someone has obviously cracked it!' Bruce hissed. 'My Toyota is witness to that.'

'Well, we haven't had anything sent through to us, yet. I'll need to make a few calls. Give me a number, I'll call you back in a few days.'

Robinson finished the tea, picked up the packet of bourbons and stuffed them in his trouser pocket, unfolded himself from the seat and, seeing that it was starting to drizzle, he donned his Peter Storm windcheater, pulled up the hood and left. Bruce was just emptying the rubbish from his red plastic tray into the bin when he saw Robinson pedalling his old pushbike out of the car park, cycle clips pinning his flapping trouser legs to his skinny ankles.

Bruce made his way back towards Bath and home, his brain awash with information, it was all a little beyond his comprehension. How could you print a gun? His own granddaughter Sharon was into her computers, maybe she could explain it better.

On a piece of waste ground alongside the railway line, not far from Bristol Scrap Metal, the fire service damped down the charred remains of a car. From the rear footwell, passenger side, the attending station officer Graham Punter removed a charred number plate the first two letters BA the only visible remains. Under these remains and protected from the worst of the fire by the shelter of the rear seat, hidden in the space once occupied by the huge speakers was the twisted plastic and metal remains of a gun.

Station officer Punter pressed the transmit button of his radio and called the information in. Within minutes the local area bobby, Brian Gowan, had arrived and summoned a detective.

About forty minutes later, the neighbours at 3 Kensal Road reported that the youth who lived in the basement flat had been playing Reggae music at full volume for most of the afternoon and was refusing to answer the door. Brian Gowan left the scene of the fire. Kensal Road was only across the park. He could hear the music from the top of Holmesdale Road. He wasn't very fond of Black Uhuru, too heavy for his taste. The front door to the basement was not locked, he pushed it open and entered. The lounge curtains were drawn shut over the window which looked out into the small front yard, below road level. He could hear the bathroom extractor fan whirring. The light must be switched on.

 He called out, 'Hello, it's the police anyone home?' There was no reply.

The bathroom was a windowless room situated between the lounge and the only bedroom. The door was open and in the dim light Nigel Gowan saw the body of Lenny Smith lying lifeless in the bath, his sightless eyes staring at the cracked Artex of the ceiling, his spindly legs hanging over the rim of the tub. Most of his brain had exited through the hole in the back of his cranium. A single bullet hole sat neatly, like a black caste mark, in the centre of his forehead.

The playlist on repeat blasted out the next track. *Don't worry 'bout a thing, every little thing is gonna be alright.* Someone silenced the ear-splitting bass emanating from the JVC ghetto blaster. A crowd of relieved neighbours had gathered outside all intent on telling Little Lenny Smith to 'keep the bloody noise down.'

The next sound to fracture the silence was not the crackle of P.C. Gowans police radio or the reprimands of the neighbours. It was the sound of Lenny's mother screaming.

A neighbour took Mrs Dolores Smith by the arm and guided her from the flat, the black and yellow tape now declaring both it and her only son a crime scene. As Mrs Smith was taken into the bosom of the community for tea and sympathy, the neighbour embraced the short brightly clad elderly woman.

'Don' worry Dolores, ev'rythin' gonna be a 'right.'

P.C. Brian Gowan wiped the vomit from the corners of his mouth with the sleeve of his coat. When Dolores imparted the news to her husband, he didn't think anything would ever be alright again.

CHAPTER 22. THE TRAIN TAKES THE STRAIN – Tansy

Bristol/London/Glasgow

The tall, leggy, and stunningly lovely woman was a regular fixture on the express train from Glasgow to London, as she was on the Great Western Service from London to Bristol Temple Meads and sometimes on the through train via Bristol Parkway to Cardiff.

She always travelled first class, and she always reserved a seat facing forwards with a table. She spent her journey time busy on one of the laptops she carried, usually the older Windows device, the expensive new Apple Mac was tucked away in a padded case in the tote bag alongside her. When she was not apparently, *'working from train'*, she read, either one of the broad sheet papers which she purchased from the news stand on the platform, or a book. The watcher would see that she liked to read historical fiction, or crime thrillers, something meaty, Phillipa Gregory, Wilbur Smith or sometimes she dipped into the violent and gun filled world of Robert Crais. To the outsider she was a businesswoman or when she stood up to walk down the aisle of the train having reached her destination, a supermodel. Her walk, on her impossibly high heels, was long striding, hip swinging, almost but not quite, a swagger. A slight smile conveyed an attitude of total self-confidence.

The watcher had seen it all before. He and Tansy Alexander had travelled the same trains, even sat within feet of each other, for months. They were on nodding but not quite speaking terms. Once he had bought her coffee. Black no sugar, instant, none of that real crap. The honey-soaked voice with the slight Scottish twang mixed with a hint of West Country had said that the lady preferred instant. She had returned the favour as they passed through Reading headed for Bristol.

She had a mobile phone. In fact, the watcher knew she had two. One was a sophisticated top of the range iPhone, only fitting for a woman such as she, a professional at whatever she was employed to do. The other was a cheap plastic number. Basic. Cheap. Disposable. This was the one she used on her infrequent trips to the toilet. It was registered of course, the watcher guessed that the person whose name appeared on the bill was probably a fictious dead relative or someone's grandfather. It was a PAYG phone used for one trip only and whose SIM card she changed at seemingly random locations along her route. She talked openly on the iPhone, sometimes for quite lengthy periods of time. Apparently.

This amused the watcher, as he heard her gabbling away in a one-sided conversation with what he had deduced was her voice recorder. The iPhone would not be loaded with a SIM card until just before her return trip and then only for one call. All this he knew. His job was to watch. For the present. He was just the student type in the army surplus parka coat, wearing the slouch beanie hat with ingrowing EarPods, he who tipped her coffee off the table and by practised sleight of hand had managed to drop the tiny tracking device into her tote bag. There it sat, nestled in the detritus which occupied the bottom of a lady's handbag along with tissues, lipstick, spare stockings, and sanitary products. If she was anything like his ex-girlfriend, it wouldn't be mucked out for months. Disguised as a single, loose paracetamol capsule, its red and yellow plastic cover disguising its identity, he hoped she wouldn't ever swallow it. It was designed to cause her more headaches than it cured.

So far all it had told them was that she got off the train, she walked or caught a cab to a better than average hotel, never the same one twice, or at least she never returned until several months had passed since her last stay. No, 'usual room? We've been expecting you.' for Miss Alexander.

She stayed for perhaps two nights maximum, sometimes attending a theatrical casting call, sometimes a fashion show or an entertainment industry event. That fitted with the portfolio of photographs which he had seen protruding from the top of her bag and the rolling screen saver on her laptop. Yet, he had never seen Tansy Alexander's name in lights. He mused that it ought to be, for she was a consummate actress and looked like Naomi Cambell and Kate Moss all rolled into one.

The crackly voice of the announcer declared *'Bristol Temple Meads. This is Bristol Temple Meads.'* all delivered in a thick west country accent. *'Passengers for London please remain on board. Passengers for Oxford please change at Didcot.'* His journey was over. In the glass of the window he saw his colleague, dressed in his smart business suit, complete with camel overcoat, seated in the coffee shop on the long platform. He would wait until the target returned to the train and take up position in one of the seats several rows behind her.

The watcher alighted from the carriage and made his way towards the railings. Just outside the exit he saw her fiddling with the iPhone after ending a call, placing the phone in its leather case back in her bag. As he watched, he saw his colleague hastily finish his coffee and fold his newspaper. Tansy was making her return trip. He was off the plot. He shouldered his backpack and looked at the empty space where he had chained his rather expensive bicycle. The front wheel was still there, the rest was gone. Was nothing in this life sacred. Never mind, it belonged to the job, it would be replaced. San fairy Ann.

Lacking two wheeled transport, the watcher caught the bus out of the city to Avonmouth. He hated the bus. Riding a bike stretched his legs after all that sitting down. He didn't mind the long ride across town and out towards the docks where their off-site office was based. Two buses later he let himself in through an anonymous brown door, into a nondescript office building.

'Kettle's on, mate.' He was greeted. 'Anything new to report?' Patricia Wilford would have seen him on the entry camera. Nothing much got past Pat.

'Our target,' he was formal, 'got on the train at Paddington and off the train at Temple Meads this morning. She seemed to have clocked me, so I stayed put and ended up in Exeter. By the time I got back she was just making her call, removing her SIM and about to board the London train. Dave White was on her case when I left. Oh, and some bastard pinched my bike.'

The watcher poured boiling water onto the brown granules in the mug. Then he added two large spoons of granulated. He liked instant, too. Black, two sugars. Tansy Alexander could be his sugar anytime. He caught sight of his unshaven face in the reflection from the microwave door. He looked like a vagrant. Time for Lee Meredith to have a shower and a shave.

'While you were swanning down to sunny Exeter, it's all been kicking off here.' Pat Welford announced from behind her bank of monitors.

'Tell me more.'

Meredith stopped in the passage, his parka draped over his shoulder. He took a step into Patricia's inner sanctum, a room lit only by the glow of the screens. Pat Welford liked the room dark, like her men and her tea. Strong and dark for the latter, just dark for the former. Lee didn't fit either of those profiles. He was small and skinny, kind of heroin chic, maybe student, maybe junky, maybe teenage runaway at a push, though he was getting a touch old for that nonsense. His hair was nondescript straight and brown. His teeth were irregular and slightly yellow, he only grew stubble in patches, making him look a little like a young Wurzel Gummidge, when he didn't shave, and yes, he dressed a bit like a scarecrow, though for this job he had cleaned up a bit. This target obviously had standards.

'Shots fired into a car outside Central. No one injured. But do you remember 'Batman?', she began.

'The comic or the film?', he asked.

'The retired D.I. – Bruce Wayne.'

'He went just after I joined the squad, very intense, bit of a ladies' man.'

'That's the one! Well, it was his car, he was dropping Sarah James off.' Pat raised a suggestive eyebrow.

'That figures. I know Sarah. She joined the job with Bruce, Is she back in harness?' Lee was unphased.

'She's one of the LIO'S in Central for her sins.' Pat paused. 'Then there was a burned-out car, and a dead body in a flat in Kensal Road. The dead body was the owner of the car, one Lenny 'Barrington' Smith.'

'What? Someone killed Big Lenny!' Lee was amazed. Big Lenny was an institution, a community figure, well liked, well respected.

'No, you idiot, this was Little Lenny, Big Lennie's son. Right little gangsta, liked to cruise the evil streets in his Ford Escort low ride playing Reggae toons at full volume.' Pat was not good at street talk. 'Anyway, they've recovered a gun, or the remains of it. No numbers, all plastic except for the barrel and the chamber. Not a rebored replica, this was one up from a disposable. Nothing we've seen here before.'

'Scary.' Lee was serious. It was.

'Very. You boys take care out there. This thing may not show up on X-ray scanners. It's virtually untraceable, made for only one purpose, oh, and there's more.'

'Go on.' Lee was all ears.

'Retired Mr. Wayne has been in touch, via a third party of course.' Pat's eyebrows were above her hairline. 'He still has his sources, and, according to him, young Lenny was tortured and talked before he died. The gun he was given looked like a toy. I don't suppose it looked much like a toy when he was looking down the end of it.'

'Little Lenny was shot then?' Lee was amazed, Big Lenny had some impressive contacts and would not take this lightly.

'Right between the eyes, and if the neighbours are to be believed, all to the dulcet tones of Bob Marley and Black Uhuru.'

'I'm getting in the shower, Pat. I'll be a while if anyone wants me, I'll write up today when I get out.' Leaving his two mobile phones on the desk next to her, Lee shuffled off down the passage towards the locker room. Towards his spare clothes and cleanliness.

'Who is likely to want you, my lovely?' Pat was laughing. Lee's personal life was a mess.

'If the job one rings - it'll be Whitey from the train, or the boss - answer it! If the other rings and it's the wife, don't answer. She chucked me out last week and she wants money.' Lee disappeared.

He stripped off in the communal shower area, the men's locker room was very much like that of a rugby club. He opened the doors to the two full length metal lockers which housed the whole of his wardrobe. He turned all the shower heads on to their hottest and most powerful, clamping the valves to 'on' to stop them automatically switching off without the pressure of a hand. He grabbed his shower gel and shampoo and stepped into the steam. My god, it was good to be clean. He scrubbed three days of travel grime from his skin, lathered shampoo into his scalp tipping his head back to let the water stream over his face. He lathered his face over the basin and scraped off three days of stubble. Ten minutes later, after soaping his crotch excessively well, he declared himself clean. He towelled himself dry on the slightly crisp towel which was hanging from the radiator. Whitey wouldn't mind, he'd only use it once. Then he would put it through the laundrette with the rest of his kit later. The office had its own washer and dryer, handy when the missus was kicking off. It was a pity it didn't stretch to bedrooms.

Lee loved his job. But it had cost him a wife and a home. The money was good, the work was interesting, but the hours stank and, when asked what he did all day at work, he could never give a truthful answer. Lee Meredith could lie for England. Unfortunately, his soon to be ex-wife was a living lie detector.

While he was drying his back with the sandpaper towel, he sighted a copy of last month's Police Magazine abandoned on the top of Whitey's locker. He assumed the innards had been removed and replaced with the latest copy of some top shelf porn mag. He pulled it from his hiding place hoping that it may be his source of gratification for the night. But no. On this occasion it was exactly what it said on the cover. Police Magazine June 2017.

He flicked the pages in a thoroughly bored manner. No titillation to be found there, then. The centre spread when he reached it made him stop.

A two-page National Ballistics Intelligence Service article about a seizure in Birmingham. Draping the towel round his shoulders he read on. When the steam cleared, and the goose pimples appeared he was still reading.

'Shit!' he thought. 'Has any other fucker bothered to read this?' In all fairness, the boxes of the monthly mag which were distributed to the various nicks around the country were more often used to hold fire doors open. It might not be relevant to their case, but it was certainly relevant to what Pat had just told him.

'Pat!' he shouted, running down the passage. 'Do you have a number for NABIS?'

'I certainly do, but you won't get any joy from them now, it's half past seven.' She lifted her eyes to look at him over the top of her screens. 'Put some bloody clothes on, can't you, before someone boils you for soup. And when I've shut this lot down, I can give you a lift to wherever you're staying, Travelodge is it?'

Travelodge turned out to be Pat's settee. They shared a takeaway and a four pack of cans and watched mind numbing TV and the news into the small hours. At about half past three, Pat's mobile rang. Pat took the phone into the kitchen. Lee heard her answer it, then heard her passing on a phone number. Why would anyone want Richie Robinson's number at this time of night. He retired years ago.

'Richie Robinson.' Pat answered. 'He contracts for our forensics, and he just happens to be our liaison with NABIS. Now get your sleepy head down for another hour or two. I have a feeling it's going to be a busy day.'

CHAPTER 23. DADDY – Siobhan

Siobhan was late finishing again. By the time she parked her car on the driveway it was nearly half past seven. It was still light. The evenings had not started to draw in yet. She could hear her boys playing some rowdy game in the garden with their father. She hoped they had been fed and were ready for bed. Ray was being a Trojan. He had once again collected them from after school club. It was not a simple journey, but the kids loved it when their daddy turned up dressed like a ninja in his leathers. It did mean that he had to make two trips, and that Josh aged twelve years always got to go first. He was considered old enough to be left alone for the half hour it took Ray to make the second trip on his motorcycle, spare helmet hanging from his arm. Josh had already heated the spaghetti bolognaise which Siobhan had cooked the day before. Ray had boiled the spaghetti and fed the boys. They had showered themselves and were now bouncing up and down like demented Tiggers on the huge trampoline Josh and Dan had been given between them for their birthdays. They were dressed in their pyjamas, but not nearly ready for bed.

Their father, still half clad in his leathers and a white T shirt, was sitting in an outdoor rattan armchair, his bare feet propped up on a low table. He had lit the wood in the fire pit and opened a cold can of lager. The garden was lit by an impressive array of solar lights strung on the fences and in the trees. In the refrigerator was an open bottle of Pinot Grigio and on the kitchen table, a glass, with ice, just how his wife liked it. Siobhan let herself in through the front door.

'I'm home!'

Her voice wasn't heard over the whooping and yelling coming from the trampoline. She walked through the house, locking the front door behind her, tidily hanging her coat and her work handbag under the stairs. It was the weekend, she had three days off. Three days to make the journey to Wales and help her brother to finish emptying their mother Lydia's house. At least she would see her brother Malcolm, and maybe she would lay some ghosts to rest. Since she had watched that video, the black man in his designer clothes, wearing a pink frilly apron, cooking for his children, she could not erase the words from her mind, 'Daddy chips,' spoken in a low smooth voice, a voice she had heard before. She would think about the rest of it again on Tuesday.

On seeing her emerging through the French doors into the garden, her boys dived off the trampoline and ran to greet her, and she was enveloped in a wave of hugging arms and freshly washed hair, smelling of coconut shampoo and raspberry shower gel. And had Josh sprayed himself with that Lynx deodorant again? He really was growing up far too fast. She hugged them back.

'Half an hour then, and then it's bed, you both have footie in the morning.'

Ray opened the refrigerator and placed the open bottle of wine in a chiller, one of those, bottle-sized, double-insulated tubes, popular as gifts, but never really used.

'It's not going to be there long enough to need chilling.' Siobhan smiled at Ray as she spoke. 'I'll get these work clothes off, and shower, I'll be out in bit.'

Ray placed the wine and the glass on the outdoor coffee table, then returned to the fridge for another lager. Siobhan, he thought, seemed stressed. She emerged from the house, her blonde hair combed off her face and still wet from the shower. She was wearing one of his old shirts tied at the waist and the most decrepit pair of cut off denim shorts he had ever seen, they were old favourites. She had had them for years, since they had had legs, which had developed holes and been shortened to knee length, and then, she said, during the one rare long hot summer, cut off to shorts. They were frayed at the edges but still fitted in all the wrong places. She refused to throw them out. Every summer they were resurrected and it wasn't summer until Siobhan got her legs out. He poured her wine, and she sat on the rattan settee, those long legs balanced on the arm of his chair, her back lying against the arm.

'Bad day, at Black Rock?' he asked.

'Not all bad, but I think eventful describes it accurately.' She took a first tentative sip, her tongue savouring the taste and testing the temperature. The sip became a decent mouthful, she swallowed blissfully. 'It's good to be home.'

'We heard the commotion this morning, who was shot, it was all over the lunchtime news.' Ray's office was just off Broadmead, handy for the courts and the police station. 'No one could get out for a sandwich there were that many vehicles in the street.'

'No one was shot. Some retired D.I.,' Siobhan was cagey, 'an old mate of Sarah's in the wrong place at the wrong time. Some little gangsta dude with a bad attitude shot up his car, all very rude! Oh my gosh, that rhymes!' Siobhan stood up and repeated the sentence, improvising a dance and chanting the words rap style. She finished her first glass of Pinot as she listened and watched Ray laughing at her, and her sons aping her, dancing on the trampoline.

'Wow mum, you're a poet, you just don't know it!' Josh and Dan were laughing uncontrollably.

'That's it! Bed boys, or you'll never get up. Give me and your dad some peace.' The two boys climbed off the trampoline. Josh took a quick mouthful of his father's lager and pulled a face of disgust. They both went up the stairs to bed.

'Do you want a story, boys?' Ray shouted after them.

'No thank you, dad! Too grown up for that!' came the reply.

'I can do the one about the Dreadful Griffin.' he tried, smiling.

'That one is so worn out we hid the book.' Dan called back giggling. The Dreadful Griffin was Ray's favourite story, but not very conducive to a good night's sleep.

'Ah, peace at last.' Siobhan sighed. 'I love those two so much, but it's nice when they're in bed.'

'It's nice when we're in bed as well.' Ray snuggled up to his wife on her settee.

'Who needs a bed?' Siobhan was looking at the trampoline in a meaningful way. One hand feeling for the zip of Ray's leathers, untucking his slightly sweaty white T shirt from the waistband. He still smelled vaguely of this morning's aftershave mixed with traffic and leather. She inhaled deeply and felt the fruits of her labours.

Ray picked her up bodily and balancing her, fireman style over one shoulder deposited her on the spring-loaded canvas. The springs stretched and squeaked and the net surround shook. 'Siobhan Williams, you are a bad woman.' he groaned. 'This is respectable Clifton, what will the neighbours say?'

'They won't be saying much if you don't help with these leathers.' She giggled, busying herself with more zips. 'How the hell do you take a piss wearing these?'

'They're a bit like the wearer, Shonnie, they don't like to come off in a hurry.' He rendered her the necessary assistance and rolling on top of her, hands laced in her half dry hair, pinned her to the canvas. The stretch of the canvas merged with the groans of pleasure and the squeaking of the springs became the rhythm of two bodies moving perfectly in sync with each other.

They lay there staring up at the suburban night sky, listening to the distant hum of the traffic in the inner city. Shonnie was happy, she couldn't say otherwise. She had Ray and the boys, she had her brother Malcolm and all of Ray's extended family. Yet in the last few weeks she had felt an emptiness, a restless discontent now polarised by those words which echoed from somewhere, 'daddy or chips.' She cleared her mind of all of it, Ray was snoring peacefully naked beside her. She crossed the garden, downed the last of the bottle of wine and grabbed the fleece throw off the chair. Climbing back onto the trampoline she curled up against his shoulder spreading the fleece over the two of them, it was plenty big enough. The night was not cold. They both slept.

'Ray.' She poked him unceremoniously in the ribs. 'Wake up Ray.'

'What is it?' he groaned

'There's someone in the house,' she hissed.

'One of the boys must be up,' he suggested.

'No, I can see a shadow, too big, it's a bloody burglar.' She was certain.

'Ray, it's gone upstairs.' She was moving now, grabbing her shorts, bugger, no shoes. She sprinted barefoot through the open doors to their house, followed by Ray, wearing only a T shirt to cover his modesty. He reached out to stop her tackling the intruder.

'Let him take it, Shonnie, it's only stuff. We can replace stuff.' Ray was practical. 'Shonnie don't.'

The figure at the top of the stairs, turned. The muzzle flash lit the stairwell, one round embedded itself in the plaster of the wall behind Siobhan's head then the gun fired again. The next round hit her in the shoulder, but she kept going up the stairs towards her target. She was hit, she might be dying, but if she was going to hospital someone was going with her.

As the figure came back down the stairs Josh appeared on the landing. Dressed in his superman pyjamas, he picked up the heavy pot containing the Christmas cactus from his granny Lydia's house. He threw it as hard as he could at the black tangle of shapes on the stairs. He heard one of the shapes groan and the heap of bodies landed at the foot of the stairs.

'Look out, Dad!' he screamed at the top of his voice. In the bedroom they still insisted on sharing at the front of the house, Dan was looking out of the window, he could see a vehicle in the street. He could hear the engine running. A black clad figure ran down the driveway, a car door opened and in a screech of tyres the car drove off. Dan started to recite to himself. BA51TRD. BA.51.TRD. That's a bad word, his young brain registered. He'd remember that.

At the bottom of the stairs his mother lay in a blood-soaked heap, his father lay on top of her clutching what appeared to be a toy machine gun. Both lay surrounded by a sprinkling of earth and shards of pottery, his father's head adorned by the dread like shape of Robert Plant the Cactus. Grannie had liked to name her plants. Josh picked up the house phone and dialled 999.

'Police please and ambulance.' Then the big brave face cracked he started to cry unconsolably down the phone.

'What's happened, young man?' the male operator coaxed. We have your number. We know where you are.

'Someone shot my mummy.'

Over his shoulder, Dan reached for the receiver, pulling it from his brother's hand he shouted at the operator, 'BASTARD.'

'Is this a prank?' The operator was angry.

'No!' squeaked Dan. 'They drove off.' He collected his thoughts, *say it like mummy taught you, in the car, on the way to school*. He tried again. A letter at a time 'Bravo. Alpha. Five. One. Tango. Romeo. Delta.' he could feel the man writing it down. 'Big black car, black windows.'

Then he heard suppressed laughter at the end of the phone

'There's an ambulance on its way, and the police. You are brave boys, both of you. Now stay with your mum.' The operator stayed on the line until the Ambulance arrived.

Through the clearing fog of unconsciousness, Ray could see only red. His head was bleeding, a trickle of claret was running down his forehead. Where was Shonnie? He heard a groan from beneath his legs. Shots, yes, there had been shots. Shonnie's arm hung at an impossible angle. Her hand seemed to be attached but backwards. There was more blood, but not his, this time.

There was an object in his lap. '*Shit!*', he thought, '*it's a fucking gun, a fucking machine gun.*' He put it to one side. Then he saw the flashes of blue and red coming up the street, the ambulance had arrived. The female paramedic carried her kitbag into the house, and he directed her to his wife, totally forgetting that he was clad only in a T-shirt. The paramedic totally ignored his state of undress, she had seen it all before, well most of it.

Shonnie would live, her shoulder was a mess, it would definitely need surgery. The bullet seemed to be embedded in her scapula. X-rays and scans would show more. He had a bruise to die for on the top of his head and a three-inch cut caused by the breaking plant pot. Sealed by the paramedic with a careful application of superglue, he would have a headache for a few days, but otherwise he was fine. He was given the standard head injury advice and advised to take a few days off work. His boys had been heroes. A message from the police control room suggested that young Dan use his phonetic alphabet instead of shouting abuse down the phone. The black car had vanished.

The man who came to collect the gun had placed it in a specially made cardboard box, marked Forensic Science Services. Ray had never seen such a strange man in his life before. Tall, thin, and cadaverous, with thinning grey hair and wearing tweed trousers and a tank top under his white paper suit and blue latex gloves. Before he left, he had shaken Ray's hand and told him in a broad Bristolian accent 'Been waitin' for one of these babies fer weeks, it was only a matter uv time.' Then he spent a full five minutes washing his hands in the downstairs cloakroom before folding himself into a nondescript white van and driving slowly away with a crunch of gears and an over revving engine. The can of worms was well and truly open.

It was nearly lunchtime. Ray found his wife's personal mobile in her bag. He knew the passcode. He searched on favourites for 'Malcolm' and dialled the number. In three rings Malcolm Taylor answered.

'Shonnie, are you and Ray coming over?' He sounded hopeful, 'I'm a bit worried. I've just arrived at Lydia's, and I think there's been a break in.'

Ray inhaled sharply. 'It's not Shonnie, it's me, Ray. Don't go in the house, Malcolm. Phone the police, but please don't go in the house

When they arrive, tell them to phone me! Before they do anything!' He went on to explain the night's events. It did nothing to allay Malcolm's worries. He would be glad when the place was sold, it was becoming a bit of a liability.

On the M4 Motorway Eastbound, a black Mercedes took the left-hand lane onto the old A48. The driver was a male IC3 in his mid-50's, his passenger was female IC3 in her late twenties. The driver pulled to a stop on the hard shoulder at the centre of the old Severn Bridge and waited for a gap in the traffic. The passenger got out and threw what looked like an old shoe box over the parapet and into the river. She smiled slightly as the papers from the box drifted like confetti on the breeze and were scattered to the winds of the Bristol Channel.

'Are you sure she's one of them?' Paul Grainger growled at his daughter. 'We can't afford another fuck up. She must never find her mother. Her mother knows far too much.'

'Why the big stress, Pops.' The woman was flippant. 'Why are you protecting that washed up old cunt in Spain?'

'Because that old cunt could send us all down for a very long time.' came the reply.

'Well, there's one simple way to get rid, isn't there, Pops.' She got back into the passenger seat, adjusting her black camel overcoat under her.

Paul Grainger gunned the Mercedes away into the traffic, accelerating swiftly but not exceeding the speed limit. He adjusted the rear-view mirror, looked then looked again. 'If only it was that easy,' he muttered to himself.

The black Toyota dropped back a few hundred yards. Paul Grainger did not need to know he was being followed. The driver of the Toyota checked that the fuel tank was on full and followed the Mercedes onto the M5 heading South.

Ward 4 of Bristol Royal Infirmary was a hive of activity. The side room by the nurses' station had seen a constant footfall of visitors, some in uniform, some bearing flowers, and grapes. The patient was sitting up in bed, her right arm connected to a drip stand, the stand both supporting the arm and carrying the intravenous pain relief.

Malcolm Taylor met Ray in the cafeteria. He had locked up Lydia's house after the police left. The burglars had searched his mother's filing cabinet but had taken nothing except that old green shoe box. They had left the jewellery, and the silver. They had not bothered to search any more than one room. Why they wanted the shoebox was a mystery to Malcolm. He had removed what he considered the 'important stuff' a few weeks ago. All that, was at his home nearby.

He patted the inner pocket of his old Barbour coat. The important stuff is safe in here, Shonnie took her envelope with her. Whoever it was is welcome to mother's old bank statements and several years' worth of old phone bills. Let's go and see Shon, shall we.'

'Please, Malcolm, don't tell her what they took yet. She has enough on her plate without digging up more of the past.' Ray was in protective mode.

'She has to know sometime, mate, it's not as if she isn't already working on it. If I know my sister, keeping anything from her will only cause trouble in the long run.' Malcolm knew his sibling well.

They sat either side of the hospital bed. Shonnie fixed Malcolm and her husband with her best interrogator's gaze.

'I know about the break in, the boys told me. Do you think there isn't a phone line between Miskin and Bristol? Wales may be what you think is the sticks, but it has come a long way since the horse and cart.' She laughed. Both men looked sheepish.

'What did they take?' She spoke to Malcolm. He remained silent.

'Just Mam's shoe box, then?' she spoke for him. Malcolm nodded.

'Malcolm Taylor, my history used to be in that box, it's not **just** a box, **it's my life**', she was starting to get really upset. 'It's the only thing I have to help me trace my history. It's okay for you. You know exactly where you came from.'

Tears filled her eyes and her whole body was shaking. Ray nodded at Malcolm, there was no sense in putting off the inevitable.

Ray reached inside his jacket and, pulled out the large, padded envelope.

'There was nothing in that box Shon, only rubbish. You took that old envelope with you last time you were over.'

'Our house and Mam's house, done on the same night, use your heads you two, maybe this is what they were looking for.'

Pass my handbag, Malcolm. Siobhan reached into the depths of the bag where she kept everything important. She pulled out the envelope and shook out the contents onto the bed. The first piece of paper to land was the press cutting. She took it in both hands and held it to her chest, wincing in pain as the stitches in her shoulder pulled and her arm moved where it shouldn't.

Then she read it. She read it all. Carefully. Then she looked at the faded black and white photo a family photo, grainy with age so faint it was almost like seeing ghosts. The words landed, filled her brain again, 'daddy and chips.' Again, in her head she replayed the video. There was no sound. Her mind had added the colour and the soundtrack.

A four-year-old child standing on a chair watching her father, him dressed in a ridiculous pink pinafore apron making the best chips in the world. She was Tony Weaver's daughter. She knew that now, all the pennies dropped. And if she was Tony Weaver's daughter, that made Cassandra Weaver her mother. That explained everything.

'Ray,' she spoke to her husband, 'you must tell Mark, and Sarah. They must find my mother. If Grainger was pulling Tony's strings, then he is behind all this and if he can't protect David Holly, he will go after Cassandra. She knows far too much.'

CHAPTER 24. PAYBACK – Peter Balfour

Glasgow 2017

Peter Balfour was angry. He was not a man disposed to outbursts of uncontrolled anger. He didn't find he suffered from this emotion frequently and when he did, he found it very hard to deal with. This morning, he was very, very angry. It was a slow burning, intense feeling which he knew would not end well unless it was followed by a period of reflection.

His day had started in its usual calm manner. He had been woken early by a full choir of birds singing in harmony, filling the woodland at the rear of his home with the chirpy sounds of nature. He had showered in his en-suite power shower, water turned up to its highest pressure, blasting the remnants of sleep from his body, refreshed and invigorated, just as the advertising banner on his shower gel bottle advertised. He had examined his physique in the mirror. Not found it wanting. Taut glutes, flat abs, the hint of a six pack, always a work in progress. Maybe there was time to hit the gym later, the thought flitted through his mind, then left. He would have enough of a workout when Tansy arrived back from her travels. The sleeper train was due in from London, she would be back in town before lunchtime. He wrapped a towel around his waist and walked barefoot down his open plan staircase to the vast kitchen.

Home for him was a renovated and sympathetically modernised seventeenth century inn. It was situated on the towpath of a canal just to the northeast of his hometown of Glasgow. It was a very special building, just the right balance of the old and the new. Ancient fireplaces and chimneys blended with modern, open plan, split level living. Bifold doors drew the outside in, opening onto the old cobbles of what had once been a stable yard, the iron rings which secured the horses still embedded in the honey-coloured sandstone walls.

From behind the eight-foot security gates in the stone-built boundary wall he could hear life on the tow path, people walking their dogs, local kids fishing, old men messing about in small boats. It was a complete break from the hustle and bustle of the city. God, he looked forward to seeing her. She had been in his life for seven years now, and not for one day had he regretted scraping her up off the street. Yes, that little shit Joey Callahan would take all the credit for finding her, for cleaning her up, for the initial meet. Peter smiled. What advice would the sophisticated Tansy of today give if she were ever introduced to the sweating, shaking, nervous junkie he had taken a risk on all those years ago. He prided himself on seeing her potential, if potential was the razor-sharp mind of a she-devil hidden in the body of an angel.

Shovelling three scoops of ground beans into the stainless steel cafetière, he waited for the kettle to boil. Out of habit he took down two drinking vessels from the cupboard. Her jar of cheap instant coffee was perched inside her mug. A large white pottery creation. A birthday present emblazoned with the words THERE IN AN INSTANT! in large black letters. The instruction underneath, Black Two Sugars. On coffee they agreed to differ. How she could stomach that cheap crap, he would never understand. He left the mug on the granite surface, made his own brew, poured it into his preferred large bowl of a cup and wandered to the breakfast bar. Picking up the remote control from the top of the bread bin he switched on the TV. What was going on in the world in the last 24hrs? The local news programme ended, Scotland had little to report. The programme looped back to the national news headlines.

He watched and listened in horror as the presenter detailed events in Bristol, developments from the previous day. Holy shit! A firearms incident right outside a police station. A burnt-out car. A murder in a basement flat, the victim shot at point blank range. A domestic burglary. Why would the national news report a run of the mill event such as that? In his racing mind, he realised that they must all be connected. The reporter was florid in her description of the scene, but the police spokesperson was remarkably tight lipped about the facts, and about the ongoing enquiry. A murder enquiry was in progress and anyone with any information should ring the number at the bottom of the screen.

A swift search of the internet. Shit! Shit! Shit! A police officer's house, children, a police officer shot, then the icing on the cake. 'A source reports that a weapon has been recovered. The police have released no further details other than they are continuing enquiries.' There was always a set of loose lips, someone who would sell words to the press for a few hundred quid.

Was Tansy on the train? Please God she wasn't involved. Why would she be? There was nothing to connect her with any of that - was there? Without thinking he dialled her number. The continuous tone of the failed connection. He stopped. Good girl. She still obeyed the rules. Peter Balfour tried to calm himself. His hands were shaking. He felt his heart rate rise. He placed his hands flat on the worktop and caught sight of his reflection in one of the steel splashbacks. Red faced, that small vein at his temple enlarged to what looked like bursting point. 'Breathe, Peter', he told himself. Suddenly he was calm, composed, his anger harnessed. He scrolled through his contacts and dialled.

The laid-back brown voice of his business partner eventually answered. Not immediately. Peter had to place the call three times before the man responded.

'I busy maaan.' The word man was extended by several 'a's.

'Get off your fucking nest you oversexed piece of shit.' Peter didn't mince his words. 'Tell me Sky News have got it all fucking wrong.'

'All under control, maaan, no trouble.' Peter heard distinctly female sounds in the background. More than one if he knew Grainger.

'Seven years it's taken, seven fucking years. The contacts are in place, and you have some low life scumbags let loose with my fucking merchandise. Did you order a fuckin' hit on a cop, in their own fuckin' home, in front of the kids, with one of my fuckin' weapons?'

'Cool it Pete, my man, it is under control, the Babylon have nothin',' Grainger lied.

Balfour knew he was lying. There were words coming out of Grainger's mouth, and Grainger was by habit a complete stranger to the truth. If Paul Melville Grainger said it was raining, it was best you looked outside before putting on a coat.

'Who let this happen, Paul?' Balfour's voice was collected.

'Hey man, it wasn't me, it was supposed to be a warnin' but ye pay peanuts and ye get monkeys. But is all under control.' Grainger prevaricated.

'Ye can'nae let the polis get their hands on anything. Paul, tell me that has 'nae happened.' Balfour paused as an incoming call announced itself on his display. Balfour reiterated. 'Can ye tell me that has'nae happened?'

Grainger hung up, and the incoming call connected and there she was.

'It's me.'

'Where are ye' Tans?' She could sense the anger in his voice. Not directed at her, surely.

'I'm in town, or I wouldn't call, I know the rules. Have you seen the news?'

Peter Balfour felt like screaming. Tansy was completely ignorant of her involvement in this part of his business. It had to be that way, but she was a bright girl, a curious girl, and we all know what happened to the curious cat.

'I'll meet you at lunchtime, usual place.' He ended the call.

What the hell was Grainger up to? His dick seemed to be running the show these days. His mind was not on business, it was lost in some form of middle-aged man crisis, the manopause perhaps. He was getting older, was he looking to step away from everything, take retirement, live out his days in clubland, partying with the surgically enhanced teenage girls he seemed to prefer to real women these days? Had he handed the reins to some rookie who didn't know Jack Shit about keeping their interests under the radar? Balfour was seriously worried. If this all went tits up, he stood to lose a fortune, not to mention lose his liberty for an awfully long time.

He pulled on a pair of Lycra shorts, a T shirt and his beaten-up old Reebok trainers. Slipping out through the door in the ivy clad wall he stepped out onto the tow path in front of the house. Breaking into a jog he set off, increasing his pace gradually. He turned left up the lane towards the golf club, a circuit of the perimeter of the course and back to base would be a swift 5k, he knew the route well. It would give him time to think, time to counter any flack which was developing down South.

He turned into the club car park, waved a greeting to the green keeper, and disappeared down the green track which ran around the boundary. It was a haven, only open to members, which of course he was, though he rarely played. Why ruin a good walk? In truth he found the golfing set overly nosey, though he did socialise there occasionally, the highly successful property developer with his stunningly beautiful girlfriend on his arm. He fed them enough titbits of his life to keep them from nosing around for more. He sponsored events and donated to their charities. He had even run a marathon dressed as a convict wearing a ball and chain all to raise money for a good cause. He was Peter Balfour, straight talking Glaswegian. He may be rubbish at golf, but he always bought a round at the bar, and he was a nice guy. Wasn't he?

Peter's thoughts went to the matter in hand. Damage limitation. With luck, the contents of that car were destroyed. There would be nothing left to be subjected to ballistics testing. Nothing there to link the round they almost certainly had from the rear of the Toyota to the shooter.

He had no clue what had been used to dispatch the kid who had fucked up big style and started this chain of events. There would be evidence left. He knew that. He would need to break any potential chain or at least divert attention from it.

The burglary where did that fit in? it seemed totally random, but it stank of Grainger and his own personal dung heap. Balfour reached the halfway point of his run, he was sweating nicely, his mind was clearing. He started to piece together all he knew about Grainger's very murky past. By the time he vaulted the wooden stile which let him back out onto the lane and back down to the tow path, he had reached a conclusion. Grainger needed to go. Grainger could carry the can for all of this. There would be collateral damage, but she would understand. A plan was forming.

He tapped in the entry code to the door and after his second shower of the day he took his second cup of coffee into his private study. He reached into the back of the desk for the ancient Nokia phone he hadn't fired up in ages. He plugged it in to charge.

Tansy was glad to be home, for this was home. She loved her little flat, it was small but perfectly formed. Everything she wanted. Peter could rattle around in his semi-rural mansion house. You could get lost in that house. It had a different bedroom for every day of the week, she had joked about it when he had taken her on the guided tour of his pride and joy. Then they had tested the beds.

She liked small and cosy, her home was a testament to the fact. It was all comfy seating, patterned throws. Joey joked that it looked like a hippie's flop out pad. In the same block as Joey's, it shared the same view out over the water and was high enough up the building so as not to need curtains, only blinds to cast a bit of shade in the summer or shut out the gales in the depths of winter. Her balcony was almost bigger than her lounge, furnished with a hanging chair suspended from the girders above. In the summer it was a riot of pot plants, colourful geraniums and bizzy-lizzies.

Letting herself in from the landing of the fifth floor, she kicked off her high heels and dumped her bag on the couch. Her mobile rang, it was Joey.

'I heard you get home. You make enough noise to wake the dead.' Joey's flat was below hers. He sounded as though he had just woken up.

'What gives, Joey?' He only ever phoned for a reason.

'Come down, we need to chat.' This didn't sound friendly.

'Give me a minute. I only just got here,' she sighed. Joey felt sidelined. He was always pumping for information. Where had she been, what had she been doing? It was tedious, he knew the score as well as she did.

She stripped off her smart Chanel business suit, hung it on its hanger and covered it with a plastic cover. Peter funded her work clothes. They were the real McCoy - no knock offs. She looked after them. If he ever cast her to the four winds, as he had done with all his other girls, she would sell them. They were worth a small fortune on eBay. Life with Pete Balfour was a tightrope. If you fell off your game, the drop was likely to be a long one. So far so good, she was balanced nicely, but one bad move could send her into the abyss. Tansy was no fool, she had other irons in the fire. She had a back-up plan. That plan did not include Joey or anything he was involved with.

She stepped into a pair of skinny Levi jeans, a clean grey Guns and Roses tour T shirt and pulled on her well-worn tan CAT boots, she hated heels, then, ran down the one flight of stairs to where Joey's door was slightly open. Coffee was already made. This must be important. Joey had been to the bakery for donuts, the proper bakery, for fresh, still warm, sugar powdered, apple and custard donuts, none of the mass-produced American Dunkin' rubbish. She perched on the stool by his small breakfast bar. Seven years ago, she had gone cold turkey in this very flat. He had looked after her then. She had no illusions, he had done it for a reason. He had, more or less, pimped her out. The deal had been lucrative for her, and undoubtedly lucrative for Joey. It was not her fault things had gone more in her favour. Now Joey was trying to work his way back in, a dangerous move where Pete Balfour was concerned. Pete did not like to be manipulated. Pete was always in control.

The TV was always on in Joey's flat, it was his background to life. Usually, it would be some daytime chat show, or a nineteen seventies cop drama. This morning it was the news. The national news.

'Current affairs, Joe?' She raised an eyebrow. 'That's a bit advanced for you.'

'It's all kicking off in Bristol, I was worried about you.' He grinned. 'Little birds tell me where you've been.'

'I've been to the smoke, Joey, I just got off the damn train. Look, I'm tired, I'm hungry, I'm meeting the boss in two hours. In words of one syllable, what do you want?'

'I don't want anything, Tansy, just givin' ye a word to the wise. Ask yourself how I know where exactly you've been, Peter certainly doesn't tell me. He tells me Jack shit these days.'

'You, Joey, are fishing, it's what you do. You cast your little hooks about until you get a bite, then you hope there's more than one fish on the line. I've been to London to visit the Queen. That's all you need know. Now pass me another donut, they're amazing.' Tansy was worried. Joey was casting his hooks way too close to the truth.

'He has you well trained, I'll say that for him, has he trained you that well in the sack?'

Thankfully, Joey didn't get an answer to his last remark. The chirrup of the standard Nokia ringtone and its accompanying vibration disturbed the front pocket of his jogging bottoms. He ferreted in the folds of his clothing and found the item in question. Tansy had opened her mouth just about to make some smart arsed comment when Joey pressed the green telephone and placed the device to his ear. He gestured to her to remain silent. 'Peter, how the devil are you? It's been months.'

The call was brief, Tansy only heard one side. Joey ended the call with, 'Later then.' and switched the Nokia off. Removing the back, he took out the SIM card, and, taking the scissors from the kitchen drawer, cut it into pieces. Walking to the bathroom, he wrapped it in toilet paper, soaked it under the tap and then flushed it down the toilet. Better safe than sorry.

CHAPTER 25. THE NARK – Peter Balfour

'Din'nae argue wi me, Joey, I'm paying ye good money tae do this.' Peter Balfour sat across the dirty beer-stained table in the darkest corner of one of Glasgow's seedier drinking establishments. Even dressed in jeans and his oldest sweatshirt, he looked too expensive to patronise this particular haunt. It was only just past midday, but the bar was already half full. It must be dole day. He hadn't really felt much like having a beer until he met Joey Callahan, but Joey was reminding him of all the things he disliked about Joey. Now he felt he deserved a drink.

'No, Pete, I will na' do it.' Joey dug his toes in. 'Ye can'nae just throw her under the bus like tha'.'

'She'll survive, and she'll have her instructions. I'll see that she's okay.' Pete Balfour knew that Joey was hanging out for more money. He knew Joey's smell. He hoped Tansy did as well. She must take the bait, and the fishing line could not be seen to have come from him.

'Double then?' Pete finished his pint and took the grubby water-stained glass back to the bar for a refill. There was something about this place which took him back to his roots. Something inherently violent, earthy, dark, the beer-stained wood and copper top tables to the vinyl covered banquette seating. He had just offered a piece of lowlife scum a large sum of money to grass up the woman they both loved, in different ways. Joey would do it. Money was all Joey really cared about apart from Joey, of course. Joey was still thinking when Pete returned from the bar with two pints of McEwan's.

'There must be another way man, I really din'nae want tae do this, ye could get her killed. Grainger will na' go down wi' out a fight.'

'You just do what I fuckin' well ask, Joey boy, I'll look after her, okay.' Pete was growing impatient. He needed to be away from this place. There were those amongst the clientele who would not let this meeting go unnoticed. He needed to get this deal sorted and move on. Then he could start to forget the guilt which was already invading his conscience.

He had thrown others to the wolves. They had been happy with a big payout and a few months off the streets. Some had even come out of the slammer having learned something. Why was Tansy different? For Christ's sake he thought to himself, what was it about her which disturbed his equilibrium? Hell, she's even made Joey find his conscience.

'You swear on your mother's life that ye will nae get her harmed?' Joey was coming around.

'I din'nae have a mother tae swear on, I din'nae have anyone bar mysel', but I swear on my own life, Joey.' Pete promised.

'I hope I din'nae have tae' hold ye tae' that, do ye have a burner fer me.' Joey held out his hand.

Pete handed him a phone.

'Is this clean?'

'It is, bin it afterwards, you know the score.'

Joey necked his pint, shoved the phone in his pocket and left Peter Balfour deep in thought, his eyes imagining patterns in the beer stains on the table. It was drizzling outside, that all pervading wet blanket of foggy rain which the Scots call dreich. He watched the drips run down the outside of the filthy windows, filthy windows with bars on the outside. In his imagination he saw a vision with high sharp cheekbones, a mass of dark curly hair, a broad smile, teeth now white with expensive dental work. The face was staring straight at him. Tansy, behind bars. A hand tapped the window, and he was jolted back to reality.

'Fuck!' It was not his imagination, it was her, in the flesh, dressed in her scruffiest jeans, hoodie and anorak, converse on her feet. Dressed for comfort. How in the name of God had she found him here? The door pushed open, and she came in from the street. A shabbily dressed youth, one of a gang of four clustered around the juke box in the corner, raised his hand in greeting. He often forgot this was Tansy's old stamping ground. As she crossed the bar to greet him, someone wolf whistled from the gloom, then shouted,

'Hey, Tanz' will ye buy the lads a drink, hen?' They tried their luck, they were all skint despite having drawn their benefits, but they still had money for a fix. If an old friend who had made good would spread some of her luck their way, they'd have another hour in the warm before Brian MacDonald the landlord threw them out into the rain.

Tansy caught Brian's eye behind the bar and nodded, 'Do the honours, Bri,' only the one mind, they never could handle their beer.' There was a cheer from the corner. Tansy bought a drink for herself, paid for the round, 'put the change in the Juke box Brian, it's like a funeral in here.'

Pete didn't look too pleased to see her, so she didn't mention that she had seen Joey leaving. She tucked the snippet of information that Pete had a meeting with Joey into her memory for future use. Pete and Joey hadn't spoken for months. Tansy had swallowed Joey's sarcastic jibes at her relationship with Peter. He was being sidelined and he didn't like it. In his book, one of them, whether it was Tansy or Peter, owed him.

Joey had been walking quickly, head down, hood up, on the opposite side of the road. It was obvious where he'd come from. She'd seen him push his way out of the big swing doors at the far end of the bar, out onto the nearly deserted wet street, deep in thought, oblivious to all around him. She lifted one cheek of her skinny jeans and propped herself on the high stool opposite him, the stool where Joey had sat only minutes before. Leaning her elbows on the table, she hit him with her smile and lasered him with a look which stirred more than his soul.

'Penny for them, a trouble shared and all that.'

He tried to raise a smile. 'You really don't want to know, hen, you're early, I didn't expect you until later.'

She took a mouthful from her pint of lager. It was flat. She held it up to the window to inspect it for bubbles. Seeing none, she picked up Pete's glass and tapped hers on the rim with its base. Still nothing

'Ugh, this is awful!' She turned to Brian behind the bar. 'Have ye tried washing the glasses with detergent, ye tight bastard?' Then she turned her attention back to Pete.

'Drink up, hen, I have news!'

Tansy was bubbling with excitement. Those who watched her on her travels around the country's rail network often saw her loitering outside photography studios and acting agencies. She frequently disappeared into the bowels of such places to reappear several hours later, often looking disappointed, sometimes a little more cheerful. Without telling a soul, she had managed to get herself an audition for RADA. She thrust the letter under Peter's nose, as an excited child would do to a proud father.

'I'm celebrating, read that!' She pointed her finger to the line which announced that she had gained a place on the course starting next September. 'Oh Pete, it's such a brilliant opportunity, a chance to make something real happen in my life. Now drink up and let's go somewhere that's at least clean.'

She took both their glasses back to the bar, both still half full, left £20 with Brian, to keep the lads happy for a few hours, and then grabbed a reluctant Peter Balfour by the arm and dragged him out onto the town. She never ceased to amaze him, it was part of her appeal, what set her apart from the others. Her total spontaneity, her joy, it was like having a large and affectionate puppy, obedient to a point but still with a knack of doing the unexpected.

What the fuck had he done, he couldn't stop Joey now, Joey had probably set the wheels in motion. How could he break it to her gently that RADA was never going to happen. By next September, she would probably be on the other side of a barbed wire fence, if she was alive at all. For now, he put his arm around her shoulder, kissed her on the cheek and walked with her to the next bar.

'Tansy, you never cease to amaze me!' Several bars and a cab ride later she continued to amaze him.

Joey did not see Tansy as he walked deep in thought along the rain damp Glasgow street. He had walked for half an hour, composing in his mind what he was going to say and then he had made the call. The number he rang wasn't saved on any phone he had ever used. It was written on the fluffy cardboard insides of a split beermat, now curled with age and nearly illegible. He kept it buried in the lining of his wallet, hard to find, nearly blending in with the lining. Now he was standing by the 'black man' statue outside the Brechin waiting for a lift.

He saw her circle twice, ostensibly looking for a parking place. The headlights flashed once and the car drove past him, then slowed to walking pace. Pulling his hood further over his face he opened the passenger door and got in.

The inside of the old Morris Marina was as battered as the outside. It was a beige and brown heap of rust. The outside rattled and let in the water. The bodywork should never have passed an MOT test. Even its owners had condemned it. The inside was the epitome of dark brown vinyl covered luxury, the foam which stuffed the saggy seats protruding through the splits in their seams. Much of the stuffing in the driver's seat had found its way out through the hole in the floor. The engine, though, was sound and performance tuned and there were three sets of spare number plates concealed in the boot, Velcro backed for ease in changing.

The driver wore well-worn hiking boots, dark blue combat trousers, a grey T shirt and body warmer. Her arms were bare to show an impressive array of tattoos, and the evidence of many trips to the gym. Her hair was short cropped and dyed white, blonde, her ears were pierced several times and sported a vicious array of spikes pushed through white, blonde earrings.

Joey's backside landed heavily in the passenger seat and with a throaty growl and a surge of acceleration which dislodged another few patches of rust, D.C. Alexa Parkes accelerated up Burleigh Street and headed for a quiet spot, to have a conversation.

'Long time no see, Joey boy. We thought we'd done something to upset you.' Alexa Parkes was suspicious. Joey's call was six years out of the blue. He changed his number so often she no longer bothered 'checking in' with him. He was seen regularly in all his usual haunts, but his once flapping lips had been silent. Word from other flapping lips was that Joey was cleaned up and straight. This was a rumour partly cultivated by Joey himself. Her murky world had put Joey Callahan on its back burner. It was not just a case of turning the gas up again. She needed to check whether the contents of the pot were likely to have gone mouldy over the years.

They found a suitably isolated spot, a patch of wasteland frequented by nobody. It had been a dumping ground for the occasional dead body. More than one freezer filled with human remains had found its way to the now deserted remains of the Govan Graving dock.

'What have you got for us, wee Joey? What has pricked your social conscience enough for it to stir your mouth into action?' She was sarcastic, doubting, testing him.

'If this is right,' He began. 'it could be big. I'd need paying, if you want more, it's risky.'

'Cut the crap, Joey. First of all, what's it about, the drugs, the street robberies, the burglaries?' Alexa did not suffer fools.

'Ha' ye seen the news?' He didn't stop talking, and she started to listen. 'Bristol, there's been a pile o' stuff gone down in Bristol. Well, the weapons they used, they started life up here.'

'What do you mean, they start life up here?' Alexa was intrigued.

'There's a girl, well a woman, good looking, you can't miss her ….' He went on to outline how Tansy travelled to London and Bristol and that she carried with her all the information needed to make guns. Guns which were not traceable, guns which were then made by an associate of Paul Melville Grainger. His conscience getting the better of him he added.

'She does'nae know what she's carryin'. She'd freak if she did. I can'nae say more, but ye need tae examine her computer, it's all there.'

Then he got out of the car and walked to the water's edge. He took the phone with which he had made the call and threw it into the fetid green water of the dock, as far out as he could. He was done with this. All he could do now was try and warn Tansy, but she was in love with Balfour, any fool could see that. Not just in love with his money. Balfour just wasn't any fool, Joey Callahan knew him too well. Peter didn't fall in love. He was far too careful for that.

Alexa watched Joey Callahan walk back towards the city. She wouldn't offer him a lift. She had a feeling she wouldn't be dealing with him again. And what he had told her, well, she would pass it down the line to Avon and Somerset. They were the ones with the problem, they could pick the bones out of it. Joey was a devious little skunk. She knew he had connections with Balfour, but she didn't think that he had the balls to grass Peter Balfour. Was this Balfour's way of removing the opposition?

Alexa parked the Marina two streets away from the office and dropped the keys into the Post Office lock box strapped to the lamp post. One of her colleagues would need the old heap of junk later. The box had a keypad and a small safe inside. No postman had ever been employed to empty it. She could smell a strong smell of bullshit attached to her conversation with Joey Callahan. Maybe she would ring the Sassenachs down south in Avonmouth before she clocked off.

Alexa found the phone on her desk hidden under a heap of uncompleted reports, notes scribbled on pieces of scrap paper. The magnetic whiteboard which happened to be conveniently behind her desk was haphazardly patterned with a mosaic of coloured Post-It notes, shocking pink for urgent, orange for not so urgent and acid yellow for matters which could wait until later. There were also a pair of magnets under which lurked information yet to be corroborated in any way. Policy stated that all information should be logged into the ancient computer system within eight hours. Policy stated that all written records must be kept secure. With one hand Alexa deftly tapped the keys of the ancient desk top computer, logging on to several databases and systems. With the other she opened one of her desk drawers and rummaged.

'Okay, which one of you has my bloody Almanac?' She addressed the empty chairs. An up-to-date Almanac, the address book of all the police offices great and small, in both the United Kingdom and the Channel Islands was as rare as rocking horse manure. She found the item in question hidden under a pile of papers on a colleague's desk.

'Might have known it was you, ye untidy bastard, ye might at least have put it back.'

'Fine words,' she thought, given the mound of outstanding work on her own desk. Sitting on the corner of the furniture using her left bum cheek to clear a space, she searched for a number. She dialled; it was unobtainable. *'Typical,'* she told herself. Departments moved, they changed offices like most people changed their socks. She dialled the number for the Avon and Somerset headquarters and waited. On the fourth floor a telephone rang, it seemed to ring for ever. Alexa drummed her fingers impatiently on the desk, she was just about to give up. *'Another three rings,'* she told herself, then the receiver lifted, and a man's voice answered.

'Central Intel, Mark Fish speaking.'

'This is Alexa Parkes, I'm speakin' tae ye from sunny Glasgow.'

'Pardon?' Mark didn't understand a word of the thick accent which assailed his ears. 'What was tha' you said, my lover?' Mark's West Country twang was equally unintelligible, but he did catch the words Glasgow.

Both parties, paused and tried again. Mark spoke first. 'Good afternoon, Glasgow, just speak a little more slowly, it's a terrible line.' Alexa answered, 'It's no' a terrible line, it's just you English have bad hearing, and din'nae call me lover just yet, we hav'nae been properly introduced, hen.'

'What can I do for you, Alexa Parkes?'

Alexa formally introduced herself, she asked him if there was anything he could tell her about the Bristol shootings.

'Okay, Detective Parkes, I'll have to ask you to put your request on an email. You could be anyone. Sky News have been all over us like a rash. I'm here until eight, oh, and include a secure phone number. Just in case I need to call you.'

'Thank you, Detective Fish.' At least they took security seriously. Alexa opened her email and started to type. Five minutes later she added a switchboard number for Police Scotland at Glasgow, together with the extension to ask for. Then she hit send.

Hi Mark,
This afternoon, I received intelligence from a source. This source has been previously reliable but has not been in contact for some time. I need to establish whether there is any credence to what he is saying or is he for some reason feeding us false information.
Checks on the nominals he mentions have all come up negative. However, he himself has connections with one Peter Balfour who is squeaky clean in paper, but warm as proverbial toast.
Do you have any local intelligence on Paul Melville Grainger which may be relevant?
What's the weather like down south? It's pretty awful up here!
I am just preparing the log if you consider it relevant.

Best Regards
Alexa

Her auto signature and the email headers confirmed that she was indeed who she said she was.

Mark was already replying.

Hi Alexa,
Grainger is also as warm as toast. Never heard of your Mr Balfour, send what you have.

Mark
PS. It's raining here as well.

He added a suitably secure telephone number and hit reply.

Back in a grey and rain-soaked Glasgow, Joey sat with the lads in the corner of the Brechin, the one near the jukebox. They had managed to stay put for the whole of the day. Tansy's £20 had seen to that. He stared morosely into his beer and wondered just what he had started. He no longer wanted anything to do with Peter Balfour and he would never be able to look Tansy Alexander in the eye again. Just before closing time, he downed his beer and stepped out into the night. Joey Callahan did not make it home. His body was found several days later floating face down in the murky water of the graving dock. Another drunk who had apparently lost his footing.

CHAPTER 26. DINNER FOR TWO

The restaurant was cosy and intimate. The manager showed Peter Balfour and his guest to a quiet table in an alcove, one reserved for their more important and regular clients. A waiter appeared with remarkable speed and offered them the menu and the wine list. A few minutes later, he returned, bearing an ice-bucket and an appropriately chilled white Rioja. Showing her the label, he uncorked the bottle at the table and poured an inch into the bottom of Tansy's glass. She swirled the contents, lifted the glass to her nose, pronounced its delicate perfume a delight, and both their glasses were filled. The wine was crisp, light and dry, the long-stemmed glasses reflecting the light of the candle on the sconce on the wall. He would have preferred red but let her choose, guiding her towards the more discerning part of the list. Despite the guidance she had still opted for this crisp mid-range Spanish white instead of the smoother, buttery Alberino he was aiming for.

Tansy was excited, she had plans. Her excitement was infectious. For a few brief moments he was swept along on her wave of childlike enthusiasm. She could take up her place on the course, study to be an actor. She could still work for him, she would have down time, she could fit it all in, she knew she could. They had said she had talent, why should she waste it. She lasered him with those deep blue eyes, their centres paler, almost but not quite green. He was hypnotised, transfixed by the kaleidoscope of colour in their depths.

'What you do for me is important, Tans.' He sounded convincing.

'I can still do that, but this is a real chance,' she smiled at him over the rim of her glass, her even white teeth lighting up her face. 'a chance for me to do something for myself.'

'You'd be in London, I'd miss you.' He started to turn on the charm.

'Pete Balfour don't bullshit me. I know I'm expendable.' She was truthful.

The waiter arrived with their Tapas. Tansy, out of habit, moved the crockery and tableware around, making space for the small hot plates that held their choice from the menu. Peter raised an eyebrow at the waiter who was clearly frustrated at the customer interference. It was his job. She should allow him to wait on her, but that was not in her make up, she would, out of habit, help anyone.

'We've ordered far too much,' she laughed, 'but if you aren't, I'm certainly starving. Its smells delish.'

She stuck a fork into a spicy meatball, raised it slowly and held it to her nose, taking in the warm scent of paprika, oregano and tomatoes. Then she held it to her lips, nibbling the slightly crusty edges, those tasty bits where the meat was slightly caramelised from the pan. All the time, she held him with her eyes. Her long dark pink tongue ran around her front teeth, then over the meatball, stripping it of the rich Spanish sauce. Then the teeth gripped it firmly and bit, leaving half the ball still impaled on the fork. Peter's left hand adjusted the crotch of his jeans where he was starting to suffer from a major inconvenience. His right foot reached out and caught her ankle under the table. He took a long sip of his wine, placed the glass on the table, then with some ceremony spread the linen napkin in his lap. When he looked up, he saw that her eyes were laughing at him. A French manicured finger wiped a stray dribble of sauce from her chin. She offered him her finger. 'Try it, it's really something.' He intended to try it, all of it. Later.

'I really need to do this, Pete. Just think, I could actually do something with my life. I can't, no, I won't, be your plaything for the rest of my days.' She brought him back to the present. He used his own manicured fingers to lift a prawn dripping in garlic butter from its bed of fresh lettuce. He examined it closely, then slowly sucked the aromatic film from its length, deftly removed the tail and popping it in his mouth, chewed on it slowly and deliberately. Two could play at this game.

'I have important business coming up, I need you to be here, I can't have you stuck in London. Believe me Tansy, you are important to me.'

He felt her long leg wrap around his own under the table. He adjusted himself to a more comfortable position.

'There are plenty of other girls who could do my job, you know there are. I'm sure Joey can find you someone who would jump at the opportunity.' She raised one eyebrow at him.

'Joey? Joey doesn't work for me anymore, ye ken.' His accent was becoming broader as his irritation grew. 'I'd rather it if ye didn't speak of him again.' She said nothing, she had caught him in a lie. He continued. 'I ken he lives in the same flats as you, and I ken ye are friends, but please din'nae get too close tae' him.' Pete's voice had become a growl. 'Ye could always move in wi' me.' He dangled a carrot.

Tansy let it lie. Breaking off the corner of a piece of garlic bread, she dipped it into the meatball sauce and offered it to him, popping it into his mouth before he could growl another sentence directed at Joey.

'You know I like my own space, Pete. Your place is lovely, but it's too big and too far out of town for me. I like my flat. I'm not moving, after all it's handy for the train,' She tried to lighten his mood. 'and it makes it more special when I do sleep over.'

'Listen Tansy, I've got important business coming up. You are my right hand, you don't let me down. Once it's done, then you could perhaps do it. Can they not defer the place for you?' He negotiated.

'This is RADA we're talking about. They don't just take anyone. You can't fuck them around, Pete. I could ask, I suppose, but I really don't want to lose my place.' She didn't want to break the mood.

'Well, if you're that good, they'll wait.' Pete poured them both another glass. 'Talking of waiting, I'm not sure I can, let's finish this and go.'

She popped a large, juicy olive into her mouth, followed by bread dipped in oil and vinegar. Then, with her mouth still slightly full, leaned towards him and whispered, 'But I need afters, Pete.'

'So do I.' He mouthed back at her. 'So do I.' He signalled to the waiter for the bill.

They walked together across the city, his arm around her shoulder, along the river, taking in the view across the industrial landscape. They did not stop at any of the inviting clubs and bars along the way. The rain had stopped and the darkness was only broken by the streetlights. She rummaged for the keys in the bottom of her bag, finding them deep in the depths of fluff and tissues which inhabited the bottom left-hand corner.

'There we are.' She produced them with a flourish and she and Peter Balfour staggered into the building and then into the lift.

He kissed her, almost savagely. He pressed her body against the back wall of the lift as she pressed the button for her floor. She felt his body hard against hers. Miraculously, she felt hers pressing back in response. Something had changed. She had never felt like this with him before. She felt herself losing her usual resistance. Was it the wine, or the food, or the anticipation? The lift doors opened and they stumbled across the landing to her flat. She kissed him slowly as she inserted her keys into the door lock. She could feel his hand fumbling with the buckle of her belt and the button fly of her jeans. Could Joey hear all this she wondered? He usually heard everything which went on upstairs. Sometimes she wondered if he had her flat bugged. Well, never mind, he could listen to his heart's content tonight.

Her bedroom was not as he had expected. Somehow, she had arranged the small flat so that her bed occupied the living area, the living area now re-located to the small mezzanine bedroom. There were no curtains, just a view out above the traffic and the bustle below to the river. The whole apartment was strewn with throws and cushions in a riot if colours and fabrics.

He started to undress her, his hands reaching to lift the T-shirt she wore over her small but firm breasts. She shook her head. 'No, let me.'

She slowly unbuttoned his shirt, kissing his chest with the opening of each button, working her way down to the belt of his Levis. Slowly, she tugged the denim downwards over his hard backside. As she undid the first button his cock sprang out to greet her. 'Commando!', she thought.

'Pete Balfour goes commando.' Sending her thought, and before she could inflame him more, he lifted her to her feet. 'I am a proper Scot, hen. My turn now.'

She danced away from him, crossing her arms, and lifting Guns and Roses clear of her lean body, she tossed the grey garment onto the floor. She rarely wore a bra, and tonight was no exception. Her nipples stood out like olive stones with arousal and the chill of the night air. She placed a booted foot on the seat of the chair positioned by the window. 'Damn', he thought, she could even make taking her boots off an art form. She ran her hands down her own body, slowly unfastening the thick black belt which held her jeans in place over her slim hips. Without the need to undo a single button, they descended down those long, long legs to the floor. 'Commando too', he noted. The long-fingered hands moved downwards to the neatly trimmed triangle of hair.

'My turn,' he groaned, burying his face in her flat belly, running his tongue downwards. He did not speak again for some time. Pressing her back into the nest of fleece throws and faux fur rugs on the bed he felt none of the usual resistance from her. She wanted him. He could feel the want blazing from every fibre of her body.

Then he was with her, merged together, one complete being. As her flesh tightened around his, her pretty white teeth loosened their grip on his shoulder and she lost herself in a cry loud enough to wake the neighbours. She only had one neighbour, and he would never hear anything again.

They lay together, her head resting on his arm, dozing peacefully, watching the lights of the working boats on the Clyde.

'I love you, Pete Balfour.' It was a thought meant only for herself.

His thoughts were equally silent.

As dawn broke, she stretched herself and, wrapping herself in his shirt, she went to the bathroom for a pee, then to the small kitchenette and started to make coffee. Tansy had no time for real coffee beans. She opened the jar of cheap brown powder bought from the local supermarket. As she placed the steaming mug of liquid alongside the bed, he opened his eyes and smiled at her.

'Sorry Pete, I've only got instant.'

'Tansy Alexander, I'll have you any instant you like.' He pulled her back under the covers, 'and you can get out of that shirt anytime you like.'

It was nearly lunchtime before he tasted the coffee. It was cold, and bitter. Not at all like Tansy.

'I'm starving.', she moaned as he rolled out of her bed.

'You are always hungry.', he replied.

'I'm a growing girl, I need to be fed regularly.' A host of ripostes sprang to mind. He used none of them.

'Let's get out of town for a drive, there's a café I know of does a great fry up,' he suggested.

'One problem. Where's your car, Pete?' She laughed.

'It's not far away,' he replied, hoping she hadn't seen it, parked in the far corner of the car park, left there when he had had other business to attend to. 'I'll nip and get it. I'll pick you up in ten minutes.'

He dressed hurriedly and, as he closed the door behind him, Tansy stretched herself under the covers. Maybe RADA could wait after all. Pete Balfour certainly couldn't. She smiled to herself contentedly. 'I love you, Pete Balfour.' She mouthed the words to herself, words she would never say to him out loud. Then she went to the bathroom and brushed her teeth. Out of the big picture window she could see the seagulls wheeling on the breeze. She had a feeling that it was going to be a great day.

She was waiting on the pavement outside when he drove around the corner in the 2-door Audi R8 convertible. She slipped into the passenger seat and then, with the roof down, they headed out of town and into the wild countryside to the north of the city. Tansy sank back, gripped snuggly by the sumptuous leather of the shell seat and stretched her long legs into the footwell. She felt the wind pulling at her hair and whipping it around her face. Peter reached into the glove compartment and pulled out two baseball caps. 'His and Hers,' she thought. She could live with that. Pulling hers down over her hair her mind toyed with possibilities

They had driven for about half an hour, both of them strangely silent. Peter pulled into a layby at the side of the road. There, hidden behind a screen of trees was a mobile refreshment van. 'Best chips in the fresh air you will find.' He ordered one large chips and a carton of curry.

They sat at a picnic table and ate with their fingers, dipping the thick, crispy, home-made chips into the tasty curry sauce.

'I need you to do a run next week.' He was quiet. 'There won't be many more after this one, I promise.' He seemed worried.

'Why all this sudden concern, you don't usually worry about me.' She picked up on his vibe.

'Well, once this job is finished, when I don't need you...... shit Tansy that came out all wrong, I think I will always need you. But when I am no longer sending you here there and everywhere, maybe you can start living your own dream.' He did not want to send her south again, but his contacts expected a delivery.

'When, Pete, when do you want me to go?' She sounded resigned.

'Wednesday or Thursday, I should have everything ready by then. London and then Bristol.'

'Why tell me now, let's not spoil today, come on, finish your chips and show me what this car of yours can really do. Show a girl a good time, Mr Balfour. I've worked for it!' She licked her fingers and loped across to the waiting vehicle, climbing into the passenger seat without opening the door.

He laughed and throwing their rubbish into the bin, he climbed into the driver's seat and started the engine.

'Do you remember the day we met?' he began.

'Of course I do, I was suffering badly. Joey was holding me to ransom for a fix. I would have done anything. I've grown up and cleaned up since then, that was at a burger van as well.' She laughed, almost engulfed by the seat as the car pulled out onto the A road, gravel rattling behind them in the few seconds it took to hit 60 miles per hour.

'You always had something special, Tansy, I think I knew it from the start. Please, let's just see this thing through to the end. One last run and be careful.' He put his left hand on her leg and squeezed. 'I never want to lose you.'

'I know what I'm carrying can't be legal. Just tell me I'm not carrying drugs. I won't mule for you. If I'm carrying drugs it's all off.' She was adamant and he knew it.

'I can assure you it's not drugs, in fact it's nothing strictly illegal, but please, Tansy, obey the rules. No phone calls, no unscheduled stops, and be observant.' He was trying to tell her something.

'As far as I'm concerned its business as usual, don't worry, I'll be fine. Now put yer foot down let's see what this thing can do.'

In his mind, Peter Balfour could do no more. He hoped that she wouldn't be swept up in the fallout he knew would happen. He depressed his right foot and heard her squeal as the Audi's engine growled into life, rattling and crackling through the gearbox, stretching its legs towards the highlands. Today would be a day for them, just the two of them and he would try and forget the guilt he was starting to feel at what might lie ahead of her. If they came through this unscathed then he wanted to spend the rest of his life with her. After this there would be no more dodgy dealings. He didn't need the money, it was the buzz which he needed, the danger. But even that had not made him feel the way he had felt last night.

CHAPTER 27. UNIT 42.

Bristol 2017

Like most students, Dean Callow was skint, needed a bit of extra cash, something to pad out his student loan. His parents struggled to find the money to send him to university. He was a very bright lad with a talent for computers and electronic engineering. He deserved his chance at a better life. These were the thoughts of his father who had worked all his life in the aircraft industry. Hugh Callow had worked his way up. He had started work with British Aerospace in the 1970's. He had worked his way up from the bottom and had seen the benefits a good and relevant education could have on a young man's career. He had encouraged his only son to study hard, do his best and now the lad was destined for a first-class honours' degree.

Dean took university seriously. He hadn't spent his first two years partying in other students' flats. He was by no means a killjoy, he loved a beer and a spliff, but not to the exclusion of everything else. Dean had other hobbies, things he far preferred to drinking himself to oblivion.

He was just starting his final year. He didn't fancy more bar or restaurant work, working into the early hours of the morning. It made his head fuzzy for lectures the following day. Neither did he fancy delivering for one of the zero hours companies which seemed to be springing up daily around the city. When he saw the small notice on the 'Computing and Engineering' faculty notice board in the student union, he had jumped at the chance. Flexible hours, early evenings and some weekdays, practical experience in design technology, and the money was excellent. He rang the number. The woman on the phone had been very helpful, the job would be explained on site, he could attend an induction session on Thursday evening. All good.

The factory unit was only a short bicycle ride down the hill from his house share at Muller Avenue. Ideal. The induction session had been thorough. He and the five other recruits, no one that he knew, none of them students like himself, had been told that the company they were working for was a start-up company called 'MelTech'. They made prototype component parts for the aerospace industry. These prototypes were manufactured in small quantities using 3D printing and were then sent to their mother factory for assembly and testing. If the components were viable then the parent company would take on the design and source mass production. Their job was to set up and supervise the printers with a programme which they would be given. In the interests of product security and potential industrial espionage they were to tell no one what they did. They were not to work on any job but their own. They would all sign an agreement to this effect. 'A bit like our own little official secrets act', she said. By the end of the induction session, Dean was not so sure about what he was getting into, but it was only eight hours a week, on his doorstep, and the money was fantastic. It would take a huge burden from his old Dad's shoulders. It also left him time to indulge in his other hobby, the one he shared with no one. The money would be handy there as well.

Dean signed the agreement. He was shown two copies, one of which was sent to the parent company, the other was filed in a locked cabinet on site. He was reassured that the reason he could not take a copy with him was because it would be a security risk. Security seemed to be a big thing, yet the unit was unprotected. It had no external fencing, it was just one of a line of five, in a large parking area behind IKEA. Curious, Dean was assured that this was to make it blend in. It was 'normal' not 'unusual.' No one would pay attention to it. There was CCTV both internally and externally. The tall, well-dressed, Afro-Caribbean lady who introduced herself as Julia Melville was growing bored of his questions. His name was added to a roster, and he was pencilled in for his first four shifts. He cycled back up Muller Road and turned left heading through the scruffy streets of Ashley Down back to the cold, damp house he shared with six other students, back to his bedroom at the back of the house, with its lovely view of the rat-infested garden and the wasteland at the rear.

Shift 1. Dean was admitted to the unit by a man who looked more like a nightclub bouncer than an office worker. He was scanned for electronic devices and allocated a small lead lined locker in which to secure his mobile phone. He consented to be searched. He was shown to a room, Room 4, which would be his workstation. The door was secured with a keypad. He was given the code and told that the code changed weekly. He would receive a new code by text message, which he was to delete. The room was small, it was painted the customary mushroom beige and was maybe 12 feet by 12 feet square. MelTech appeared to have the use of the whole line of units, divided into similarly sized work cells. The window was above head level, one wall was occupied by a large extractor fan, like a giant cooker hood. Under the hood were six 3D printers. Dean could see that they could be wired together to work from the same lap top computer, but they were not. Each machine had its own data stick inserted in the USB port. This would contain the programme which instructed the extruder heads. There was a stool and a work bench and a water dispenser with plastic cups, and one area marked, 'Food Only.' He assumed that if he was going to eat his sandwiches anywhere, then it should be there. There was also a box of latex gloves, size large, and a sign advising, 'For your own protection, wear at all times.'

The 'doorman' had supplied him with the key code for the door to his cell, log on details for the Apple Mac and a set of instructions for the day.

The toilet was at the end of the corridor. Dean had a feeling there was CCTV monitoring use of the toilet. It was that sort of place. The doorman said nothing, just left him to it, and disappeared into his troglodyte cave to the left of the door, the windows covered with black film and the glow of CCTV monitors the only light.

Switch on all equipment at the mains – printers need to warm up. Switch on the extractor. There was a handy diagram showing the sites of all the switches. Dean suddenly wondered whether the workers in the other rooms did not speak English, maybe they needed diagrams to assist. Personally, he was certainly able to find the 'on' switches. They were standard metal electric switches, wall mounted in industrial trunking which ran down the walls from the suspended tiled ceiling at intervals around the room. Load the printers with filament, black only. Remove Data sticks from printers. Log on to Apple Mac and, using the adaptor provided, download ONLY the file listed on your worksheet onto each stick. Make six copies. One for each printer. Replace sticks into USB port of each printer and press 'start'.

When each printer has finished, box up part in the boxes marked 4. Dean presumed that as there were six different rooms, there would be six different components being made. It seemed logical enough.

It did not take Dean long to set up his printers. He swivelled his stool round on its axis and got out his course work while the extruder did its work, guided by the commands from the data stick, slowly building a black object on the base plate. Layer upon layer, upon layer. It needed minimal supervision just a visual check every few minutes to make sure nothing had dropped offline.

This wasn't half bad, it was warmer than the house, it was certainly quieter than the house. Dean decided he could get plenty of revision hours in and earn plenty of spare cash at Unit 42. After four hours he boxed up his first six components. That would do for today. He let himself out to find the doorman waiting for him. He placed the fruits of his labours in the greet crate marked 4. The doorman handed him an envelope containing £50 in £10 notes. Dean wrote his name in the book for more shifts and unchaining his bicycle from the railings on the far side of the car park, he made his way home. It wasn't late, his wallet was full. He continued past his usual turning and called in at the Foresters Arms for a beer. He had earned it. It was Friday tomorrow. He had a day on the range planned, he hadn't handled a rifle for weeks and he was getting stale, out of practice. Dean Callow was a competition marksman. Forced to keep his pride and joy in the armoury at his club, he took every opportunity to travel the hour and a half journey it took to get to Exeter where he could keep his eye in and chat with likeminded gun geeks. Now he had some disposable income he could afford to go more often. Ammunition was expensive, but now he had a source of income he could afford to live a little.

    The rifle range was where Dean honed his skills. He loved the feeling of firing a high-powered rifle. The accuracy, and the control, he felt as one with the weapon, as if it was an extension of his body. It was not until he was disassembling the gun that he noticed the similarities in the shapes. He had never questioned what he was making in unit 42. It was just a plastic part. He had not really looked at it as anything more. His nimble fingers went instinctively through the field stripping process, he could do it with his eyes closed. He knew all the parts by touch, his fingers remembering their shapes and their place, their orientation in the complex mechanism of a rifle. He had been taught well, the discipline, the precision of movement, and the speed acquired competing with other army cadets.

    Job completed, he replaced the rifle in its case, returned it to its place in the rack of guns, secured the clamp which held it and, signing out of the gun club, he walked back to the railway station. His subconscious had stored away the snippet of information. It was Sunday afternoon. If he was quick, he could catch his housemates in the Foresters for a drink. He needed to catch up on things like washing his clothes, he could always put a load on in the laundrette opposite the pub and have a beer while he waited for the machine to finish. He smiled to himself. That seemed like a good plan. He would probably pick up a Chinese takeaway or at least a Spring Roll on his way home for the night. He sat back in his seat and contemplated the rest of his day. Catching sight of his reflection in the glass of the carriage window he realised that he also needed a shave. Well, that could definitely wait until the morning.

Dean walked quickly across the city, past the hospital and up the Gloucester Road, turning off into Dongola Avenue and winding his way through the side streets until he reached the decrepit rented house he and his housemates called home. He pushed his way past the heap of bicycles chained to the railings just outside the front door and let himself in with his key, pushing the door over the lump in the carpet caused by the loose tile underneath. The smell of damp was pervasive. It overpowered the smells of greasy cooking and takeaway cartons which came from the shared kitchen. He joked that his room at least had cold running water, but most of it was running down the chimney breast from the leaky lead flashing on the roof. He unlocked his bedroom and dumped his bag on the bed. There were none of the usual noises which indicated that the others were home. No music from any of the other bedrooms, no sound of the TV from the communal lounge. The boys were out! He quickly combed his hair, picked up his bag of laundry, checked his wallet for cash and ran back down the rickety stairs two at a time. It was only a short walk down the street and round the corner to the Wash House and then the warmth of the pub.

Chores done, Dean found several of his mates clustered around the table in the snug behind the chimney. Two had their heads deep in their books, trying vainly to catch up on required reading for lectures on Monday. Gavin Holmes, who was on his engineering course and who, like Dean, had no lectures until Wednesday, had switched on the TV above the fireplace and was browsing the channels looking for some sport to watch.

'Yo! Dean!', he greeted his housemate. 'Good shooting, man?' It was a question.

'Not bad mate, I got some good scores in. It's Bisley next month, team trials, what's news here?'

'Nothing much, mate, it was all kicking off on Friday, closed the centre, police everywhere, some dude had his car shot up, right outside the police station.'

On the TV on the wall, the volume turned down so as not to disturb the other customers, the subtitles announced that the police were seeking information. Gavin's finger hovered over the remote, eager to change the channel to something more interesting.

'Hold on one minute, Gav, I want to see this.' Dean put his hand over the remote.

'Its old news now man, nothing to interest us. Let the police get on with it, it's their job, not ours. I'm missing the football, man.' Gavin pressed the button and found what he was looking for, highlights of the football match between Manchester United and their last opponent. The result a forgone conclusion. Man- U. won everything. It was why Gavin liked them. Dean memorised the number which had appeared on the bottom of the screen. He had no lectures tomorrow and he had a shift booked in at Unit 42 for the afternoon. His curiosity was piqued. What was he actually making? He knew he could not ask but he was sure he could find out.

Sunday evening progressed as Sundays do. Dean adjourned to the launderette to rescue his washing just before the Wash House closed at eight pm. The landlord of the Foresters asked them bluntly if they were actually customers or if they had only come in to warm themselves.

Dean and Gavin watched the rest of the football and stretched their cash to another pint of Flowers ale. Phil and Duncan bought half pints and kept their heads in their books.

It was nearly eleven o'clock before they wandered back around the corner to number thirty-three. As they rounded the corner, they were welcomed into a street illuminated by blue flashing lights, amber streetlamps reflecting off the fluorescent chequerboard livery of the riot van, shouts of female voices hurling abuse at officers in riot gear, the slam of the riot van doors.

A large, uniformed officer wearing body armour and carrying a riot shield stepped out in front of them. 'Stop here, lads, it's a bit busy up there at the moment.'

'But we want to get home.' Gavin started to remonstrate. 'It's our fucking street, man, you can't stop us.'

The officer drew a long breath in, the kind of long breath which conveyed the fact that he had had a long day and did not want it lengthened by an argumentative student.

'Just do as I ask, son, please, it won't be long. You and your mates wait there.' The officer was polite but firm.

Gavin began to speak. The officer clicked the ratchets on his handcuffs as a warning. Gavin thought better of the smart comment he was about to make, opting instead to sit on the low garden wall with the rest of them instead.

Half an hour later, the riot van left, taking with it the occupants of number 34, the house across the street. Gavin shoved Dean in the shoulder. 'Shame about that.'

'Shame about what?', Dean asked, pushing past the bicycles for the second time that evening.

'Weed will be in short supply for a while.' Gavin looked across at the site of the former grow house. 'Real shame, it was good gear.'

Such was life on Muller Avenue.

Dean disappeared into his bedroom, opened his window and, lying on his bed, lit up the remains of the reefer which he had been keeping in his sock drawer. Taking a big draw in and exhaling he sighed to himself, 'Good gear.'

He fell asleep with his headphones on to the sounds of the Rolling Stones coming to his emotional rescue.

It was ten in the morning before Dean woke up. He showered in the freezing swamp which passed for a bathroom. He dressed and made himself a quick slice of toast and jam for breakfast, then, unchaining his bicycle from the pile outside the front door, he cycled down the hill to Unit 42. This morning, he was a man on a mission. He had his books in his backpack and his lunch in a box. A tinfoil lined box.

Dean was a regular, he had been working there for over a year now. The huge, monosyllabic Rasta on the door trusted him.

'Morning Bruce.' Dean was cheerful as he walked in through the door and tapped in the key code to his work room. The guy's name wasn't Bruce, but he smiled back anyway, his white teeth with their gold incisor crowns gleaming back at Dean. First time ever, Dean got a reply.

'Good mornin' to you too, Dean, an' me name's not Bruce, it's Trevor.'

'Yo, Trevor!' Dean saluted him in jest as he disappeared into his locked room for the day.

Dean switched on the printers and went about his work while they warmed up. He laid his books and lecture notes out on the work bench in preparation for a day's study. Then he linked up the waiting computer to the printer. He loaded the extruder with black raw plastic coil. Then he selected the file as per his work sheet and pressed send. Then he settled down to his course work, lulled by the gentle hum of the extractor fans.

The printer sprang into life. The extruder head began its journey, back and forth, up and down, building slowly layer upon layer, stopping, then changing direction, following the instructions fed to it by the programme in the Apple Mac.

Dean let the six printers run on. He sat down on the high stool and began to study. It would be several hours before he needed to tend his machines again. At the end of the afternoon, he boxed up the parts which he had produced. The last one off the last machine miraculously broke into three large pieces, possibly a result of slightly rough handling. Dean marked his work sheet as having one breakage and slipped the broken piece into his sandwich box. Then, he packed up his backpack and let himself out. Trevor had left for the day. The CCTV was monitoring the door.

Dean cycled back to Muller Avenue, stopping en-route at the corner shop to purchase a tube of superglue. Later that evening, he made a phone call. He sent photographs of the reconstructed piece of plastic to the email address they provided. Continue as normal, they told him, don't change your routine, don't change your habits. Thank you for calling Crimestoppers.

Dean did not sleep well that night. He worried that he had been seen. He worried that they would know what he had done. But he kept on booking shifts at the unit, obeying all the instructions. Nothing happened.

After a few weeks of nothing happening, he wondered why he had bothered. Maybe Gavin was right about the police. Maybe they just weren't interested. Then it happened.

CHAPTER 28. OPERATION RAGWORT.

Bristol 2017

The chatter of anticipation in the briefing room faded out slowly as the officer in charge rose from his seat at the front of the room. He quietly pulled the papers from his folder in front of him and composed his thoughts. He would not need the crib sheets. He had rehearsed what he was going to say in his head a hundred times. The PowerPoint presentation on the screen would answer most of the inevitable questions. He had been thorough, leaving nothing to chance. But then there was always the unexpected.

The intelligence case was strong. Months of surveillance had corroborated what the source had said. Their target most likely knew nothing. It was what she carried which held the evidence. She would be collateral damage. She was a pawn in a bigger game. Expendable to her paymaster, whoever that was.

Detective Sergeant Joel Knight composed himself, ordered his thoughts and began.

'Firstly, a word on operational security. You all have a copy of the briefing, the copies are numbered, they are signed for, they do not leave this room. They will be signed back in before you leave the building. Nothing in relation to this operation leaves this room. I cannot stress that enough.'

Officers shifted in their chairs and adjusted their positions, leaning against the furniture at the sides and back of the room.

'Lights please,' he nodded towards the back of the room and a convenient hand dimmed the main lights, enhancing the images on the pull-down screen behind the speaker.

Joel stood to one side, allowing his team to see the short documentary film which best conveyed his message.

'This is what we are dealing with.' On the screen, an image of an assault rifle revolved in slow motion on the screen. From every angle it appeared authentic.

'Consider the effect of this would have, in a post office, a bank, your local corner shop or in a school.' There was a rumble of throat clearing and an intake of breath from the audience.

The presenter on the screen, a forensic scientist, an expert in his field began to disassemble the weapon. As they watched, the component parts were laid out on a bench and itemised.

'As you can see, and for those of you who are not intimately familiar with the inner workings of a gun, I can assure you, all the working parts are there.'

The on-screen demonstration continued. The weapon was reassembled, care taken when inserting every machine screw into its correct hole. The casing sealed tightly, the completed item appeared again on the screen.

'Watch and learn.' Joel focussed his team's attention.

The weapon had been mounted on a jig. It was clamped into a frame, in a controlled area. Some meters distant was the figure of a human head and torso - a ballistics dummy.

The weapon was loaded firstly with a blank round of ammunition, the trigger pulled remotely for safety reasons.

'Its construction will stand pressure.' Joel commented.

Then a live round was loaded, the trigger pulled, the ballistic dummy vibrated with the shock of impact. A trickle of fake blood emerged from a hole penetrating deep into the torso. The presenter removed the round and measured the depth of the wound.

'If you need to know, it penetrated a full eight centimetres into the dummy, a potentially fatal injury.' Joel paused the film.

All eyes were now focussed on the screen.

'Now the scary part.' Joel continued. He pressed play. On screen appeared a lap top computer connected to some form of apparatus. It looked as though it would be more appropriate in a high school physics laboratory.

'For the uninitiated, this is a 3D printer. Those of us with school aged children may be familiar with them. Mine have produced some lovely models of snowflakes and dinosaurs using the same sort of kit. The lethal weapon we have just seen tested was made on such a printer.'

There was an intake of breath around the room, mutterings of 'Bloody hell, and Jesus Christ,' were punctuated with other pithy epithets.

'The weapon you have seen demonstrated, and others like it, are made almost entirely of plastic. Yet they are not in any respect toys. They have a small number of machined metal components. The design has been refined so that the metal components may be removed and transported separately. This makes what you have just seen largely undetectable on an X-ray scanner if packed correctly. The metal components can be distributed so that they appear innocuous to the untrained eye. These weapons have been used on the streets of our city. They cannot be allowed to circulate amongst the criminal fraternity, for they are comparatively cheap to produce, easily disposed of and untraceable.' Joel paused for a few minutes to allow the facts to sink in.

'We have an intelligence case which suggests that these weapons are being manufactured in the city. The main player is believed to be this man.'

The screen flicked and the image changed, a picture of Paul Melville Grainger appeared.

'Paul Grainger,' Joel continued, 'has not had so much as a parking ticket or a speeding fine since he was a lad. He is now fifty-five years old. He is Mr Squeaky Clean. He is also very well connected. Some of you may remember the Weaver case.' There was another wave of crusty epithets from the older officers present. 'We do not know who his potential customers are, but as I have said, he is *very* well connected.' He emphasised the *very*.

'We believe that Grainger has handed some of his business dealings to his daughter Julia.' A grainy still from a surveillance video appeared, showing a tall black woman with the appearance of a young Naomi Campbell. 'It is Julia who has proven to be his weak link.' Another pause

'The technical expertise is sourced from Glasgow. The computer programmes used to run the printers are written and refined on the banks of the Clyde. We have Police Scotland to thank for our intelligence.' He cleared his throat.

'A number of months ago, we were made aware that this man' A picture of Joey Callahan appeared on the screen. 'was involved in running a network of couriers using the railway service between Glasgow, London, and Bristol. Several of the couriers were stopped and searched, some have been convicted of minor offences in relation to the courier service, others for more serious unrelated offences. None of them would countenance talking to us. They were all terrified of the consequence of informing. A surveillance operation was set up. The team on the plot pinpointed this young woman as taking over the role of courier.' A picture of Tansy Alexander appeared on screen. Male and female offices alike gasped.

'Yes, exactly.' Joel continued. 'This lady is smart, astute, careful, and very, very convincing. She travels on average once a week from Glasgow, sometimes direct to Bristol but mostly via London. She gives the appearance of a businesswoman. She carries two laptops with her, one on which she appears to work during the journey, the other, an Apple Mac, she never touches. She deposits the bag with the Apple Mac at a boutique hotel, to be collected by an individual. Then, if she is in London, she spends the day mainly visiting acting agencies and casting calls. Sometimes she goes to a music venue. Never the same routine. At a prearranged time, she returns to the hotel and picks up an Apple Mac and either returns to Glasgow or travels on to Bristol. Analysis of her mobile phone data shows that she carries two phones. One is kept without a SIM card until she is back in Glasgow. It is kept switched off unless it is in use. The other is changed weekly. SIM and handset. It is this phone which has connected her to Callahan. He was not so hot on phone security as she is. I say this because Joey Callahan is dead. He was found floating in the Clyde a few weeks ago. Take a short break, relieve your bladders, and get some refreshment, back in ten minutes.' Joel nodded to the back of the room and the lights came back on.

D.C. Alexa Parkes had been standing unobserved in the shadows at the back of the room. She was an avid watcher of people. The team assembled was a balance of age and experience combined with youth and enthusiasm. Hopefully, there was also the necessary expertise. Her appraising eye had run over Joel Knight. She had seen his type before. He was tall, well over six feet, built a little like Lynford Christie. She tried not to imagine him dressed in skintight Lycra. The man definitely worked out. He positively glowed with health and wellbeing. He was confident, self-assured, very professional, she hoped he had the balls to do the job.

Ten minutes passed and the team filtered back to their seats and perches around the room. Alexa walked to the front of the room and awaited her introduction. Someone dimmed the lights in anticipation and Joel resumed the briefing.

'I will now hand over to our colleague from Policing Scotland in Glasgow, Detective Alexa Parkes.' Joel invited her to join him at the front.

Alexa began. 'Firstly, tell me if ye can'nae hear me at the back, I din'nae usually get this much of an audience, ye ken.'

'ALEXA! Say something in English!' some wag called out from a dark corner by the filing cabinets, followed by peals of laughter from the room.

'Okay folks, that's enough of the jokes.' Alexa spoke more slowly. 'For the benefit of those of you have difficulty in understanding, I will try to speak with subtitles.' She paused, hearing Joel stifle a laugh as he sat at the small desk behind her. The man had a sense of humour then. She began again.

'So, what do we know about Tansy Alexander?' Alexa flashed her picture onto the screen. 'She was a teenage runaway. She is now eighteen. She was reported missing from her foster placement by her carer, Marcia Alexander, nearly two years ago. Marcia Alexander is dead. Tansy slipped below the radar. She was a good student, quite academic, also very musical. Reading between the lines, she ran away after she was abused by Marcia's boyfriend. But that is by the by.

In school Tansy was close friends with Joey Callahan. Surprisingly, she has no criminal record. She is the connection with Callahan. It is Callahan who seems to have been running things at our end. In the last few years, he has gone from minor drug dealing pimp living off the backs of a gang of youngsters, to having his own harbourside flat and a degree of status. He had apparently cleaned up his act.' She paused. 'Joey Callahan was also the source of our intelligence. Why would he grass himself up, why would he throw Tansy to the wolves? It all fits in, timing wise, with shootings here in Bristol. It is pure speculation, but I would say it is damage limitation. Someone at this end has gone rogue on him.' She heard Joel grunt in agreement behind her. 'Joey Callahan was murdered. He was'nae drunk, but his blood contained enough opiates to fuel a Derby winner.'

She handed the room back to Joel. 'Over to you Sergeant Knight.'

'This is Unit 42.' A picture of a nondescript factory unit on a nondescript industrial estate appeared on screen. 'Until last week, we knew nothing about its use. It is out of the way, the same front company rents all of the units in the block. They are all interconnected. This is where we believe the weapons are made, or at least it is part of the process. The intelligence is Crimestoppers. But the source has given lots of detail and seems to know their guns well enough to realise what this is.' A picture of a plastic component appeared on the screen.

'Today's op. The surveillance team has its eyes on Tansy. They are currently on the train from London to Bristol. Tansy has picked up an Apple Mac from her London contact, on this occasion, Julia Grainger.

Team One. You will wait for her to get off the train at Temple Meads. Once she is clear of the station, you will arrest her and seize any technical devices she is carrying - tablets, phones, computers.

Team Two. You will hit Unit 42. Detain anyone on the premises. Search any cars which can be connected with the persons or the property. I take it we have warrants already sworn, Mark?' Joel looked to Mark Fish for a confirmation.

'All done, skip.' Mark assured him.

'Right, you lot, get into your teams, get kitted up, get some food if you need to. We will have a phone call when the train is an hour away. Any questions?'

The teams broke off into their separate huddles. The firearms team began their familiar routines of checking and re-checking weapons and ammunition. Hopefully, they would not be needed. Body armour was adjusted. Boot laces tightened. The entry team went through their check list, the contents of their tool bag itemised, each piece of kit counted, checked and found to be in working order. It was not unknown for the Rammit to be missing, removed from the bag to prop open a door or borrowed by another team and not replaced. It would not do to arrive at the job with no means to open the door.

The factory unit had been recce'd. It was a wooden fire grade door, inward opening, spy hole but no glass. There was also a roller shutter door padlocked down from the outside. No escape route through that then. Four reinforced glass windows at shoulder level at the rear, all with external bars and only three feet from the steel boundary fence. The office window next to the entrance door was covered with one way film. Whoever was in there could see out, but no one approaching could see in. A week of surveillance with a conveniently placed camera had recorded a maximum of eight persons on the premises at any time. Most of them young males, possibly students, most arrived by pedal bike or moped. There was one man seemingly in charge of the door who let everyone in and out. Once a week a van arrived. The roller shutters were opened and the van was reversed into the loading bay at the end of the run of units. The door was closed. The van left about an hour later.

The van was a hire van, hired by the same company which rented the units. There was no regularity to the van's arrival. If it was there, then it was a bonus. Satisfied with their preparations, the teams prepared to wait for the train, stopping at Bristol Temple Meads.

Mark Fish was on the fourth floor reviewing the day's intelligence when the phone rang.

'Dave White here.' The caller was brief. 'Tell the boss that we believe the London contact is Julia Grainger.' The call ended.

Mark did not have far to go to pass on the message, Joel Knight was in the next office pacing his size 12 magnum boots wearing a track in the carpet. Alexa Parkes was sitting in his chair, Doc Martin encased feet resting on the desk. 'Don't worry Sarge, it's all going to work out fine.'

Siobhan Williams was already primed. She was part of the interview team who would deal with Tansy Alexander. Alexa Parkes had briefed her well. Siobhan had a good grasp of all things technical and had also liaised with Danny Young in the Hi-Tech unit. He would take whatever devices they seized. Extracting their secrets may take a while but a basic interrogation would be enough for a first interview. Anything seized from Unit 42 would also need examining.

Siobhan read the background package on Tansy Alexander again. Something was bothering her, but she was not certain what. A strange hollow feeling crept into the pit of her stomach.

CHAPTER 29. JULIA GRAINGER

London 2017

Julia Grainger was certain she knew the courier. The striking looking woman in the smart expensive business suit had a face that was familiar. It was the eyes that reminded her, but of what? They were incongruous with the colour of her skin, eyes which looked right through you. Subliminally, some piece of information had found its way in, just in the few brief glimpses she had caught, as the woman handed over the merchandise to the receptionist, at the hotel, and had asked for it to be kept in the safe for collection, by a Mrs Melville Brown.

A memory had started to gnaw at the back of Julia's mind. She needed a better look. Julia Grainger needed a way back into her father's good books. She realised that she had overstepped the mark. In her view her father was overcautious. His caution in a practical test of the product they were starting to market was resulting in a stockpile of what were effectively prototypes. There was no test of their effectiveness. Yes, they had been tested at short range on ballistics dummies, and they certainly looked the part. No self-respecting post-office clerk would hesitate to open the safe if confronted by a hooded robber carrying one of her guns. For that's how she viewed them. This was her baby. Her father wanted out. He was getting too old for the business. Hadn't he told her that she would be in charge?

She had her contacts as well. She had heard rumours of a move to get the Weaver bitch off the hook. With her name cleared, there would be no way to ensure she remained silent. She also suspected that David Holly had enough dirt hidden away to cause a load of aggravation, probably enough to see her father sent down for the rest of his life, unless he continued to protect Holly's interests. She watched discreetly from behind the scenes as the receptionist placed the soft zip-up case containing the Apple Mac into the safe and took a brown A5 envelope from the bottom shelf. She handed the envelope to the courier who tucked it away in the depths of her soft leather shoulder bag. The courier zipped up the bag, slung it carelessly over her shoulder and with a long hip swinging stride pushed her way through the old wooden revolving doors, leaving the old wood and overstuffed leather furnishings of the hotel behind her. Julia knew that she would see the woman again later, in a different place, but the same woman. Their drop off points changed, irregularly, never the same one twice, unless it couldn't be helped. Meanwhile, she would drop the laptop off to be updated and ponder on her knowledge of Tansy Alexander. She ran the name over her in her brain Nothing sprang to mind.

The receptionist handed Julia the laptop in its case, it was not her place to ask questions. Julia handed her an envelope which contained a substantial tip, for services rendered, and headed for the car park. It was business as usual for her. She had no regrets about Little Lenny Smith and the farce which he had caused outside the police station. In her mind it had all been tidied away. The Police were as clueless as usual. She was, in her mind, always one step ahead of the game. The idiots responsible for that fucked up burglary were a bit of a mistake, but they would be sorted when she got back home. All she needed now was to clear the air with her father and all would be right with the world.

In her handbag, her mobile rang. 'Hi pops, how are you this morning?'

'Julia, what the hell are you playing at, child?' She hated it when he called her child.

'Me? Pops! Nothing, I'm just on my way out of town, takin' the Apple to the teacher.' She was surprised that he had broken all his own rules and called her.

'I just had a call from Spain, 'bout a dead body in Glasgow. Tell me it is nothing to do with you girl.' Julia could feel the wave of suppressed anger in his voice.

'Nothing to do with me, pops, I can promise you that.' She lied, convincingly.

'You are making too many waves, daughter. I want you home tomorrow. We need to talk.' The call ended.

Four hundred miles away, Peter Balfour turned on the TV just in time to catch the regional news bulletin. The newsreader was just concluding an article. 'The body of the man has yet to be formally identified but is believed to be that of Joseph Callahan. A Police spokesman for Strathclyde Police has appealed for any information but at this stage the death is not being treated as suspicious.'

Peter Balfour stared at the screen incredulously. 'What the fuck!' The words hung in the air. 'Stupid wee bitch, ye were only supposed tae scare him!' He cursed Julia Grainger roundly. She really was a fucking liability. Pulling on his running shoes, he started out on his usual lap of the golf course behind his house, stopping at the greenkeepers' office to make a quick phone call. Someone down south needed to get their house in order. It was not his call to make. Eighteen hundred miles away a weathered brown hand lifted the receiver. A voice cracked with age but still conveying an inherent air of authority answered. 'Holly.'

'Glasgae', was the one-word reply.

'What the fuck do you want?' Holly was rattled.

'Have ye no' seen the news this mornin'?' Balfour was calm. There was no response from the other end apart from the sound of heavy breathing. 'Have a fucking word with him, this has his wee daughter's smell all over it. Get her sorted or the deal is off.'

The call ended.

Meanwhile, Julia Grainger drove out of the city to a house in the suburbs where a mouse of a youth with thick glasses and the pock marked skin of untreated teenage acne, pallid from a life lived permanently indoors, relieved her of the Apple Mac. She handed it to him through the window of the house, into a dim room lit only by the glow of monitors.

'Four o clock.' The resident troglodyte spoke with a slight stammer. 'I need the cash, you owe me.'

'Three o'clock and I'll pay double.' Julia haggled.

'Half past three, I can't do it before. That's not me, it's my supplier.' The troglodyte was firm.

'Don't fuck me around on this.' Julia threatened.

'Half past three, double bubble, or nothing.' The troglodyte sensed a weakness. He had what she needed. He already had the programme, updated, tested by his source. He could upload it now, while she waited, but he wouldn't tell her that. His supplier said his other customers were very happy with the product. No technical issues. The Americans should know. They sure loved their guns.

'You'd better be being straight with me, I'll be back by half three, with your cash.' Julia curbed her temper. Two minutes later she was parked up outside the health club. She would chill amongst the warmed towels and therapeutic rocks, have a massage, perhaps a glass of Prosecco and think some more about Tansy Alexander.

Start at the very beginning. While the strong hands of the masseuse worked their scented, oiled magic in the knots in her shoulders and slid in a professionally sensuous manner down the muscles either side of her spine, she cleared her mind of the irritation which was her father's voice. He had not been the same since her mother died. He had always been overprotective of his only child. Julia, on the other hand, had tried to fill in where she could, taking on her mother's role, but to no avail. Her father had taken his refuge in a succession of escort girls, all high maintenance, expensive, there at his beckon call. Julia had tried her best then, changed horses, trying her best to be more like her father, more like the son she thought her father always wanted. Well, she thought, he could have ended up with a son like Lenny Smith's. A complete waste of skin. A right little TV gangsta boy. She felt she could do no right.

It had always been the same. Her mother had tried to protect her from life, her father had just terrified people. She had been bullied at school, she was the posh girl, the girl who arrived by car, not by bus like everyone else. She remembered the cringing embarrassment of her mother walking her into the classroom on her first day, the hostile crowd of girls who had encircled her on her way to the canteen that first lunchtime, and who had ruined her schoolbooks and her expensive uniform, uniform from the proper shop, not from the clothing department of the local supermarket.

'But I survived, and I will survive. Pops will come round, won't he, he always does,' she thought to herself. How had she survived, who had taught her survival? Her one friend. Tracy Brown from the homes, Tracy who her father had disapproved of. Tracy who her mother had actually quite liked, who had taught her the survival skills she needed. Tracy who had disappeared. Where was Tracy now, she wondered, her feisty friend with the impossibly long gangly legs, that huge mop of insane curly hair and those…. eyes? 'It's her.' The penny dropped. The blue-green eyes. Tansy Alexander was Tracy Brown.

The masseuse was working in her calf muscles and her long slender feet, pulling and stretching her toes. Julia was supposed to be feeling suitably relaxed and drowsy, but all of a sudden, her brain was working overtime. Remembering an angry conversation between her mother and her father not long after Tracy Brown had disappeared, Julia remembered that she had been inconsolable when her friend had vanished. Her mother had offered to take Tracy in when she was eventually found. Her father had been incandescent with rage at the thought. Julia remembered the last thing she heard him shout at her mother before the voices became hushed. 'Do you know whose daughter that girl is, woman?' Then her mother's reply.

'She is just a girl, like our girl, she deserves a break in life.'

'Well, she can't come here, that's final, she's………..' His voice had gone deathly quiet. So quiet Julia could not hear the final words.

She had solved her mystery. Tansy Alexander the courier was Tracy Brown, she would put the troglodyte's money on it. Maybe her father needed to know just who the Glasgow connection was using to carry his precious information up and down the country. She saw a way back into daddy's good books. Had she identified a weak link in the chain? Lying face down on the massage table she stretched out her body, and as the masseuse finished his work in her toes, she decided what she would do.

A light salad lunch with a Perrier water and a fruit smoothie later, she drove back to the troglodyte and collected the Apple Mac. Good as her word, she paid him the arranged money. She did not stay while he counted it. She would carry it back herself. Fuck Tansy Alexander. She had an old machine in the cupboard, one which had some very distasteful photographs in its latent memory. Her father had told her to get the troglodyte to dispose of it. Julia had never seen the contents. She didn't want to. Now it might just come in useful. She stopped at her flat and picked up the old machine and deposited it as previously arranged in a locker at Paddington Station. She set the locker door to the prearranged code and sat in the café with a clear view of the concourse and waited, just to satisfy herself that she was correct.

Dave White spoke into his covert microphone. His partner was only a few yards behind him. Their target had just alighted from a taxi and was headed onto the concourse. But someone else had caught his eye. Always best to be on the ball, *'cafeteria table in the window,'* anyone watching would think he was only making a phone call. The earpiece would double for an expensive hearing aid, blue-toothed to a smart phone.

The reply came back. 'Julia Grainger, if I'm not mistaken.'

'Thought so.' Whitey remarked. 'Where's our girl?'

'Left luggage, I'm just getting a paper, she's opening a locker, parcel acquired, I'll get on the train, you see what Miss Grainger does.'

Dave stopped at the Subway kiosk and bought himself a foot long roll filled with meatballs and cheese. He hated the things, too much fat. It would repeat on him all the way to Bristol, but it served its purpose. He saw Lee Meredith walking in amongst the passengers a discreet distance behind the lovely Tansy, headed for the first-class carriage. How did Lee get the best half of the deal? Dave would be slumming it at the other end of the train. He was back up just in case anything went seriously wrong and Lee's cover was blown.

As he took the first bite of his Subway roll, looking at the selection of best-selling novels in the window display of WH Smith, he saw the reflection of Julia Grainger walking purposefully towards the exit. He depressed his transmit button again, 'Miss Grainger has left the concourse.'

He heard the announcer calling the stations enroute to Bristol Temple Meads and accelerated his pace, boarding in the second-class carriage behind his colleague just as the guard slammed the last door.

'I'm on,' he whispered to his jacket.

'You cut it fine,' came the reply. 'I'm across the aisle from the target. She's reading.'

Looking down the train through the glass sliding doors he could see Lee sitting with his long legs stretched out, pretending to read the newspaper. He felt the wheels of the train turn into action and the jolt as the carriages started to move. 'Next stop Bristol', he thought, and a reception committee.

Julia Grainger drove herself out of the station car park and took the signs for the M4 westbound. If she didn't hang around, she would get to unit 42 before the train arrived at Bristol. She would speak to her father about Tansy. She could also put the wheels of production into motion.

CHAPTER 30. POLICE, POLICE, POLICE!

Bristol 2017

Police! Police! Police! The sliding door of the van slammed open on its runners, the force making it crash against the end stop. Three officers clad in protective gear wearing helmets and body armour ran the short distance to the front door, the first officer carrying the sixteen kilo Rammit like a twig.

Bang! The door shuddered on its hinges. Two more strikes and the locks caved in, the door flew open.

Two more officers ran to the rear of the building, weapons holstered, armed with side arms and Taser. The windows at the rear were no feasible exit route, they were secured with bars, bars which prevented entry, but also prevented an exit.

A second van, a second team, ran to the roller shutter door, crowbar at the ready, disc cutter to hand.

Police! Police! Police! Stop what you are doing. Stop it now!

Dean Callow could hear the commotion outside. Standing on tip toes he could see the two officers on the narrow path behind the building. Dean had no intention of trying to escape. Best to go quietly. He could hear shouting from the corridor as officers began to smash their way into the other work rooms.

Police! Open the door! Open it now! Bang! One hit with the Rammit and the internal doors opened. Dean opened his from the inside. He pulled it inwards so that the officers could see into the room. Then he sat on his stool and waited. He left the machines running. The police might find that useful.

An officer entered and unceremoniously took him by the arm, pulled his hands behind his back and placed him in a set of handcuffs. Then the officer searched him, thoroughly, placing the contents of his pockets in a bag. The officer stayed with him, but said nothing.

All through the building, there were shouts, bangs, crashes.

The entry team had hit a snag, the office door was reinforced. Trevor the doorman and Julia had sought to lock themselves in and climb out through the window. Their exit was covered. Two armed officers stood, weapons drawn, a short distance away.

'Armed Police! Step away from the window! They shouted a clear warning.

'Armed Police! Stand clear of the door!'

The entry team cut their way through the steel reinforcing plate which was preventing their entry.

Julia Grainger calmed herself. She gave Trevor a look that instantly made him cease his protestations. When the noise died down, both were sitting quietly waiting, compliant with every request.

Across the city, the Paddington train pulled into to platform 13. Tansy closed her book and rose from her seat in the first-class carriage. It was a warm day and she carried her suit jacket hung between the handles of her shoulder bag. Book safely tucked away, she slung the bag onto her shoulder and made for the door.

The platform was busy. Doors slammed behind her as other passengers joined the multitude heading for the exit. She was unconcerned about the man who followed several yards behind her. He was a regular on this train, sometimes he even spoke, or bought her a coffee.

'Target is off the train.' Lee spoke to the covert microphone in his coat collar.

'I have eyes on.' Dave picked up the trail.

Just outside the exit, plain clothes officers alighted from a nondescript blue Ford Sierra. They covered the distance to the exit doors in a few strides.

'Tansy Alexander?' It was a question demanding a response.

'Yes, why?' She was surprised.

'Tansy Alexander, I am arresting you on suspicion of being involved in the manufacture and supply of prohibited weapons.' Handcuffs closed around her delicate wrists. The bracelets nearly too large at their smallest to prevent her pulling her hands through.

Tansy fainted. Her long legs on their high heels folded like Bambi on ice. When she came to, she was surrounded by a sea of faces. None of them seemed friendly. In that moment she could have easily taken a fix, anything to magic her away from all of this. It was time to face the truth.

'You do not have to say anything…..,' the officer cautioned her, the rest of his words lost as she tried to calm her thoughts. What was it Peter had told her? Had he known this was going to happen?

'What am I supposed to have done?' she asked.

She did not get a reply. The officer was too busy securing evidence.

Tansy was searched, her mobile phone was seized. 'Why two?' the officer asked.

She remained silent.

'Why two laptops?'

Again, she remained silent.

A female officer with a face like a dyspeptic baboon sat beside her in the rear of the car.

Tansy's mind was racing. What had Peter involved her in? She knew that whilst most of his business ventures were legitimate, he did not tell her everything. She might be his current girlfriend, but she was always mindful that she was first and foremost an employee. Where Peter Balfour was concerned it paid not to forget your position in life. Too late to cry about it now. Tansy made her decision. She decided what she would do. She hoped that the truth would not be too catastrophic.

In the rear of another police vehicle, heading for a different police station, Julia Grainger was having the same conversation with herself. She, however, had a different problem.

She had arrived at Unit 42 precisely five minutes before the entry team. Her car, engine still warm from its drive down the M4, was parked conspicuously in the car park. The latest versions of the STL files were installed on the Apple Mac which was in her large black leather tote bag. There was only one mobile phone in that bag. She was happy that they would find nothing there, but that was the only thing she was happy about. Her other phone was in the car. The phone she should have destroyed, the phone which could connect her to her father's businesses, the data which could collapse the whole chain, and those number plates, BA51TRD, whatever had possessed her? They had seemed like such a clever touch, at the time.

Julia Grainger thought carefully. She sat in silence and quietly decided that there must be a scapegoat. A scapegoat and a smoke screen. She had the very person in mind. Julia toyed in her mind with what she would say, how she would divert attention away from herself, maintain her innocence, cast suspicion on the woman she knew as her childhood friend, Tracy Brown.

The search teams worked their way through Unit 42 in methodical fashion. one room at a time. There was a video walk through of the whole building. There was a video of the work room where one of the workers who was arrested had conveniently left one of the printers running. One of the team watched in amazement as extruded plastic built itself, layer after layer into a black object, a thick sided plastic part, with precision made holes and indentations. A nondescript piece of plastic, which, unless you knew its identity and its place in the complex mechanical jigsaw, would pass for a piece of a child's toy or something to be thrown into the recycling bin, the whole process now captured on film and labelled with an exhibit number.

There were four young men and two young women in custody. Three of them proved to be illegal immigrants, overstayers on their visas. Three were students subsidising their student loans with this highly lucrative job. Amongst them was Dean Callow, the one who had let his machine keep running, the one who seemed to want to talk. All the others were tight lipped, one might even say terrified.

D.S. Jimmy Fox sucked on his bottom lip. He would speak to Dean Callow later. He organised his interview teams. One for Unit 42, the other to concentrate on Tansy Alexander.

Then they would assess what evidence they had and see where it led. Danny Young and Mark Fish were dealing with the phones and computers and the other technical devices. These would, Jim felt, be the keys which unlocked this case. They might also unlock two murders, one shooting, a burglary, and the wave of corruption which he could feel building, a tsunami of trouble coming inexorably towards him.

Data would take time to acquire, access to phone records was hamstrung by paperwork, forms to be filled in. Every application must be Justified, Proportionate, Legal and Necessary. Wording them was an art form. It was a skill Mark Fish had in spades. He also had contacts with the service providers which might speed up the process slightly.

Danny Young might be a whizz with computers, but extracting the secrets from Windows based laptops and Apple Macs took time. It was pointless trying to rush Danny. It would take as long as it took!

But they could at least get the minor players interviewed. The drones who ran the machines and the monster Trevor who guarded the door. Then to tackle the ladies.

There was a myriad of exhibits to be catalogued, photographed, and stored, vehicles still to be searched. There was also a lot of background reading to be done in other connected cases, all to be done to the time of the custody clock, a clock which had already started ticking.

Jimmy left the scene at Unit 42, the search teams and scenes of crime officers still hard at work. He made his way back to the office, logged on to several computer systems and began to read.

He had already picked and briefed his interview teams.

Fraser and Dawes would deal with Tansy Alexander. Marcus Fraser was a no-nonsense Scot. He had a direct manner and was born in Glasgow. He still had a good knowledge of the area, he was a Rangers supporter after all. He spoke the language. Alison Dawes was an empath.

She had a way of coaxing information out of people. Even the most hardened of criminals ended up telling Alison things they didn't really want to, just because they liked her. Alison was easy to talk to. Alison was their friend! She and Marcus knew how to work an interview.

In a room the other side of the wall to his own, they would be planning, looking at what evidence they had, deciding what they needed, waiting for Mark Fisher to download phone handsets, and for Danny Young to extract the data from the computer hard drives.

Roger Guest and Kim Lucas would deal with Julia Grainger. Again, Jimmy chose carefully from the strengths in his team. From all the background reading Jimmy had done, Julia Grainger seemed to be the weak link. All the arrows pointed to her as being arrogant, hasty, hot tempered and the maker of unconsidered decisions. From what Jimmy knew of her father, Paul Grainger was careful, he liked a low profile. He had kept himself under the radar for many years, making a good deal of money with fingers in many criminal pies. Julia was the heir to the throne. Paul was getting older. He had taken his finger off the pulse.

Kim Lucas looked like a shrinking violet. She was tiny. How she had ever managed to convince anyone she was tall enough to join the police, she did not know. She professed to be five feet four inches tall, the minimum height for an officer, at the time. She wore thick spectacles and had mouse brown, short, cropped hair. Appearances were deceptive. Kim was probably the most intelligent person Jimmy had ever met, though she never advertised it. She would suck the arrogance out of Julia Grainger, let her talk herself into a corner, then let her try and talk her way out.

Roger Guest? Well, laid-back Roger would play the idiot. He was a Bristol born boy, he knew the culture. He DJ'd in his spare time in one of the clubs, he had family who lived in Bedminster and in St Paul's. His knowledge was encyclopaedic, and he would use it.

Once the formalities of booking in were completed and once they were fully prepared, his teams would get an initial interview with Julia and Tansy. Neither knew the other was in custody. It would remain that was for as long as possible.

Jimmy himself would interview the workers and Trevor. His partner would be drawn from the intelligence office. D.S. Siobhan Williams came to mind. He knew she still had her arm in a sling, but she had seen one of these weapons up close and personal. He didn't expect to get much more than silence from Trevor, but hidden in amongst the others, and to be treated like all the rest, was Dean Callow. Though they didn't know it, several of the others, apart of course from the illegal immigrants, would owe their freedom to Dean Callow, provided, of course, his story checked out.

CHAPTER 31. ONCE MORE UNTO THE BREACH

Bristol 2017

Jimmy and Siobhan had nearly finished interviewing. The illegal immigrants had been handed over to immigration. The students sat in the cells, contemplating their fate. None of them had ever been arrested before. After all, they were law-abiding students of engineering. They had all said the same thing.

They were looking for part time work. They had seen an advert on the notice board at the student's union. They had been interviewed. The job required some knowledge of computers. Then they had signed an agreement or a contract about not telling anyone what they were doing, in case of industrial espionage, they had been told, making prototype parts for the aerospace industry. They were paid well, in cash, at the end of the day. Each and every one of them had said the same thing.

Trevor Clifton was employed as door security, he told them in his smooth baritone voice, his very white teeth with the gold incisor smiling at them across the table. It was his job to monitor the CCTV, let the kids in and out, make sure the place was unlocked in the morning and locked up at night. Oh, and pay the kids. He, himself, was paid cash at the end of the week. On the subject of Julia Grainger, he said that she was the boss, but he rarely saw her. She had turned up today because her courier had let her down. No, he didn't know what they were making. No, he didn't know the name of the courier. Usually, Miss Grainger arrived with a new laptop. She re-programmed the machines and she left. He didn't know, or was deliberately stupid, about the computer side of things. His other job was to help load boxes onto the van which came to collect them. He didn't see what was in the boxes. He didn't know where the boxes went.

Siobhan and Jimmy sat across the table from Dean Callow. Dean seemed anxious to talk to them. He had asked them insistently to look in his backpack. His version of events was the same as all the others.

'The first work room,' he said. 'I left the kit running, I did that on purpose, for you to see.'

'Dean,' said Jimmy, 'don't you think we would have tested it anyway?'

'But it helped you. You could see the actual process, couldn't you. You could actually see what it was we were doing.'

'We could. Thank you for your help, Dean. Now what else do you know?'

'I got to know Trevor.' Dean began. 'I was there a lot, I worked a lot of shifts, see, I wanted extra money for my hobby, and that's how I knew what they were making.'

'You knew?' Siobhan's eyebrows raised.

'After the first week.' Dean continued. 'I shoot rifles. I'm good. I shoot in competitions. I went to range practice. I was cleaning my gun after. Then I realised what I had been making. In plastic.'

'What did you do?' Siobhan held him with her eyes, willing him to say the right thing.

'I was watching the news that evening. I saw the appeal for information and I rang the number. I didn't give my name. I was a bit scared.' Dean was trembling.

'Go on.' Jimmy let Siobhan lead.

'I told them exactly what was going on, and I sent a photo of what I was making. I broke one of the parts and took it out in bits in my sandwich box, wrapped in tinfoil. I have other stuff, in my bag, with my books.'

'With your books?' Siobhan raised an eyebrow.

'Trevor let me take my books in. It's warmer than the house, and it's quieter, I'm revising for my finals. I'm at Uni, doing Engineering.' Dean's look was pleading.

'Get his backpack, Jimmy, it's in the pile of stuff in the office. Let's see what he's got.' Siobhan rubbed her shoulder. It still ached like a fiend.

Use it, the surgeon had said. It still hurt. She wondered if it would ever be pain free again.,

They suspended the interview and Jimmy went to retrieve the battered old rucksack in which Dean Callow carried his books. It had been separated into two clear bags, the rucksack itself in one and the contents in the other.

'In there.' Dean pointed to a large engineering textbook. 'In the centre pages.'

Jimmy opened the book at the indicated place. There, folded neatly was the advertisement he had removed from the engineering notice board.

'Get this bagged for prints, Shonnie, please.' Jimmy separated it from the pile. 'Is there anything else?'

'I took a copy of the contract. It's in that folder, with my lecture notes. Trevor wasn't supposed to let me take it home, but he was in a hurry, it was late. I promised to fetch it back, but I copied it first.' Dean looked hopeful. 'My dad, see, my dad likes paperwork for everything, he told me to make sure it was legit. He worked for BA. I think he smelled a rat.'

Jimmy retrieved the contract and handed it to Siobhan with a latex gloved hand. 'Well done, Dean.'

Dean spoke up. 'Look, you can't be going to do me for this? I risked my life. The others told me. That woman, she's heavy, man, she has people wasted. If they find out it was me….'

'Dean, calm down. My colleague and I need to go and discuss a few things. We have to treat you exactly like the others, for the time being. Get it?' Jimmy was firm with him. 'Back to your cell, we will talk again later.'

They ended the interview and adjourned to Siobhan's office on the fourth floor.

'So, he's the informant.' Jimmy sat back in the spare chair.

'Seems that way. He's told us near enough everything from the Crimestoppers info. Who else would know about how he smuggled that part out.' Siobhan could see the problems coming.

'Well,' said Jimmy, 'our illegal friends get to go home. That's one burden off the taxpayer. As for Dean and the other two, we can't caution them, they haven't admitted anything. We can't charge them. We'd have to charge Dean as well. That could endanger him.'

'Coffee, Jim?' Siobhan suggested. 'I need to check on Mark and the phone work.'

'Can't stand the stuff. Tea for me, please, weak and black, no sugar, just dunk the teabag once.' She laughed at him.

'Not strong and black like your good self, then, Jim?' She winked as she left him and walked down the corridor to the kitchen.

In the end, they decided that they would release the three students on bail. All their phones needed to be examined. Dean would be treated no different from the rest. They would examine the advertisement and the contract, but it would not be brought into evidence unless it was essential. It would be in the unused material in a sealed envelope marked NOT TO BE DISCLOSED. It would take a closed hearing and a brave judge to authorise its disclosure. Dean Callow would be protected. Eventually, if nothing incriminating was found on their phone data, they would all be released. There were bigger fish to fry. Fish who were being interviewed less than a mile away from each other.

'How long with their phones, Shonnie?' Jimmy enquired.

'Knowing Mark, it will all be done and written up in about three weeks.'

'I'll bail the lads for a month, then.' Jimmy's hand went to the phone. He pressed the speed dial button for the custody office. 'They will be safe enough. Julia's father will see to that. He won't want any more waves on his pond. He will ride the storm for the present.'

Custody answered the phone and Jimmy made the arrangements.

'No conditions, bail for a month pending phone work. Have them back within an hour of each other and get a contact number for each of them. Thanks Mike.' Jimmy replaced the receiver.

Now let's see how they're going with Julia.

Julia Grainger. Interview 1.
Interviewing officers:
D.C. Roger Guest
D.C. Kim Lucas
Legal representative – none. Ms Grainger states she has done nothing wrong and does not need any legal advice.

D.C. LUCAS: 'For the benefit of the tape, please confirm your full name and your date of birth.'
D.P. (Detained Person): 'You know full well who I am.'
D.C LUCAS: 'For the tape please, Ms Grainger.'
D.P.: 'I am Julia Melville Grainger. My date of birth is 21st July 1990.'
D.C. LUCAS: 'You have declined legal representation. You have agreed to be interviewed without a solicitor present. Are you still happy to proceed?'
D.P.: 'I have done nothing wrong. I should not be here. Ask your questions, girl.'
D.C. LUCAS: 'You were arrested today at Unit 42, the business premises of a company called MelTech. What is your involvement with that company?'
D.P.: 'It is a company started by my father, but it is now run by me.'
D.C. LUCAS: 'What does it do?'
D.P.: 'We make plastic prototype parts. They are sent to the mother company we make them for and tested. If they are suitable, then they are made up in other materials and used in the aerospace industry. That is what we do.'
D.C. LUCAS: 'How are the parts made?'

D.P.: 'We use 3D laser printers. They build the parts from a programme which is on a computer.'

D.C. GUEST: 'Where do the designs come from?'

D.P.: 'They are sent to us in computer form, already loaded onto a device, an Apple Mac. A courier picks up the laptop from a secure location, leaves it at a secure location for me and I load the programme onto separate data sticks which drive the printers.

D.C. GUEST: 'What is the name of the parent company, who do you work for?'

D.P.: 'I really don't know. My father told me the work was very hush hush. That's why we employ security.'

D.C. LUCAS: 'Yet you employ students and people who are not legally allowed to work in this country'

D.P.: 'The work is not constant. It depends on demand. It's a bit like zero hours, but we pay well.'

D.C. LUCAS: 'When you were arrested, you had an Apple Mac in your possession. Where did that come from?'

D.P.: 'I don't know. The courier let us down. I had to pick it up from the locker myself, in London.'

D.C. GUEST: 'Tell me more about the courier.'

D.P.: 'It used to be a different one each week, now it is the same one. I don't usually see them, but I knew today's courier.'

D.C. GUEST: 'I thought todays courier let you down.'

D.P.: 'I knew her. She was unsafe. I thought she would endanger our work.'

D.C. LUCAS: 'Who was she?'

D.P.: 'Tracy Brown. I was in school with her. I remember my father didn't trust her family.'

D.C. LUCAS: 'So what did you do?'

D.P.: 'I did the run myself. Whatever is on that machine is what she was supposed to be delivering. It's nothing to do with me.'

Kim and Roger decided that this would be a convenient place to stop for the time being. They had Julia's initial explanation. Until they had the technical data, they couldn't disprove what she was saying.

A few miles away, Tansy Alexander sat on the hard bunk of her cell, not so much a bunk as a low shelf wide enough for a human being to lie on, covered with a wipe clean foam mattress which was all of two inches thick. *'Such comfort'*, she thought to herself. There was also a wipe clean pillow, and a grey, army style blanket. She folded the blanket around the pillow and, resting it on her knees, sank her face into it. It was rough, like sandpaper on her skin, a reminder of where she was. She shut her eyes from the glare of the fluorescent ceiling lights and the sight of the unshielded stainless steel toilet bowl in the corner. The plastic covered dome in the corner of the ceiling announced that this cell had CCTV. There would be no privacy here. None at all. Except her thoughts.

Tansy began to order her thoughts. She had declined a solicitor. She knew she could change her mind. but she had done nothing illegal. She did not need one. She began to go through where she had been, and what she had been doing stage by stage.

She was employed by Peter. He paid her expenses. At first, she had been purely one of a number of other couriers doing the same sort of job. She had never met any of the others, but Joey had told her they existed. Some of them had messed up. They had either disappeared, or they had gone to prison. Those who had gone to prison were well looked after when they came out, though they never worked for Peter again.

She had earned enough money in seven years to pay for her flat. She had bought it cash, from Peter. He was a property developer. He could give her a good price, and, after all, he did like her. Nothing illegal there.

Peter booked her rail tickets, always first class. Peter paid for her expensive clothes, clothes which painted a picture, clothes which sent a message - professional, aloof, busy. Do not disturb.

When she was required, she received a text message on a phone she used only for that run. Again, supplied by Peter. The only thing sent to her on her personal phone was a six-digit code, the code for the lock of a storage locker and its post code location. Her burner phone would be there, in the locker. This was also the signal to turn that phone on. One call from Peter would tell her the train times, the destination and the drop-off point. Nothing unlawful there.

Tansy collected an Apple Mac from the storage locker. Never the same locker twice in a row, never any continuity or routine. Suspicious, yes, but no laws broken.

She travelled by train to her appointed destination. She dropped off the Mac usually at a hotel. Then she picked it up several hours later, usually from the same hotel, sometimes from a luggage locker. Again, she was sent the location and the combination for the lock by text. She was never told the account name or password details for the device, never told what data it contained. She then carried it to its destination. Another locker. She never saw who collected it.

While she was not travelling, her time was her own. She could occupy herself in London and in Bristol, sometimes in Cardiff. The only rules were that she never phoned Peter from her personal phone if she was not in Glasgow. When she was working, she took the SIM card out of her personal phone and switched it off. The burner phone she was given for that run would be dismantled and disposed of before she switched her own back on. Only she knew these rules. They were just rules. Suspicious? Maybe, but just his rules, rules to protect her, and his business.

Tansy easily worked out that it was the contents of the Mac which were the issue. Well, she knew nothing of the contents. She was just the messenger. Then, she also knew what had happened to several other messengers. She was Peter's girlfriend. Would she suffer the same fate? While she was pondering, the door lock turned and the door was pulled open.

'I am D.C. Alison Dawes,' a friendly female voice addressed her. The speaker was casually dressed and carrying a leather folder and a sheaf of papers. 'Time to get you interviewed. Come with me.'

D.C. DAWES gestured her to leave the cell and proceed her up the narrow passage through the alley of closed doors on either side, the smell of disinfectant mixed with air freshener and unwashed bodies not fading as they approached the sergeant's desk.

'Going for interview, Sarg.' They walked past the desk and were buzzed through a locked door into another corridor. D.C. DAWES pushed open a door on the right. The Perspex plate on the outside of the door declared it, 'Interview Room 4'.

Sitting at the small table was another officer. He rose from his seat and introduced himself. His accent was familiar and reassuring.

'I am Detective Marcus Fraser, hen, it's Alison and I am goin' tae be interviewing ye today. Have a seat. Do ye no want a brief hen? Ye can have one if ye like.'

Tansy sat on the plastic chair he indicated. She didn't need a 'brief.' She intended to tell the truth. She had nothing to hide. If Peter intended to throw her to the wolves, then she would make sure he got bitten as well. Did he even know where she was? Did he even care?

The interview started with the usual formalities. They asked her about her movements, where she had been, what she was doing. She told them. They asked her about her background, where she came from. Marcus commented that her accent was slightly West Country for a Glaswegian. She told him that she was born in Bristol and that she had moved to Glasgow as a teenager. She omitted that she had come from 'The Homes'. That was, in her mind, not relevant.

They asked about her phones, why she had two. Why was one switched off? She told them, quite reasonably, one was her work phone supplied by her boss, the other was her personal phone. She switched it off because she didn't want her boyfriend tracking her movements. They would soon find out that Joey Callahan was in her contacts. He wasn't her boyfriend, but she knew he kept tabs on her. Boyfriend would do as a descriptor. He was a friend, and he was a boy. With luck they would see him also as her boss.

They asked her for the log-on details for the Mac. She told them she did not know it. She wasn't given that information.

Then they reminded her of the reason for her arrest. They stressed the serious nature of the offence: being involved in the manufacture of prohibited weapons. The words had not sunk in totally until Marcus showed her a picture. A picture of a gun. A machine gun. Tansy didn't know the name of it, she had only seen them on the news or in films and TV programmes. A bad feeling started to grow in the pit of her stomach. She felt slightly sick. She was glad when they put her back in her cell. After Alison Dawes had locked the door, Tansy threw up, the stream of vomit dividing itself equally between the stainless-steel receptacle in the corner and the front of her smart suit jacket.

In the custody office, two detectives watched the monitor, one of many in the bank of them behind the big desk.

'She's terrified,' Marcus began.

'Mentioning the G word did it,' Alison added. 'Well done, Marcus. If she's wise, she'll lawyer up now. She's scared, but she's not stupid.'

'She's kept in the dark for a reason, ye ken. Her masters think what she doesn't know won't kill them. She does'nae realise that she is expendable.' Marcus was confident. 'She'll keep talking.'

Tansy pressed the 'call' button. The custody sergeant looked at Marcus. 'I bet I know what she wants. Go on, go and find out.'

Marcus walked the short distance to Tansy's cell and opened the hatch.

'Room service!' He tried to lighten the mood.

'Would ye tell the Sergeant I've changed ma 'mind. I think I'd like a brief. I think he said there's one on call. I've never needed one before.'

Marcus hid his dismay well. Any brief in these circumstances would probably advise her rightly or wrongly to make no comment. That would make life more difficult for the investigators. But it was her right.

Back at the custody desk, the sergeant was already making the phone call.

'She can sign the record when you get her out again. Looks like she's got Ray Williams.' He looked knowingly at Alison Dawes. 'Can your hormones cope with that?' Then he raised an eyebrow at Marcus, 'Or yours for that matter?'

The second interview steered clear of the events of the day and concentrated mainly on phones, mobile phones and computers. Tansy was obliged to surrender the unlock codes for both her mobiles. She was confident that the information on the new burner phone was minimal. But her own phone? Well, what that was her personal life. There were things on there that only she could know about, but apparently the law said it was an offence not to disclose the passcode for the phones. So, she did. When asked for the log-on details for her own laptop, she complied. She did not and had never known the log-on details for any of the Apple Mac devices. She answered their questions briefly and honestly, guided by the advice given to her by Raymond Williams.

She would not be drawn on the content of the devices which had been seized. After all, how could she remember absolutely every call she had made. She would not itemise the names in her contacts list. If she was allowed reference to the handset, then she would assist. But without that she was not going to guess.

The interview concluded and after another hour or so of waiting Tansy Alexander was released from custody.

CHAPTER 32. CAST ADRIFT- Tansy

Bristol 2017

'Tansy Alexander, you are being released on bail to return to this police station at 3pm in one months' time.' The date was written on the forms but drifted over her head in the mental fog and anticipation of release. 'You are being released as there are further enquires which need to be completed before a decision can be made as to whether you should be charged.'

The custody officer read out a list of conditions by which she must abide during this time of freedom. They included that she lives in Scotland and that she does not enter the city of Bristol except to see her legal representative or to attend court.

'No great hardship there,' Tansy thought to herself, 'and my phone?', she asked hopefully.

'Stays with us until we have finished with it. It is part of the further enquiries.' The man sounded bored now, 'Sign here, and here.' He marked the official pieces of paper which spewed out of the printer with crosses in the required places.

'And my laptop?', she queried.

'Same as the phones.' Came the brusque reply.

Ray Williams hovered in the background, listening intently while the formalities were completed. He was intrigued by his client. In some ways she was harder than the granite of Edinburgh, in others extremely naïve. She seemed to place an almost childlike trust in people but had a deep suspicion of authority. He had only known her for less than half a day, yet he felt he needed to find out more about her. He watched quietly as she signed for her property and was handed the anonymous plastic bag, still sealed with its numbered tag. He watched as she went through the inventory in front of the sergeant behind the desk, making sure all was there, without opening the bag. A novel approach.

He watched the desk sergeant's impatient eyebrows raise as she turned the lining of the big black leather shoulder bag inside out. A pile of fluff and assorted detritus fell onto the desk. A kaleidoscope of pieces of sweet papers, make up and other rubbish. She turned the bag right way in and placed the pile of property back into its depths, leaving the rubbish in a neat pile on the counter. 'Keep that pile of crap, Sarg,' she quipped, 'it seems at home here.'

The Sergeant's stern expression did not quite break into a smile. That would have been too much. Instead, with a flourish he lifted the metal wastepaper bin from the floor behind the desk and swept the jetsam of Tansy's life into the trash. She placed the sealed bag inside the leather one. She took her shoes off the counter, straightened her clothes, shouldered the bag.

'See you in a month then.' Tansy stepped into her heels and smiled at the bemused policeman. 'Which way is out, Mr Williams?'
The exit door buzzed, and prisoner and lawyer stepped into the outside world.

'Coffee before you go?' Ray offered. 'We need a chat where there's no chance of being overheard.'

They crossed the road and Ray guided her into a small café, not a big chain coffee shop. He sat her at a table and went to the counter, returning with two mugs of coffee, a small jug of milk and a bowl of sugar.

'Instant, okay?'

'Sounds good, my train isn't for hours, I need to buy a mobile. I'm still not quite sure what's going on here.'

'In what way, not sure? You were arrested for a serious offence. The police need to make more enquiries, so, they've given you bail.'

'Guns! I have nothing to do with guns. I won't have anything to do with guns.' Things started to sink in, her voice started to tremble, 'I could go down.'

'You could.' Ray commented. 'You could go to prison for a very long time.'

'What will they do? I mean, my phone, what can they prove with that?'

Ray took a mouthful of his coffee and then a deep breath in. He returned to the counter and returned with two donuts.

'You were carrying two phones. The police have asked themselves why. You have told them one is your personal phone. One is for work. One your boss pays for. The other is yours. They have asked you who your boss is. You have told them Joey Callahan. If that is true, then they will want to find connections between you and him, patterns of calls, other contacts.

They will download both phones, they will have lists of your contacts, details of your text messages, your voice mails. Did anyone tell you, Tansy, Joey Callahan is dead?'

Tansy was shocked. Much as she despised Joey for what he had become, she couldn't think of him as dead. 'When?' She asked.

'Last week, they found him in the Glasgow graving dock. He was drunk and full of drugs. They think it was an accident.'

'Not Joey, not drugs. If there were drugs in Joey's veins then that was no accident. Joey liked a drink, and he supplied H to half the city, but he never touched the stuff. Never.' She shook her head to make the point.

'What is on your phone, Tansy, is there anything I should know about?'

'My personal has all the usual stuff. Calls to friends, business contacts, customers. The other is clean. I was supposed to contact Joey when I made the drop. It never happened. Oh, and there's a text telling where to pick up.' Tansy was certain.

'And the laptops?' He asked, 'I have a feeling the police are very interested in them.'

'One is my own, I write songs, I have music software on it. It also houses my portfolio of photographs. It's easier than carrying a huge folder everywhere. The Mac, I don't know. I was told it was business records and computer programmes which needed to be transported securely. I can't access any of it, I just pick up and drop off, as and when requested. I'm paid well, and in between drops I get to pursue my dreams.'

'Your dreams, which are?' He was curious.

'Acting, music, modelling. I don't intend spending my whole life travelling on the Glasgow express.'

'Who is Peter Balfour?' The name hovered in the air. Tansy was silent, blanched, and inhaled crumbs from the donut she had bitten into, coughing them back onto the plate.

'Don't answer that, they've obviously got others in custody elsewhere. I overhear things all the time, but think about that. I don't know who else has been arrested, or who they are looking for, but that name was mentioned. His and Julia Grainger.'

'Julia Grainger. I was in school with Julia. Her father is...' She stopped.

'What the hell am I involved in, Mr Williams?'

Ray looked at his client. He saw a vulnerable woman, a very attractive, very vulnerable woman hiding behind a façade. For the first time that day he believed her.

'If you want my opinion, someone is trying to use you as a scapegoat. If you want my advice, if you are trying to protect that person, don't. Think of yourself, look after you!'

Tansy finished her coffee and her donut. She delved into the depths of her bag and found her purse. 'I'll get these.' She rose and went to pay. Suddenly she felt the need to talk. She bought two more drinks and two more donuts, resuming her seat across the small table in the window of the café, with its stained melamine top and pink plastic flowers displayed in a disused vinegar bottle.

'Mr Williams, may I call you Ray? Without your lawyer's head on, what would you do?'

'Miss Alexander: Tansy. You are one of those people whose face makes it clear when they are lying. You have what some people call a glass face. You are plainly intelligent, plainly capable. I don't know who you work for, but they don't deserve you. If it is Joey Callahan, which I doubt, given your reaction to my mention of Mr Balfour, then with Joey dead, there is nothing to be gained by lying. As for Julia Grainger's involvement, I do not know what evidence they have to connect her with anything. It would be unprofessional of me to speculate.'

'I shall go home then to Glasgow. I shall take stock of my life and wait. With Joey dead, and all of this,' she shrugged her shoulders, 'I have no job, no employer. Maybe I should take a holiday?'

'As long as you are back here on the prescribed date, that's fine. But don't draw too much attention to yourself, and be vigilant. It wouldn't surprise me if they have you tailed, to see where you go next, what you do, who you run to.'

She was easy to talk to, those piercing blue eyes, unusual in her dark skin, that mass of hair, the long nimble fingers curled around the plain white cheap pottery mug, the way she licked the donut sugar from her lip and deftly stopped the escaped eruption of jam from running down her chin onto her blouse. Ray didn't want to stop talking.

'What is your connection with Julia Grainger then?' He asked.

'I told you. I was in school with her, but I went north when I was fourteen. I haven't seen her since. Her home was the complete opposite to mine. Her mother was lovely. Her father was, well, he was a bit scary. We heard things about him. Not nice things. She had everything we didn't. Where it came from, we didn't ask.'

'Why did you leave?', he fished.

'Family stuff, you know, I needed to go,' she evaded., 'like I need to go now.' She looked at her watch. 'Look, I need to dash. I have to buy a phone and catch a train, but thank you, Ray, you've been very helpful.'

Bag slung over her shoulder, she left the café, her long striding walk in those high heels visibly distracting the workmen on the scaffolding across the road. Ray heard the whistles and shouts of approval as she passed.

Her first stop was the Phone Shop where she bought a new iPhone handset. A call to her service provider arranged for it to be uploaded with all the data from her old phone. A few settings later, she had programmed her old phone to erase. Next time it connected to the wi-fi it would remotely reset itself to factory settings. Her next purchase was a change of clothes: underwear, jeans, T shirt, sweatshirt, jacket, trainers. She left the heels and business suit hanging on the changing room hook. Then she headed for the train.

Her ticket was open ended, flexible. Peter thought of everything, including unexpected delays. Delays of this sort, though, Tansy wondered. She plugged her new phone into the USB port by her seat. She would not insert the SIM card until she was home in Glasgow. Then she would ring Peter from a clean phone with a clean number.

Behind her in the carriage Lee Meredith took his seat, his back to her, nothing but a few seats between them. Spare clothing for several days stuffed into a backpack, hair freshly cut, clean shaven, he was quite looking forward to a month in Glasgow. Lost in thought, Tansy didn't notice that he was there.

Doors slammed and whistles blew, and the Glasgow train lurched into motion. Wedging the soft leather shoulder bag between her cheek and the window Tansy Alexander fell asleep, the sway of the carriage lulling her into a false sense of security. A small smile reached her lips as she thought of Peter.

CHAPTER 33. CLIENT CONFIDENTIALITY – Ray Williams

It was drummed into me at law school and all through my years learning my trade, as it were. Client confidentiality. Yet, as I drove home after my day spent with Tansy Alexander, I had never felt the need to breach this trust more.

There was something about her which intrigued me. She drew me in, fascinated me, even. It wasn't the way she looked, though she was stunningly beautiful in a quirky way, distinctive looking yet still able to blend into a crowd if she wanted. She had demonstrated this ability as soon as she left me in the back street café where I had bought her coffee and donuts and given her the benefit of my off the record advice.

In a hurry to catch her train and needing to buy a new mobile phone, she had left me sitting at the table. Her goodbyes were short but polite, her smile as she made them, dazzling. Then she had glided through the door and into a street crowded with shoppers.

During our meeting she had taken the trouble to organise the contents of the huge leather shoulder bag she carried. While she had been in custody, the police had emptied it, searched it, removed anything they thought might contain evidence. They had handed the remains back to her in an impersonal clear plastic bag, sealed with a numbered tag, the contents of which she had signed as being correct. Tansy had placed the whole plastic bag in the leather sack, not bothering to reinstate the contents in her haste to be free.

She was unconcerned that half the customers of The Jerry Can, knew exactly where her plastic bag had originated. Most of the clientele were familiar with the serial numbered blue plastic property tags. No eyebrows were raised, no eyelids batted. Replacing cash and credit cards into her wallet, a man's fold over wallet not a lady's purse, he noted. She had winked and smiled at him, reading his thoughts.

'Fits in the back pocket of ma' jeans, I'm a jeans girl in ma spare time.'

Her accent was West Country but with a slight Scottish twang at the edges. Then she had sorted through the rest, seeing the enforced emptying of her private property as an opportunity to de-clutter. A bright red neck scarf cum bandana appeared, the sort a motorcyclist might wear to stop the draft getting into their throat. I had one myself, I thought. Again, she read my thought.

'Keeps the thatch under control,' She laughed and demonstrated. 'and hides the chaos if it needs a trim.'

Then she folded it neatly and filed it away in the depths, to be followed by a wide-toothed comb and a small tin of cherry flavoured lip salve, this only after she had applied a fine coating to her lower lip and rubbed it in with her upper one. She placed the dog-eared remains of several old business cards and an over stretched elastic hair bobble in the ashtray which adorned the centre of our table, alongside the menu and the tomato sauce bottle. A large leather-bound diary was placed on the table. I was surprised the police hadn't kept it.

Again, she read my thought. 'It's empty,' she remarked. 'Bastards kept the full one, and my bloody notebook. I write everything in there, all my thoughts and stuff. That'll be an eye opener for someone!'
As she dropped a set of keys into the interior side pocket, I realised that subconsciously I had not been watching my client, I had been watching my wife. The similarity of movement, the economy with which she did everything, the raise of an eyebrow, the mannerisms of her hands. Yes, that was it, she talked with her hands, just like Siobhan. And there was something about those blue eyes, the tilt of the corners. If I could ignore the madness of dark curly hair and the olive brown skin and just view the bright blue windows situated in the four inches of face at the bridge of her nose, the eyes section of a photo fit, the ones they show in crime dramas, Tansy Alexander and Siobhan Williams had the same eyes.

I watched as she slung her bag over her shoulder and vanished down the street. Then I took the tea mugs and the rest of the crockery back to the counter. On my way out I removed a hair bobble tangled with a mass of strands of black hair from the pile in the ashtray. I slid it into the small plastic bag I keep in my pocket for emergencies. Who knows when a client might produce a piece of evidence which needs saving. Then I walked, deep in thought, back to the office, changed out of my suit and into my motorcycle leathers and made my journey home.

By the time I arrived at our house, the boys were fed and watered and playing upstairs, their presence in Joshua's bedroom marked by the occasional 'thump' on the floor. As I stashed my helmet in the hall cupboard, I heard Siobhan shout up to them from the kitchen to, 'Calm it down, you heathens!' There would be ten minutes of quiet after a reprimand, then battle would resume in earnest. Boys would be boys. The noises of teenage rough and tumble between brothers was the punctuation to our domestic life.

I could smell the smells of something garlicky coming from the kitchen. Dinner was underway.

'Red or White?' My wife asked my preference on wine. 'Get changed, it's nearly ready. Simple tonight, just chilli and garlic bread. It's been one hell of a day.'

This is where the talking in great generalities started. There could be no, 'How was your day in detail?' conversation, our worlds overlapped far too much for that. However, we did trust each other not to overstep the mark, I knew that nothing we talked of over dinner would leave our house. Nothing told in confidence could slide into a conversation over a glass of Rioja.

So, I heard brief details of a raid on a factory unit, the mountain of technical work it had generated, and the prospect that, despite all their best endeavours, nothing might come of it.

In return I told her of an intriguing client, whose apparent naivety seemed completely genuine. I gave Siobhan no details, just the bald statement that I did not think that my client was capable of lying.
We were curled up on the sofa together finishing the first bottle of red when I broached the subject.

'In many ways my client scared me, Shonnie.' It was a throw away remark.

'I thought you said she was naïve and not a liar. How is that so scary?' came the reply.

'I took her for coffee and a bit of a debrief before she got out of dodge. She is bailed not to enter the city unless it's for legal visits or to attend court.' I paused. 'I got to know her a bit better, her personality and such.'

Shonnie wriggled into the corner of the settee and sat up, bristling.

'Ray Williams - don't tell me you fancy her! I thought those days had gone.' She was suspicious. Since the burglary and the shooting, she had been very insecure about everything. 'Don't do this to me Raymond, don't spoil this evening!'

'No, no, nothing like that.' I lied slightly. Well, a man is allowed to look, isn't he? 'There were bits of her that reminded me of you.'

'Are you telling me, your client, a scumbag escort girl from bloody Scotland, was like your wife, the woman you are supposed to love?' She was upset.

I took her by both arms, I pulled her towards me and looked her straight in the face. There was no way to hide what I needed to say, no dressing it up. 'Shonnie, I think that Tansy Alexander may be your sister.'

'*Fuck off!*' She spat the words at me. 'Just *fuck off*, my sister couldn't be her. My sister is.....' She burst into tears. 'I don't know what the fuck my sister is, or where the fuck my sister is, but she's *not* a fucking escort girl from fucking Glasgow.' Shonnie gulped down her glass of wine and poured the rest of the bottle into her glass. 'If you want a refill there's another bottle in the rack, open it yourself.'

I decided against wine and poured a large scotch for myself. I thought I might need it. If I knew my wife. She would sit for a while and brood, then she would think, reason would kick in and she would examine the facts. It might take minutes, or hours, but I would have to wait until the storm clouds cleared. Then maybe she would talk reasonably. I wondered whether Tansy had this trait as well, or whether her temper came from a different set of genes.

I turned the television on and watched the news, then scrolled up and down the channels looking for something new to watch. Hundreds of channels yet nothing interesting, just endless repeats.

It was several hours later before Shonnie came round. She turned to face me, unfolding from the curled up protective heap she had rolled into in the corner of the upholstery. She was emerging from what I sometimes called, 'Hedgehog Mode'.

'What does she look like, this Tansy woman?' Shonnie's voice was a whisper.

I described as best I could the woman I had drunk coffee with and whose virtual hand I had held all day, in strained circumstances.

'She's tall, she's dark skinned, has very blue eyes and a mass of black curly hair, not quite an Afro, but nearly. She's built like a supermodel, legs like a racehorse.' As soon as I paused, I knew that that was completely the wrong thing to say. The response was cutting.

'Oh, so you fucking noticed the legs then. I suppose she has a tight little arse as well, watched it wiggle as you put her on the train, did you?' Siobhan was angry. In the early days of our relationship, I had not been an angel. There had been times when I had caved in to temptation.

'As a matter of fact, she did.' I made light of it and laughed at my wife, 'very pert, quite disturbing in fact. No, I didn't watch it for long, only out of the café door, and I didn't walk her to the train. I thought about offering her a lift, but I only have the one helmet.'

Siobhan laughed, her face broke into a lopsided smile, it reminded me of Tansy! 'You remember that, Raymond. You have one helmet, you stray, and I may just cut it off for you.' She ran her hand down my cheek over the emerging stubble. 'So, she's good looking then?'

'Very.' I replied.

'How can you possibly think we are related based on a few gestures and some eyes? Loads of people are similar in those ways.' She was on side now, sense of humour restored.

'Things she said about her past. She's not Scottish by birth, she went north when she was fourteen. She ran away. She found a place in Glasgow, but it went wrong after a few years, then she ran away again. She's been a missing person, so she says, since she was sixteen.'

'I'm going to bed,' my wife whispered to me through a yawn, 'can we talk more about this in the morning, I've a day off. I'll get all the paperwork out, maybe call Malcolm. See if he can remember anything Mum said on the subject'. Then she took me by the wrist and dragged me off the couch and towards the stairs. 'Come with me Ray, it's not a night to be alone.'

I followed willingly, watching another pert backside, the legs were not quite as long, but the wiggle was just as seductive. 'Hmmmm.' I ventured.

'Enjoying the view?' came the giggly reply. Red wine was taking effect. 'Maybe a wiggly arse runs in the family.'

Well, I thought to myself, not wishing to break the mood, 'The world loves a smartarse.'

I followed my wife past the doors of our sleeping sons' bedrooms into our own and proceeded to show her exactly why she would always be the woman for me.

In the morning there was the reality of family life, two nearly teenaged boys to be sorted for school. I saw them safe onto the bus. It was a journey they were very familiar with. The other end saw a short walk to the school gates. By the time I returned, Siobhan had the island unit in the kitchen submerged in paper, everything she knew about herself. It was a lot of paper, but not a lot of information.

Siobhan was making notes in a blue hard backed book, probably liberated from work's stationary stores. Every detective I had ever met carried a 'blue book'. She was writing down what she knew was fact, what she actually knew to be true.

Her father was Tony Weaver – he was dead, killed by her mother. She had learned this from the documents they had found in their office and from the newspaper clipping in the old shoe box.

Her mother was Cassandra Weaver. Cassandra had served her sentence, had signed papers to have her daughters adopted, had been released after eighteen years. Then she had dropped off the radar. She had been free for ten years but had made no effort to find her children.

Why? Siobhan wrote in the margin. Why hadn't Cassandra come looking?

Where? was her next question. She had asked Mark Fish to make some enquiries in that direction. Then work had overtaken them and enquiries of that nature were put on the back burner.

She had a dim memory of a children's home, but that place no longer existed. It had been demolished years ago. The adoption papers sent to her mother told her little more than what she knew already. She had a sister, somewhere out there, unless that sister had died, a sister whose name had probably been changed, a sister who had been found a home, but separated from her sibling, a sister whose birth name she no longer remembered - unless she was the Amy who sometimes arrived in her subconscious.

'There is one way to find out.' Siobhan looked up from her scribbling. 'DNA. We could go through one of those companies, you know the ones that they use in those programmes on the telly, or Ancestry. I'm sure Malcolm will know more. He has done his family tree. I suppose I am part of it. I can submit mine easily. Problem is, getting hold of your client's. Do you think she'd give another sample. Did they swab her before she was bailed?'

'You will have to wait until she comes back. The honest thing to do is ask her but not until she knows where her life is headed.' I had a feeling my wife was considering something which was highly unethical and definitely unlawful. I did not tell her about the elastic band and its entanglement of torn out hair, the hair bobble which I had removed from the ashtray at The Jerry Can. Maybe I could make use of it.

Lawyers, after all, were not as accountable as police officers, were they.

CHAPTER 34. THE RAIN IN SPAIN – Paul Melville Grainger

Paul Grainger dialled a number he had not used for several years. In fact, he wasn't even sure it was still the man's number. It rang out...... that was an encouraging start. There was an answer. Terse as usual. No change there.

'Who is it?'

'Is that you, Holly?' Grainger wasn't sure.

'Who wants him?' The voice was old, not as forceful as it had once been. Tired even.

'It's me, yer old friend Paul. I need you to pull in a favour, my man.' Grainger's voice was honey smooth and mildly threatening.

'Sorry, wrong number.' Holly replaced the receiver; the line went dead. Was there no peace for an old man? He thought he had left it all behind him, hoped he had cut himself free of the tentacles of his old life. He was happy to live on the proceeds. He had a nice lifestyle, a stunning apartment with a roof terrace and unobstructed views of the sea and the mountains. He ate in the best restaurants. He had few friends, but that was not unusual for him. Most of the ex-pats who engaged him in conversation only did so once. He had only two subjects of conversation, himself, and himself. Most of the time he managed to combine the two in one.

His phone rang again. Same incoming number. Holly did not answer. Maybe it was time he changed his number. He would do that this afternoon. Changing a SIM card was easy, he could buy one for a few euros in the shop next to his apartment block.

Paul Grainger was incandescent. Much as he despised Holly, he had been useful in the past. All useful things in Grainger's book had a shelf life. Maybe Mr Holly was past his 'use by' date. Grainger made another call. The conversation was short and to the point. Then he called his daughter Julia. That call too was short

'Julia, my darling, best you come see me NOW.'

He did not wait for her response. He terminated the call and paced the floor of his office, mind focussed on damage limitation.

He was waiting for her when she arrived, the big electric gates to his house opening before her, no need to press any buttons. He must be watching the camera. She parked the Mercedes on the crisp, crunchy gravel of the driveway and, collecting her thoughts together, prepared to face the music. Julia had fucked up, and she knew it. He was sitting at the breakfast bar in the kitchen, his huge hands knotting and unknotting a tea towel. The devil was in his mind and his idle hands were itchy. She dropped her shoulder bag on the counter.

'What's up, Pops?' It was the wrong question to ask.

'What's up? You are fucking up! Big time. Please tell me you haven't spent a pleasant day in the cells, Julia. Please tell me that Babylon have not been crawling all over us like a nasty rash. No. You can't, can you.' He spat his words out in a vicious torrent. His eyes fixed on his hands which were now gripping the edge of the granite work top like a vice. 'Say something, daughter, explain.'

'I don't know how it happened, nothing has been out of the ordinary, nothing to connect the factory with any of the rest.' She fumbled for words.

'And just who started all, *'the rest',* may I ask, what did you think would happen? Not even the cops we own are able to ignore shootings and murder on their patch. Tell me, Julia, what do you suggest we do? Your father does not intend to spend time over the wall, but I see it coming, girl, yes, I see it coming.' He was shaking as he spoke.

'The courier, you *must* know about the courier, she's got to be the weak link. I know her, Pops! You know her too, from years ago. Do you remember Tracy Brown?' Julia was thinking on her feet.

'What about her!? I don't know any Tracy Brown. Tell me!' He was still now, only his lips moving, his whole-body rigid with tension.

'I was in school with her, remember? She used to come to the house, she was my friend.' Julia let him think. Better if he remembered by himself.

'The girl from the children's home? The one who ran away?' He was rubbing his chin now. 'I remember, she was ……..' it all came flooding back to him. 'Are you sure it's her?'

'I would know her anywhere, Pops. I didn't think you would want her in our business. I know all about her father. I don't know who he was, but I heard you talking about Tony, how treacherous he had been. I remember all the trouble, the fuss when you found out who my friend was.' Julia was soothing. Her father let her speak. 'In London, I swapped the machines, I did the run myself. I gave her a different Mac, one with a bit more than STL files for her to think about.'

'So, you handled the one for the work unit?' Paul spoke quietly.

'There was no other way.' His daughter replied.

'And tell me where it was when the police crashed the door?' His voice was nearly a whisper.

'In my bag.' The words hung in the air. 'I had only just got there. They must have been following me.'

'So, my darling daughter, your stupidity has just cost me a lucrative business, and when the wooden tops figure out exactly what they've got, I might be looking at spending my retirement behind bars.' His face was in his hands

'But there is nothing to link you….,' she began.

'Nothing to link me - are you that dense?' He was thinking. 'If this courier is anything to do with Glasgow and she talks, it comes right back to my door. I need to know what she said, Julia.'

'Maybe you should phone a friend, Pops.' Julia made light of it with a feeble attempt at humour.

'My dear, I already did, and I am clean out of lifelines. Those days are gone. You keep your nose clean, let me deal with Glasgow in my own way.' He ended the conversation. 'You do as I say for once, Julia. You do not put one foot out of place, do you hear me?'

'Loud and clear.' Julia crossed the room and taking two glasses from a cupboard and a bottle of good whisky from the cabinet alongside them, she poured two healthy measures. Reaching into the ice dispenser of the huge American fridge, she dropped a cube into each. 'I know it's early, but I need this. Don't worry, Pops, I shall keep my head down.' Julia lied; she was already planning her next move.

'Now tell me, quietly, what exactly do the police have on you?' Rage had passed, he was thinking reasonably once more.

Julia told him everything, about recognising Tracy, deciding to carry the goods herself, about the journey back from London. She was almost certain she was not followed. Arriving at Unit 42. Then before she had time to do anything more, the raid.

She had given a prepared statement in interview. It said that she was the manager of a firm who manufactured prototype parts for the aerospace industry. The work was highly secretive. That there was a likelihood of industrial espionage, so she couriered the new designs herself, by car from a secure drop in London. That was all she was willing to say. She did not know what the parts were for, or where they were sent after they were completed.

They had asked their questions anyway, as she knew they would. She had kept her answers tightly to the script, not wishing to seem unhelpful.

She had been released on bail to return in a month, once the police had investigated the phones and technical devices seized. She knew that the illegals were being deported, and that the students had been given bail on the same terms as her own. Now it was a waiting game.
Julia left her father's house with a plan in mind, a plan to find out what exactly Tracy Brown was up to. A plan to find out who and what exactly went on in Glasgow.

Paul Grainger finished his whisky, pouring the last of the liquid in the glass down his throat in one. He breathed in deeply. There was one last avenue he could try. One man who might be able to call in a favour for him, though he doubted very much that Big Lenny Smith would do anything to help him. But Lenny did owe him one from many years ago, and a debt was never left unpaid. He owed Lenny an apology at least, for his daughters' behaviour. He owed him an assurance that the death of Little Lenny could not be laid at his door. Maybe Lenny Smith would listen to his old cell mate and come through for him.

Paul Grainger rinsed the whisky tumblers and left them to drain, then he went to the walk-in wardrobe which adjoined his huge bedroom. He found his black suit, black tie, white shirt, and his black overcoat, they had not been worn since his wife's funeral. They would fit, he prided himself that he had not run to fat like so many of the brothers. He was just contemplating another cup of coffee before he hit the gym, when his mobile rang.

'Grainger.' He answered brusquely.

'It is done,' the anonymous voice in heavily accented Spanish replied. Then the call ended. The number had not identified, he didn't think it would. He smiled quietly to himself and filled the kettle. Today, he decided, he would visit his wife's grave, leave some flowers. Tomorrow would be another day.

Julia, too, was making phone calls. She could find no trace of Tracy Brown. Why was she searching for a name? It was the person she wanted. Surely, she knew enough about the courier to find out where she lived. She had heard her father talking to a contact in Glasgow. That seemed to be a good place to start. For once her contacts were good. Julia would not leave this to chance. She was going in person. Her target had been found. It would only be a matter of time before it let its guard down. The Mercedes she had acquired was a saloon, an anonymous black, tinted glass. The boot was large, large enough to carry enough luggage for a family of four going on a two-week holiday. She was assured that it was clean, not stolen and had not been used in the commission of any crime. The registration plates were swapped with those from an identical model, the donor vehicle currently resident in the long stay car park of Bristol Airport, purely a precautionary measure.

Julia began the long trip north. She would meet Andrew Fairclough, her pet hunting dog, on the banks of the Clyde. He had located the courier and was keeping tabs on her. She had paid Andrew well for his services. He knew better than to fuck this up.

She did not tell her father where she was going. She was a grown up. She didn't need to 'clock in' with him. He had other things on his mind these days. The least he knew, the better.

CHAPTER 35. PLUNGED INTO DARKNESS – Tansy

Glasgow 2017

She had been home five days. She had not spoken to a soul. Peter was keeping his distance. She knew that. He was putting space between himself and the chaos which was breaking out at the other end of his empire. No doubt he was cleaning up any of the loose ends that could be traced back in his direction.

Unable to sleep, she had spent the night listening to music and staring out of the huge window and out across the river and the city. There had not even been Joey to talk to. Tansy had not felt this alone for years. Not since the bad days. She steeled her mind. She would not go back there. She knew where to go, she knew who to see. She could get fixed up within an hour if she really wanted that kind of oblivion. But no. She would not.

She listened to the sounds of the seagulls shuffling their webbed feet along the overhang above her window. The raucous yap-yap-yap as one launched itself into the dawn, in search of food, whether it was fresh from the Clyde, if that were possible, or foraged from an overfilled rubbish bin. The scavengers of the sky would be fed. Dawn was breaking. It was a new day. '*Stay in,*' he had ordered her in the only call he had made. '*Don't go out.*' Well, she had to eat, didn't she. Now she needed fresh air, or she felt she would disappear down the old rabbit hole of addiction. She would not go there again.

Tansy donned her old joggers and trainers, an oversize hoody over a scruffy T shirt. Carrying only her phone she left her flat and made for the riverbank. She needed to stretch her legs, get some air, clear her mind. The morning mist swirled off the river. It hung in grey wreaths over the shoreline, not even the seagulls were visible in its depths. By breakfast time it would have lifted to reveal the true nature of the day.

The watchers stirred in their cramped old transit van. It was parked a good distance away. They were alerted by the device they had installed on the entrance door to the block. It told them whenever any of the residents entered or left. They had not had the opportunity to wire her flat itself. Too risky. She had obviously been warned they might be watching her. The alarm buzzed, as it had buzzed many times in the last five days. Each time a false alarm.

Dave White did not see the tall figure dressed in grey emerging from the doorway. Dave was tired and irritable, eyes still adjusting to the dim light of the morning. The figure had bent to adjust a shoelace, taking her out of camera view, just for a second. As his vision cleared, what he did see was a figure in a camouflage pattern sweat top, and a khaki pull on woolly hat stride out along the path towards the river. Dave clicked the shutter button of the camera more for something to do than any sense of efficiency.

'False alarm,' he grunted to his partner, Lee. 'Not her.' He wrote the movement in the log sheet. 'Take over for five, I need a pee.'

He slid quietly out of the side door of the van, breaking wind silently as he left.

'Have more than a pee while you're out there, you smelly bastard, and pick up some breakfast. I'll hold the fort.' Lee growled after him. After all, this was their last day on the job. This evening, they could pack up. They could hand back the rusty builders' van which was used for surveillance by their Scottish friends. BAG OUR PIPES plumbing and heating would be hidden away in some back street garage and its exterior re painted for another job, no doubt.

The target had done nothing of note in the five days she had been back. She had bought food. She had bought coffee. They could see the light go on and off in her apartment. She had not been out. She had not phoned anyone. Their presence was no longer justified. The boss had pulled the plug. Lee was relieved. He didn't think he could survive another night with Dave White's bowel habits. They both needed a shower, and he definitely needed a pint. The door slid open and Dave slipped into his seat.

'Coffee and MacDonalds breakfast.' He handed Lee a cardboard tray. 'Sorry about the guts, should be okay now. Greasy food. Plays havoc with my insides.'

'Dropped the kids off, have you?' Lee replied, dryly raising an eyebrow. 'I wondered where you got to.'

The alarm buzzed again, and Lee noted a tall male figure entering the flats. Tall, blonde, middle aged, collar up. Features not visible. He wrote in the log and automatically pressed the shutter button again. The camera clicked several times.

'Not seen him before,' Lee muttered, reaching for the folder which contained the list of residents and their descriptions, 'but he looks familiar and he's not on the list.'

'Probably a visitor.' Dave replied.

'It's a bit bloody early for visitors. Wait until he comes out.' Lee wiped a dribble of egg Mac muffin from his chin.

They did not have to wait long. The alarm buzzed and the tall man left the building. He walked straight past the van, close enough for them to see plainly who it was.

'Shit!' Lee formed the word in a mumble of breadcrumbs.

'Fucking Batman!', Dave echoed as a fist pounded urgently on the door of their mobile workplace. Dave had not bothered to lock the door and it slid open. Bruce Wayne's face was worried.

'You pair of fucking idiots! She's gone! You missed her!' He spoke slowly enunciating the words syllable by syllable.

'She hasn't!' spat Lee, crumbs flying towards the retired D.I.s face.

'Watch back if you like. Some guy in camo and a woolly hat went out earlier, but no woman, and not her, we'd know her, wouldn't we, Dave.' He looked to Dave for back up. 'What's it got to do with you anyway, you're ancient history, a civvy now.'

'Your target is out and about. Do you have the slightest idea where she is or what she is up to?' Wayne raised an eyebrow.

'You don't know that.' Dave argued.

'Well, her flat is empty. I've been there. I checked.' Wayne was concerned.

'But we only saw that guy, he was alone.' Lee scrolled back through the morning's footage. Back to where the buzzer had first woken them. He zoomed in – there she was bending below the level of the camera, a millisecond of curly black hair caught in the corner of the frame. Gone. Just before the other male appeared. Bruce was not surprised they had missed it. He was more concerned that his instinct told him that the other male was following her.

'Put out observations for the guy in camo gear. Sightings only. Do it now. If she has gone for a run she'll be back, and no harm done. Just hope she appears soon.'

Bruce issued instructions. Dave and Lee looked stunned. But it made sense, and when the job was examined, it was their arses covered. No mention would be made of Bruce Wayne. Dave lifted the phone and made the call. Minutes later the two-way radio hanging in its harness from the roof crackled to life. 'Observations were requested.'

Tansy had re-tied her laces out of habit. Flexing her hips as she did so, she stepped forward still slightly crouched, then shook her head and walked out of the unseen camera's range. Then she broke into a jog, heading for the river. Her route took her along past the graving dock where Joey had been found face down in the stagnant water, over the footbridge and out towards her old home, Marcia's flat. She lengthened her stride, hood up and oblivious to the man jogging several yards behind her.

Eventually her route turned back towards home, back through the industrial wastelands and the riverbank. The male behind her waited for his moment. It might not come today. He would bide his time. He had waited for Callahan, had he not. He felt the phone vibrate in the small pack he carried at his waist.

'Do you have her?' The voice was demanding.

'Be patient, not yet., he replied through the Bluetooth hands free.

'It must be today. It can't wait longer.' He sighed and hung up. He sensed that his boss was in a vehicle following him, issuing orders, making demands.

Tansy stopped for a moment, leaning on the railings and looking out over the water. She would weather this storm, then she would follow her dream. Break free, go to London. She could model, she could act, and she knew she could sing. It was time for a change. She pushed herself away from the railings and turned into the alley which was a short cut back to town. Engrossed in her own thoughts she did not hear him.

The world went dark, a hood was pulled over her head, a hand like a vice clapped over her mouth. Her scream was muffled in the taste of latex gloves, a metallic prod in the ribs conveyed a message far more direct than words. She peed herself in fright. She was gagged, a rag stuffed into her mouth and bound with some other form of tie. Her arms were pinioned behind her back. Hand cuffs, she had felt those on her wrists before. The rigid type. Unyielding, painful. Then she was lifted bodily and slung into the rear of a vehicle. Hard landing on steel, the smell of diesel, the bounce of the suspension. Her legs were curled up and foetus like she lay on her side. The boot slammed shut. She could hardly breath, only her nose allowed air into her body. She tried not to cry, tears led to snot, snot would restrict her air. Breathe Tansy, keep calm and breathe. Count the bends, concentrate. She mentally mapped each turn in the road, imagining the route in her mind. It may help if she survived. It was something to occupy her screaming mind if not.

The car stopped. Silence. The boot opened. She was lifted. Slung face down over a shoulder. She sensed high walls around her. The creak of a door. Then headphones. No, these had no music, they were ear defenders. Taped on over the hood. She heard the screech of wide tape unrolling. Duct tape, that was what they called it. More duct tape around her ankles. Then nothing. She was dropped again. Another steel floor. Then nothing.

Tansy lay in a heap. She straightened her legs, ran an inventory of her body parts. She was tied up and handcuffed. She could not hear, or see, or speak. Total sensory deprivation. She had seen it on a documentary. Keep calm. Think. Find a weakness. They had not beaten her. She was not injured. Just restrained. Deep under the folds of her hoodie, wedged in the armpit of her sports bra she still had her phone. She could feel it. That bastard who had lifted her off the street had been in a rush. He hadn't searched her properly. She had some means of communication, at least. If not a signal.

She wiggled herself onto her back and pushed herself until she hit a steel wall. Ridged in places. 'Shit,' she thought, a shipping container. But the floor was at least dry, though it stank. She found a ridge in the metal and like a pig scratching its ear on a fence started to work on the headphones. Little by little the tape started to fray. She felt movement. Have a break, then start again. It took what seemed like hours but eventually she shook her head and heard the thud as they landed on the floor. 'Thud' she heard it. Her ears were back online.

She pushed and wriggled herself into a standing position and began to hop inelegantly around the internal perimeter of her steel prison. Her shoulders were burning with the pain of being pinned back. She arched her back slightly and rotated them in their sockets. Some relief but not much. Still blinded by the hood she could see nothing but could feel the ridge in the wall where the door hinged. She was tall, she ran the side of her head along the edge of the metal, working upwards, her ear feeling the rubber seal. The butt of the hinge caught on the cloth of the hood. Jerking her head back she felt it rip. Then a little more, but still no light. She needed to get out of the hand cuffs. A tall order for anyone of any size. Tansy however was blessed with slim hands and wrists. Long elegant fingers kept strong and supple from playing guitar. One cuff was tight, so tight her left hand was starting to go numb, but the left had not been ratcheted to its smallest.

Experimentally she wriggled the restraints up her wrists then flexing her fingers she curled the thumb towards her little finger, rolling her palm inwards, pointing her fingers, and straightening her knuckles. Then she wiggled the metal bracelet downwards. Pinning it against the metal wall at waist height she continued to work her right hand upwards. There was pain as her skin stretched and the steel scraped and broke the surface. She gritted her teeth and felt the single bar of the cuff give a little, it would never break she knew that, but the millimetre of room allowed the knuckle of her thumb through the gap.

She felt the blood returning to her fingers and, also, running down her hand as it came free. One hand back. No – both hands, though one still had the black hand grip hanging from it. Frantically she ripped the gag and the hood from her head and the tape from her ankles. Exhausted with the effort she leant on her hands and allowed herself the luxury of tears.

She was just taking stock of her predicament. A shipping container, she decided. She reached into her underwear for the phone and switched it on. That's why he missed it. The man had scanned her for devices, but she'd kept hers switched off. Peter insisted on it. He didn't want anyone tracking their movements.

No signal. She left it switched on. If anyone had missed her. It was there. She had just readjusted her clothing, squatted to relieve herself in the corner, the call of nature would not wait, when she heard the creak of the hinges on the outside. They were expecting a trussed up helpless body. She hid in the darkness, holding the handgrip of the cuffs like a dagger in her left hand.

The door swung outwards allowing the light in. Tansy shielded her eyes against the glare, unused to the brightness. A large torch was shone into the darkness.

'Where the fuck is she?' Tansy recognised that voice.

'Julia,' her voice caught in her throat. 'Julia Grainger?' Tansy leapt at the figure like a panther, lashing out, using the handcuffs as a weapon. Julia Grainger fell to the floor. Tansy felt male hands grabbing at her, but her own hands were fixed to Grainger's throat. She could hear herself screaming, 'Why, Julia, why?'

Then a sharp pain in the back of her head and more darkness. They did not bother to tie her as before. The cuffs were removed and replaced with tight cable ties. The gag was tightened. She was again placed in the boot of the Mercedes.

It was Bruce Wayne who made the call. 'Unidentified number' appeared on the display of Peter Balfour's phone. 'I told you no calls!' He was angry. No familiar voice answered. 'Who is this?', he growled, his accent thick and almost unintelligible.

'She's in trouble.' It was a male voice he did not know.
Peter was silent. Should he help or let her sink? 'What do you want?' he asked. He didn't question who he was asking.

'Find her phone, we know you keep tabs on her. She may have it with her.' Bruce was to the point.

'Who the fuck is this?' Peter was cagey.

'A friend you shouldn't have, a friend of hers.' Bruce was vague.

'It will be switched off, it's what we do.' Peter heard the strain in Bruce's voice.

'Check and keep checking. If it goes live ring this number.' Peter wrote down the given number on a post it. 'Don't fucking ring her.'

'Hold on, I'm looking.' The screen refreshed, and a blue dot appeared.

'Why the fuck is she in the dockyard?' Peter's heart lurched. 'Who are you for gods' sake, and where are you? I need to find her.'

'I'm in the black Toyota parked outside.' Bruce Wayne introduced himself, looking up from the steering wheel as Peter dropped into the seat alongside him. 'Belt yourself up.'

Peter Balfour decided that he could like this man. The cavalry was on its way. They would find Tansy, wherever she was. The metallic bulge in the leather pouch under his left arm was a comfort. He felt Bruce depress the accelerator and kept his eyes on the screen of his phone as the one blue dot left the city and headed for the M74 motorway, travelling south.

They had been driving for about twenty minutes and had just crossed over the river Clyde when Bruce took his foot off the accelerator. Peter could just make out the rear of a black vehicle ahead of them, travelling at the maximum of the speed limit, blending in with the traffic. He noticed that the blue dots on his screen were not far apart.

Bruce spoke. 'That's the car, that Merc, black, four cars ahead.'

'How do you know?' Pete was curious.

'I know the car, and I know the driver well. I know her father. He's a friend of yours, or so I've been told.'

'Who?' Pete was shocked. 'What friend of mine would do this to Tansy.'

'Paul Grainger. But it's not his style. This has his daughter's mark all over it.'

'So, what do we do?' Peter was at a loss.

'Did you know that the Police have been watching Tansy? But they messed up this morning, they lost her, they're probably still chasing their tails around Glasgow looking for a jogger in a woolly hat. They are trying to connect her to you. She's been a good girl so far. They have nothing to go on.'

'We can'nae involve the Polis then, can we.' The Glasgow accent thickened. 'Who the fuck are you, then?'

'I'm an interested party. My interests are in Bristol. Let's say they are personal rather than criminal.' Bruce was circumspect. What could he say? His goal was to find Cassandra, to protect Siobhan Williams and her team and to expose the corrupt, Holly in particular. 'How much do you really know about Tansy Alexander?' Bruce continued.

'She's smart, she's beautiful. She makes my head spin. Joey Callahan was her pimp and her dealer. I paid him well to get her clean and in my employ. She's reliable, good at what she does.' Pete could have said more, what he didn't say resonated in Bruce's mind.

'She wasn't always Tansy.' Bruce left the statement hanging in the air as he changed gear and moved into the outside lane.

'She never talks about her past, but Callahan was always picking up runaways from the homes, nothing would surprise me.' Pete expanded. 'I din'nae really care, she's an adult now, she could go places. I should let her, after all this is over.'

The car accelerated. Bruce closed the gap slightly. 'Under your seat, see if you can see her in the car.'

Pete did as he was asked. Under the passenger seat he found a gun sight. He placed it to his eye and adjusted it. The rear screen of the Mercedes came into view. 'No rear seat passengers. Just the driver and a guy.' Peter fell silent. 'They've killed her, haven't they, her body is in the fucking boot.'

'She was alive when she switched her phone on. Julia will need her alive. Julia is taking her home.' Bruce was confident. 'Julia had fucked up. Daddy is not pleased with Julia, oh, no. Julia is trying to clear her name without implicating her daddy. She is trying to place everything at your door.'

'But how does she know Tansy?'

'She doesn't. She knows Tracy Brown. They were school friends in Bristol. But it runs deeper than that. It all goes back to Tony Weaver. Tony and Cassandra. That's where it all started.'

'Din' nae talk in riddles, man, I can'nae understand it all, tae me she's just Tansy, and I may even be in love wi' her, her past dis' na matter a bit.'

'It's her past that could get her killed.'

They drove for over six hours without a break, much of it in silence. As Bruce turned off the M4 motorway and onto the M32 heading for

Bristol city centre, he wondered where Julia Grainger would take her captive, like a spider taking her prey back to the centre of the web. In her airless metal prison, Tansy heard the crunch of gravel under the wheels of the car, then they stopped. The engine was switched off, two doors opened and through the steel and plush carpet which muffled the sound she heard voices.

'He never goes out at this time of day. He should be in his office.' It was Julia.

'Well, his car's not here, maybe he had a meeting,' a male voice answered.

'That, or he's shacked up with one of his harem.' Julia again.
'No wait, isn't it that memorial thing today, said he needed to go to the cemetery, something about Big Lenny's boy?' The male voice again.

'Get her out then, we'll just have to wait. We can ask her a few questions while we wait.'

The boot lid opened. Tansy shut her eyes unaccustomed to the light. She felt slightly sick. Her legs felt like pieces of string, knotted at the ends. The same man pulled her roughly out of her prison. As her vision cleared, she could see him. He was short and stocky, built like a bulldog, his face half covered with a neck scarf, sandy coloured like those worn by desert soldiers. His hair was buzz cut, what remained of it was black, and his skin was swarthy and pockmarked. Or were those black dots tattoos? His eyes were a strange light brown, almost amber in colour. He was strong, arms like a wrestler, and encased in dark green combat trousers and a cameo pattern parka. All he needed was an assault rifle and he'd be an extra in a Rambo movie.

Rambo frogmarched her towards the rear of the house, a house where she had once played as a child, added to over the years, but still the same stylish property. The gym was in a separate building, a set of detached garages, with an office space and a spare bedroom suite above, and a comprehensively equipped workout area. Paul Grainger liked to think he kept himself fit.

Rambo tapped in a code to the keypad lock. The door opened. She was shoved without ceremony into the building. He sat her on an incline bench, the back fully raised, pinioned her arms behind her back and around the seat back. Her shoulders burned and she winced in protest. It was pointless struggling. He taped her legs to the metal frame. Only when she was totally immobilised did he remove the gag from her mouth.

Air rushed into her lungs, the shock of it making her vomit down her front. Bile burned up her throat and down her chin as she retched, unable to move against her bindings. Rambo laughed at her in disgust.

'Give her a drink, before she chokes to death.' Julia threw him a bottle of water. 'I need her alive.'

Grudgingly he poured water into her arid mouth. She savoured the cool clean feeling. She swallowed gratefully. He let her drink half the bottle. Then the world went dark again as he covered her head with another hood, securing it with another cloth gag wedged into her dry mouth.

More wheels on gravel. She heard car tyres crunch on the surface. 'This must be the old man back.' Julia headed for the door to greet him. Tansy heard the tramp of boots, several sets of boots.

'Julia Grainger?' The man's voice was formal. 'I am Detective Inspector Lawrence Coleman.' Tansy could see in her mind that he was showing his ID. 'May I come in?' He was polite. 'I think you need to sit down. I have some bad news for you.'

Julia was cool. She showed no sign of emotion. 'Come into the main house, detective. Can I get you refreshment of any kind?'

Tansy heard them heading for the door to the kitchen. She envisaged Julia ushering the policeman into the huge open plan room with its granite work tops and stainless-steel appliances. Then she heard the scream.

Julia's scream from the house was drowned by the crash of six armed officers through the door of the gymnasium. 'Armed police!' The warning was shouted. 'Lie on the floor! Do it NOW!'

Tansy heard Rambo hit the deck. She heard his grunts and pointless protests as he was handcuffed.

'What on earth is going on here?' The voice sounded amazed but friendly. 'Don't panic, luv, I'm a police officer. I'm going to untie you. The gag is coming off. Don't scream.'

Slowly the officer removed cable ties and duct tape, unbound her hands and feet, removed the hood from her head and sat her on one of the crash mats with her back against the wall. He handed her a fresh bottle of water and broke the seal on the top for her. 'Drink it slowly, one mouthful at a time.' His voice was kindly. He had removed his protective helmet. His black fatigues fairly dripped with armaments: handcuffs, baton, taser, side arm. He wore body armour and a camera. He was a fearsome sight, but Tansy had never been so pleased to see a copper as she was at that moment. Then she heard a familiar voice behind them shouting to her over their heads.

'Are ye alright, hen? If she's harmed ye I'll...', his words stopped, muzzling the threat. 'Can I no' just see her before we go, just tae see she's alright?'

Looking up from her seat on the floor, Tansy saw Peter. He too was accompanied by an officer. Peter was handcuffed and unprotesting, his hands in front of him. 'It's all fine Tans,' din'nae worry fer me, ay. Are ye OK!?'

She struggled to her feet, still unsteady on her legs. Wobbling over to him, she hugged him. 'You know me, Pete, I'm a survivor. Six hours in the boot of a car won't kill me.' She tried to make light of it.

The officer at his elbow ended the conversation before it started.

'There you are, you've seen her, she's fine, we have to go.'

'I'll call you later, Tans'. Leave your phone on! There's a guy waiting for you called Bruce. He'll look after you 'til I get out. Do as he tells ye, aye!'

Then Peter was gone ushered out of the door into a waiting plain car. Several hours later, certified as medically fit and having made a formal statement, Tansy was released. As Peter had predicted, there was a tall blonde man waiting for her outside the nick. He drove a very smart Toyota sports car and looked a little like James Bond. He introduced himself as, 'Bruce Wayne; you may call me Batman.'

CHAPTER 36. RETRIBUTION – Lenny Smith

Bristol 2017

Lenny Smith eased his huge shoulders into the black suit jacket. He had worn this suit too often in the last few weeks. Jesus, he had buried his wife, Dolores, only two weeks ago. Poor woman, she had lost the will to live after the death of their son and had found no comfort despite the best efforts of family and community. She had gone to bed one night and simply not woken up. The cause of her death had been unclear. Maybe it was possible to die of a broken heart. Coroner's report pending.

He straightened the waistcoat, breathing in gently to fasten the buttons over his less than athletic waistline.

Now, at last, his son's body had been released for burial. The community church where Dolores had been a pillar, and Little Lenny had attended Sunday school as a small child, had organised the service and memorial.

Lenny Smith had lived in the area all his life. He had graduated from minor crime to drug dealing via a short custodial sentence, then to marriage, the church and redemption. He had been a community councillor for many years, flying the flag for the young people. Self-educated and remarkably well-read courtesy of Her Majesty's Prison, he now counted the great and the good amongst his friends and acquaintances. But he never forgot his roots.

Outside his three-storey terraced house, the long black car waited. The car which would take him to say a last farewell to his family, for Dolores and Little Lenny were the only family he had. Well, the car could wait a moment longer.

Lenny poured himself a large glass of neat rum. He savoured the feeling as the liquor burned a trail down his throat and the vapour filled the back of his nose. He hadn't eaten, he couldn't face food. He hadn't eaten for days. The rum made him lightheaded. He drained the glass and looked studiously at his reflection in the mirror hung on the chimney breast above the gas fire. He saw an old man.

His thoughts turned to his son. Lenny. Twenty years old. So much to live for. Lenny who lived for his car and his girls. Lenny who liked to smoke weed, too much weed. Lenny who was indulged by his mother, always forgiven by his father, never held to account by his own peers or his father's peers, everyone too scared to tell the father about his son's misdemeanours and gradual descent into the criminal underbelly of the city.

Big Lenny knew who had sanctioned the killing of his son. He knew that person well. They had grown up together. He fully expected the man to turn up today. The man would be brazen enough to pay his respects, brazen enough to think he was untouchable, that he could get away with murder. Maybe he hadn't pulled the trigger himself, but he had ordered it. Big Lenny had learned to bide his time. He had learned to control the volcanic rage which burned in him as a young man. His body may have gone soft with age and business lunches, but his mind was still hard. It didn't do to upset him.

The chauffeur adjusted the mirrors and wiped dust off the walnut dashboard of the waiting car. He looked at the front door of the house anticipating the arrival of his only passenger. No movement yet. He sat back in his seat and waited.

Lenny opened the back door and crossed the small back yard to the outdoor privy. He had forbidden Dolores to get rid of it as the rest of the street had done. He kind of loved the old Victorian plumbing, it was solid and reliable. He stood on the small steps he kept in the outhouse for this purpose and reached into the toilet cistern. The Glock 19 Compact was wrapped in plastic, the bullets were kept similarly dry. Lenny spent time in his privy, door locked, cleaning it. He had not used it for a while. He supposed he should have disposed of it, handed it in, in one of the many amnesties the local plod organised in an effort to keep guns off the streets. But Lenny could not bear to part with it. Now it would come in useful. He loaded the clip and checked that the safety was on. Then slid the semi-automatic into the inner pocket of his suit. Shame it spoiled the hang of the jacket, but he would be wearing an overcoat. It would not be seen.

He walked back into the house, locked the back door, removed the family photo of the three of them at Weston Super Mare from its frame and, folding it carefully, placed it in his wallet. Then he locked the front door and walked out to the waiting car. The hearse carrying the body of his son was parked a short distance away. As Lenny slid into the rear of the chauffeured car, there was only one word in his mind. 'Why?' He smiled at the chauffeur and thanked him for waiting. The driver pulled away from the kerb. The wreath bedecked hearse followed.

The community church was packed. The seats were full. Mourners stood in the side aisles and those who could not find a place inside the building stood in the small remembrance garden outside. Amongst the crowd Lenny could see friends and associates of his own. Friends of Dolores, dressed in colourful Caribbean style, there, to celebrate the life of the dynamo that had been Dolores and the youth who had been Little Lenny Smith. Little Lenny's peers arrived dressed respectfully in formal suits, no sign of the gang colours they usually sported, no baseball caps, no hoodies. Big Lenny's eyes scanned the crowd. No sign of him yet then.

Six of his son's friends carried the coffin, draped in a flag of red gold and green, shoulder high to the front of the church.

The service was moving. The pastor spoke of the tragedy of a young life taken too early. One of his friends spoke of the camaraderie they shared, his love of music, his passion for cars. The reading was from the lyrics of Black Uhuru. What is life?

Cars in convoy snaked across the city making their way to the cemetery to the south of Bristol. The cemetery, too, was already filled with mourners, many out of respect for Big Lenny, community figures, councillors, dignitaries, those not wishing to intrude on the privacy of the service in the church.

Big Lenny clocked him as he was driven in through the big, gothic style, iron gates. There he was, sitting, waiting, in his low-slung black Mercedes, the privacy glass obscuring the side view, but clearly visible through the windscreen. Lenny held his cool. He stood at the graveside while his son was lowered into the ground, the same hole into which they had lowered the coffin of his wife. The pastor completed the service.

Earth to earth, ashes to ashes, dust to dust. Once again, Lenny threw a handful of earth onto a coffin lid. He heard the hollow thud of similar handfuls landing as he turned away from the graveside. Mourners came and shook his hand, gave their condolences and sympathies.

Seeking a moment's solitude, Lenny stepped out of sight of the main body of people. The crowd seemed to sense his need, no one followed him. He was standing in the shade of one of the huge yew trees, staring down at his Sunday best shoes, the ones Dolores had cleaned and polished and kept in a cloth bag in the bottom of the wardrobe. Lenny sensed the man's presence, smelled the expensive sandalwood and spice scented aftershave. When he looked up, he was looking at a man nearly as large as himself. Paul Melville Grainger.

'I am truly sorry for your loss, Lenny.' Grainger offered his hand in friendship. 'You and me, Lenny, we go back a long way, if there's anything I can do?'

'Thank you, Paul.' Lenny was cool. 'My Dolores was always friends with your Alicia, always wished my Lenny would be close with your Julia.'

'As I said, if there's anything.' Grainger turned to walk back to his car.

'Maybe there is.' Lenny turned to walk with him. 'Let's talk where no flapping ears can hear us.'

Grainger gestured towards his car. 'There is as good a place as any.' Grainger slid into the back seat, more comfortable for a chat. Lenny slid alongside him.

'I've heard a lot of talk,' Lenny started, 'not very pleasant talk.'

Grainger said nothing. Lenny continued 'You know my boy was murdered, shot through the head, in his own flat.'

'A terrible business. I heard it was retired Babylon who pulled the trigger.' Grainger was quick to volunteer information, too quick.

'That's what I was told, too. But the Police, the Babylon, they say different. They tell me to look closer to home, your home.' Lenny adjusted his position in the seat, pulling the gun from his coat. He pressed it hard into Grainger ribs. 'Tell me you didn't order the kill, Paul.'

'With my hand on my heart, I did not.' Grainger was truthful, though he knew what the next question would be.

'Now tell me your family had nothing to do with it.' Lenny placed the muzzle of the gun to Grainger's head.

'Why do you believe the Babylon, Lenny? They lie to us. They defend their own.' Lenny had heard enough.

The sound of the gun was muffled by the airtight insulation of the car. What sound there was, was lost amongst the dispersing mourners. Big Lenny climbed into the driver's seat of Paul Grainger's Mercedes, the lifeless body of the car's owner still in the rear, his brain spread like an explosion of redcurrant jelly over the white of the headlining and the cream leather of the seats.

The keys were in the owner's pocket. The car started on a push button. The engine growled into life. Lenny selected drive and pulled smoothly away, leaving his chauffeur sitting waiting for a passenger who would not materialise any time soon.

Lenny parked the Mercedes in the disabled bay. It seemed appropriate. He drew in a breath and walked up to the glass front doors. He pushed the door open and stood for a moment on the blue Lino tiles. He read the posters on the walls, framed behind Perspex screens, the appeal for information alongside the photograph of his son, an old photograph. Lenny was still wearing is school uniform. He approached the reinforced security screen and pressed the buzzer requesting attention. A weary looking woman in her mid-thirties raised her head from a computer screen.

'How can I help you, sir? she asked in a most unenthusiastic and unhelpful manner.

'I need to speak to an officer.' Lenny asked. His voice was completely calm. He knew exactly what he was doing.

'What is it you need an officer for?' The woman was persistent.

'Please, fetch an officer.' The woman had left her seat and now recognised Lenny Smith, Councillor Lenny Smith. She also saw what she thought was blood spattering his usually smart clothing. She pressed a button under the counter, the one which summoned help from the depths of the building. Then she opened the door to a small side room. 'Have a seat, Mr Smith. Someone will be with you directly.'

Lenny calmly sat himself at the cheap office table, on the plastic office chair, and waited. He still had a gun in his pocket. But he waited patiently just the same.

He had been waiting for about twenty minutes when the front doors crashed open, and a uniformed officer burst into the foyer.

'Let me in, Betty!' His voice was urgent as he called to the desk clerk.

'Before you disappear, can you have a word with Lenny Smith, he's in the interview room.' No officer had answered Betty's earlier summons. Not unusual. At this time of day, they would be in their pre-shift briefing.

'Lenny Smith, Big Lenny? I will if you get the Serg out here. Someone needs to explain why Paul Grainger is in the disabled bay.' P.C. Graham Lloyd was going slightly ashen.

'Shall I call the traffic warden then? She's not scared to give him a ticket.' Betty's voice dripped with sarcasm. God almighty, student officers had no gumption about them these days.

Lenny Smith rose from his seat and drew himself up to his full six feet seven and nearly twenty stone. He completely filled the doorway of the tiny square side room. 'I think you'll find he needs more than a ticket, man.' The deep West Indian drawl held a hint of humour. 'I tink you might fin' that he is dead.'

Grahams Lloyd's mouth opened and closed like that of a goldfish. His face bore an expression of complete disbelief.

Betty took control. She emerged from behind her counter and bustled her way out into the street.

Lenny Smith spoke again. 'Young man, I have come to confess my sin.'

Graham Lloyd was physically sick in the wastepaper bin. To cover his embarrassment, he followed Betty through the door to the outside world.

The inner door to the interview room opened and Sergeant Billy Price appeared. 'If you need a priest, Mr Smith, you need to try the church. It's not a service we offer.'

'Sergeant Price, William. Don't you remember me?' Lenny was smiling nastily. He did not appreciate the smart answer.

Billy Price's memory dredged for information frantically. Lenny spoke again. 'Sergeant Price, please take me seriously, or I may just hang you from another set of railings. Do you remember me now?'

It all came flooding back, the embarrassing recollection of a young Constable being rescued by his colleagues, having been lifted bodily by a much younger Lenny Smith and hung by his trouser belt from the park railings, his size eleven boots suspended six inches from the floor.

'I have come to confess to the murder of Paul Grainger. His body is in the back of his car, which is parked in your disabled bay. The keys are in his pocket.' Billy Price sucked a breath in. Lenny continued 'I shot him in the head, with this.' Lenny took the gun from his pocket, removed the bullet clip, made it safe and placed it on the table. 'I have made it safe for my protection, not yours, you wouldn't know which end was which, now would you.'

'Well, Mr Smith, under the circumstances, the confessional is this way.'

Billy Price opened the door to the inner sanctum and ushered Lenny inside. 'Betty, be a love and get the duty CID in from wherever they are, and get SOCO to deal with the car, and a firearms officer for that gun. Oh, and make sure that idiot Lloyd isn't sick over anything else.'

Taking Lenny Smith by the arm he guided him through three sets of double locked doors. 'Lenny Smith, I am arresting you on suspicion of murder.' In reply to the caution Lenny replied, 'Sergeant Price, there is no hint of suspicion about it.' Billy Price opened the flap of the custody counter and started the formalities of booking his prisoner in.

'Before you start, I don't want a brief. I know I'm not coming out for a very long time. I did it, there is no more to say.' Lenny Smith still knew his way to the cells even though he hadn't been there for many years. Some things are never forgotten.

He took off his shoes, left his jewellery and his belt on the counter along with his wallet and his other personal possessions. He walked in his stocking feet down the passage where he knew the cells were. Number four, that was the one they had usually kept for him when he was a delinquent teenager. Number four would do just fine. As he lay down on the hard bunk with the thin foam mattress and stared up at the grubby beige paint of the ceiling, a great feeling of peace descended over him.

'Everything was goin' to be a 'right.' He felt that his son and his wife were close to him. He had done right by them. He would gladly pay the price.

CHAPTER 37. SPANISH FLY

Marbella 2017

Wheels screeched on melting tarmac, engines thrown into reverse thrust, the rhythm created by the joints in the runway gradually slowed and a ripple of applause filtered through the cabin. Over enthusiastic children bounced in their seats. Fathers stood in the aisle reaching down Ninja Turtle backpacks from the overhead lockers, eager to be first off the plane and into the sunshine. The two slightly shy men in Row 8, Seats D and E remained seated. No rush. There was luggage to be collected, immigration to pass through. Not a problem with freedom of movement and open borders. Brexit, as they were calling the exit of Britain from the European Union would change all that. It was the only thing on which they really differed in opinion. Stevie was for leaving. Chris was not. Time would tell who was right. They were in love with each other, why let a small thing like politics come between them?

Stevie and Chris were on their first holiday together. They had not been a couple for long. They were still unsure of how to behave around each other. And as for being a couple, in public? Well, that was a whole new ball game.

The flight from Bristol airport had been uneventful, less than two hours. Smooth take-off and landing, no turbulence to report. The male cabin crew had winked at them in a conspiratorial manner when Stevie had ordered a bottle of champagne. They had drunk it flying over France, it was all very exciting. Very romantic.

The taxi from the airport to the apartment they were renting for their week in the sun had taken just under an hour. Now, here they were, standing outside the whitewashed low-rise block with their shared suitcase waiting for the apartment manager to furnish them with keys, take their registration details and show them up to their accommodation. Stevie had rented the place from a friend of a friend. Well, not so much a friend as a business acquaintance. It had been highly recommended. The apartment was huge, open plan, and had a view out over the sea. If the boys didn't want to venture out to the clubs in the local town, then they could relax by the rooftop pool, watch the sun set over the ocean and just be by themselves.

Juan, the manager, completed his checklist and put their suitcase in the elevator. In minutes he was showing them around their home for a week. They were not disappointed.

The lounge was huge, all marble tiled flooring with understated furnishings in sandy browns and pale blue. Glass sliding doors opened easily and quietly onto a wide expanse of private terrace which housed a small plunge pool - just big enough for two, thought Chris. There was an open plan, well equipped kitchen. Stevie didn't think that would get used much. The refrigerator was already stocked with fizz. Oh, and there was a bottle chilling in an ice bucket on the counter, with two glasses alongside.

There were two bedrooms, the boys only needed one. The huge bed was scattered with rose petals and decked with artistically arranged pillows.

Welcome to Spain. Julia really had thought of everything.

Juan pushed their suitcase into the room, swiftly demonstrated how the air conditioning worked and reminded them that it did not work with the doors open, then handed them the keys and wished them a good stay.

Stevie fell backwards onto the bed, pulling Chris down with him. They rolled around together like a pair of puppies, playful at first, but the play rapidly developing into more.

'I think I'm going to enjoy this week.' Chris nipped playfully at Stevie's left nipple. 'Thank you so much, Steve, I really do love you.'

That night they didn't bother to explore the club scene of the town. They opened the bottle of fizz and explored each other instead.

Dawn blasted her way in through the open doors, no slightly tinted glass to hinder her progress. Chris patrolled the kitchen and located a supply of bread and olives in the refrigerator, along with goat's cheese, milk and coffee. This would do for breakfast. They could pick up something more traditional on their travels. He found the cafetière, put the kettle on to boil and prepared the first meal of their holidays. They sat naked at the table on the terrace, out of sight of everyone except themselves, and ate, both looking forward to what the day might bring.

'I wonder if we have neighbours?' Stevie began. 'There's definitely an apartment next door, must be a mirror of this one though, terrace and pool at the other end.'

'If we have, I didn't hear anyone, but then I was a bit distracted last night.' Chris kissed Stevie gently on the lips. Stevie thought it tasted of goat's cheese and coffee and fresh bread. He felt his body responding.

'Put me down, Christopher. Today is a day to explore. You can abuse my body later.' Stevie did not intend to spend the whole of his week away in bed, though there were worse ideas. He intended to make the most of the sun and the sea and get to know his lover with his clothes on. 'Let's walk the prom later, we need supplies, Julia won't have shopped for a week. We can check out the beach, find a friendly bar, perhaps have a dip in the sea. It looks marvellous.'

The sea did look enticing. It shimmered blue and green, with low silver and white wave crests, gently whooshing onto the golden sand of the newly cleaned sea front. Large floral parasols stood in neatly ordered ranks and files, their symmetry not yet disordered by the morning's influx of sun worshippers.

Two hours later, Chris having had his way with Stevie, a matter which had not taken much persuasion, they ventured out. Clad in shorts, obligatory multi-coloured shirt and flip-flop sandals, they walked, hands just touching, along the paved promenade.

When they returned mid-afternoon, slightly drunk on Spanish beer and Spanish life, laden with shopping bags and struggling with keys, Juan let them in, bidding them good day in his broken English. They took the stairs up to the apartment. This route took them past their neighbour's door, situated at the opposite end of the marble tiled corridor, hidden in the darkness and the cool of the belly of the building.

It was Stevie who noticed the smell first. He said nothing. 'Probably the drains,' he thought to himself.

Chris let them into their abode and opened the big doors, they abandoned their purchases on the kitchen counter and headed out to their private terrace to christen their private pool in a most private way. In the evening, they dressed in long open shirts, linen shorts and sockless loafers and strolled down the strip, sampling a different restaurant each night, then deciding whether to find a bar, or to have another 'early night'. If Chris had his way, then the early night usually won.

This was to set the tone for the week.

Six days flew by. It was Sunday afternoon, about half past four, when Stevie announced that he had a terrible headache. There was paracetamol in the apartment. The bar they were drinking in was only a short walk away.

'Get me another San Mig, Chris. I'll nip back home and take a tablet, then I'll come back. It's a shame to spoil the day.'

They had met up with another couple earlier in the week. They had hit it off straight away. Julian and Phillip were Welsh. Julian was an architect and Phillip or Phylis, as his partner of twenty years called him, was an actor. They reminded Stevie a pair of old-time film characters. Julian wore trousers even in the Spanish heat. Admittedly they were very stylish, impeccably tailored linen trousers, but trousers none the less. He wore them with a hippy style waistcoat a white T-shirt and a multitude of leather necklaces and bracelets. His hair was slightly too long, it was grey and wavy and fell endearingly over a pair of very brown eyes. His voice was cultured, the Welsh lilt evident only when your ear became attuned to its presence.

Phylis seemed like the polar opposite. Where Stevie was small and wiry in frame, Phylis was tall; he was over six feet. He was well built but not fat, he obviously looked after himself well. He too, was dark haired, his obviously assisted by visits to the colourist.

'Well darling, it gets dyed regularly for my work, so I'd just as well keep up appearances. One week it's blonde, the next it's dark. But I'm a ginger at heart, collar and cuffs, the lot, aren't I Jules?'

This caused the less flamboyant Julian to inhale his San Miguel and snort it out through his nose. Amid the laughter, Stevie's lilt floated in, 'Phylis, too much information! These youngsters really do not need to know!'

They had met in Amigos Bar on the Tuesday of their stay and had enjoyed each other's company. This afternoon Phylis was just getting into his stride. A natural raconteur he was telling tales of stage and screen, actors he had met, those he'd like to meet, tales from behind the scenes from Cardiff to California. It would be a shame to break up the gathering.

Stevie walked quickly and let himself in through the front door of the block. Waving to Juan who was behind the concierge's counter, he didn't wait for the lift. He took the stairs. Two at a time.

Leaving the stairwell at the top floor, the smell of drains was awful. He really must tell Juan about it on the way back down. As he passed the door to the second rooftop apartment, he noticed that there was a bluebottle fly crawling along the floor at the foot of the heavy mahogany door. Intent on curing his headache, Stevie let himself into their flat, took two paracetamol and half a pint of water, washed his face and grabbed his forgotten straw hat, the one Chris said made him look like a beach donkey, and ran back down the stairs headed for the bar.

He stopped in the foyer and spoke to Juan who was nearly mid-siesta, nodding quietly in his armchair in the office, desk fan quietly blowing cool air at his face.

'Ola! Juan! There is an awful smell on the stairs, like bad drains only worse, I think there is something wrong there.'

'OK, my friend, I take a look later, I'm sure it is nothing. Señor Holly prob'ly left food in his fridge again. He has gone back to England for a few weeks.'

Stevie was, by this time, half-way down the street. He did not hear Juan shout after him, 'You English, mad dogs the lot of you! Too much sun, too much sun!' Juan had no intention of checking anything out today. He put his feet up on his desk, laid back in his comfy chair and turned the fan up to full blast. Let the English go drinking in the sun. The Spanish knew better.

It was late evening that the four Amigos fell into the apartment, well regaled with tales from Phylis and with Julian eager to check out the design and architecture of the lads' plush accommodation. They had a bottle of tequila and they intended to drink it. There was salt and limes in the kitchen. The plunge pool and the view of the sunset called.

The four of them drank to the sunset, they drank to each other, to the pool, to the sunset again, to the beach and the sea.

'And to the poor dead bastard in the flat next door!' slurred Phylis

'What dead bastard?' mumbled Julian.

'Can't you smell it? Dahling, that smell of death. The body of a dead enemy always smells sweet.' Phylis brandished his glass theatrically.

'Is that Shakespeare?' Chris asked, amazed that their new friend had such a vast command of the classics.

'No. Certainly not.' Phylis bridled. 'Titus Vespasian, if you must know.'

'Well,' chipped in Julian, 'whoever it is, they've been there a while.'

'Juan told me it was probably some guy called Holly, gone home and not cleaned his fridge out.' Stevie added. 'I told him about the smell this afternoon, and the flies.'

'Well, he won't be any less dead in the morning, dears, let's finish the shots. Its way past our bedtime, Julian, are you coming boys?' Phylis divided the remains of the tequila by four and handed one to each waiting hand along with a small herbal tablet. 'May your nights last forever and all your flies be Spanish.'

Four sprawled bodies lay naked on the huge bed. Sheets were wrapped around legs, but mostly discarded onto the floor. The sun was just lifting her head and encroaching on the marble of the floor when they were all rudely awoken by the crash of the Spanish police breaking down a door. Not their door.

'Fuck!' groaned Julian, reaching for his abandoned trousers, 'I'm too bloody elderly for this, Phylis.'

'Jesus, Julian, you've still got a hard on.' He lowered his head in the general direction of his partner's groin. 'Let me ease your pain darling, put you out of your misery'.

'Oh my god, my head!' groaned Chris. 'Shit we need to pack! Our flight is this afternoon.'

Stevie just groaned and turned over. 'I think I'm dying, leave me alone.'

Chris rolled off the bed. He was sore in a great many places. He silently pondered on how much of a sheltered life he must have led. He began to make coffee, lots of coffee. Meanwhile, Phylis had immersed himself naked in the plunge pool. 'It's the only way to wake up, dear.' Julian was in their en-suite shower, and Stevie was in the bathroom.

Chris dragged their suitcase from the closet and began to throw clothing at it in a haphazard manner. Creases no longer mattered. It was all going to be washed at the other end. Pulling on shorts and T-shirt he made for the door. 'I'll get some fresh bread, while you lot use all the hot water.'

He could have shared a shower with Stevie, but there wouldn't have been much bodily cleanliness involved. He needed food. The shop a few hundred yards away sold great fresh bread. If he hurried, he might just catch the last of it.

Stevie got no further than the landing. The door to the other apartment was open. The smell was nauseating and the flies buzzed in the passage, coming to rest on his hair. He swept his arm across his face and started to breathe through his mouth. The inside of the property was a hive of activity. A crew of medics was just packing up their kit. It was unused. The casualty was well past the benefit of their ministrations. Several uniformed policemen in latex gloves and face masks were standing looking at a body hanging from the wrought ironwork of a set of spiral stairs.

'We don't have stairs.', Stevie mused to himself. 'Must go up to the roof.'

Wherever the stairs went, there were now the remains of a human being suspended in the stairwell, swollen and rotting, fly infested and emitting that sweet, cloying, stomach turning stench of death. Stevie lost the contents of his stomach there and then, all over the marble floor. The results of a day's heavy drinking and a night of debauchery burned his throat and made his stomach try and escape his body. He almost fell down the stairs in his haste to reach fresh air.

In the lobby, Juan was sitting at his reception desk, unconcerned. He beckoned to Stevie. 'Señor Steve, I call the police, it looks like Señor Holly he decide not to go home after all.'

The interviews with the Policia National were brief and to the point. Julian and Phylis could provide no information. Stevie and Chris told what they had smelled and seen, and that they had told Juan about the smell and the flies. Juan seemed unconcerned. In his interview he swore he had seen Señor Holly with his suitcase. A new suitcase. He swore that he had let no one into the building who did not belong there. No, he did not have a spare key to Señor Holly's apartment. He was a permanent resident not a visitor. Maybe they should speak to the owner of the building.

Juan delved into the filing cabinet in the corner of the office. He was being most cooperative when he provided the authorities with a Bristol number. 'Call this number, speak with the owner, they may be able to help you.' He smiled grimly through broken teeth. He had no more to add.

Stevie and Chris were booked onto a later flight home. Their transport to the airport was a police car. They were ushered swiftly through check in and straight onto the plane.

As the airbus accelerated down the runway, the nose lifted, and they felt the satisfying clunk of the undercarriage lifting. Chris placed his hand over Stevie's on the armrest, chuckling. 'Well, that was a week to remember.'

'Don't, go there,' replied Stevie. 'I love you, Christopher, but don't ever Spain and flies in the same breath again.'

Less than two hours later, the tarmac of a rainy Bristol rose up to meet them. They were back to reality. As they stepped out into the waiting area, intending to catch a taxi back to their home, there with a cardboard sign bearing their names was Julia Grainger.

'Welcome home, boys, I need to have a chat with you about your week away.'

On the other side of the city Sally Holly was answering the phone. In broken English she was informed that her estranged husband was dead. It was of little consequence to her. In fact, becoming a widow freed her from the encumbrance that was David Holly. Now she could truly live her life. Perhaps find love again with someone less complicated, someone at least honest.

In a few months she would be told that she had inherited the lease of a beachfront apartment in a fashionable area of southern Spain.

'Sell it,' she would instruct the lawyers. 'Sell it and give the money to the widows and orphans fund.' There were no flies on Sally Holly, she knew that her late husband and his colleagues had created a few. Maybe his money could be used to relieve some of the misery he had caused.

CHAPTER 38. HELP AND RESCUE - Tansy

Just outside Bristol, 2017

She felt sick, that feeling of sickness you get from reading in the car, not quite on the point of vomiting. Her body felt bruised and exhausted from lying on rough carpet in the dark. It was like the after-effects of a bad fairground ride, or maybe the result of being put through a washing machine, an extra rinse and a short spin, perhaps. She desperately wanted a shower but didn't think she could stand up long enough to take one. Tansy Alexander was battered and bruised, tearful, confused, and very angry.

She wanted nothing more than to go home, curl up in her bed and hope that in the morning it would all have gone away.

They talked little as Bruce drove through the lush countryside just outside Bristol. Green hedges seemed to close in completely over narrow lanes. Her saviour handled the car with the ease of one who had spent many hours behind the wheel. He did not so much drive, he became part of the machine, almost totally absorbed into the leather and polished walnut cocoon. The Toyota ate up the miles, its engine growling to itself contentedly.

Tansy was exhausted. She craved a soak in a hot bath, the familiar feel of her fluffy pyjamas and the comfort of her own space. She was worried, worried about Peter. Why she should be she really couldn't work out, he was quite capable of looking after himself. It was complicated, she decided, too complicated to ponder for the present. Yet ponder she did.

She knew he cared for her on some level, yet in the back of her mind she knew she was expendable. Would he throw her to the wolves now? If that was his intention, why had he ever come after her? Was he just afraid she knew too much, afraid she would crack under whatever Julia

Grainger had planned for her? That did not make sense. He had been careful that she knew nothing.

Did he keep her as some sort of pet, an adornment for his arm, an escort to accompany him socially, for he lived life like a hermit, rattling around in his big fancy house.

He had bought her from Joey Callahan. He had cleaned her up, seen potential. He had saved her. He had saved her for his own selfish reasons.

Tansy mulled all this over, silently. The man in the seat beside her appeared to read her mind.

'He loves you, you know.' The statement came out of the blue, just as Bruce was changing gear to negotiate a junction. 'He doesn't want to, but he does, or he wouldn't have broken cover for you.'

'And just who are you, that you'd know that? Who are you anyway?' she replied from the depths of the leather passenger seat.

'I'm a friend, and right now you need friends. You weren't always called Tansy Alexander, were you?' He was conversational

'How the fuck would you know that?' She spat the words at him. 'My past is the past. It should stay there.'

'Did Tracy Brown never wonder where she came from?' He was curious.

'That was a long time ago, Tracy is gone, Tansy is the present, and I hoped it was the future. All the rest is ancient history.' She didn't want to pick open the scars which were not long healed. 'I have a good life, and I have opportunities, I don't need baggage.'

'Being on your own can be a lonely place. People need people even if they think they don't.' He spoke with the voice of experience.

'Well people have only ever shit on me, and from a great height. They either abused me, or they died, or they didn't want me anymore. Oh, and don't forget the feeding me with drugs and selling my body to men. No, Mr Wayne, I don't need people. Even Peter bought me. He bought me from my pimp, the pimp who was my best friend. Does he love me, or just the idea of me? The Tansy Alexander he created.'

'I don't think he quite knows himself.' Bruce turned the car into the car park of the pub. 'When he thought you were in danger, he was willing to…, well, look under your seat.'

Tansy felt under the seat. Her hand grasped what felt like a large wallet. In it was a metal object which felt like what it was. A gun.

'Oh shit, he would never have used it, would he?'

'He would have. I made him take it off, made him see sense. You don't need any more aggravation, not in the gun department. He'd do time for you, Tansy. He doesn't know it, but he would.' The Toyota came to a stop.

'I can't face a drink, Bruce. I'll stay in the car.' Tansy yawned.

'I live here, stupid, it's my home and my business. Come on, there's a bath, and fresh clothes, and if we are lucky some food and a comfy bed, on your own if course.' He winked at her, a conspiratorial wink, like a friendly uncle, or a father.

Tansy followed him from the car and allowed him to escort her into the building. He had showed her to her room, found her an assortment of clothes, his granddaughter's, she thought he said. Then he had left her to her own devices.

'There's the shower and the bath. There should be everything you need to feel human again.' Those had been his parting words.

Tansy had sat in the walk-in shower with the water turned up to full blast and as hot as she could bear it. She sat there under the flow of water for what seemed like an age, letting the tears mix with the coconut and lime shampoo suds.

'Pull yourself together,' she told herself. 'Peter will phone, he will find you, then he can answer your questions.' She snorted to herself, turned off the water, wrapped herself in one of the fluffy towelling bathrobes hanging on the bathroom door. Who was she kidding? Peter would tell her nothing she couldn't work out for herself. He certainly wouldn't tell her why Julia Grainger had reappeared in her life, or why the bullied schoolgirl she had befriended had turned on her. But maybe that was something not even Peter knew. Whatever it was, Julia thought she was dealing with Tracy Brown. Tansy's carefully constructed life was falling apart. She felt the pull of the past. The lure of oblivion called her. This man, Bruce, he could fix her up, couldn't he? He seemed like a nice man, but nice men never stayed that way. He moved in the right circles. He would get her what she needed.

They sat in the pub kitchen and ate. Bruce managed to rustle up a tasty lasagna and garlic bread and a bottle of red wine which Tansy drank far too easily. Then they sat in the empty snug by the fire, waiting. Waiting for what she wasn't certain. There was no word from Peter. Her phone remained silent.

'I think I had a sister, once.' Where the words came from, she didn't know. Was it too much red wine, or the atmosphere, or just sitting with this man who seemed to make her want to talk?

'If you had one once, you still have one now,' he grunted. 'Where did you hide her?'

Tansy's eyes were continually drawn to the black screen of the iPhone sitting on the table in front of her, willing the screen to light up, waiting for some contact from the man she had subconsciously pinned her life to.

'Pardon?' She hadn't heard the question, lost in a world of her own.

'Where did you hide her, your sister?' Bruce asked again.

'I don't know, honestly, I don't know, maybe when I went to search for her, and she wasn't there. I lost hope. Why wasn't she there?' The pain of the past began to creep back into her mind. 'Then I forgot.'

'You should never forget, Tansy.'

'Maybe when all this is over, I can start to remember again. When I was little I used to hear her voice, but then it was lost in the screaming, so I shut it out.'

'Life has a habit of getting in the way, if you let it.' He was philosophical. 'Sometimes you need to focus on what you want, not what people expect. Stop being swept along by circumstances.'

Tansy grunted into her drink, exhaling a long, tired, emotional breath.

'Like, stop the world, I want to get off?'

'No..., not like that.., more like, get out of the traffic, take a quiet road and find your own way, don't follow the herd, be true to yourself. I should have been, years ago.' He took a long swallow and stared into his glass. He could see what Peter Balfour saw in this woman. Beyond the beautiful exterior, she had that certain something, that manner which made you want to talk to her, engage her in conversation, tell her things you had hidden for years. He could bare his soul to Tansy Alexander. He could probably bare his body as well, but that would be unforgivable. So, he kept talking.

'I was in love with a woman once. I should not have let her go. Life had me by the scruff. Life told me not to chase her. Then she was gone. I became one of life's wanderers. Either that or I have a taste for wedding cake, and here I am, on my own, happy in my skin. Most of the time.'

'And the rest of the time?' She floated out the question.

'Loneliness has no hiding places. So, I keep busy, I have projects, I kill time.' He drained his glass. He felt like getting out the whisky but said nothing, just stared at the dying ashes in the fire. There was still no call from Balfour.

Her turn to mindread, she rose from her seat and let herself into the serving area behind the bar. Her practiced eye ran along the top shelf where the bottles of single malt lived. The heavy tumblers were stacked along the bar back, there was still ice in the bucket, just enough, one cube in each glass. She took down the bottle of Dufftown Singleton, it was her favourite. She carried bottle and glasses over to the table. Bruce noticed she brought three glasses. He raised an eyebrow in question.

'He will call, you know.' She poured three generous measures.
They heard the crunch of tyres on the gravel, the slam of a door and the sound of a car turning around in the car park, then disappearing into the night, the sound of its engine taking it back towards the city. It was well after midnight. The pub was empty. The old building began to creak to itself, making noises which would usually signal the end of the day. Bruce

had added a log to the embers in the grate, the dry wood was catching light, the rough edges glowing with the beginning of flames. He lifted his glass. 'Absent friends.' He made the toast. She raised her tumbler in salute and sipped, letting the smooth amber liquid trickle down her throat, its vapour warming her lungs and dancing in her nostrils.

'Mmmmm.' She sighed her appreciation.

'Less o' the absent, ay.' The voice came from the back door. Peter stood, nearly invisible in the shadow. As he stepped into the room, she could see that his clothes were rumpled, his hair was messy, he looked tired and in need of a good ironing. Before she could rise from her chair, he reached them. Picking up the third glass he drained it in one and reached for the bottle. 'By Christ, it's been a bloody long day.' He poured another large measure. Then he pulled her into his arms and kissed her. He tasted of whisky and he smelled of commercial air freshener and stale air. He detached himself and pulled up a chair. 'I should 'na be here, ye ken, I should be on ma way back tae Glasgow, but there's no' a train until the mornin'.'

'You're not on bail for fucks sake, are you?' Bruce was concerned.

'No, I'm not.' Peter began. 'That's what took the bloody time. They could na' let me go back until they'd searched ma' house, they said. I'm sure they thought that once they'd found what they thought they'd find, they'd have me fer good, any road. But they found nothin'. I told them as much, there's nothin' tae find. So, they've released me. If they want me again, they'll be in touch, but they told me tae get on the next train back.'

'No conditions then, you aren't breaking any conditions.' Bruce muttered. 'They'll be following you. You know that don't you?'

'My driver couldn't have been more set up if she tried. Din'nae worry man, she knew where ye were anyway. Seemed like ye were an old friend. I don't think she was supposed tae bring me here though.' He poured another scotch. 'Any chance of a shower, man? Then Tansy and I need to talk.'

Bruce showed him upstairs into his own flat. It didn't seem appropriate somehow to assume that he and Tansy would be sharing, but his instincts told him that the jury was still out on that matter. He opened the door to his wet room. 'Help yourself, there's towels on the rack. My clobber will be a bit big for you, but it'll have to do. Pass me your dirty stuff, I'll chuck it in the wash. It'll be dry by the morning.'

Peter Balfour stripped himself naked, threw his clothes across the room to the waiting man. If he didn't know different, he would put money on Bruce being gay. But he knew otherwise. The man had mentioned several wives on their journey south. If he was anything, he was a serial divorcee with a passion for fruit cake. The man had the brisk efficient manner developed by those in the hospitality industry. Like a six-foot mother hen, he thought as he turned on the shower and stepped into its spray. Reaching for the sandalwood scented shower gel and the new sponge that Bruce had thrown him as an afterthought, he had to admit the man had a certain class about him. As he washed his hair and let the fragrant suds run down his athlete's body, he wondered why Bruce Wayne, a man who had retired some years ago to run a country pub, would involve himself in the affairs of a Glaswegian call girl, for that's what the police believed her to be. Peter hadn't disillusioned them. It puzzled him. What was Bruce doing, and why?

The day's grime disappeared down the plughole and he towelled himself dry with an enormous, navy-blue fluffy towel from the rack. On the equally enormous bed outside the en-suite was a pair of burgundy coloured jogging bottoms, thankfully with a drawstring waist and a matching hoodie. He didn't opt for the extra-large boxer shorts, they were far too big. His own trainers were still serviceable. They had spent the day outside the cell door.

He followed his nose back down the passage towards the business part of the building. He could smell cheese toasting. He could almost taste it. He could also use another dram. He needed to speak to Tansy. Some Dutch courage was in order.

'I'm for bed.' Bruce placed four rounds of Welsh rarebit on the table. 'Help yourselves to what you want. I leave the sleeping arrangements to you. I'll leave you to it.' He winked at Tansy,

'Goodnight, Uncle Bruce,' she teased him, blowing him a kiss as he left the room. They listened to his footsteps disappearing up the stairs and along the passage and heard the click of his door closing.

'Pete, I've been so worried,' she began. 'I'm past exhausted. I need to know….'

'Din'nae fret yersel' they've nothing on us, nothing they can use.' he came back, gently. 'They asked me a lot. They wanted the ins and out o' the cat's arse, so I told them.'

'What did you tell them, Pete? Maybe it's stuff I need to know.'

'Hen, the less you know, the better. If ye din'nae know it, they can'nae tease it out of ye.'

'Pete, what the fuck have you told them?'

'They asked me about ma businesses. I told them that I had many business interests. They asked about computers and the like. I told them I had a legitimate supplier for Apple Mac computers, I even offered to supply them if they liked. That's the truth. I would na lie about something they can check. They already had a list, ye ken. I told them I had a regular customer, a guy called Joseph Callahan. That he bought several machines a month, new. He was a good customer, aye, but I had' na heard from him in a few weeks.

They asked me had I no' seen the news, that Joey had been found dead? I said I had been busy and had nae.

Then they asked me about you, hen. They had your phone records already, they asked about why you only called me from Glasgae city centre and why, if ye were ma girlfriend, there were so few calls, and no texts.'

He took a big breath in. 'So….. and I'm sorry ye ken, before I start, ye must know, I'm sorry.'

'Sorry for what exactly?' She held his eyes with hers, the blue lasers blasted into his mind trying to read his thoughts. 'What did you tell them? Tell me, it can't shock me any more than being kidnapped, trussed up like the fucking Christmas turkey and brought to this fucking shithole of a city in the boot of Julia fucking Grainger's Mercedes! Tell me that was not connected to you!'

'I told them you were a call girl, a prostitute.' He paused. 'I told them that I bought you from Joey Callahan, who was my customer, and your pimp. I told them you still worked for Joey. I'm sorry.'

'And Grainger?' Tansy's face was ashen and her lip was trembling. She had curled up in her seat like a terrified puppy, trying to hide from the world.

'I know nothing about Julia Grainger,' he lied. Lies came easily. 'Maybe it's about time you started to talk to me, Tansy. This is a two- way thing, ye ken. How does she know you?'

It was her turn to breathe. 'Before I came to Glasgow, before I was Tansy Alexander, I was Tracy Brown. I lived here in Bristol. Julia Grainger was in school with me. I was her friend. She was bullied. I helped her. I had sleepovers at her house. Then I had to leave. She was always so nice. Her mum was so lovely. Her father didn't like me, he was scary.' She sounded like a little girl again. 'She saw me, in London, at the last drop off I did. She changed the pick-up point. She sent me to a different locker. When I got off the train, they must have been waiting for me.'

Peter thought fast. 'Tansy, where is the machine you picked up that day.'

'It's with the police, they took it.'

'Was there anything different about it, from what you normally carry?' He was concerned.

'It was just like the others, but it looked older, like it had been used. It was still new looking, but it had lost its shine. Oh! that's it, the protective film was gone from the case, why?'

'Why the hell didn't Julia's father like you, Tansy?' he probed.

'I don't know, I overheard something when he argued with her mum over me. He didn't want his darling Julia being friends with me. Something about my father, but I don't have a father, I had foster parents. I was from the homes.'

Peter said nothing. It was a puzzle. It was information he was not willing to share, not yet. If Paul Grainger said he knew Tansy's father, then it was certain that he did. If Tansy was in foster care, then how could he know. That would be confidential information. Information Grainger had taken to his grave.

'She said she was taking me to her father, for some reason.' Tansy added.

Peter rose from his seat, he shouted up the stairs, loudly. 'Bruce, I need a phone, I need one now.'

There was a shuffle of feet on the floorboards above them. They heard the sound of a drawer being opened, then footsteps stumping heavily down the passage. Pete went to the bottom of the staircase. Bruce threw him a phone and charger.

'It's clean, it's not new. Do what you need to do, then I'll dispose of it. It will need juice.'

It was an ancient iPhone, but it charged and it had a SIM card and a signal. From memory Peter dialled a number. In a semi-detached house, just outside London, a voice answered.

'Are you still up?' Pete questioned.

'Up all night, me. Sleep in the day, what do you want?' The voice answered.

'The last machine you sent out?' Pete didn't finish the question.

'Already done, mate. I couldn't see your lovely lady tucked up by that bitch now, could I?' He paused.

'All clean?'

'As a whistle.'

The phone went dead.

'What the fuck was that all about?' Tansy's voice was curious.

'You have nothing to worry about, Tansy Alexander, or Tracy Brown, or whoever the fuck you are. You are the cheap, drug dependent prostitute I cleaned up, remember. I call yer when I need a fuck. You perform a service. In return you are paid well. That is all you are. Get it?'

Tears rolled down her cheeks. 'I get it, you fucking flash bastard.' Pete had said it like he meant it. Was that what he really thought of her?

Tansy uncoiled herself from the chair and fled up the stairs to her room. Peter heard the door slam, so did Bruce.

'That,' thought Peter, 'was the most painful thing I have ever done.'

'I wasn't expecting that,' thought Bruce who had heard it all through the floorboards.

'Fuck you, you bastard, fuck you and the horse you rode in on. Fuck you, Peter Balfour. I thought you loved me.' Tansy sobbed herself to sleep.

In the morning, Peter was gone. She pretended not to care, but a piece of her had died last night. Some of her heart was missing, or had it just gone hard. She pushed away the breakfast Bruce offered her but accepted the lift to the train station.

Bruce saw her onto the train.

'There's really no need, Uncle Bruce'. She tried to raise a smile.

'He didn't mean any of it, you know.' Bruce kissed her cheek and hugged her. 'And I do need to. Don't get off before Glasgow. Remember, you are still on bail.'

The train pulled out of Temple Meads. Bruce felt a bit of his heart die, too.

CHAPTER 39. STRANGERS IN THE NIGHT - Tansy

Time hung heavy. Tansy was bored, she was worried. Peter had blanked her completely. No calls, no contact, she had neither seen him nor heard from him since he had been left her in a small pub just outside Bristol. It was as if he had eradicated her from his life.

She passed her time reading, endlessly reading, and waiting. But the phone never rang. There was no knock at the door. She would have loved to go for a run but she was scared, terrified that she would be bundled away again, kept somewhere in the dark, abandoned.

After two weeks of this enforced isolation, she had driven out to Peter's house. Feeling like a stalker, she had parked a short distance away and dressed in her old running shorts and trainers. She had run his route around the golf course, the green keeper had even waved to her as she loped past, her long golden tanned legs eating up the yards with ease.

She would never know but he had seen her. He had watched her lean figure disappearing up the lane and out of sight. He had so nearly joined her, but he knew they would be watching him, watching for the chink in his armour, looking to destroy his alibi, his cover story. He was cross with her for not seeing through his silence. But he would not break the silence. It was not yet time.

Sweating and slightly out of breath, Tansy leant on the roof of her Mini. She pulled on her oversized grey hoodie, took one last look around and, seeing nothing, she drove back to her flat.

'I need a break,' she told herself. 'I need the sun.' She still had her passport, not that she needed it these times of open borders. She had nothing to do and a week to do it in. It would have been nicer if she had been accompanied by Peter, but she was happy in her own company. Thinking with some trepidation about her uncertain future, she pushed open the door to the Thomas Cook travel agent on Gordon Street. Half an hour later, her ticket to the sunshine was booked. An hour later she was neatly rolling the cheap and cheerful clothes she had purchased and packing them in her newly acquired cabin-sized suitcase. Tansy could wear high street brands like Primark and New Look with panache, and travelling light was what she had always done. Keep baggage to a minimum. She half laughed at the thought. It depended on what baggage you were referring to.

Her flight left Glasgow early the following morning. She would be in the sunshine by lunchtime. She could almost feel it already. For the first time in weeks her spirits buoyed. She booked a taxi to get her to the airport in plenty of time, her tickets were already in her wallet. The break to the newly refurbed hotel had been a cancellation. The young lady behind the desk had made the necessary changes to the booking and had entered her passenger information into the system. All Tansy needed to do was turn up.

She boarded the flight amongst the overtired and overexcited children off for their summer holidays. Stressed parents hefted heavy suitcases through check in. She was entertained for the whole flight by a cheeky six-year-old lad, Gordon Macrae, whose parents and younger sister occupied the row behind. Gordon's older sister was welded to the window seat and, despite requests to share with her red haired and freckled sibling, was ignoring him with a grim determination. Gordon turned his attentions to the tall elegant young lady sitting in the aisle seat. Gordon's mother could sense that her husband was rather wishing he could swap seats with his son. The doors closed and the cabin crew cross-checked and made one last run through, a cursory glance at each passenger's lap to confirm that seatbelts were indeed fastened.

'Welcome aboard this EasyJet flight to Malaga airport, Spain. I am your captain, Graham McAndrew. The flight should take about three hours and twenty minutes. The weather in Malaga is reported as a balmy 26 degrees. Please observe the seatbelt and no smoking signs. We should soon be given clearance to take off. Our landing will be at around ten thirty, local time.'

Gordon's sister Ailsa made sure her brother was strapped in, then turned back to her view from the window.

The Boeing 737 started to move, taxi-ing towards the end of the runway. Tansy could feel the rumble of the wheels on its surface, the gentle, repetitive thump as the undercarriage of the plane rolled over the joints in the concrete, gradually increasing their cadence. The jet stopped at the end of the runway, rocking just a little as it turned on its axis to face the outstretched runway. The pitch of the engine fell as the pilot awaited permission to depart, the whole plane vibrating and whining as if impatient to get going. Tansy tightened her grip on the armrest between her and the boy.

'Are ye scared, miss?' young Gordon piped up, his blue eyes looking up into hers. 'Hold ma hand if ye are, I'm no' afraid of anything.'

'What's your name, young man?' Tansy asked him formally. 'That's very kind of you.'

'I'm Gordon, I'm goin tae be a pilot when I grow up, I'll look after yous.' His accent was thick, Glaswegian.

Tansy let the boy hold her hand. 'Can I tell you something?' She looked down at him conspiratorially and winked. 'I've never flown before.'

This news promoted a flood of information. 'Well, hold tight. The pilot will rev up the engines, ye ken, then we'll be off down the runway, then he'll put on full power and ye'll feel it push ye back in yer seat, just like a rollercoaster. Then the nose will lift up, then the whole plane. Then ye'll hear a clunk as the wheels are folded away. Then we will be flying. It's a braw feeling, aye!'

Ten seconds later Tansy was surprised at the accuracy of her new friend's description.

'See miss, I was right, wasn't I? What's your name then? If we are goin' tae be flight buddies, I must know yer name.'

'I'm Tansy.' She found herself smiling at him as his sister poked him in his ribs and told him to be quiet. 'Pleased to meet you. Are you off on holiday?'

The flight passed remarkably quickly, passed in conversation with a six-year-old who knew everything there was to know about flying and was more than happy to share his knowledge with her. He offered to share his boiled sweet with her as the plane began its descent. Tansy declined the offer and was supplied with her own by a very obliging Donald McCrae, Gordon's father, before his younger son could hand his friend a half sucked Werther. Gordon held her hand when they landed and supplied a running commentary from final approach to disembarkation.

As the steps were pushed into position and the doors opened, Tansy unfolded herself from her seat and reached for her bag in the overhead locker. Mrs MacRae started to apologise for her son. 'I'm so sorry if our Gordon has been a nuisance. He loves tae talk.'

Tansy lifted down her bag. 'He's a grand wee lad, it's been a pleasure tae meet him.' She winked at Gordon. 'Maybe see you on the way back.'

'See, Mam, I told you she did'na mind.' Tansy heard the lad telling his mother as she made her way towards the exit, carried along by the flow of passengers.

The heat and the Spanish sunshine hit her as she emerged onto the top of the steps. She donned her Ray-Ban aviator sunglasses, one of the few designer items she possessed which were suitable for a trip to the sun. Following on in the line of passengers, she made her way towards immigration. Passengers with hold baggage filtered off towards the baggage carousels and Tansy, with her one small case, headed for the exit doors. The previous owner of her trip had pre-booked a taxi to take her to the hotel. There, just outside the main doors was a short stocky man with a two day beard wearing an ID tag and carrying a sign which read in capital letters, T ALEXANDER.

Tansy made herself known. The man looked her up and down and then spoke in good English with a strangely cockney Spanish accent.

'Hotel Amàre, yes?'

'Yes,' she replied. 'are you not Spanish?' she queried. 'You sound like a cockney, from London.'

'I am from Ecuador, my wife she is cockney. I speak Ecuador Spanish, and I learn English from her. I like to practice on my customers, you are from…..?'

'Scotland.' She filled in the gap for him. 'We speak very fast, one word rolls into the other.'

He carried her bag for her and placed it in the boot of the waiting white Mercedes taxi. Then he opened the rear door for her. She could feel the cool of the air conditioning and sank into the plush leather interior. Then he slid into the driver's seat and started the engine. She saw that he switched the meter on to tariff two.

'Is just for my bosses. I have to show where I have been. This is courtesy taxi from the hotel, is very nice the hotel, have you been before?'

She told him that it was her first time in Spain, that she was just here for a week.

The 40-minute journey down the coast from the airport was punctuated with 'oohs' and 'aaaah's' from Tansy as Eduardo the driver pointed out some of the landmarks to be seen enroute. It was all new to her and she was enjoying every second.

Amàre Beach Hotel did not disappoint. Attentive staff greeted her at reception, took her case to her room and made her feel more welcome than she had felt anywhere for a several weeks. Feeling like a teenager again, she waited until the porter had left the room, then bounced on the huge firm double bed, explored the simple, minimalist en-suite bathroom with its walk-in shower, huge square wash basin and low level loo, opened the built-in wardrobe and hung her few items of clothing on the hangers provided. Then, pulling back the net curtains, she slid the huge window open and stepped out onto the balcony. She was five floors up. Her room was at the side of the building, the view out over the promenade stretching towards the harbour, and if she turned to her right she could see out across the beach and the sea. The sunbathers were packing up for the day, the great pink-orange orb starting to fall from the sky and disappear into the sea. The tall palm trees which lined the promenade swayed gently in the warm early evening breeze. She would, she decided, dine early then make her way up to the roof-top bar and watch the sun set, maybe have a few glasses of Sangria or just a cold beer. Tansy had a whole week to spend exploring. Tomorrow would be the start of her Spanish adventure.

'Fuck Peter, fuck Glasgow, fuck Bristol and all the horses they all ride in on!' she thought to herself. She had heard a lot about the scene in 'Marbs'. She would seek it out, have a little fun before she had to return and face the music. Then she would need to find a job, a source of income. Her bank balance was healthy at the moment. Her flat was hers. Peter had put it in her name from the start. She had no rent to pay and no mortgage, but Tansy was a realist. She couldn't live on her savings for ever. A week then to put all that shit on the back burner. She still had her dreams. She would pick up their trail and follow them one day. She was certain of it.

Leaning on the balcony rail, she let the warm wind ruffle her dense black curls. As she shook her head she noticed the courtesy bottle of bubbly in the ice bucket on the small table in the corner, positioned in the shade so as not to get warm. One bottle, and two glasses, this hotel really did think of everything. Tansy popped the cork and poured for one. It would be rude not to.

Staring out across the sea, she raised her glass. 'To me, to Marbella, and fuck them all.' She drained the crystal flute in one and re-filled it. She was hungry. It was nearly time to shower and check out the dining room.

'To you, to Marbella, and how you say 'eet, fuck them all!' The owner of the voice was not visible, but if he, for it was definitely male, was as deep, dark and sultry as his heavily accented English, if he was anything like his voice, Tansy decided she would love to get a better look.

The invisible man was evidently on the next balcony. Tansy heard the scrape of a chair being pushed backwards on concrete, the clink of a bottle on a glass and the 'glug' of liquid being poured, perhaps with a slight hint of fizz.

'Salud!' The voice offered a toast, and a glass appeared around the corner of the dividing wall. A champagne flute identical to her own held by a dark brown hand, long fingered, strong looking, with well buffed nails and smooth skin.

'Slainte.' Tansy clinked her glass against his. 'Looks expensive,' she thought to herself, mentally checking her own manicure. She was still contemplating her appearance when a head appeared from the next balcony. He had been leaning on the handrail, drink in one hand like her staring out across the bay, lost in his own thoughts.

His face was dark, Mediterranean brown, naturally tanned from years in the sun, black hair worn shaved at the sides, the long upper layers tied up in a fashionable, 'man bun'. His brow was unlined, cheekbones sharp enough to cut paper, black eyebrows neatly divided over his nose by strategic use of a tweezers, no doubt. Nose slightly damaged, she noticed, it's once narrow bridge decidedly flattened and pushed to the right. Below the character adding nose, he did not wear a beard but could be in need of a shave. He had a broad white smile, naturally white, not fake. The smile, like the teeth, seemed genuine. He placed his glass on the table and extended a hand.

'Joachim Parral, at your service, senorita.' He had noticed the lack of rings on her fingers.

Tansy took the hand. It was cool and firm in hers.

'Tansy Alexander. Charmed, I'm sure.' She stammered over the words, blushing slightly.

'Shall we drink to this lovely view together? It is sad to drink alone.' His eyes were not directed at the Spanish vista spread before them from adjoining balconies.

'To Marbella.' Tansy raised her glass again, clearing her throat and making contact with his eyes, dragging them north from where they'd been resting and back to her face. 'The view is truly breathtaking.'

'Indeed, it is enchanting.' He refilled her glass from his bottle. 'I could enjoy it for hours.'

'I love to watch the sun setting, the colours of the sky, the darkness in the clouds, darkness has always fascinated me.' She sipped her drink. 'And when the darkness lifts, the sun will rise on a new day.'

'I think we are both here to forget. I too have a list of, as you so politely said, "fuck yous". Will you join me at dinner, Tansy Alexander?' He purred at her like a sleek, dark cat.

'Maybe compare notes, you mean? Let me check my diary.' She refilled his glass from her bottle. 'Oh, look! Mine's empty!'

'Your bottle or your diary?'

'Both.'

'Mine, too.' He turned the vessel upside down in demonstration. 'I need a shower and a shave. Shall I meet you in the bar at say, eight o' clock?'

'Joachim Parral, Tansy Alexander will be pleased to join you for dinner, be warned.' She twinkled her blue eyes at him. 'I am ravenous, and I can eat a lot.'

He snorted the remains of his drink most impolitely. 'I'm sure I can more than accommodate your appetites.' She heard him chuckling until the sound of the water from the shower drowned out the noise of his laughter. If the rest of the man which accompanied the head and shoulders lived up to expectations, this was going to be a very pleasant evening. She drained her glass and placed the empty bottle upside down in its ice bucket. Painting mental pictures of her new acquaintance, she too headed for the shower, the cool water hardly dissipating the steam of the atmosphere.

CHAPTER 40. SPANISH INQUISITION

The complete article didn't disappoint. Tansy observed him at a distance as she glided into the lobby from the stairwell. He would have expected her to take the lift. Indeed, there he was seated on a high stool at the corner of the bar, chatting to the barman in animated Spanish. An unopened bottle of very fine Cava stood in an ice bucket by his right elbow. After every few words his eyes would flit towards the entrance doors, his line of sight on the just visible elevators.

From her vantage point she could see that he was tall, perched with one long leg extended to the floor, the other hooked around the leg of the stool and his right buttock on the seat. He wore skinny black jeans which left little to the imagination. They fitted snugly in all the right places. Narrow hips ran upwards to a trim abdomen dressed in a tight black T-shirt. Broad shoulders, well-muscled but not overly so. Black hair worn long, now freshly washed and tied up in that man-bun on the top of his head. He had shaved. 'No,' her inner devil said to itself. 'Not a disappointment at all.'

Her better self-replied. 'What on earth are you doing, Tansy? You only met him an hour ago.'

'It's only dinner and a few drinks. Where's the harm?' The devil egged her on.

'Think of Peter.' She pushed that thought out of her head.

'Fuck Peter!'...

'Tansy you look devastating.....'

She had been spotted. She hoped she did not look like a rabbit trapped in headlights. She pulled herself up to her full height and glided towards him, walking like she owned the place.

The washed-out turquoise dress had travelled well, a few minutes hanging in in the steam from the bathroom and any unsightly creases had dropped out. It draped itself sinuously over her shoulders, falling in blue green waves skimming every curve. Hanging from perilously thin spaghetti straps it ended mid-thigh, a slightly indecorous distance above her knees but not so short as to look cheap. It emphasised her height and the impossible length of her legs, worn with white sneakers. Tansy hated heels.

Her hair was loose in a huge curly mane, still slightly damp from the shower. She wore no makeup except black eyeliner and red lipstick. She examined him from his black loafers upwards. Her eyes met his and she hit him with her best blue gaze.

'Still enjoying the view, Senor?'

'Immensely.' He pulled up a stool alongside him and signalled to the barman for two glasses. The barman swiftly produced two crystal flutes from the shelf under the bar and set about uncorking the chilled bottle. 'Shall we start from where we left off, perhaps?'

Tansy was not quite sure why, but the only thought which seemed to register was the fact that Joachim Parral wore no socks. Her mouth was moving but no words were coming out. So, instead, she took the offered drink and, sipping the chilled elixir, let the bubbles tickle the back of her nose. Gathering her thoughts as she sipped, it was Tansy who broke the silence.

'There is a word for men like you where I come from.' She allowed her accent free rain, making him strain to understand the words. He was not phased.

'In Spain, there are many. Before you use any of them, for I fear you are about to. I do not make a habit of chatting up ladies on their hotel balconies.'

'Why me then?'

'I was expecting someone else.' His voice was a whisper. 'But…… '

'So, the champagne was not really for me….'

'Cava…, we are in Espana after all, you will have a courtesy bottle on arrival, it comes with the room. But what you and I were drinking. That was my doing.'

Tansy was intrigued. She fixed him with a gaze and raised an eyebrow.

'Tell me more, please.'

'I heard you on the balcony. I was already out there.' He started. 'When I realised you were not who I expected, I had already heard your toast. You seemed sad. I was sad. We could be sad together.'

'You did 'nae sound verra sad tae me.' Tansy growled at him in her broadest Glaswegian accent.

'Pardon?' He queried. 'English please, what kind of language is that?'

'Sorry, but you didn't sound very sad.' She repeated herself. 'Who was I meant to be?'

'A lady I have been meeting here for several years. She is a business partner, and yes, she is my lover. Every year the same two rooms, we have dinner, we talk business, we drink, we party, we fuck. This year was to be the last. I was sad because I was ending something. Then, when she did not turn up, I was.... Well, I was relieved. Then you were there! I am sorry if I have intruded. Now tell me about you.'

She outlined the chaos of her life, leaving out what she felt he should not know, and what she felt too personal to tell. No names mentioned. She was a young lady who was taking a last minute break from it all. A week to clear her head of clutter, to find some enjoyment after several months of stress. She told him she was from Glasgow. She told him her aspirations, the place she had achieved in drama school, that the turmoil she was involved in might scupper those plans for good. He listened. He was a good listener. They missed dinner.

'Let's walk.' He suggested. 'I know a place we can eat, there is music and dancing, a few more drinks.'

'What then?' She was direct. 'We talk a little business, we party, then we fuck! I tell you now, I'm not that type of girl.'

He laughed then, so hard he nearly fell off his perch by the bar. He grabbed her by the arm. 'And I am not that kind of guy... Come, let me show you Marbella.'

Carried away on his cloud of enthusiasm, she went with him. They walked for a while, the night air clearing both their heads. They talked more, they ate at a small exclusive restaurant away from the main buzz of people. The staff seemed to know him. A table was not a problem for Senor Parral. They drank crisp, fresh, Spanish white wine. The fish was fresh caught that day, so fresh it nearly leapt off the plate. The music was low key, not the banging club music she expected. He laughed at her often. 'Not in this part of the town, Tansy. Those places are for the plastic people. Maybe we will go there tomorrow. But tonight, we are here.'

'Here is fine, here is exactly where I want to be.' She raised her glass to him, smiling with her eyes, feeling the pleasant glow of food, wine, and a little expectation of things to come.

'Let me show you something,' He had already paid the bill. 'it is not far to walk.' They walked in companionable silence, his arm draped comfortably over her shoulder. She nestled into his armpit, their strides evenly matched. Ten minutes later they stood on the broad walkway outside the building, he pointed upwards.

'We could see the stars from anywhere along the front, why here?'

'Not the stars, it's a building, well an apartment. My business contact...'

'She who didn't show up?'

'Yes, her....'

'Your ex-business contact....'

'I suppose you could say that....., yes. Well, she told me that the penthouse is for sale. These places are like, how do you say, 'hens' teeth'.'

'If that's as rare as rocking horse shite, then yes that's rare'.

'They don't come on the market often, only when some ancient British ex-pat dies. They are mostly owned by Brits. The Spanish could not afford to buy them when they were built. And, well, the people who built them, built them to launder their money.'

'So, you want to buy a flat?'

'Will you come and see it with me?'

'Like she was going to, you mean?' Tansy baulked at the thought.

'No. Because you seem to have a natural sense of style. I want an independent opinion. Julia would just have me buy it blind.'

The name slipped by in conversation, Tansy thought no more about it. She agreed to view the apartment with him. They turned and strolled back towards their hotel, stopping every now and then to watch the sea, and the stars. They took the path down onto the beach in front of the hotel. The loungers were neatly stacked for the night except for one which had been left behind. It seemed to have their names on it. They sat beside each other, her sneakers alongside his loafers. No socks. Bare feet feeling the damp sand.

'May I kiss you, Tansy.' He asked, very old fashioned.

'You may.' She replied. 'Thank you for a wonderful evening.'

His lips were cool on hers, his teeth nipped slightly at her bottom lip, hardly any pressure, light as a feather. She nipped back, feeling her whole body start to react to him. He pushed back the curls of her hair, tucking them behind her ear, rattling the huge hoop earrings she wore. He kissed her behind her ear, down her neck and across her shoulder. She sank her head into his T-shirt, her own hands sliding under the soft material, feeling the hard lines of muscle each side of his spine. First running upwards towards his shoulders, then downwards to the waistband of those well-fitting jeans. Her long fingers undid the button. His hands slipped under her dress, pushing the fabric up over her hips. Her hands slid down the back of his jeans, there were no soft parts to this man.

'Inside,' he grunted.

'No.... here..... now.'

'But..........'

Sometime later, when the concierge let them into the lobby, he smiled to see Senor Joachim with the young lady who had booked his adjoining room. So much unlike the 'business partner' he usually entertained. He did not mind that they brushed the sand from their clothing onto his pristine marble floor. Senor Joachim deserved some happiness. He did not know the stunningly beautiful young lady, but she carried a sadness with her as well. They looked good together. It brightened his night to see it.

'Buenas noches, Senor, Senorita !'

'Buenas noches Miguel'

The lift doors closed behind them and the elevator carried them upwards.

Tansy woke early. The Spanish sunlight was just starting to penetrate the gap in the heavy hotel curtains. The bed was huge, yet there did not seem to be as much space as she expected. There was something heavy lying across her belly and her legs could not move. Cautiously opening one eye, the first thing she saw was the top of a head of jet-black hair, long, no longer tied up, flowing in a straight ebony wave to join with the curls at the joining of her thighs. A lithe brown muscled arm lay across her belly and a long brown leg lay over both of hers. Slowly, memories of last night came back to her. She moved, extracting a leg from beneath him. He awoke, his dark brown eyes found her blue ones and before she could wish him good morning she was assailed by his lips.

'Buenas dias, mi amor.' He kissed her lightly on the lips. She had learned through the night that he was subtle with his kisses, deft, almost desultory, always leaving her wanting more. And more she had received. More she was about to receive. He rose above her and she lifted her hips to meet his. Those nipping teeth grazed her breasts. He arched his back and met her as she opened herself to meet him. With a flick of his arms and the grace of a gymnast, she was now on top of him, astride him, her turn to set the pace, her turn to use her teeth. He held her hips firm, he reared up against her and bit her nipples hard, first one then the other, then sinking his teeth into her shoulder. He flipped them both over and thrust hard. The noise he made was that of a wounded dying animal. She heard herself cry out. She had cried out before, but never like this. Now she felt like her soul was bare. When he looked down at her and she looked up at him, it was through tears, they had both been crying. They did not make breakfast.

Tansy showered. She dressed in denim shorts, a loose white linen shirt tied at the waist and her habitual sneakers. She had not thought to pack a business suit. Apartment viewing would have to take her as she was. She met him in the lobby to find him dressed in beige linen trousers and jacket with a white T-shirt. Brown loafers. No socks. Hair neatly tied up once more. She kissed him on the cheek. It seemed appropriate. He kissed her on the mouth. Miguel stiffed a laugh and turned to open the doors for them.

'Tu auto esta afuera, Señor Parral.' Miguel gestured to the waiting BMW convertible.

'But we can walk.' Tansy protested.

'I am meeting the agents in town, it is more, how you say, professional to take the car.' Today he was all business.

Tansy only heard snippets of the conversation. The apartment had several bedrooms, it had a roof terrace with a pool, it was in need of a refurbishment, nothing had been altered since it was built. The vendor was the ex-wife of the owner. The owner had died. Yes, it was a bargain. The widow wanted a quick sale. A Mrs Holly. From Bristol.

The name registered in Tansy's brain, it sat there in limbo, unconnected to the other name she had heard. Julia. Both names unconnected, for the present.

CHAPTER 41. AN APARTMENT TO DIE FOR

Tansy only heard snippets of the conversation between Joachim and the real estate agent. As they talked, she browsed the window display of properties on offer. All very high end, luxurious, marble and gold fittings. All way above her budget, even if she had a budget. Not, she decided, her style. She preferred something more homely, less flashy.

The apartment in question did not seem to be displayed in the window. She leant over Joachim's shoulder as he sat across the desk from the young woman who was dressed like an air hostess, hair scraped up into a bun, heavy makeup, bright lipstick, business suit, high heels. A uniform, she thought, a uniform to create an image. Who was she to judge, she had once worn such a uniform. It could cover a multitude of sins.

Reaching across the desk, she picked up a copy of the glossy brochure which advertised the specifications of the beach front apartment.

'May I?' She asked as she lifted it, and smiled widely at Vana as the young woman's name badge identified her. Vana said something in rapid Spanish to Joachim. He smiled at Tansy, then nodded at Vana.

'Si!' He finished in English, 'Señorita Alexander will be viewing the property with me. She has excellent taste, and maybe she will want to live there with me one day.'

Tansy's eyes widened, and her eyebrow raised at him in question. He winked at her and went back to negotiations in his native language.

The apartment had five bedrooms, and three bathrooms a roof terrace accessed by a spiral staircase, with a pool. The kitchen and living areas were large and open plan with huge sliding windows leading to a balcony with views across the bay and, to its left, to the harbour. The roof terrace had a 360 degree view of the bay and the town. Beneath the building, and accessible by a sizeable lift, a secure underground parking area offered space for two large cars. The property had not been refurbished since it was built and had only had one previous owner, the ex-husband of the current vendor. It was in need of a complete refurbishment, a blank canvas on which the purchaser could stamp his or her own style. Nothing had been altered. The vendor was the ex-wife of the owner. The owner had died. Yes, it was a bargain. The widow wanted a quick sale. A Mrs Holly. From Bristol.

The other apartments in the exclusive block of six were all owned by the same management company. The company had been instructed to sell on behalf of the current vendor. Mrs Holly herself wanted nothing to do with the sale.

'Señor Parral, this is a unique opportunity. Properties such as this do not appear on the market often. Shall we go and see what it has to offer?' Vana was done with the sales pitch.

'What do you say, carino? It looks a fine prospect, it has potential.' Joachim stretched back in his low chair and placed an arm around her hips.

Tansy suddenly had the feeling that she was being used. He was asking her subtly to play along, to be his partner in this venture. She could play a game too, she thought.

'It looks a little run down, Jo.' She shortened his name and flicked through the pages of photographs in the brochure. 'It would cost the earth to put right. Are you sure it would be worth it?' She saw the lovely Vana have an intake of breath, then reach into her desk drawer for a bunch of keys. 'There must be room for negotiation, it is still a big investment.'

'At least view it in person.' Vana spoke perfect English. 'It is a very impressive property. The vendor would like a quick sale. I can say no more.'

Joachim rose and taking Tansy firmly by the arm, frog marched her to the waiting car. 'Please stick with the script, my dear. Let me do the talking.'

'I had no idea there was a 'script'. What the hell is going on?' She pulled her arm free and dropped into the car without opening the door, long legs pointing skywards.

'Sorry, it was a sudden thought I had. It would be fun, to live here, wouldn't it?'

'Joachim, I have a home, in Scotland, and there are reasons why I must go back. I am here for a week, that's all.'

He looked at her plaintively. 'Can I not dream a little?' He started the car and they followed the agent through the streets of Marbella and eventually down the slope to the electric shutters which secured the parking garage.

Vana in the car in front raised the roller doors with a press of a remote-control fob. The shutters raised silently and interior lights came on, casting delicate shadows over the gleaming bodywork and tinted glass neatly stowed and waiting for fun. She parked her little red Fiat Uno in a bay marked VISITORS and gestured for Joachim to use the one marked PENT.

They followed Vana to an elevator and were swiftly transported upwards. Behind them Tansy could hear the garage doors quietly closing. She had noted the CCTV cameras on the entrance and by the elevator doors. Was everything in Marbs this hot on security? Her mind was still playing with names. They were swirling around her subconscious, unconnected in mental limbo, for the present.

As they approached the door to the property, Tansy could see that it was new. It had no signs of wear and tear. It was pristine, dark, varnished hardwood, no telltale marks from shopping bags and sticky fingers. First question. 'Why the new door?' She began making a mental list of things that needed to be asked.

Vana spoke as she inserted the key in the deadlock. 'You will have to excuse the mess. The vendor has not yet removed what she wants of her ex-husband's belongings. There are still many boxes cluttering the floor, but they do not detract from the property itself.'

Next question thought Tansy. 'Why does the vendor not want the contents of this place?'

Vana ushered them through into a small atrium, then into a huge open plan space. 'This,' she announced, 'is the living space and kitchen.'

'Wow!' Tansy couldn't help herself. The room was fantastic. It was similar to her own little loft only in a grand scale, and without the cosy furnishings. She walked to the huge windows and saw the panoramic views. While Joachim went on the formal tour with Vana, she took the brochure and wandered, drawn instantly to the spiral stairs to the roof. She climbed slowly upwards and eventually emerged through the doorway onto the terrace, separated from the property next door by a wall and a small service building which housed the workings of the air conditioning, the solar panels and the plunge pool. All neatly tucked away and disguised. This apartment's utilities were sharing part of next door's roof, for the apartment next door was not half as large. The views were as advertised, 360 degrees, a total view of the town and the bay and the harbours. Vana had not exaggerated. She heard Joachim calling.

'Are you okay up there, carina.'

'Just coming down, darling,' she played along.

She was halfway down the spiral stairs when she noticed the smell. A little like drains, but more pungent. It stopped her mid-step. It hung in her nostrils. It was a smell she had smelled before. A smell which could take years to leave a building. The smell of death. By her right foot, just by the toe of her sneaker, she saw a mark in the paint of the wrought ironwork. Paint had been touched up, but not well, something had marked the stairs. Reaching the bottom, she looked upwards into the spiral. There, stuck in the ornate ironwork, was a thread, just a tiny thread. She reached upwards and detached it. Not cotton from someone's clothing, or a stray towel dragged up the stairs to the pool. It was hemp, from a rope or cord. She was sure of it. Another two questions raised. 'Has someone died here?' If so, 'How did they die?'

The bedrooms were spacious, the bathrooms a little old fashioned but serviceable, as was the kitchen. All the furniture had been removed making the living area echo slightly. The smallest bedroom was filled with boxes containing what looked like police memorabilia, on the top of which was one envelope sealed with tape and marked as confidential. It did not appear to have ever been opened. Tansy shivered. A chill ran down her spine. She felt the urge to run, to get out of this place. In her mind the dots were getting closer together. Holly…. Julia…. Holly……Julia.

'Well, mi amor, do you like it?' Joachim was descending the spiral steps from the roof. 'It is fantastic, isn't it.'

'Can we think about it? This is a big decision. It certainly has potential. I mean, the location is amazing, the views are to die for, but I'm not sure. I have a few questions.' Tansy put an arm around his waist.

'Sure carina.' Then he addressed Vana. 'Can you leave us for a few minutes, to get a feel of the place by ourselves, to talk a little, in private.'

'I will wait downstairs. I need to stay to lock up after us but take all the time you need.' Vana sensed a sale. She let herself out and Tansy heard the lift doors 'ping' and the elevator begin its descent.

'Someone has died here, and recently.' She looked directly into Joachims brown eyes.

'The owner died here, Mr Holly. I know that.' He was unconcerned.

'He did not die peacefully in his bed, Jo.' Tansy squeezed his arm.

'Dead is dead whatever way it happened. This place is a bargain. Don't look a gift horse in the mouth, as you Brits say. And please do not call me, 'Yo'. If you must shorten my name call me, 'Kim.'

'So, you have made up your mind then?'

'I have.' He looked down at her and kissed her on the top of her head. 'I would love it if you would stay here with me. I think you have stolen a bit of my heart. That bit is getting bigger each day. Think about it, please, Tansy.'

'I have told you. I have a life in Scotland, not much of one at present, but it is my life, my home is there. I have to go back. Maybe once my life is more sorted…..'

'It's not a no, then?'

'It's a maybe….. in the future… but I have questions…'

'Fire away…' They were standing on the balcony admiring the huge sweep of the bay in front of them.

'Who is Julia? She seems like more than a business contact.'

'Julia Carrera. She is an entrepreneur. She has fingers in many pies. She invests in businesses, in properties. She has interests in several of the night clubs in Banús and in the town. She deals in commodities. Every now and then she puts a matter of business my way.'

'She is Spanish? If she is Spanish, how did she book a hotel from a firm based in downtown Glasgow?' Tansy was suspicious.

'No, she is not Spanish. She is English. I do not know much about her life in her home country. We met here in Spain several years ago. Yes, we were lovers, once, but she is a complicated woman. Even so, she has put many good ventures my way.'

Tansy was not convinced.

'I don't get it. You chat me up on a balcony in a Spanish hotel. We spend one night together, and now you want me to move in?'

'We Spanish are very, how you say …. spontaneous. You and I, we have a bond, we are good together, I do not want to lose you.'

'But I don't know you. I know your name, if that is your name, and nothing else. Who is Joachim Parral.'

'My family is originally from Castile in the north of the country. My father now has a ranch breeding horses near Cordoba. He also breeds fighting bulls. I have an older brother. He will take over the ranch when my father dies. I love the horses, but the bulls… no… I may be Spanish, but the bullfight is cruel. I do not have the passion for it that my brother and my father have. I have some money which my grandfather left me and a small house back in the mountains near Castile. It is so remote I would never choose to make my home there. I choose to make my own way. I have done some modelling, a few photo shoots. That is how I met Julia. I did some work for her, promoting her club in Banús. I invested some money there. Things have gone well. Now I can afford to buy my own.'

Tansy cut straight to the point. 'She deals drugs doesn't she.'

'Tansy, I swear I have never heard that of her, and I have never seen anything to suggest it.' He was defensive. 'Maybe you should tell me more about your life. How you know so much about the seedier side of things.'

'Not here and not now. Let's put Vana out of her misery at least. Kim, this is a beautiful apartment, but it gives me the chills. It is an investment, but I could never live here. My gut says a man hanged himself from those stairs. I can smell death here, and fear. Maybe he didn't hang himself. Maybe he had help to do it. Now let's go. Please.'

She knew his mind was made up. He would buy the place. But she would never cross the threshold again.

CHAPTER 42. THE DEATH OF HECTOR PARRAL

Vana was waiting for them in the garage. She and Joachim made arrangements for a further viewing in a week's time. He needed to consider his options and check on some minor financial details. He told her he loved the apartment and was definitely interested in making an offer. Were there other purchasers interested? He knew that the asking price was still a large amount even if the property was a bargain at that price. He could afford it. His last deal with Julia had seen to that.

Tansy waited in the car, fidgeting and uneasy, ordering in her mind what she would and would not tell him. Joachim made her slightly nervous. She found him very intense, slightly too affectionate. Tansy had never been a touchy-feely kind of girl. Yes, she could touch, and she could feel, but she was reticent of her past. His seeming need for constant physical contact, a hand on her shoulder, an arm around her waist, felt controlling. But he was right, they did have 'something'. She was just not sure it was something she wanted. In the back of her mind was Peter. She felt guilty leaving him. But he had cut her off. He had left her, hadn't he.

Joachim lowered himself into the driver's seat. He reached into the glovebox and produced two baseball caps.

'Put this on. We are going for a drive. I need to show you something.' He had already pulled the black headgear down over his brows. He started the engine and they followed the estate agent's Fiat back out onto the road.

Tansy eschewed the cap. She reached into her bag and produced a headband, red, paisley patterned. It held her hair off her face in her own style, a little signal that she was her own person, not completely under his spell.

She saw him smile slightly. 'Nice.' His face broke into a grin. 'Sometimes I presume too much. I am sorry.'

'Nothing to be sorry for.' She slid her sunglasses onto her nose, the arms secured under the scarf. 'Now where are we going? I don't much like surprises.'

'To my father's place. Maybe then you will see who I am. It is a fair drive. We can talk on the way. You can tell me all about Tansy.'

They left the coast and drove inland, past the Plaza de Toros, which she was informed was built in 1964 and was now no longer used for its original purpose.

'It closed its doors two years ago. No bull has met its death there since 2015. The authorities would turn it into another place to hold events but there is resistance to the change. Old Spain loves her traditions. Maybe one day they will resurrect the bullfight in Marbella. Until they decide, the place will be left to rot. That is a shame, it is a fine building.'

Tansy looked to her right to see the walls of the stone built, whitewashed stadium on the other side of the roundabout. Now surrounded by apartment blocks, a supermarket and an infants' school, it seemed slightly out of place.

'I bet the animal activists are up in arms about that!' was about the only comment Tansy could muster as they passed the headquarters of the Policia Nacional on the A-355 and headed away from the coast into the Spanish countryside. The road took them north into more mountainous terrain. He drove with one hand on the steering wheel, the other on the gear stick, left elbow resting on the door. He drove fast but not recklessly so, covering the miles at a steady pace. Built up areas gave way to small farms; small, whitewashed houses with a few hectares of neatly ploughed land surrounding. The further from the coast, the larger the farms became. For a while he was silent, intent on the road ahead or simply lost in thought.

'Tell me then, who is Tansy Alexander?' The question came out of the blue.

'Just me,' she replied.

'International woman of mystery?'

'I wish.'

'Who am I taking to meet my father? A beautiful woman with a history about which I know nothing, or may I at least have some meat to flesh out the story of your lovely bones?'

'This was your idea. You don't have to take me anywhere. How about we go back to the hotel. Call it quits. I don't really need to meet your family. Do I?'

'It might explain a few things about me, explain my choices better than I can in words.'

He slowed the vehicle and changed gear to negotiate a roundabout, then accelerated again, pulling out to overtake a lorry loaded with boxes of vegetables. He adjusted his cap and put a hand on her thigh. She felt a charge like a low buzz of electricity running up her thigh muscle. It made her squirm deeper into the half leather seat, not in an unpleasant manner.

'Please, Tansy, tell me, who are you? One minute you are like wildfire in my arms, the next you have turned into an ice maiden. Questions, so many questions.'

'To tell you the truth, I don't really know. I haven't always been Tansy Alexander.....' She told him her story, what she could remember of her childhood, her life in the children's home and in foster care. Marcia and Joey. Half an hour later she finished. 'So, I booked a week in the sun. I got a cheap last-minute cancellation, whose I don't know. I could never have afforded this trip otherwise. The rest is, as they say, history. Now, your turn.'

'My father is a man called Hector Parral. His family are from the mountains in the north of the country. My grandfather left me a house there, but it is remote, miles from anywhere. My father moved to more fertile country. He married my mother, Felicia. She inherited her father's ranch about twenty miles from Cordoba in the fertile lands of La

Campina, a better place to do what my father loves. He breeds fine Andalusian horses and also bulls for the bullring.'

'Is that why you told me about it?'

'About what?'

'The bullring, it wasn't exactly on our way out of town.'

'No, it was not. Bulls are part of my heritage and Spanish culture. I felt that if you met my family, you might understand me a little better.'

'So, is your mother alive?'

'No, there is only my father and my brother, but my brother, he is out of the country. He has gone to your country to learn more about the bloodlines of good cattle. The market for Spanish fighting bulls is getting smaller. The ranch needs to adapt, breed hardy cattle who can survive the Spanish heat and produce good beef. We have to be more commercial. Less sentimental.'

'So, your father is there alone. Why do I need to meet him?'

'Hector Parral is a very old-fashioned man. He has very old-fashioned values. My brother is older than I. He will inherit everything. That is why I must fund my own way or take the path my father chose for me. The path I chose not to follow.'

'He is not pleased with you then.'

'Last time I came home, he was very angry. We did not part on good terms.'

Tansy's female instincts kicked in.

'Am I some sort of peace offering?'

He was strangely silent. She continued. 'You think you can present me as some sort of girlfriend, to say that you are settling down?' Her eyebrow raised. 'Turn this damn car around now, I won't play along with your games. Don't I have enough on my plate without pretending to be your 'significant other' for the week?'

'But Tansy you don't understand. Just roll with it. You have run away from a past. Come and see what I am running away from.'

'Why would I be interested?'

'Well, I thought......'

Lost in conversation and intent on his passenger, Joachim lost track of the road.

'Aaah! Watch out!' Tansy screamed and instinctively ducked away from him. Eyes instantly back on the road, he swerved to avoid an oncoming truck. There was a squeal of tyres and a blast of air-horns and 30 tons of ready mixed concrete missed them by inches.

'Shit...... slow down can't you.... You'll get us both killed... OK, I'll play along with you. But I make no promises.'

They sat in frosty silence for the rest of the journey, Joachim keeping his eyes on the road and Tansy watching the ever changing landscape. Gradually the dry fields gave way to greenery as the hills rose in front of them to the north. The occasional signposts directed them towards Cordoba and the fertile area of La Camina.

After about three hours of driving, they arrived outside the ornate iron gates and the high terracotta topped whitewashed boundary wall of the Hacienda Parral. The gates were closed. While they were not chained shut, gates which have not been opened show signs of their inactivity.

The remote speaker phone in its metal housing looked dusty and unused. The coat of arms with its leaping horse and charging bull emblems was rusting at the edges. There were no fresh tyre tracks leading towards or away from the gate.

'How long is it since you came home, Joachim.'

'A little over a year.'

'When did you last speak to your father.'

'Just before I left.'

'And your brother.'

'I have not seen Xavier for several years, since.....' His voice faded into silence.

'Since what.....?' Tansy prompted.

'Since I quit.'

Joachim climbed out of the car, the engine still running. Two strides took him to the buzzer. He pressed it and rattled the gates. They were secure. Back to the car, he reached in over Tansy's lap and opened the glove compartment. His black leather wallet had been hastily thrown in amongst the clutter. In one of the small pockets designed for credit cards behind his driver's licence he found a slip of paper.

X1864J it should be easy to remember X for Xavier, 1864 when the ranch was built, J for Joachim.

Back to the gates, he tried the code, pressing the keys on the pad deliberately. Then the faded green, ENTER. There was a few seconds pause, as though the gates were thinking. Then there was a creaking, a squealing of metal parts moving which had remained still for months. Slowly the gates started to move inwards, a few inches at a time, sometimes assisted by Joachim's shoulder. The driveway to the Hacienda opened up before them.

'I must tell father to get the gates fixed properly. He is letting things slide in his old age.' Joachim made light of the situation.

'Surely they should be in constant use.' Tansy's was the voice of concern.

'My father has probably been using the farm entrance. It is further up the hillside, closer to his beloved bulls. The front gates. They are more for visitors, and for show.'

He drove slowly down the winding driveway, nearly half a mile long, tyres crunching on the earth and gravel surface. On either side were paddocks, neatly fenced, low hanging branches of well-established ancient cork and Algerian oak trees. Shady places away from the heat of the day. The thin trickle of the stream boosted by the addition of a galvanised trough provided water, but the paddocks were empty save for two old horses, both white, standing nose to tail in the shade, heads occasionally nodding, tails flicking the flies from each other's faces.

'This is not right. These fields should hold the brood mares and foals. Those two old soldiers should be in the back paddock behind the house.

Something is wrong here, Tansy.' For the first time he sounded concerned.

The house came into view. A long, low, whitewashed building, two wings either side of a central front door, the driveway sweeping around a small fountain in the central courtyard, a curved wall separating the grounds and garden of the house from the farmland. The gates to the courtyard were open but there were no obvious signs of life. The dense purple bougainvillea hung like an untrimmed fringe over the windows. No colourful plants flourished in the huge tubs either side of the door.

Joachim stopped the car. Tansy followed him up the steps to the front door, right hand placed on the huge oak edifice in front of him. He froze. She took over and pushed.

The doors moved, both of them opening inwards.

'So, this was his home,' she thought.

The tiled entrance hall had a high vaulted ceiling. It was painted traditionally white. The oak furniture was now dusty but still showed evidence of the deep patina of years of love and elbow grease. The narrow table just inside the front door was worn from polishing, the silver candlesticks at either end giving it the air of an altar. Against the wall opposite, two long benches a little like the pews of a Scottish church were made more comfortable with cushions covered with colourful cloth in shades of orange, brown and red, all now faded with age and sunlight.

Another set of huge double doors led into a further reception area, its walls hung with paintings, oil paintings of matadors, the heroes of the bullring. High on the walls above the paintings, the heads of bulls, their razor-sharp curved horns still in place. From the oldest to the most recent, the history of the family of Parral from the eighteenth century to the here and now.

Tansy's eyes took in the depictions of handsome men, graceful and lithe as dancers, some dressed in the finery of the suit of lights, some less flamboyant, formal in their stance, proud, each portrait bearing a name engraved on a brass plate screwed to the frame. Except one.

Whether by design or by accident, hanging nearly out of sight, looking down at her from an alcove was Joachim. A younger Joachim, his nose then undamaged, dressed in a tight fitting suit of royal blue and bottle green with heavy gold piping and embroidery of red flowers over the shoulders, hair much as he wore it now, tied up in a small tight bun. In his hands a black montera hat, the blue and gold short cape, the 'capote de paseo' over his left shoulder partly covering the dark green sequin encrusted jacket, the 'chaquetilla', flowing down snuggly into tight fitting blue silk 'taleguilla' anchored in turn to pink medias or stockings, pink being a lucky colour for the matador. The whole outfit was shod with shoes like ballet flats, Zapatillas. The dancing shoes of the bullring.

She was frozen staring up at the portrait. Then glancing sideways at the man beside her, he spoke softly.

'Yes,' he answered her unspoken question. 'that is me, before I quit.'

He took her arm and pulled her gently away, stepping further into the cool depths of the house.

'Padre! Father!' He called into each room. There was no answer. The kitchen was tidy. No dirty plates, no sign of domestic life. 'Consuela!' he called. 'She is my father's housekeeper. She at least should be here.'

But there was no answer.

Out through the kitchen door and into the working part of the ranch, the stables, once filled with aristocratically bred high stepping Andalusian horses, now empty. In the back paddock where the two old soldiers Trueno and Focos should be seeing out their retirement, a lone brood mare grazed with a foal at foot, the youngster destined to be dark grey but still bearing its chestnut roan foal's coat, his mother herself a deep red chestnut. His father had always liked a red horse. A change from the traditional white but not as saleable. The mare was called Dama Roja de Parral. Her bloodlines could be traced back generations, but she was not fashionable. Had his father sold everything except that which he could not bear to part with.

The stables were gated off in a separate yard from the huge round arena. Joachim approached. He slid open the small, shuttered window in the heavy doors. It allowed him to see into the testing arena, the scaled down bullring with its protective double walls where the three year old bulls are tested for aggression and those fit for the bullring are separated from those who are not.

'Holy mother of god.' Joachim crossed himself and shut the aperture. 'He is in there.'

Tansy reached up and re-opened the wooden shutter. Slumped against the far wall of the arena, just short of the entrance to the protective Barrera, she could see the figure of a man. He was silver haired and dressed in working clothes, a chequered shirt and jeans held up with belt and braces, worn with western style cowboy boots. His head was tipped forward and flies circled his aristocratic profile. He was dead.

'Your father?' she questioned.

'I am not referring to my father, I can see that my father is dead. Old fool that he is. Look to your right.'

Tansy did as she was told. This was her first sight of a Spanish fighting bull. 'Shit.' She shut the hatch. It was black as midnight, its coat stained with sweat. Its horns perfectly symmetrical, the huge hump of its neck covered with tight, harsh, curly hair, its huge shoulders tapered back to the body of an athlete, an athlete weighing nearly 700 kilos, its hind quarters muscled to propel its bulk nimbly around the arena in frightening bursts of speed. It was breathing lightly and a thin stream of slaver hung from its nose. As she watched, it casually licked its nostrils clean and stood, tail resting against the wall, a picture of calm.

'There is nothing we can do for the old man, but we must get his body out of there at least.'

'The bull seems quiet enough.' Tansy ventured. 'Can we no' just drive it to a shed or somethin'?'

'That is not one of your placid highland 'coos'. That is nearly a ton of potentially very angry fighting bull. That is the now four-year-old novilla he called Fuego. A more evil animal you would not wish to meet. But I will have to.' He crossed himself in catholic fashion.

'If we move behind the barriers, could we not drag your father behind one and move him from there.'

'Fuego will be across that sand before we can get the doors open. For this I will need a horse, much skill and more luck. Come with me while I get changed, there is nothing we can do as we are. And if there is no one else to hand I will need you to distract the bull.'

Tansy had seen films of men dressed as clowns at American rodeo shows distracting half crazed cows and horses, preventing the cowboys from getting injured. She did not relish the prospect of avoiding capture by a purpose bred fighting bull.

'Can't you just shoot it?'

'Find me a rifle and I will, but my father did not keep such a thing. With him it all had to be done by tradition. You kill the animal as it was destined to die. With a sword.'

'You are going to kill it!'

'No, I am going to try to drive it out to the pasture. But he knows where he is, he expects to fight.'

Joachim was walking quickly towards a sheltered area at the end of the yard. Tansy could see that it was hung with harness and loose capes. The tools of the vaquero.

'First we must catch one of the old boys out there and hope he has not forgotten his trade.'

'I can ride,' Tansy volunteered, her equestrian skills limited to days of pony trekking in the highlands in the days when she lived with Marcia, but she had become quite proficient.

'Then we must catch both of them.' Joachim smiled. 'You can help me round up his harem. Then if we are fortunate, he will go quietly.'

Trueno and Focos ambled down the field at the summons of a whistle and the rattle of a feed bucket. They submitted themselves to being brushed and saddled up without a fuss. Tansy searched amongst the old clothing hung on the various pegs in the tack room and emerged wearing a pair of jeans about two sizes too wide and several inches too short secured with her own belt and covered with a pair of leather chaps. She rode in sneakers, the toes of the leather stirrups being closed in. Safe enough she thought. Joachim wore leather chaps over his jeans and boots similar to his father's. He helped her to mount Trueno the older and steadier of the retirees. He sidled and danced a little, getting accustomed to the weight on his back. Arching his old neck, he shook his mane and snorted, then stood still.

'Good man.' Tansy settled into the Spanish style saddle, more western than she was used to, but comfortable. She felt safe, confident. She could do this.

Focos skittered about under Joachim's weight. He half reared and wheeled beneath him. The horse could feel the tension in his rider and the old anticipation of his life in the ring was returning. His rider sat easily in the saddle, moving with the old horse as he made his token protest at this unannounced return to work.

The two riders ventured out into the fields at the rear of the house. In the furthest pasture they found the remains of the Parral herd, now reduced to less than two dozen cows, some old and barren and some still with yearling calves. Joachim whistled shrilly through his teeth. The older cows lifted their heads. He and Tansy circled behind them and gradually drove them down to the pasture immediately behind the house.

Securing the gate to prevent their escape, he dismounted and bid Tansy do the same.

Give the old boy a rub down and leave him in the stables until we have finished. I have to go in with **him**. I want you to open those doors. I will ride in. You close the doors and hide behind the Barrera. You must make your way to the door which is just behind my father's body. See it? That leads to the tunnel. The tunnel leads through the crush where they weigh the bulls and the veterinarian handles them if necessary. I must drive him through the crush and straight out to the pasture. Your job will be to open the door to the tunnel and then attract his attention.'

'How do I do that exactly?' She knew she would not like the answer. He handed her a small red cape on a rod.

'Wave this at him and shout his name. He will charge. Take refuge behind the wooden wall. He cannot get to you there. Once he is moving, I can do the rest.' He disappeared back into the harness room and reappeared with a heavy leather apron which he threw over Focos's hind quarters. Tansy looked surprised, 'Protection,' he clarified. 'Fuego may choose to fight before he smells his herd.'

Tansy stabled Trueno. She found him a scoop of oats and a bucket of water and removed his saddle and bridle. Rubbing his ears he responded by nuzzling his nose in the front of her borrowed clothing. Leaving him to his feed she went back to the testing arena to do battle with Fuego.

Tansy pulled the huge doors open. They swung easily on their hinges. Joachim rode the old work horse into the arena like some medieval knight, horse fully armoured for the fray. She pulled the gates shut. The slam of the gates closing alerted Fuego who raised his massive head and scented the air with his bovine nose. He shook his horns and stamped one foot like a giant toddler about to throw a tantrum. Tansy slid her slight frame behind the thick wooden wall. The space behind it was only a few feet wide. She could now see why it would be impossible to get Hector's corpse out by manoeuvring him through this gap. Hector was not a small man. She was tall enough to see over the barrier. With the occasional glance sideways, she made her way to the tunnel entrance. The visible movement did not go unnoticed. Tansy did not see the bull start to move, she merely felt all 700kgs of him pound against the wood in front of her. The whole arena seemed to vibrate.

Joachim was quickly into action, wheeling Focos on his haunches and moving Fuego around the arena away from Tansy, his legs making the horse half pass from side to side, preventing the bull from reaching his intended target.

Tansy pushed the tunnel doors open, then dived back into cover. Picking up the red cape from where she had left it behind the body of Hector Parral, she waved it tentatively towards the enraged black beast, which was stamping and snorting, waving its horns back and fore trying to unseat Joachim from his horse. The bull charged again straight towards Tansy. Focos lunged sideways, years of experience recalled to his equine memory. Joachim moved with him, horse and rider seamless. For an instant, Tansy and the red cape were visible in the mouth of the tunnel. In a cloud of sand and earth Fuego was on her, horns lowered, his bovine brain filled with nothing but rage. He emerged into the pasture to be greeted by the calming scent and the lowing of cows. He stopped and turned through 180 degrees. His target lost. His anger abated as suddenly as it had started. Joachim slid from the old grey horse and began to pull the doors shut.

'Tansy, Tansy, where are you, Tansy are you okay!?'

Her head appeared from inside the cattle crush in the tunnel. He looked down and saw the trampled remains of a red cape and a converse sneaker at his feet.

She pushed her hair out of her face, wiped the dust from her eyes with her hand and picked up the sneaker.

'That was a bit too close for comfort, aye.'

He looked at her, slightly amused as she hopped on one leg and replaced her footwear without undoing the laces.

'You have talent.'

'I also have brown stains in ma pants.'

He shut the doors, confining Fuego to the field. Leading the horse and with an arm around her shoulder they made their way back across the arena.

'Now we'd better restore a bit of my father's dignity.'

She was not surprised when he found a canvas stretcher in the harness room. Accidents were not uncommon when dealing with fighting bulls. Even the calves could cause a substantial injury if handled badly.

'I will have to call the authorities. It looks like a foolish accident, but they will want to be certain. We cannot lay him to rest until they say how he died.'

They carried him back to the house and laid him on the huge ornate table in the formal dining room. Joachim covered him with a matador's red cape. They retired to the kitchen and waited for the Guardia Civil to arrive.

CHAPTER 43. A GREAT DISAPPOINTMENT

News travels fast even in remote areas, by the time the local Guardia Civil arrived, the elderly housekeeper, Consuela, had found her way to her employer's house from the nearby village. She let herself in through the kitchen door, surprised to find Senor Joachim in her kitchen. She flung her arms around his neck and greeted him profusely in rapid Spanish which Tansy could not understand. The sentiment was plain. Joachim had been sorely missed by some members of the family and Consuela at least was glad to see him. In a flurry of efficiency, she began cleaning and tidying and pulling together a rudimentary meal for them.

As she worked, she continued to talk, Joachim in his turn translating for Tansy's benefit.

She says that my brother Xavier wrote to our father from Britain. He instructed him to begin to sell all of the stock. Xavier has sold a large portion of the ranch for development as a tourist attraction. He said that that father would be left only with a few hectares and the house. Xavier told father that the days of the fighting bulls were over. Father read the letter and she says it broke his heart. He found homes for his Andalusians but he would not part with Roja. Then he sold off all the bulls and the breeding females to Manuel Diaz. The last of them went only a month ago. He did not get much money for them, but at least they would be kept well until it was their turn to fight. Consuela was visibly upset by what she was saying. Her hands shook and there were tears in her eyes. She paused and turned to the kitchen sink and pretended to be busy with something while she composed herself. Then she continued.

'*Luego le dijo que ya no tenía que venir à la casa. Todavía le pagaba, pero no quería que cocinara ni limpiara. Podía verse a sí mismo. Pagó a todos sus vaqueros. Las acciones que no había vendido las podía manejar él mismo. Eran solo unas pocas vacas y terneros, los viejos estériles y Fuego. No se separaría de Fuego.*'

Joachim translated. 'Then he told her that she need not come to the house anymore. He still paid her, but he did not want her to cook or clean. He could see to himself. He paid off all his vaqueros. The stock he had not sold he said he could manage himself. It was only a few young cows and calves, the old barren ones and Fuego. He would not part with Fuego.'

Consuela was crying, tears were running down her cheeks. She wiped her face in her apron and continued.

Hacía un mes que no veía al señor Héctor. Se suponía qu'el señor Xavier volvería a casa para concluir el negocio. Él y su socio comercial. Pero no había llegado. En la semana antes de irse, me dijo que mi padre había pasado mucho tiempo en su estudio hablando por teléfono con sus abogados. Había mandado preparar muchos documentos legales, que había firmado y enviado a una dirección en Inglaterra.

Again, Joachim translated for Tansy. Consuela had not seen Hector for a month. Senor Xavier was supposed to come home to conclude the business. He and his business partner. But he had not arrived. In the week before she left, she said that my father had spent much time in his study on the phone to his lawyers. He had had many legal documents prepared, which he had signed and sent to an address in England.

Then in broken English she added. I asked him to contact you, but he would not, he was too proud. He said that he was an old man, he had but one son. It was time for him to hand over the reins. Time for the young to take over. *Yo quería mucho a tu padre, pero era un hombre difícil.*

The Guardia Civil arrived, Joachim showed them around the property. Showed them where had found the body.

The Guardia concluded that it was a foolish accident but there would need to be a post-mortem. Joachim watched and waited as his father's corpse was placed in an impersonal black body bag and loaded into a small black van and taken to the mortuary In Cordoba.

Consuela made up beds, senor Joachim would have his old room.

'Si Consuela,' he had replied, resigned to spending the night at his father's house. The Senorita would have the guest room at the end of the landing. Consuela was as old fashioned as his father. Consuela would, she said, stay over and see to their needs. It was only proper. It was a sad time for all of them.

Tansy was exhausted. Joachim coaxed the ancient plumbing in the old house into producing enough hot water for two baths. He left Tansy soaking up to her neck in the huge tub in the en-suite bathroom attached to the guest room. He himself went to his father's study to investigate what his avaricious and scheming brother had been up to.

Soaked clean of sand, dust and the smell of cows and the stables, Tansy had made use of the camomile and lavender shampoo which occupied the cupboard in the bathroom, along with the soap and a variety of towels and dressing gowns. She wrapped her hair in a towel and selected the biggest and fluffiest of the bathrobes and a pair of towelling slippers which appeared to have been liberated from the Hilton Hotel in London. Consuela had insisted on washing her clothes. They would be laundered and ready by the morning. Tansy went downstairs to explore. Passing the open door of the study she saw the back of Joachim's head bent over the huge desk, poring over papers. She could hear him tutting and cursing to himself under his breath in his native language. He heard her passing the door. 'The sitting room is next door,' he remarked, 'it is more comfortable in there. If we are lucky, you may find a bottle of wine in the rack by the sideboard. The glasses are in the cupboard. The corkscrew will be on the shelf above the fireplace.'

The room was small, cosy, furnished very much to Tansy's taste. It was informal. Her eyes took in the array of family photos on the long piece of furniture along the wall adjoining the study. Pictures of a family, two small boys riding first ponies then riding the fine Andalusian horses their father bred. Two boys, one obviously the younger dressed as a matador. In Scotland or England, it would look like gaudy fancy dress, but in Spain it was a statement of intent. The older boy, Xavier, graduating from college, Joachim holding a bullfighter's cape and dressed in the suit of lights. Their father, once dark haired, now greying, his waist thickening but obviously proud of his sons. What had gone wrong? The next picture made her blood run cold, made her freeze to the spot. One hand picked it up for a closer look. It was Joachim sitting on the edge of the fountain in the courtyard. With a woman. With Julia Grainger.

Picking up the picture she went into the room next door. She thrust it under his nose. 'Is this your Julia?'

'Not now, Tansy, it seems my brother is up to his neck in something. He has sold the whole estate to some development company, even before father had died. It does not make sense. He was not entitled to sell anything. Not while Padre lived. Pass me the phone.'

Tansy passed him the ancient Bakelite telephone.

'I asked you if this is your Julia.' He dialled a number and gave the photo a cursory glance.

'Yes, it is, why.'

'This is the Julia that had me kidnapped. Julia Grainger.'

'No, that is Julia Carrera. I used to do business with her. Then he continued in Spanish …. ¡Holà es ese Capitán Pérez…. Se trata de Joachim Parral…. Creo que mi padre fue asesinado…. ¿por qué ? ……. Entonces, alguien podría tener en sus manos su propiedad… Por la mañana…. Sí, por supuesto… Hay muchas irregularidades en las cuentas…. Estoy seguro de que los verás…. Hasta la mañana, capitán.

Hello is that Captain Perez….. this is Joachim Parral….. I think my father was murdered….. why? ……. So, someone could get their hands on his estate…. In the morning…. Yes, certainly… there are many irregularities in the accounts….. I am sure you will see them…. Until the morning, Captain.

'Joachim, this Julia is Julia Grainger. I was in school with her. She did not meet you this week because she is in prison. She is a criminal Joachim, a very nasty woman. Please say you aren't close to her.'

'There was a time I might have been. But I am afraid she chose my brother. She and Xavier have been joined at the hip since …… well since I quit. It was only as a favour she put odd bits of business my way. Now I think maybe it suited her more than me. I think I may have been duped.'

'You keep saying that you quit, what did you quit? Why was it such a big deal?'

He placed the papers in a neat pile and switched off the desk lamp. He guided her out of the study and into the sitting room. Switching on the lamps he gestured to the sofa.

'Sit, I will tell you.' He uncorked a bottle of Rioja, poured two large glasses. It was strong and red, fruity tasting, full of the vanilla oak it had once been in, and smooth across her palette.

'I am the second son of the house. My brother Xavier was always destined to inherit the Hacienda and all that goes with it. As I explained before, I inherited a small remote house in the mountains from my father's father. That is about all.' He paused. 'But I loved the horses, and the bulls, especially the bulls. I had a gift. My father said I could ride before I could walk, and I could read the young bulls better than any vaquero before I was ten. He sent me to matador school. I was a star. Soon, my picture was on the posters advertising the bullfights from Marbella to Madrid. As you saw, my portrait was painted, my proud father was the father of a hero of the bullfight. Then there was Fuego.

Fuego was my father's pet. He was sired by a Pérez bull. His mother was a young Parral cow, he was her first calf. She was not a good mother. She rejected him. Father reared him, father turned him into a pet. He followed father around like a dog. But I read that calf, he had a mean streak in him. I warned father about him.

Fighting bull calves stay with their mothers for a year. Then, when they are weaned, they are separated into herds. Males in one, females in another. Father never turned Fuego out with the herd. By the time he was two years old he was bigger than all the rest of the young bulls. He still followed father around wanting milk like a calf. Again, I warned him.

Father did not like it. We fought. He started to spread it that I had lost my nerve. I started to get listed to fight only the sub-standard bulls. I could only get on the bill at the lesser rings. There I saw the terrible cruelty of what some of my countrymen loosely refer to as sport or tradition and culture. The treatment of the horses, sewn together, their wounds packed with straw, gored by the bulls and then allowed to die in pain.

The bulls not killed cleanly die a slow and painful death. It is not heroic. It is awful. Last time I saw my father I brought with me the suit of lights. That very suit in which I had proudly sat for my portrait. I told father I was quitting. I burned the suit of lights in front of him. He hung my picture out of sight where he would no longer have to set eyes on it. He removed my name from its frame. He did not speak to me again with love.

The bull Fuego was now four years old. He was my father's pride and joy, he hoped that he would be one of the rare bulls who escaped slaughter in the ring. He had hoped that I would fight Fuego and he would be indulato – in bullring talk this means pardoned – spared at my request as a matador and allowed to live out his life siring many calves. This is sometimes a privilege given to a great matador and a very brave bull. The bull will then be used to improve the breeding of the bulls of the Hacienda.

It was after I had argued with father, I tested Fuego's temperament. It is something we do with all the young bulls, the novillas. He was big, he was lazy, and he was hard to anger but I sensed that he was a bull who would kill. When he did charge, he was quicker than any I had seen. He was so used to people he could read my movements before I moved. He would follow the person and not the cape. I told my father to send him to slaughter. I would not fight him. He was too dangerous for the ring.

That was the last time I saw my father. But I do not think it was Fuego who killed him. I do not know how it was done, for he was certainly killed by the horns of a bull, but it was not by Fuego. My brother Xavier is heavily in debt, he has sold everything before my father was dead. For any money to change hands, Hector Parral must be in his grave. That is motive is it not?'

'You say your brother is involved with Julia. Well, I can assure you she is capable of murder. Whether she goes by Carrera or by her Grainger she will do anything for money. She is ruthless. If your brother owed her then she would see to it that she is paid. I would also fear for your brother's safety'

'The police will be back tomorrow. I must show them all the papers. I must give permission for them to see all that is held with the lawyers. I need to explain to them the accounts. I may need your help, Tansy. You will need to tell them how we found father's body. Ah, y no te preocupes, porque mi hermano Xavier puede valerse por sí mismo' He lapsed into Spanish at the end. But Tansy got the drift of what he said.

'But I must be on a plane home in two days. I cannot stay longer. I cannot break my bail.'

'The day after tomorrow I will drive you back to the hotel. Then, I fear I will have to return here for a while.' He pulled her against him and she snuggled into his shoulder. 'Thank you for today, Tansy, you are a very brave girl. Oh, y Tansy, creo que te amo.' He lowered his face to hers and kissed her. 'Cama?' It was a question. She understood completely.

'Separate rooms,' she kissed him back.

'Consuela is a heavy sleeper, and what is it to do with her anyway. I have always been a great disappointment.'

'Not to me.' She replied breathing in deeply. He still smelled of horse, of dust and male sweat, with a hint of fighting bull. She slid her hand under his shirt and began to undo the buttons with her teeth. 'Who needs a bed, anyway?'

Outside in the passage, Consuela closed the study door hard and coughed loudly. They paid her no attention and heard the slap of her loose leather slippers on the tiles and the stifled laugh as she disappeared into the kitchen. *Como padre, como hijo, entonces. Ambos con apetitos de toro.* Hector Parral had never been a disappointment to her either. She would miss him more than life itself. But it was good to have Senor Joachim back. He would sort things out, she was sure of it.

In the depths of Tansy's handbag abandoned in the front of the car, forgotten about in the heat of the day, Tansy's mobile rang.

…………..*Tansy Alexander is unable to take your call please leave a message after the tone.*

………..Tansy this is Ray Williams, I don't know where you are, but please don't forget you need to be in Bristol on Thursday. Meet me in the café an hour before. I have important news for you

Second message……….. Tansy this is Peter where the fuck are you? Come home, I miss you.

Tansy had forgotten she even had a handbag, she was far too busy with her matador. He was definitely living up to expectations.

CHAPTER 44. AN UNEXEPECTED PACKAGE - Cassandra

Pen y Banc.
Near Fishguard.

It had been ominously quiet of late. Well, it was never exactly busy in an obscure solicitor's office in a small West Wales town. Even by these standards work had been sparse.

I worked exclusively for one client. The senior partner, Andrea Atkinson, knew this. Andrea knew too much about my life altogether. Sometimes I wished Andrea would have some form of terrible accident. What had happened to Simon Hastings? I never found out. I had accepted the warning, taken on board the message, asked no questions. For seven years I had towed the line. I had tried in my own way to look for my girls, but the doors were sealed shut. The players who had sealed them and muzzled me were still alive and active and as long as they remained so, I must let sleeping dogs lie.

There had been no work sent from our master's office in Bristol, no documents to work on, no dodgy dealings to hide. I had become good at hiding things in legal jargon and mounds of paper. I had, over the years, been given access to most of the dealings of the Grainger empire. There were still some cupboards closed to me, but not many.

I had managed to ensure that my home was solely mine. One day, while Andrea had been at a family funeral, I had completed the Land Registry transfer of the freehold my cottage stood on. The building had been gifted to me by Grainger, payment for my silence and my time served. Now it was all mine, there in black and white. I had moved my money, the blood money he had paid me with. That was now hidden well away from his grasp in case he chose to take it back. I was nearly ready to make my move.

It was eight a.m. I looked out over the shimmering, calm waters of the bay. The view was incredible. There was even something serene in the passenger ferries in the channel waiting to dock at Fishguard and the oil tankers heading for the refineries at Milford Haven.

Ernie the postman was on his way up the path. I heard the gate creak and the crunch of his Royal Mail boots on the gravel. Post was rare. Correspondence for Sandra Weaver usually arrived at the offices of Atkinson, Hastings and partners, Hamilton Street, Fishguard.

Ernie handed me a large brown envelope and asked me to sign for it. I had no idea what it contained, but it didn't look like a bomb. I hadn't ordered anything by post, at least nothing I could remember, and strangers were not in the habit of sending me gifts. It was a mystery. I turned the package over in my hands and felt around its edges for clues as to what it might contain. Nothing exciting, my fingers told me it was either a book, or a magazine. Maybe I had forgotten to cancel a subscription to some book club or other, though for the life of me I couldn't remember joining one. Placing the package on the kitchen counter, I picked up my car keys and handbag and drove down into town for another boring day at the office.

The bell attached to the door off the street jangled merrily, announcing my entry. Gwen the secretary and receptionist looked up from her typing and wished me good morning. I walked through to my little office at the rear of the building, nothing more than two terraced cottages converted into office space. I hung my jacket on the back of the door and started to look through my 'in' tray. There were a few searches to do for local property sales, but nothing which would occupy a full day. I logged on to my desk top computer. I checked my email, nothing of importance there, except perhaps an email from a Spanish property firm regarding the sale of an apartment in Marbella. I would look at that after coffee, I knew of no holdings the Grainger's were disposing of in Spain. Maybe Andrea knew more. She had the boss's ear for most things.

At about eleven thirty the phone in Andrea's office rang. I heard her answer it after about five rings. The tone indicated that it was her direct line.

'Atkinson and Hastings, Solicitors at Law, Andrea Atkinson speaking.' Sandra could hear her boss breathing while the caller spoke, the silences punctuated by 'hmmm' and 'aaah' then finally, 'Oh my god, how!?'

There was another pause while the caller spoke at length. Then Andrea's tearful voice.

'Thank you, Julia. Let us know if you need anything. OK, I shall see you at the funeral.' The call was ended.

About three minutes later, Andrea opened the door to my office. For once she knocked. Her mascara was running, she had been crying.

'What on earth has happened?' I feigned surprise.

'He's been murdered, Paul is dead.' Another tear ploughed a furrow through the summer bronze of her make up, seeding it with ultra lash 1000 calorie eye make-up. 'Shot, in his car, by Lenny Smith of all people.'

My pulse skipped a beat. Whilst I hated to gloat on anyone's death, this one was different. The light at the end of my tunnel had just become brighter. I wanted to say a lot of things, but what came out was, 'Oh Lord, I'm sorry Andrea. Have they got the bastard? When is the funeral?'

'Lenny handed himself in, so, yes, they have the bastard. The funeral will be when they release the body, so not for a few weeks. Please don't tell me you are upset by the news. Quite honestly, I know of several reasons why you would be pleased by it.'

'Andrea, I'm upset for you, not for him. I knew you were close to him.'

'He was my boss. He wasn't a bad man really. All the shit that's gone down lately is not down to him, it's down to his darling daughter.'

'What shit is that? Not much big city news makes it to this backwater.'

Andrea proceeded to tell her in detail about the police raids and the arrests, the shootings, and the latest event, the kidnap of some escort girl from Scotland. 'Julia has caused a lot of strife out there, trying to be daddy's brown eyed girl.'

'So, what happens to us? I know we are just a front. This firm does very little in the way of legitimate business. Downtown Fishguard is hardly the legal centre of the universe. We are the out of sight out of mind doers of the Paul Grainger dirty work. With him gone, what next?'

'We wait. He made a Will. It is in his safe, he told me that much. There's a copy deposited with some city firm, just in case. Funny, he only did that a few weeks ago, when Julia started her antics. He may have left instructions for us, so we wait, and in the meantime put the kettle on and get the brandy out.' Andrea sniffed and wiped her eyes on a wad of Kleenex she pulled from the box on the corner of my desk.

I did as she asked. We drank endless mugs of instant coffee and waited for the phone to ring. While we were waiting I broached the subject of the email from Spain. I printed it off and handed her a copy.

'This came through this morning. I didn't know he was selling any of his Spanish portfolio.'

'Just this one, and it's for a client. The client owned it on paper but Paul had control over it, as he retained control over most things. The money goes to the client's wife. He died last week.'

'That's very quick. I thought property sales in Spain took an age.'

'They do, but if you read this, it's just a valuation. The client's wife is to receive that as an agreed amount. It pays her off. The property can be sold at leisure. It's what the ex-Mrs Holly has agreed to. She just wants rid of it. Silly woman is giving the money to charity, a bloody police charity.' Andrea laughed. 'Her ex will be spinning in his grave, when he gets out of the mortuary.'

The name sent a shudder down my spine. I felt physically sick. Opening the door to our little kitchen I stepped out into the sea breeze which was stirring the leaves on the tree overhanging our small back yard. I looked out over the low stone wall, out across the ocean, a vacant stare which could have reached Ireland. Andrea seemed to realise what she had said. 'You didn't know Holly was dead then?'

'I didn't, but good riddance. How did he die?'

'The Spanish police are convinced he hung himself. It takes a lot of euro's to do that much convincing.'

'When?'

'A week before Paul.'

'Karma,' I whispered to myself.

'Pardon?' Andrea had not heard me.

'Nothing, I'll sort the bank transfers out by tomorrow. It's a good wedge of money for a seaside apartment.'

'It was the bloody five bedroomed penthouse, with the roof terrace and the panoramic views of the Mediterranean. Would a man of his calibre live anywhere else?'

'I hope it made him as happy as he made others miserable.'

'I think that's just about what his ex said. Lovely lady, Sally, you would get on.'

'Are they sending his body home.'

'I think not. His sins have come back to haunt him. Every murderer he ever convicted is suddenly appealing. It's going to cost the police a fortune in compo and apologies. No one will draping a flag over Holly's coffin.'

There was nothing else to say. There was nothing left to do. For once I took charge. I picked up the office keys. Told Gwen to take a half day on the firm. It was Friday after all. I thrust Andrea's jacket at her and picked up her tote bag. 'Lunch first, at the pub?'

'Good Idea, let's do it.' She followed me out of the door and we made our way down to the harbour, heading for The Royal Oak.

I should not really have driven home that evening. I had made my way through several glasses of house white wine, a very drinkable Chardonnay, and followed it up with a large, spicy gin with a chilli garnish. I parked, or rather abandoned, the car at a jaunty angle in my small parking area and let myself in. I let Andrea in as well. Neither of us had wanted to spend the night on our own.

I had known Andrea in her capacity as a lawyer since Simon Hastings had disappeared. His name remained on the headed notepaper and in the name of the firm. I often wondered whether he had actually driven into the sunset in his camper van, or whether he had met some sinister end. Simon had, apparently, worked hard on my behalf, to no avail. Or had he? Andrea had taken the baton from him and, unwanted by me, become my liaison with my paymaster. Then she had become my boss. She was shrewd, talented and very good at her job. What would she do now? She had told me that she did not relish the thought of plying her trade for Julia Grainger. Julia's father had been trying to legitimise all his interests, was looking to retire. Julia on the other hand seemed to be intent on escalating her scale of criminality.

Andrea wanted out. She would conclude her dealings with Paul's estate and then she would get out, if they let her. If Julia Grainger knew the extent of Andrea's knowledge of the family skeletons, she feared for her safety.

'If little Julia knew how much I know, there would be a bullet with my name on it.' Andrea flopped into one of my huge sloppy armchairs and kicked off her shoes.

'How about my skeletons, Andrea, do you know about those?' I slurred slightly.

'Cassandra Weaver, they are not skeletons, Paul would not allow that, as he would not countenance your murder, for that's what Holly wanted.'

'So, they are alive?'

'Unless they have died, but if they have, Paul had no hand in it.'

'Where are they Andrea?'

'That I do not know. Once that judge's order was made, that was job done. Holly was gone to Spain. You were in prison. He could manipulate you from outside. He used you.'

'If I had not complied?'

'We would not be here having this conversation. Murders are common amongst prison inmates, especially of those who have abandoned their children.'

'Drink?'

'What have you got?'

'Whisky?'

'Fine, just a splash of water, no ice.'

'That's good, there is no ice.' I laughed. It was a laugh born of the hysteria of the situation.

We talked about everything and nothing into the small hours. My recollections of Amy and Charlotte, they would be grown up now. Were they married? Did they have families of their own? Did they even know each other? Andrea and her aspirations to be a criminal defence barrister before she became romantically involved with Andrew Toller, what of that? That was a long time ago, she said. 'By the time I ended it, he had introduced me to his paymasters, and to his cocaine habit. The two went hand in hand. I was forgiven my debts, at a price.'

'That price was?'

'My services to Mr Holly and Mr Grainger, sine die.'

'And if you did not agree.'

'Pay up or die.'

'Not much of a choice there then.'

'They set me up in this backwater and here I have been ever since, hiding their dirty little secrets under mounds of legal loopholes and paper.'

The bottle of Penderyn was empty, the glasses were drained and both of us fell asleep fully clothed where we sat. I am not sure I really slept. A cacophony of sparrows chirping from the hedge outside the kitchen window added to the pounding of the frogs in the confines of my skull. It was half past five. The day was beginning. I went to the kitchen sink and filled two pint glasses with fresh cold water and dropped two Alka-Seltzer tablets into each glass. I drank mine down in one.

Andrea was still sleeping, her skinny frame folded sideways into my armchair, disappearing into the cushions, her usually immaculate black graduated bob of a haircut in total disarray. I looked at the curly mop it had turned into and wondered how anyone could spend that much time with hair straighteners every morning. He smart business suit was as creased as her hair.

I opened the back door to let the fresh air in and the whisky fumes out and put the kettle on. If we were lucky, I had enough bread for a slice of toast each and there was half a pint of milk in the refrigerator. Today was shopping day. My cupboards would be bare until I had made my weekly pilgrimage to the local cooperative stores.

I had nearly forgotten about the big brown envelope which had arrived in the post yesterday, but there it was, an ominous object taking up space on my work top. 'Open me,' it seemed to say, 'I dare you to open me.'

It was postmarked Bristol. No clues there, most of the post I received at the office came from there. The label was printed and stuck on. It looked official. The seal was reinforced with packing tape. The sender wanted it well sealed, then. There was no AMAZON logo on the front or the back.

I poured boiling water on the teabag I had thrown into a brown pottery mug. I added a splash of milk from the half full carton.

I picked up the parcel and carried it like an unexploded bomb out through the back door and into my small back yard. I placed it carefully on the old wooden table which served as patio furniture. I pulled up one of my cheap but indestructible green plastic chairs and sat down. I stared at the brown paper covering, hoping it would speak to me. But all it said was, 'open me, I dare you, open me.'

I accepted the challenge and tore open the tape which sealed the mouth of the package. Inside were two further envelopes, packaged separately.

I heard the shuffle of feet in my kitchen, the rattle of crockery and the open and close of the fridge, the whine of the electric kettle as it heated the water. Andrea was awake. I heard her locate my jar of Douwe Egberts instant coffee, heard the tink! tink! of the spoon as she mixed boiling water with granules. Then the scrape of a second chair as she sat down opposite me.

I pulled the first envelope from the package. It was marked in capital letters, CONFIDENTIAL HOLLY ONLY. The flap which sealed it shut was signed across the sealed edge with a signature I knew from years ago. The signature was unbroken. The date was stamped with the official police date stamp, the ink had faded and worn. I could not make out the day or the month, but the year was 1993. Suddenly I felt sick. The second envelope was identical, sealed, signed, dated, then, to judge by the ingrained dust, forgotten.

There was a third envelope wedged between the larger ones. It was pale blue, letter sized and addressed to me. It was hand written in neat, careful handwriting, in ink, not biro, a bit spidery as if the hand that wrote it shook slightly as it wrote, but still very legible. The envelope was not sealed. It contained a number of sheets of good quality vellum note paper.

I felt my stomach heave uncontrollably and staggered from the table to retch over the garden wall, anointing the grass on the other side with a fountain of paracetamol laced bile and half-digested whisky. It burned my throat on the way back up, more than it had on the way down.

I returned to the table, trembling, and swallowing down the next wave of nausea.

'That bad, is it?' Andrea pushed her pint of water in front of me.

'Worse.' I swallowed a mouthful of the offered water.

Then I pulled the contents out of the blue envelope. The two sheets of Basildon Bond were neatly folded in half. The top sheet was headed with an address, in Clifton. The typeface was fashionably ornate. The letter itself was handwritten. It was dated a week ago.

Dear Cassandra,

Firstly, I am sorry I did not find these earlier, for they must have been in my ex-husband's hands before he fled to Spain. But then most of his life and his work was kept secret from me. I was just his wife, the little woman.

You may be aware that he is dead. He had no next of kin other than me and had not changed his will. The contents of his flat were cleared and his personal belongings including his safe and its contents were shipped by the Spanish authorities to me.

These folders were taped to the floor of the safe. They were in a plastic wrapper marked WEAVER.

I remember your case, Cassandra. It was his last 'hoorah' before he ran away. I do not know what is contained in these envelopes. Your address I found in a notebook containing the addresses of several of my ex-husbands 'customers' all of whom are now dead, some not of natural causes.

The instincts of an old lady once married to a crook told me I should send these to you. My old instincts tell me that is the right thing to do. If I am wrong, then forgive me.

Yours, Sally Holly.

PS – we did meet once, at a function. David said you were talented but you were trouble, a thorn in his side. My instincts say that he thought you too honest for your own good.

I handed the letter to Andrea, she read it slowly.

'Go on then, you can't put it off. Open them.' She placed her steadying hand over mine. 'Go on, do it, I owe them no loyalty now. I'm as much a victim as you.'

The first envelope contained a green cardboard folder. I had seen thousands like it in filing cabinets, but this one was special. The outside of the flap was marked in black felt pen: Amy WEAVER 2yrs. The second was marked: Charlotte WEAVER 3yrs.

Both files were nearly an inch thick, surly there was enough information here to find them.

'Simon tried,' Andrea spoke quietly in my ear. 'Simon really did try. He trod on too many toes, he got too close to the truth.'

'What happened to Simon?' My mental picture of him driving into the sunset was disappearing fast.

'I suspect his name was in that notebook, the one Sally found your address in.'

I staggered once again to the garden wall and spewed the meagre contents of my stomach onto the waiting dandelions.

CHAPTER 45. GOTCHA

Intelligence Office
Bristol Central

'Got her!' Mark Fish punched the air and rose a few inches off the seat of his chair.

'Got who?' Sarah James looked over the blue baize wall which separated their desks.

'Sandra, you idiot, I've found Cassandra Weaver.'

'Mark, you were told not to keep on with that. We were to concentrate on the phones, on the Op. Ragwort stuff.'

'Yeah, well, I put a recurring search on Land Registry. They just pinged me, it found her.'

'Keep it to yourself then. The only one who will want to know is Siobhan. It could be classed as misuse, Fish. Don't cross that line, be careful.'

Mark sat down. He forwarded the email to his sergeant and started to work his way through his in-box. Five minutes later he raised his head again.

'That's fucked it, then.' His language was terse. He continued to swear under his breath using a turn of phrase he last used in the navy.

'My god Mark, it's too early for all that profanity, what's up now?'

'Read this!' He pointed at his screen. Sarah trolleyed her chair on its castors to where she could see. 'The bastard's dead. Holly is fucking dead,'

The email from the Spanish police did indeed confirm that the body of a male found hanged in an apartment in Marbella had been identified as that of David Holly, former Detective Chief Superintendent. Cause of death given as suicide by hanging.

'Best we all stop what we were doing then. No further enquiries to be made. Pity that, but shit happens. Now get on with the Ragwort stuff. Sarah was practical. Holly was on the back burner anyway.'

'Best let Siobhan know. She can tell the boss, it will be a load off his mind, even if it's been a load of wasted budget.' Mark was not happy. He had been secretly keeping the Holly investigation up to date in amongst all his other ongoing work. If there ever was an enquiry into the working practices of Detective Chief Superintendent Holly, then their work may be relevant. Mark did not want to be found to be anything other than thorough.

He paged through the rest of the incoming emails, found nothing of note and settled down to go through the downloads from the phone of Julia Grainger and the hard drive of the laptop she had been carrying. Operation Ragwort was also a case fast disintegrating into dust. He had heard that they had nothing on the courier save an empty laptop, slightly used but suspiciously clean of all except its operating system. Her personal phone connected her with a man who was probably her pimp, but who was dead. What else? Some contacts in theatreland in London. Her work phone connected her with the aforementioned dead Joey Callahan and Peter Balfour.

Peter Balfour had checked out as squeaky clean. There was nothing on his phone to connect him with Paul Grainger or Julia. He said that Tansy Alexander was an escort he used, and that she was sold to him by Joey Callahan, who was dead. He said that he did business with Callahan and supplied him with computer equipment. Balfour had a legitimate business in that field. Balfour was clean.

Paul Grainger was dead. Lenny Smith had been more than cooperative. Julia Grainger had been behind the hit on his boy. Paul had told him that, before Lenny plastered his friend's brains all over the inside of the Mercedes.

If there was music to be faced as a result of Operation Ragwort, then the conductor's baton pointed at Julia Grainger.

Mark opened a spreadsheet and started to go through the data, feeding in details, adding names to the numbers, organising texts into conversations, looking for patterns of calls, looking for evidence they could use.

The courier Tansy Alexander was answering bail in a few weeks. There would be questions she needed to answer, but unless Tansy Alexander admitted to anything criminal, she would be walking free. It wasn't an offence to catch the train. Well, Mark would check, but he was pretty certain it wasn't, but you never knew these days.

Why the girl had been kidnapped by Julia Grainger remained a mystery. Tansy had said it must be something to do with their schooldays and something about Julia's father. But then Julia's father was dead. He couldn't shed any light on the subject. It seemed to Mark that Julia was after a scapegoat and Tansy Alexander was being set up.

A reply dropped into his in box. It was from Siobhan. All it said was 'Thank You.'

The kitchen was where most of the off the record discussion took place. The world was put to rights in the office kitchen. Disputes were settled, apologies made, small grievances aired, titbits of gossip shared. The main office door was open and Mark saw movement in Siobhan's office as she rose from her chair and headed for the kettle. It must be time for a brew.

'Coffee, Sarah?' He tapped the base of his mug on the desk. Sarah's head was bent over her work.

'Is it that time already? Milk and one sugar please.'

'Black for me, please!' Alfie stirred in his corner by the window. 'I'm slimming. Doctor told me if I didn't lose two stone, I wouldn't see many more birthdays.'

'You won't be wanting donuts, then?' Sarah teased. 'The boss brought a dozen in this morning. Is that jam on your shirt, Alfred?'

Alfie went scarlet. He had already eaten two. Sarah didn't miss a trick!

Mark joined Siobhan over a tray of dirty coffee mugs. He ran hot water into the plastic bowl in the sink and added a squirt of washing up liquid. As he cleaned the crockery Siobhan looked out of the window and down into the back yard.

'Penny for them.' Mark remarked.

'For a penny you can have the first one.'

'Go ahead, over.' He gave her the signal to speak.

'Fuck!' was the one-word reply.

'I'd better have ten bob's worth, then.' Mark laughed.

'What the fuck do I do next, now I know where she is? Do I go there, do I just turn up? Do I even want to see her, she forgot me didn't she? If she had reasons, do I really want to know them? There, that's a quid's worth.'

'Talk to Ray. Maybe get someone else to make the first move. Was there someone close to her who could sound out the ground? Sarah worked with her, maybe she.....' Siobhan cut him off mid-sentence.

'Not Sarah, she's too good a mate, and we work together. That's a good idea, Mark, but it needs to be someone who isn't involved. Sarah is too tied up in the case.'

'Involved in what, may I ask?' Sarah appeared in the doorway. Three in the kitchen was a crowd. All they needed now was Alfie's bulk searching for more carbohydrates and the whole of the department's staff except the boss would be in the kitchen. 'Is this a tea break or a bloody retirement function?'

'Just chatting. Who put you in charge, Ms James?' Siobhan was sharper than she needed to be.

'Sorry I spoke! But if you are on the subject of that email, I'd keep it out of office time if I were you. The boss will have enough of a strop when he finds out Holly is dead.'

'Well, that's hardly our fault now, is it. I can justify the rest. We've found a prisoner on a life licence who dropped off the radar. That's our job, isn't it?' Siobhan sounded stressed. There was a slightly frantic edge to her voice

'Only problem there, is that there is no life licence, not one in existence that we could find. It was mentioned in her release, but no one has ever rubber stamped it. It was never issued. It doesn't exist.' Sarah spoke quietly.

'As long as we believed there was one, which I did, the enquiries were justified. Oh, and when did I actually find out that she was my bloody mother? I think there's a few dots to be joined there.' Siobhan reasoned.

'Stick a teabag and some water in there, could you.' True to form D.I. Perry had manifested himself in the passage. 'Is anyone doing any work this morning?'

'We all need a break, boss.' Mark took the proffered mug and dropped a pyramid bag into its depths. 'Would you like the water boiling, sir?'

'I find boiling works best. Fill it to just short of the rim, Mark, please. That's a lot shallower than the hot water you lot may find yourselves in. Now, break up the party. Sergeant Williams, when did you intend to tell me that the target of your investigation was dead.'

'We only found out in the last hour, sir.'

'My office, now, bring your coffee. We need to talk.' He turned on his heel and almost marched back to the big wood panelled office at the end of the corridor, annoyance bristling from every step.

Siobhan followed, quietly composing herself. Her shoulder was aching. She rubbed the newly healed scar which itched like the devil when she was stressed out. She massaged her trapezius muscle at the base of her neck. Doing it herself didn't feel at all as nice as when Ray did it, but it relieved the ache slightly. What did her boss want to 'talk' about? The Holly case was dead in the water. Did the force want to suppress the fact that they knew of the extent of the corruption? She was sure that some reporter would pick up on the links between all the recent shootings and the high profile raids and arrests, and research a chain of events back to one person. Were they planning a funeral with honours for the man? Some would say that not to bring him home would raise more questions than to give him the expected level of respect.

She shut the heavy door behind her and walked slowly across the still sumptuous carpet. D.I. Perry gestured to two armchairs and a low table arranged in what was once the typist's office, open plan with the main room, the door always open. She sat, he sat. Two mugs sat.

As if reading her mind he spoke. 'Who are the real mugs here, Siobhan? You have worked hard to prove your case, only to have it fall apart at the last minute. You cannot prosecute a dead man. I have been told, not asked, told from above. All that you have found must be boxed up. That means everything. Every last scrap of paper, notebooks, intelligence logs, the contents of those bloody filing cabinets. All of it. It is being collected at the end of the week.'

'Is that for the IPCC, sir?'

'Don't ask who it is for, Detective Sergeant Williams. For once in your career, just do it!'

'Are they bringing him home, then?' Siobhan's temper was incensed. 'Are they bringing the bastard home!? Is this all being swept under the carpet!? Am I to be the fucking brush, sir!?' She slammed her coffee down on the table slopping brown liquid over its highly polished surface. 'No sir, I will not be the fucking brush, neither will I be the fucking mug!'

'Siobhan Williams, you will not address a ranking officer in this manner!' It was D.I. Perry's turn. He agreed with everything his sergeant had said but he had a career to think of, promotion prospects, his family, an early retirement in the sun perhaps.

Siobhan curbed the invective. 'Sir, I'm sorry for the language, but I will not stand by and watch my department's work be for nothing. I admit I may be too close to this. Did you know sir, my mother was one of Holly's cases? His last one. That man blew my family apart, sir. He systematically destroyed three lives, just to hide his greed. I cannot stand by and watch while his stench is buried with his body, with a police flag draped in ceremony on the top. I cannot, and I will not.'

'You have a week before they collect it, Siobhan.' A weak willed, spineless D.I. Perry looked her in the eyes. 'You have a week. This conversation will not leave this office.'

'A week is a long time in politics,' Siobhan quoted as she left the room.

'A day is a long time in policing,' he thought to himself as she left. Then he walked to the door and called after her, 'Harold Wilson 1964.'

He thought she had read his unspoken message. He knew what she thought of him. It made him feel slightly ashamed. He knew what he was, and she was right. He was a coward, he was a 'yes' man, but he was sticking his neck out for Siobhan Williams. Her honesty scared him.

Siobhan closed her office door quietly. She was shaking with a variety of emotions: rage, disappointment, frustration, and grief. She sat in the big leather chair and put her head on her desk and cried. She felt drained. There was a tap on the door, it was Sarah. She walked in without invitation, armed with coffee and biscuits, placing Siobhan's coffee mug on the already ring stained corner of the desk. She placed her own mug on the dried out beer mat which occupied the opposite corner, the logo of The Fleece public house fading with the absorption of any number of beverages since it had been liberated from its home in the dockside music venue.

'What was that all about?' Then she noticed Siobhan's tear-stained face. 'More to the point, what are they all about.' She nodded, mid-biscuit at the pile of file jackets on the end of the desk.

'We have a week to box up the Holly case, all of it. Some department or another is collecting it on Friday. Ours is not to reason why. That was made clear to me, in words of very few syllables.' Siobhan saw Sarah flinch.

'But we have a week. That's five working days. Sarah, do you know anyone in the media?'

'Not personally, but I know a man who may. You can't be thinking of going public, that's career suicide, Siobhan. Its stupidity.'

'Just find me a contact. Let me do the rest. Don't tell Mark. Just tell him to start saving his work, but I need access to it until the last minute.'

'Shonnie, think of your future. You have family, don't make rash decisions. You have found your mother. That's a start. Holly is dead, Grainger is dead. They can't hurt you anymore. You mustn't make it personal. Not ever.'

Siobhan wiped her face on her sleeve. 'I won't let them hide the truth any longer, it's more than Holly. Do you really think the rot didn't spread wider than him. I can smell it from here. This whole organisation is decomposing from the top down. Even Perry has a paymaster. He's shitting his well pressed trousers, but he's given me the time and I can find the opportunity.'

'I think you are a fool. I suppose I've always been one. Fancy some company on your ride? I won't let you go to the wall alone. You can always blame me, after all my time is borrowed. Let's do it for Cassandra.

'On that subject, what do I do Sarah? One piece of me wants to head off down the M4, the rest of me wants to run a mile in the opposite direction.'

'Get Bruce to speak to her. They were more than close once. If you don't ask the questions, you will never get the answers. If I ever knew her at all, she would never have willingly abandoned you. There will have been reasons, and good ones. I'll ask him when I ring him about a pet media bod. He's the man with the contacts.'

'Thanks Sarah, now leave me to it, I have a great deal of work to do. Close the door, this is for my eyes only.'

'You aren't on your own in this. I'm with you all the way. I'll make the call.'

CHAPTER 46. NOT STRICTLY LEGIT – Ray Williams

Ray Williams had good news for Tansy. He was quite looking forward to meeting up with her again. He had faith that she would not fail to make their appointment. She was too afraid of the consequences to skip bail. He hoped that she had received the message he had left on her mobile. Maybe he should reinforce it with a text message, at least he could see if she had read it.

Today he had taken a day off. He had sat down and instead of watching the usual mainstream programmes he had switched on BLoB, Bristol Local Broadcasting that his wife had told him was a progressive local station. It was a streaming offshoot of the BBC. News and Views from on the doorstep. It had not disappointed. He wondered what the fallout would be.

He had pushed the vacuum cleaner around and tidied the downstairs of the house, made a shopping list and started checking the refrigerator for ingredients for their evening meal. The boys were both at a sleep over this evening. Ray was thinking he would cook something special. Or maybe they should go out. They hadn't been to that little Clifton Bistro Siobhan liked recently. He dialled the number and made a reservation for two. Job done.

It had been preying on his mind, constantly. He would wake in the night, with Siobhan, the woman he loved lying beside him, haunted by another set of blue eyes. The same eyes, the same shape, the same tilt at the corners, the same twinkle in their depths, the same penetrating stare when required, but in a darker setting. When viewed in the blonde and fair landscape of his wife's face, they were so different. Surrounded by the dark curls and deep olive skin of Tansy Alexander they seemed unearthly, haunting. And they were haunting *him*.

Tansy had told him her history as far as she knew. She was perhaps the most open, frank and brutally honest client he had dealt with.

He had no doubt that she was being set up by someone to carry the can. Who that someone was he still wasn't sure. He had a few hours until Siobhan came home. He reached into one of the spare kitchen cupboards and pulled out Siobhan's cardboard box of personal papers. He read through her doodling's detailing what she knew and what she thought she knew. The more he read and the more he fed in what he had learned from Tansy Alexander about her past, the more he believed that Tansy was his wife's long-lost sister. A DNA test would solve the puzzle. He still had the knot of hair he had picked out of the ashtray in his wallet. There were plenty of sources of Siobhan's around the house. He could forge Tansy's signature. He had seen it often enough and had copies of it in her file but that would not be legitimate. No. He would ask her next time he saw her. He would lay his cards on the table and ask her.

He heard the front door open. He looked down the hallway to see the bottom of a bag land in the hall with a resounding thump.

'You're early.'

'Yep, needed a half day, it's been eventful.'

'I expect so. I saw the programme on BLoB this morning, I bet that ruffled a few feathers.'

'Too right! That old dinosaur McTavish is after my blood - and yours. I'll be lucky to escape with demotion to traffic warden.'

'Don't insult the traffic wardens, they work hard for the abuse.'

'What are you doing with all that?' She pointed to the papers spread over the work surface.

'Shonnie, how would you feel about doing a DNA test? Putting it on ancestry to see if your sister turns up'.

'Already have, my brother had me do it. I know I'm not biologically linked to him, but he thought it would help complete his research. So, I humoured him.'

'Great. What would you say if I told you that I think I know who your sister is.'

'I'd say you were mad. Is that what you are saying?'

'Yes.'

'Come on then, spill the beans, who?'

'Tansy Alexander.'

'Oh! Fuck off, Ray. I know you fancy the woman, but this is pushing things a bit far.'

'No, seriously. From what she has told me about her life, what she remembers of it, it all fits. I'm going to ask her to take a test.'

'Is that why you still have that chunk of black hair in your wallet? That wouldn't be very ethical would it.'

'I did think about it. But no, I think I'll just ask her for a sample. I'll send for a kit today. It should be back by the time she answers bail.'

'And, at least I have good news for her in that direction.'

'Don't tell me, I shouldn't, and anyway, I don't want to know'.

'If it's any comfort to you, Julia Grainger is going to cop for the lot. I was chatting with her brief in court the other day'.

'Nothing to do with me now, Ray, but at least not all the work was wasted. She has left a trail of destruction up and down the country, maybe even abroad. I shouldn't ask, but what about Peter Balfour?'

'He's a canny customer. Managed to cover all his tracks. Has a reasonable alibi and a cover story. It won't endear him to my client but, as long as she keeps to her part of the bargain, as he obviously has, then he's in the clear.'

'Typical Scotsman, playing things tight.'

'Pietro's tonight? I've booked for eight o'clock. The boys are going to a sleep over straight from school.'

'Lovely....... you do spoil me, Ray Williams.'

'When did you submit that DNA?'

'Only last week. I never seemed to get around to it and it didn't seem important. Why?'

'Just curious as to whether any long-lost relatives have turned up.'

'It's linked to an app, Ray. If anything pops up, my phone or my tablet will ping. It'll send a notification. I will also probably get an email.

You know what curiosity did, don't you. Now let me get out of these clothes. I want to spend an hour in the bath, at least.'

'Can I join you? Please?' Ray made puppy eyes at her.

'Given what I did today you may find the water a little dirty.'

'Tell me more.'

'I need to download this and make an insurance copy. Its Malcolm McTavish completely losing his shit with me.'

'You recorded it?'

'All of it, from the *Enter* to the *Get out*. If he makes waves then he's fucked, but it won't stop others doing it for him.'

'That's my girl! Ever fancied a job as a PI? We'd make a great team!'

'Theres only one sort of private investigation I like to get involved in.'

'Why do you think I married you?'

'For my wiggly arse and my sparkling personality. Or have you been lying for all these years. Pour me a glass of red and join me. You can scrub my back if you like.'

Later, over a bottle of Chianti and perfectly cooked lasagne with crispy crusted garlic bread dripping with butter, they talked about Cassandra.

'You know Bruce is going to see her, don't you?'

'Yes, I do. Sara says that they were always close. Maybe he can sound the ground out for me'.

'Maybe there's things she needs to know as well.'

'I'm sure there are, but I need to know why she didn't move heaven and earth to keep tracks on us.'

'Maybe she did, but it must have been difficult from where she was.'

'Well, from what Mike says, she came out of that fairly well set up. She has a house and a job. Not many ex-cons come straight out to that, do they?'

'Only she knows the reasons. Maybe she would tell you if you went to see her. Ask Bruce to set up a meeting. I'm sure he would mediate.'

'I'll think about it. Maybe she knows more about what happened to my sister.'

'Again, its stuff you'd need to ask her. Lots of wheels have turned. Several of the main players have left the field. Holly is gone. Grainger is gone. Julia is going to be away for a long time. I would say that your mother is safe now. She was protected because she knew too much and was paid not to queer the pitch'.

'I'll think about it. What's this Tansy really like?'

'You've seen her, she's beautiful, she's talented, she's intelligent. She is also remarkably naïve, a bit of a romantic. You'd like her.'

'Well, if you can't persuade her to part with her DNA, I can always take an extra sample when she answers bail.'

'Don't even think of it. You can't afford to break any more rules. Leave that to me. She wants to find you. I'm sure she'll play ball'.

They ordered dessert. Pietro's special was a huge lemon sorbet topped with lemon mouse and whipped cream, decorated with sprinkles, studded with almond biscuits. They ordered one and requested two spoons and fed each other, giggling. Having paid the bill, they wandered down through Clifton, weaving their way through the students weaving their own way out of the Coronation Tap, some obviously unused to the strength of the farmhouse cider, the speciality of the house. Then they wandered back up the hill towards the Downs, turning right onto Upper Belgrave Road towards the Black Boy Inn at the top of Whiteladies Road. They reminisced about nights out they had had when they were younger, a while back, before the children.

'Are you happy, Shonnie?'

'Why do you ask?'

'You seem to have the cares of the world on your shoulders.'

'Well, there's a lot going on at the moment. You know that. I suppose if I could sort things out with my mum and find my sister then I wouldn't give a fat rat's arse about the job. How about you?'

'It's always been you that made me happy, and of course the boys. Shonnie, I'd do anything to make it happen for you.'

'Okay then. Let's take some time off. How do you fancy a trip to West Wales.'

'Great idea. I'll ask Mrs Sullivan if she can have the boys for the weekend. I'm sure her Alan would love company when they go to their caravan. She's often asked if they wanted to go.'

'I need to sort a few things out in the office. Make it next weekend, ay.'

'That's fine. Tansy will be off my books by then as well.'

'The news is that good?'

'Don't believe a word you hear about her. She is a lovely woman.' They walked the rest of the way home in silence.

CHAPTER 47. WE CAN BE HEROES -Sarah James

Sarah had been brief and to the point, but the call had still taken more than a few minutes. She mused to herself as she waited in the waiting room of the oncology clinic. She would love to see the contents of Bruce Wayne's Filofax. Did anyone even have one of those leather-bound monstrosities anymore? Whatever. Knowing Bruce, he would have most of his contacts committed to memory.

She smiled wryly to herself as she waited for the results of her latest scans. Her future might not be bright, but she could at least spread a little happiness before she departed. As always, she expected the worst, believing that expecting it would be preparation enough. She already felt slightly sick, but she swallowed the feeling with more pleasant thoughts as she recalled the conversation.

'She wants to do what?' Bruce had been astonished. 'For fucks sake, is she fucking mad, or what?'

'She wants to blow the whole bloody thing open, Bruce. Take them all down, no prisoners.' Sarah had sat back in her chair and taken a deep breath in. She had heard a similar deep breath being exhaled at the other end.

'She has a family, for god's sake. Does she even have enough dirt to throw?' Bruce sucked air through the gap in his teeth.

'She has Holly and Grainger bang to rights, but they are both dead. Mark has found enough to make that old buffer, Judge ap-Meredith hand in his wig and apply for his bus pass. He has also found evidence of payments to several CPS lawyers, one of whom is standing for Parliament. Rumour has it *she* is potentially a future prime minister. She believes she has enough.' Sarah heard a deadly silence.

'If she leaks all that………'

'She knows what may happen. She's willing to gamble that they will just let her go quietly to avoid a scandal'

'That is a big set of dice to roll.'

'She's determined to do it. She can have all your contact needs ready to go, but it has to be before Friday.' Sarah could hear the cogs turning in Bruce's agile mind. She could feel him paging through his mental directories.

'Tell her I'll pick it up on Thursday morning. Breakfast TV could do with a bit of a shake-up. I think I know just the woman for the job. That CPS lawyer, I take it it's the lovely Penny Major.'

'I do believe so.' Sarah had raised an eyebrow.

'She is fighting a by-election as we speak, has a media appearance scheduled for Friday morning, prime time morning slot. She may have some awkward questions to answer.' Sarah could feel Bruce making plans.

'Oh, and Bruce, there's one more thing, she knows about Cassandra. Mike found her. She doesn't know what the hell to do.'

There was silence on the other end. 'Bruce... are you still there?'

In that moment's silence, Bruce had felt the pain of many layers of sticking plaster being ripped from the hole in his heart.

'I'm not the fucking social services. She has a husband doesn't she, she should talk to him. I can't help her. It's not my place to visit.' Then he hung up. That was only a few minutes ago.

Sarah looked at the clock on the waiting room wall. She still had ten minutes to wait. She checked her phone. No signal. Picking up her bag she wandered casually out into the passage and to one of the many windows which looked out over the city centre. The text message she sent contained all the information Bruce didn't want. Sarah was certain he would use it. Postcodes were wonderful things. He would know who lay at the end of the road. Sat-Nav would take him there. Batman would do the rest, she was certain of it. Maybe she should apply for the job as Robin. Sarah leant on the narrow sill for a minute. Then, choking back a wave of unexpected emotion she steeled herself and walked purposefully back to the clinic.

'Sarah James?' The receptionist smiled at her. 'Go on in.'

The words did not quite compute the first time. Mr Roylance enunciated them in his broad Yorkshire accent. He looked at her over the top of his heavy framed half glasses and from under his huge bush eyebrows. Prof Roylance looked a little like David Bellamy the naturalist, his beard definitely had wildlife of its own. It was so engrossing that she didn't hear exactly what he was saying until his third attempt. 'It's definitely shrinking, Sarah, its good news.'

'What? Oh………, what next, then?…….. How long do I have, Prof.'

'More of the same…. Ms James. We have it on the run…it's good news, Sarah….., good news.' His eyes twinkled at her. As the words sank in, she thought he sounded a little like David Bellamy as well. 'See the girls outside. They'll sort you out with a clinic appointment.'

Sarah looked at him slightly incredulous. Good news was scarce in her life these days. All she needed now was a reconciliation call with her ex. Then her joy would be complete. In her bag she heard her phone 'ting'. She rummaged in the depths and read the text message. It was only a few words. They were from Bruce in shouty capitals.

OKAY! OKAY! I'LL GO.

He's going then, she thought to herself as she waited for details of her next round of chemo.

Sarah walked slowly back across the city. The old limestone buildings seemed to have taken on a new life, their mellow brown walls no longer oppressive. They seemed to nestle happily amongst the modern tower blocks. The shops of Broadmead called to her. She hadn't felt the need to treat herself for years. Seagulls swooped in from the docks, picking up the remains of Subway rolls dropped next to a group of benches. They perched on the statue of Edward Colston waiting for opportunities to scavenge. Anything was fair game for the herring gulls. If you dropped it, they would eat it. Sometimes they didn't wait for it to be dropped. They sat on Colston's head, watching for scraps and shouting raucously to each other. Sarah walked on in a wave of optimism. Looking upwards, she found herself imitating the call of the herring gull performing its aerial ballet above her head. She was sure she saw it wink before is deposited its load on her shoulder.

'Bastard!' she shouted after it as it accelerated away back towards the docks at Guinea Street. Wiping the mess off her shoulder with the crumpled remains of some blue hospital paper towel hidden in the depths of her bag she laughed. Bird shit was supposed to be lucky, wasn't it! A quick window shop on her way back to the nick. She had news for Siobhan.

The spring was still in her step when she mounted the steps to the front doors. They opened as if by magic before her. She flashed her warrant card at the newbie on the front desk. The youngster's supervisor nodded an acknowledgement and pressed the buzzer to open the doors to the inner sanctum. Four flights of stairs later she was back in the office with Siobhan and Mark.

'He's going to need everything you have on Penny Major.' Sarah raised an eyebrow and fixed Mark Fish with a meaningful stare. 'And anything you have that connects her with Holly and Grainger. She's doing a TV interview on Friday morning. We need enough for the odd awkward question. Something to bring the C word into play.'

'Not that C word, muttered Siobhan seeing the horrified look on Mark's face, Corruption... that's the word. Corruption with a capital C.'

The closed door to Siobhan's office opened, unexpectedly. Inspector Perry's head appeared, unwanted and unannounced. 'Am I interrupting something?' His enquiry was expectant of an answer. 'There is a smell of a conspiracy about this room. D.S. Williams, a word, if I may.'

Sarah and Mark made an exit. Whatever was to be said was for Siobhan's ears alone. They would be cut into the loop if needed. But the D.I. needed to be humoured, as far as possible.

Three words was literally all it was. Not even spoken. D.I. Perry slid a folded sheet of paper across the desk to her. 'Use it carefully.' Then he looked at her, his serious face to the fore. 'You are a good Officer, D.S. Williams. It has been a pleasure working with you.'

'You too, sir.' She lied. 'What was that all about?' She wondered. Unfolding the paper, she saw a list of names, all high-ranking officers including the Police and Crime Commissioner himself. She never saw her boss as a whistleblower. In fact, she would never see him again. The man had handed in his resignation, cleared his desk and would be gone by the end of the week. Friday was set to be an interesting day. Siobhan read the list and pondered on the size of the can of worms she was about to open.

She was so engrossed in the matter at hand she nearly forgot where Sarah had been for most of the day. Looking up from her work she could see her colleague through the open door. Her gut feeling told her that Sarah would put her ticket in once all this was over. But what then?

Sarah's boys were grown up. She and her partner led separate lives. Sarah had made her bid for freedom, investing in her new harbourside appartement, but Siobhan knew it was not a freedom Sarah really wanted. She would give her eye teeth to have her old home life back. Sarah, fearing the worst, had run away from life. She had buried her head in the sand. She insisted that she be treated just like normal. If she was well enough to come to work, then she was well enough to take whatever the job threw at her. She didn't complain. She didn't moan. She was rarely late, and she arranged her appointments outside of work hours when possible. Today had been different.

It was half past five. 'Sufficient unto the day is the evil thereof.' Siobhan thought to herself. Logging off her computer and tidying her workspace she picked up her jacket from the rickety old hatstand in the corner. 'That's me done for today,' she called through the main office door. 'Anyone else fancy a drink? Sarah?'

'Count me in!' Mark was already halfway into his coat.

'I can't stay long,' Sarah looked up. 'I'm meeting my boys and their father later.'

'Come for one?' Siobhan encouraged.

'One it will be, and only one! I know what you lot are like. I really can't be late tonight'.

It was a ten-minute walk across the city to the Golden Guinea, the small but perfectly formed dockside pub, which was convenient for Sarah's current home, her small flat in the nurses' home of the recently converted Bristol General Hospital. The Guinea had been tastefully modernised in the last few years but still retained its cosy, local atmosphere, nestled on the edge of the Guinea Street dock, next to the gates to the old hospital courtyard and in the shadow of St Mary Redcliffe church. The three amigos took a route past the old corn exchange, down Welsh Back and over the Redcliffe Bridge. It was turning into a pleasant evening and the after work drinkers were congregating on the tables outside the many hostelries they passed enroute. They waved greetings to several colleagues, already enjoying a social evening in the heart of Bristol's old dockland area. Live music was starting to be heard over the clink of glasses and crockery and the hum of conversation. Siobhan, Mark and Sarah were headed for a quieter more intimate atmosphere, the beer garden of the Guinea where Siobhan intended to extract information by hook or by crook, even by the application of thumbscrews, from her friend Sarah.

CHAPTER 48. IT'S ALL IN THE NEWS – Bruce Wayne

Bruce was as good as his word. Janet Carmicheal was the lead presenter for the breakfast news programme. She already had her PR prepared agenda for her interview with Penny Major.

A standard interview, nothing to taxing or stressful for the budding politician and one time CPS lawyer to tackle. Some easily deflected questions around her plans to improve local services. What plans did she have to tackle to growing problem of the homeless sleeping in the city's doorways? That sort of thing. The interview would be suitably bland. Nothing her producer and editor would find too controversial.

Janet was bored. She ached to break free of the straitjacket her production team had put her in. Don't make waves, nothing too radical. Then Bruce had been in touch. She and Bruce had history going back several years. He had fed her the occasional titbit of information before. He had been one of her more interesting sources. He seemed to have many fingers in many pies and was often willing to 'spill the beans' on a controversial subject, anonymously of course.

His call had come in on an unidentified number. 'How do you fancy making a few ripples on the pond?'

'Bruce is that you? Long time no speak. What have you got for me?'

'Meet me in the park by the Cabot Tower in half an hour. This could be big, but it has to be broadcast on Friday.'

'Friday's show is already scheduled. The content has been decided. It's not down to me to make changes.'

'Janet Carmicheal, I never had you down for a bosses' *yes* person. This could be *really* big, but I've a feeling your producer would never sanction it.'

'I'm on my way.' Janet slipped off her office shoes and pulled on her trainers. She dragged on her faux Barbour jacket. It was a good twenty-minute walk and it was drizzling. She took an umbrella from the selection left by various of her colleagues in the huge china plant pot by the office door.

When she arrived, slightly damp and dishevelled, Bruce was leaning against the wall of the Cabot Tower. He had a thick brown envelope tucked under his left arm.

'What do you have for me then, Bruce? I haven't got long, I'm supposed to be prepping for Friday's programme, doing my background on our Penny. I don't see the point, frankly. They haven't given me anything meaty to ask her, just the usual, mundane, morning TV interview stuff. I really do need a change of job, Bruce. Do you know of any vacancies?' she joked.

'This lot will blow your socks off. The Hope & Anchor is quiet at this time of day. Let's adjourn there and I'll talk you through it.' They walked across the park, down Brandon Hill, avoiding the roads. Five minutes later they were seated at a secluded table in the bar. They were the only customers. Two hours and a ploughman's lunch later, Janet wasn't sure.

'Bruce, you expect me to hijack the Friday Morning political interview with uncorroborated accusations of corruption directed at the interviewee and most of the judiciary in the local area. Based on what? A case which is nearly twenty years old. There is nothing current, Bruce.'

'But there is, Janet. The Police intend to bury Detective Chief Superintendent Holly with full ceremonial pomp and a memorial service, the lot, right here in Bristol. The file you hold in your hot little hands is destined to be swept under the carpet. The corruption continues. Penny Major was, and probably still is, involved. Believe me, Janet, this is the blue touch paper which lights the fuse to a very large explosion.'

'And what's in it for you, Bruce? You aren't doing this from any sense of community spirit, are you.'

'Well, no, let's just say there are people important to me who have suffered either directly or indirectly as a result of Mr Holly's actions. His death has put an end to their efforts to expose him. You are my last resort. Please Janet, for old times' sake.'

'Old times' sake won't pay my mortgage and my bills. If I do this I will either be hailed a revelation in broadcasting, the next Laura Kingsland with my own show, or I'll be drummed out of the BEEB faster than you can say knife. They don't much like whistle blowers, the BEEB.'

She sat and thought for a while.

'Come on Jan, where's your spirit of adventure gone? You used to love to shake things up a bit.' He smiled his best winning smile and bought her a large brandy.

'It's a shit job anyway. I could do with a change.' Janet drained the brandy in one swallow. Took a deep breath in. Placed the brown envelope in her shopping bag, then kissed Bruce on the cheek. Make sure you are tuned in on Friday.'

Bruce watched her as she hailed a passing taxi on Jacobs Wells Road. There seemed to be more of a spring in her step. Bruce smiled to himself. He seemed to have that effect on people.

Janet sat back down at her desk and, with a renewed zest, dug into the background of Penny Major. She had two days to complete the research. Digging deep into the archives, she began to research her career with the Crown Prosecution Service. Penny had been a high-flyer, a first-class law degree. She had chosen to prosecute rather than defend. Defence was where the money was. There would have been any number of chambers who would have accepted her as a pupil. Ms Major had a strong social conscience. She liked to put the bad guy behind bars.

From the outset she had only been engaged on high profile cases, first as second seat to a more experienced barrister then as lead counsel. It helped that she was related to Judge ap Meredith. A small newspaper article from an even smaller local paper highlighted this fact when they wrote a column about alumni from a small school in Wales who had done very well for themselves. The Welsh liked that sort of article. Penelope Major, law graduate, following in the family footsteps. It documented a family tree riddled with small town solicitors dealing in conveyancing and wills, whose heritage could be traced back to Cardiff's 'hanging' judge from the early 19th century. The Honourable Gwilym Williams on one side and a few generations later to His Lordship, Llewelyn ap Meredith. Wasn't the old circuit judge mentioned in Bruce's file?

Slowly she began to pick the threads. A case won here and there far too easily. A defendant sentenced to a harsher sentence than would be expected. A record of winning tough cases for a few years.

Then there was the occasional high-profile case where the defendant was either acquitted or the case discontinued before it ever got to trial. She was careful though, she never appeared before the old judge, her great uncle. That would be unethical. Her downfall was her lifestyle, she loved the high life, oh, yes. There were sojourns to the Costas of Southern Spain. Janet's font of dirt found relationships with several of the lesser officers mentioned in the package she had safely locked in her desk drawer. She scrolled through the digital archiving system, searching for photographs. She had just given up hope of finding the golden nugget she wanted when up it popped. There, sipping cocktails on the terrace of a bar in downtown Marbella was Penelope Major dressed in a sea green cocktail dress. Standing alongside her with his hand placed protectively on her waist but turned conveniently to face the camera lens was the newly retired David Holly. There were several versions of the shot in question, taken by a bored paparazzi from a nearby rooftop. The last of the series showed Holly and Major engaged in an embrace which appeared to be rather more than platonic.

'Are you nearly done with the Major interview?' Her editor shouted across the newsroom. 'I need to check the content before its filed to go live.'

'Just doing background checks, Barry, she called back. 'She's an interesting woman, our Ms Major.'

'Well don't make her too interesting, we need to be in her camp on this, and that's come from London.'

'Don't worry, Barrykins, it will be the standard bullshit on Friday. Now go and polish your fairy wings or whatever you do on your lunchbreak. You'll have it by four o'clock.'

Janet realised that she had probably committed career suicide. Barry Davies was camp-er than a row of tents, but very, very good at his job. He had connections in all the right places, darling. What he said went. Calling him 'Barrykins' was not likely to endear her to his better nature. If indeed he had one.

'Fuck it!', thought Janet, *'I'd just as well go out with a bang!'*

CHAPTER 49. FOR OLD TIMES SAKE – Bruce Wayne

Bruce had supplied the proverbial explosives. He had left Janet Carmichael to plant the bomb and set the timer. The explosion would be devastating, he had no doubt about that. BLoB was only a small station, but it was progressive. It had a loyal core of local viewers. If the initial interview did not stir the pot, the planned 'special' would. If not, one of the papers would pick up the story. He was sure one of the tabloids would be only too glad to run with the corruption angle. 'Up and Coming MP in Bung Scandal!' He could see the red banner headlines. For now, his involvement was done.

Bruce threw a few things in his overnight bag and fuelled up the Toyota. Better check my email he thought, before he left. He would go on this fool's errand for Sarah. He had a great respect for Sarah James.

Logging on, he saw that he had several items in his in box. Several were junk mail, one was a request for him to read his gas meter. He was sure he'd asked Sharon to do it last week. He would leave a note on the cash register for her. The last one was a notification from Ancestry.com. Notification of a DNA hit. Interesting he thought. I'll just have a quick look before I head west. He opened the genealogy site and logged in.

You have a familial DNA match.

'Holy Shit. Wot the fu….' His mind started to run in overdrive.

He read the email carefully. Then went back to the web site. Bottom line was that the science was telling him that DNA submitted only in the last week by Siobhan Williams formerly Taylor born in 1989 was a familial link with his. Siobhan Williams was his daughter.

Bruce Wayne felt sick, then he felt elated, then sad, then angry. He knew who Siobhan's mother was. He had been in love with her. If things had been different all those years ago, who knows what might have happened. Why didn't Sandra tell him? Did she even know? If he thought about it, he could even pin down the night of her conception. Cassandra had been at a loose end. For old times' sake they had gone out for a few drinks. Tony was in work. There had always been a spark between them. The inevitable had happened. It had been a night of as much passion as two adults can manage in the confines of an old Volvo estate partly filled with sailing gear. The following month she had married Tony Weaver. Next time he saw her, she had told him that it meant nothing, she was just getting him out of her system.

He took another look at the screen, took in the details and swallowed. Oh well, he thought, better go and face the music. He was going there anyway. A bit of a coincidence mind, agreeing to go and speak to Cassandra Weaver about this very daughter, at this time. Bruce did not believe in coincidence.

He shut down the laptop and stowed it in its case, he'd just as well take it with him. Lord knows if Sandra even had wi-fi where she lived.

Sliding into the driver's seat, he turned the ignition key and the engine sprang to life with its customary growl. All the little dashboard lights out, quick screen wash, he flicked the indicator, selected first gear and pulled out onto the main road. The satnav was set for a location somewhere west of Carmarthen. He headed for the M4 Westbound. He liked this car. Maybe even loved it

Settling into the journey, radio tuned to play sounds of the eighties, Bruce mused on having a daughter like Siobhan. She looked like Cassandra, though she was taller. There was something about her chin which reminded him of his own mother. How hadn't Tony questioned how a daughter of his could be so fair? Maybe he didn't want to think badly of his wife. And after all, Siobhan did resemble her mother in many ways, just a lot taller. As he drove, the thought of fatherhood grew on him. He had other children. He had never settled down happily with any of his wives. He had been an awful part-time father. Never consistent. Blowing in and out of people's lives like a passing tornado. Here today, gone tomorrow, leaving a trail of emotional destruction behind him. Maybe Siobhan had been lucky to have avoided his attempts at parenting. Wherever she had grown up, whoever had raised her, they had done a better job than he ever would.

He decided he quite liked the discovery. But how would Cassandra take it? More to the point, how would Siobhan?

The Toyota growled its way through the miles. Bruce took the A38 out of the city, then the M49 by passing the congested M5. He paid the toll on the Severn Bridge. He was in Wales. Through the Brynglas tunnels, past the Celtic Manor on its hillside perch.

'*Looks like a refugee camp from the road,*' he mused to himself as he tuned in the radio, which had lost contact with any station he recognised. He knew the hotel, with its red awnings and championship golf course, was the height of luxury inside. But its exterior, well in his view, it was planning disaster, an eyesore, but what can you do?

Traffic grew lighter as he drove west, past the junctions for Cardiff and Bridgend. Siobhan's adoptive parents had lived not far from here, hadn't they?

He had been driving for just over an hour when the industrial wasteland of Port Talbot came into view, the blast furnaces of the steelworks taking centre stage, a hundred years of fumes having killed the trees on the mountainside to his right. When the industry eventually left, which it would, soon, of that he was sure, would the hillsides recover? Would they be green again?

To his left, over the protective concrete wall, he could see the chimney pots of the houses just outside the town centre. How could people live this close to the road, in some cases, underneath it? Never mind, the sea was blue today and the sweep of Swansea Bay went right round to Mumbles. He slowed to the required fifty miles per hour. If memory served him well the speed limit here was well enforced. The cameras were active.

Half an hour later he reached the end of the motorway and continued his journey on the A road. Lush green countryside rolled out on either side. This was countryside the Cassandra he knew would love.

He knew that she had always dreamed of living in the country and by the sea. He began to wonder who had provided her with her paradise once she had served her time. The only thing missing from her personal utopia was her children. How had they been lost in the wash?

He was lost in thought when a tractor towing a trailer, laden with hay, pulled out in front of him. Jolted out of his reverie, he hit the brakes, allowed the vehicle behind him to overtake and then did the same, offering a blast on the horn in frustration. If there had been a collision it would have been his fault. He was tired. Surely, there must be a café close by. After another five minutes' drive he pulled into a lay-by. There was a small picnic area with a wooden table with attached bench seating bolted to a concrete base. The table looked newish. The brick-built toilet block was fairly clean. He relieved himself, leaning his head on the wall above the urinal, scanned the graffiti offering an array of personal services, then approached the white utilitarian trailer from which a homely looking woman dressed in a striped apron was serving snacks and burgers. A colourful image stuck to end of the trailer proclaimed, 'Try Emma's Baps'. Impressive. Well, why not, he thought. The smell of braised and caramelising onions was tempting. He ordered a cheeseburger and a Flat White.

Denise, for that was who the name badge declared her to be, regarded him as though he was mad. 'We don't do fancy stuff like that, mind you. Coffee is black or white. If you need sugar, it's white or sweetener. They are in those boxes, there. If you want sauce or mustard with your burger, they're on the shelf, see.' She smiled and gestured to the condiments on offer.

'White then, please Denise.' She shook up the onions with a spatula and flipped the burger with a practised hand, then took a large white pottery mug from the row on the shelf and attended to the coffee.

'Instant, OK?'

'As long as it's hot and wet, that's fine.'

'Where you off to, then?'

'All the way down to Milford Haven.'

'Be thankful it's not school 'olidays. Roads are chaos. Catching the ferry, is it?'

'No, just visiting an old friend.'

Denise was as nosy as a Welshwoman ought to be. She placed his burger bun face down in two halves on the griddle just long enough to toast it lightly, then placed a slice of tomato on the bottom half, added the burger, then a cheese slice. She then produced a blow torch, not one designed for the kitchen, one straight out of a plumber's toolbox. She lit it from the gas flame and deftly grilled the cheese before adding the lid. She placed the whole thing on a paper napkin, green and white decorated with small red dragons. Wales – what's not to like?

'£4.95 please.'

Bruce handed her a fiver. 'Keep the change.'

The extra 5p was already half-way into the charity box fixed with cable ties to the counter, its cancer research wrapper showing signs of grease stains. It was nearly full to bursting.

'They'll be round to collect it soon, I hope.' Denise followed the direction of his eyes. 'Otherwise, some little bastard will rock up on his moped and nick it. I've been robbed once this year already.'

'And you are happy to be here on your own?'

'No choice. My daughter will be here next week, after the schools break up, but otherwise it's just me.'

'Top burger!' Bruce licked a stray thread of the cheese from his lip. He took a mouthful of his coffee then walked over to the table. He didn't much feel like making small talk. He wondered whether perhaps Denise's daughter was the legendary Emma, imagined baps in the back of his mind, chuckled to himself and took a pew.

'Fetch the mug back when you're finished, won't you, love. I should use the paper ones, but no one empties the bins. And china is, well, nicer, isn't it.'

He raised the mug in salute and gave her a thumbs up sign.

He sat and watched the traffic for half an hour, passing the time of day with a young family who wanted to use the table. He finished his coffee, returned the mug as instructed and continued his journey.

The sat-nav began to direct him down ever narrowing country lanes, through small villages with unpronounceable names, did the Welsh not use vowels!? There were signs advertising campsites and caravan parks, onto roads which were more like rough tracks running between steep, bracken clad banks, across mountain tops. Sheep grazed completely unfenced, sometimes standing at eye level to the driver. Then, like an expectant child going on holidays, he saw the sea and immediately stopped the car. In front of him the huge sweep of Cardigan Bay stretched before him. He wasn't far away now.

'In two hundred yards turn left onto unmade road.'

He followed the instructions.

'In half a mile you will arrive at your destination.'

In front of him was a small cottage, its front garden bounded by a low wall to prevent invasion by local livestock. It backed on to the mountainside, what appeared to be mountain grazing rising behind its whitewashed walls. The window frames were dark green, as was the front door. A stable door. The top half open. Someone was home then. An old Ford Fiesta was parked in the small, gravelled turning area at the end of the lane. He pulled the Toyota onto a flat grass area next to it.

He saw an upstairs curtain twitch. Someone had seen him. No point in putting things off any longer. Bruce climbed out of the low-slung vehicle and stretched his long legs, then approached the green painted wooden gate to the garden. He was half way up the path when the lower half of the front door opened slightly.

The woman who spoke to him from inside the house was thinner than he remembered, her face more worn. Her hair was hidden under a headscarf, the wind picked up straying strands. It was still blonde, but he could see it was streaked with grey.

'If you're looking for the campsite, you've gone wrong. You'll need to turn around and……' She was leaning against the door jamb but suddenly straightened. 'Bruce, is that you?'

'Cassandra, am I in the right place? This was hell to find.'

'I don't want, neither do I get, many visitors, Bruce. How the hell did you find me?'

'I still have my contacts, aren't you going to ask an old man in?'

'I suppose I'd better, but if you came all this way for a bunk up after all this time, forget it, those days are gone.'

'Sandra, I have news for you, and we definitely need to talk.'

'After twenty years of nothing, you think we really have anything to discuss?'

'Let me use your loo, then put the kettle on or get the glasses out. I think you'll want to hear at least half of my news. You've been the devil of a hard woman to find.'

She opened the door fully and invited him into her kitchen. The twelve-bore behind the front door did not go unnoticed.

'It's through that door and down the garden.' Sandra directed her to her outside privy, the Ty Bach as the wooden sign on the door declared. Whatever news Bruce Wayne could have for her, good or bad, it would probably need medicating with something stronger than tea. She reached in the cupboard and emerged with a bottle of Myth single malt and two squat, thick bottomed tumblers. By the time he let himself back in through the garden door she had poured two good measures, added spring water ice from the freezer and had placed two chairs by the kitchen table.

'Sit down, Bruce. Have a drink then tell me what this unexpected visit is all about.'

He sipped his drink, tapped on the table with one large hand, then he began.

'We've found your daughter, well, our daughter, Siobhan….. Charlotte… whatever…she's found, we found her.' He looked at his hand wrapped around the glass. It was shaking slightly. He tightened his grip on his drink.

Cassandra went slightly pale. 'Why would you even be looking? My children are nothing to do with you. Hold on. Our daughter you said?' Her ears were still working then, he thought.

'Funny, I received this in the post a few weeks ago.' She delved into a cupboard and pulled out the brown envelope she had received form Sally Holly. 'I was about to start looking again. But I didn't know how they'd take it. You know, where I've been, all the shit that happened after.'

'What shit? Siobhan, as she has been for all her adult life, is desperate to find you. Yes, she is curious about why you never searched for her. She has been searching for her sister for over twenty years. She has known where you were for the past year. She also knows you were released seven years ago. She can't understand why you haven't tried to find them.'

Cassandra went on to tell him the whole story. She showed him the contents of the folders she had received. She told him about the deal with Grainger. She told him what she believed had happened to the lawyer who had tried his hardest to fight her corner. When she'd finished, she wiped the tears from her eyes with a tea towel with a stereotypical Welsh lady dyed into one side and a map of Wales on the other.

'What about Amy, has she found Amy?'

'Not yet,' he replied, pouring both of them another inch. 'but Siobhan is on the case. She's on the force, you know, damned good at her job as well. Theres a lot gone on in the last few months. A large amount of 'IT is about to hit the fan. Karma is a wonderful thing, Sandra.'

'I never stopped thinking about them, my girls, Tony's girls.'

'Tony's girl. Singular'. Bruce mumbled.

'What the fuck?'

'Siobhan has a brother, Malcolm. He is younger than her, but he is the biological child of her adoptive parents. He is big on his family history. Just as I am. My DNA has been on a genealogy site for years, just in case I have some long-lost cousins in a remote part of Australia or the States. Malcolm persuaded Siobhan to put hers onto the same site. She did that a few weeks ago. Today, before I came here, I had a notification. Siobhan is my daughter. Not Tony's. Mine.' Bruce became quite animated, thumping his glass down of the table. 'Did you know? Did you even suspect? Because if you did, you really should have told me, I had a right to know.'

'You and I would never have worked, Bruce, and no I had no idea. Do you think I would have been able to lie convincingly to Tony if I had. He was suspicious at first. But I believed the baby was his from the start. When I told him Charlotte was his, I wasn't lying, I believed it was the truth.'

'But you don't seem that surprised.'

'After the life I had, between one thing and another, nothing surprises me anymore. So, Holly is dead?'

'Yes.'

'And Paul Grainger?'

'Yes.'

'And Siobhan's parents?'

'Yes.'

'She's married?'

'Yes, to a lawyer and has two lovely sons, teenagers now. She lives in Bristol.'

'And what of Amy?' She seemed resigned to not finding her other daughter.

'You know as much as we do, but Siobhan has never stopped looking. What shall I tell her?'

'If you can stand the settee for the night, then I will write something for her. I need to explain it all, and I need to tell her that I never stopped loving her. They were both stolen from me. I will write two letters. One for each of them. Amy deserves to know it all as well, if we ever find her.'

Bruce fetched his belongings from the car. He sat up and watched into the small hours until Cassandra Weaver finished writing. He watched her add a recent photograph of herself to each envelope and then seal them and write a name on the front.

'Will you keep Amy's for me, Bruce?'

'If you want me to. Better you keep it here. Who knows what may happen to an old stray dog like me?'

He left in the morning. Cassandra did not hear him leave. She was still asleep with her head on the table, the empty bottle and two glasses alongside her.

CHAPTER 50. THE BREAKFAST SHOW

Janet Carmichael straightened her skirt and adjusted her blouse where the battery pack and the microphone were attached, then slid her elegant shoulders into the plain pale pink jacket. The sound techs always managed to disturb the hang of her suit. She had done her homework. She had done a meet and greet with Penny Major in the green room beforehand and had found her a pleasant and engaging woman, dressed to impress in a deep purple dress and jacket teamed with killer heels. She was clearly intelligent and educated. She was also enthusiastic and, for a change, seemed to have some good ideas for improving the lot of her constituents.

Janet had left her with a cup of green tea, sitting with the other guests, perusing the set of expected questions and chatting about this and that while waiting to appear on the mid-morning section of the show. Confident strides carried her into the studio, and she took her seat on the blue settee. Her guest would sit opposite. She heard the opening music and her producer counting down.

She looked straight down the lens of camera three, which was currently displaying the red light, and began her introduction.

'Thank you, Bethan and Rhodri, for what has been a wonderful start to this Friday Morning. You will definitely be a hard act to follow. I am Janet Carmicheal. Welcome to News and Views on Friday. Today I have the pleasure of interviewing the new candidate for election as member of parliament for Bristol South, Ms Penelope Major. Welcome Ms Major.

Penelope Major walked briskly onto the set and after a brief shake of hands with Janet took her seat on the opposite sofa.

Janet opened as she was expected to.

Penny, may I call you Penny? Firstly, it is a refreshing change to have someone so youthful standing as member of parliament. What inspired you to change from your successful career as a barrister to standing for election to government?

Well Janet. Call me Penny by all means. Having been involved with the law and the criminal justice system for many years, I have met a large cross section of society. In my dealings with them I have seen that there is a great deal of social injustice in the world we live in. My mission is to fight for the little people. I aim to get poverty off the streets and fairer living conditions for everyone.

'Penny, does this mean that you are ceasing your work as a high-profile CPS Lawyer after a successful career of more than ten years?'

Well, Janet, indeed it does. I am afraid I shall be hanging up my wig and gown for the foreseeable future and devoting my time to working in my constituency.

'Ms Major, is that not conditional on your being successful in the upcoming by-election? You speak as though your success is already a foregone conclusion.'

Penny Major's jaw dropped. She recovered swiftly. 'What I mean is, should I be elected. I am campaigning on matters involving getting the homeless off the streets and into accommodation and working with private landlords to keep rents fair, and properties in a good state of repair. Canvassing has shown that these are matters which greatly concern the residents in my prospective constituency.

'Ms Major, Janet continued. 'Is it not so that you resigned from your job with the CPS some weeks before you were nominated for the candidacy?

There was no immediate reply, so Janet pressed on. 'Is it not also correct that you were required to hand in your notice due to technical irregularities in some of your recent cases, some of which have yet to come to trial.'

Penny Major bridled. She looked helplessly at the producer, expecting someone to shout 'cut' or 'stop', or something, but there was silence.

Janet sensed an opening. 'Penny, what can you tell me about your involvement with Retired Detective Chief Superintendent, David Holly.'

Penny Major composed herself. 'Of course, I know of Mr Holly. I have successfully prosecuted several of his high-profile cases. I know him only on a professional basis. His recent death was a tragic event. It is fitting that he be given a police funeral with full honours.'

Janet continued. 'Cast your mind back to the year 1999. Did you spend the millennium eve at Mr Holly's Marbella apartment, being entertained by Mr Holly on a rather more personal basis?'

'I have never been to Marbella with anyone, let alone with David Holly. So, no I did not spend Millenium eve with him. Of that I am sure.'

'Are you aware that the police have recently been conducting an enquiry into Mr Holly's working practices and have found evidence of large amounts of money being paid to members of the judiciary by certain criminal elements in exchange for certain court cases to be, shall we say, manipulated.'

'Ms Carmichael, I must object! This is not what I came here to talk about.'

Janet continued. 'Penny, what is your relationship with Judge Llewelyn ap Meredith?'

'I must object to this this line of questioning. It is completely out of order.'

Janet's attention was attracted by her producer who was frantically giving her the thumbs up signal. Not the finger across the throat signal she expected.

She waited for an answer. Eventually Penny Major spoke. 'Judge ap Meredith is my great uncle. He has recently retired after an auspicious career. He was a revered judge for many years.'

'There is evidence that Judge ap Meredith took several very large payments which were processed through Mr Holly regarding several cases which he excused himself from hearing. These were cases for which you were appointed lead prosecuting barrister and several of them are those which are now subject of a case review due to their unexpected outcomes. Did you benefit from any of that money?'

'I certainly did not.'

'Did you yourself benefit from a payment of some £25,000 which can be traced to you from the account of Mr Holly during a case involving a notable Bristol citizen, Mr Paul Melville Grainger? An amount which can be shown to have originated from a business MelTech which was owned by the late Mr Grainger.'

At this point Penelope Major ripped off her microphone and stormed out of the studio. The producer shouted down her earpiece 'Keep Talking, we are cutting to a commercial.'

'That, ladies and gentlemen, was Penelope Major, the new parliamentary candidate for Bristol South. After the break our next guest will be the singer Jamie Alonsi, fresh from his sell out appearances at Bristol's Ashton Gate and Cardiff's Millenium Stadium. Can I have a warm News and Views welcome for Jamie Alonsi singing his hit song, 'Tell it Like it Is'.'

Cue canned applause. Jamie Alonsi stepped up to the microphone and Janet Carmichael stepped into a storm.

'That was marvellous, darling, where did all that come from? The phones have gone mental, darling, mental!' Barry Davies was positively crowing with joy. 'I hope all of it was corroborated or she will sue the balls off us.'

'Believe me it's all corroborated and there's more. There is enough evidence to have them twitching right to the top. My source has provided most of it, but I found loads more in the news archives, little snippets which when put together paint a very grubby picture.'

'How about a news special tonight? Can you put it together, have it ready for half past seven, the slot after the news?'

'Why not make it half eight, Barry, gives me an extra hour and it won't clash with the mainstream soaps. It will be ready.'

'Great stuff, Janet. I'll get a bit of a trailer done. Prepare the ground, try and generate interest. I have a feeling this could be big.'

'What I propose is a taster. To do this properly will need a few months of work, Barry. It needs interviews with those affected. It all needs to be checked by the legal team. How about we give the viewers an outline of what is to come? Then hit them with a 'Crime and Corruption', an On Your Doorstep Special.'

'Janet Carmichael, are you writing yourself into your own show? I see it now. *This is Janet Carmichael, On Your Doorstep......exposing the grubby underbelly of the city and holding it to account!*' I love it, love it, love it.'

Across the city, telephones were ringing in high places. Hushed conversations were being had in high places, and the wrecking ball was beginning to swing.

Siobhan Williams added one last box to the pile which she and Sarah had made in the out of town storage unit, copies made of everything, copies made using copiers in different offices, smuggled out sometimes a sheet at a time. She locked the door and let herself out of the compound. She caught the bus back into the city and walked from the bus station back to the office.

Mark was waiting for her. His face wore an expression of concern. Siobhan noted that the pile of brown document boxes which had been neatly stacked behind his chair was gone.

'They've been then?'

'They've been.'

'Who collected them?'

'Two anonymous porters in brown overalls, with a sack trolley. They had visitors passes.'

'Didn't you ask?'

'I did, they didn't answer, they just showed me a letter of authorisation and took the lot!'

'Ah well, Mark, we knew it was coming, it's not a surprise.'

'Shonnie, it's starting. Your presence is required in the Chief Super's Office.'

'Give me a chance, Mark, I haven't got my coat off yet.'

'I'd leave it on Sarg! He wants you up there yesterday. He's got a full head of steam worked up. I'd go now if I were you.'

Siobhan took her coat off and hung it up on the old hatstand in the corner. Then she went to the kitchen and made herself a coffee. She took it into her own office and tidied her desk. Everything in neat piles. She looked at the photo by the flatscreen computer monitor. Ray looked back at her, and the boys. Then she placed it face down by the keyboard. They didn't need to see her cry.

Twenty minutes later, she lifted her head off the desk. Leaving the coffee to go colder, she hadn't really wanted it, she steeled herself.

Straightening her clothes and her shoulders, putting on her carefully tailored jacket, and checking that the charity tie pin, which was acting as an emergency button, was securely in place, she made her way to the other side of the building, 'The West Wing' as they called it, the habitat of the senior management team.

Chief Superintendent Malcolm McTavish was not known for his friendly demeanour. He was at best dour and at worst downright rude. Not far off retirement, he prided himself on being the longest serving officer in the force. Forty and a half years. His father had served for forty. Malcolm intended to make it to forty-one, then he could retire with a feeling of satisfaction that he had beaten the old bastard at something, even if it was only length of service. Now this whippersnapper of a detective sergeant was about to jeopardise it all. If the Holly scandal, as it was being called, broke loose and the true extent of it was ever revealed....... Malcolm took a deep breath and his pension and his retirement home just outside St Mawes flashed before his eyes. He could see the disappointment in his wife's eyes. But that was not unusual. He had been a constant disappointment.

Siobhan slid her left hand into her trouser pocket and felt the comforting, cool aluminium case lying against her leg. Once more, she checked that the carefully adapted 'Help for Heroes' pin was secure, strategically filling in for a missing button at the cleavage of her blouse. As she tapped quietly on the boss's door, she pressed the small switch connected to the wire which ran invisibly up her sleeve and over her shoulder.

'Enter.' Mr McTavish didn't sound remotely happy. He rose from his seat and spread his palms on the desk. 'Ah, Detective Sergeant Siobhan Williams. Take a seat!'

He paused and seemed to grow an extra few inches. He was a huge man, six feet six in his stocking feet. Now run to fat, he had a massive girth much like Haggred the character from the Harry Potter films. His black beard, the colour now artificially maintained, was neatly barbered. His hair was neatly trimmed. He uttered one word. Spat it out with venom. 'Explain.'

'Explain what, exactly sir?' Siobhan showed no fear. To even suggest that you were intimidated would only add fuel to the fire. This misogynistic dinosaur loved to intimidate.

'Explain how this organisation has become a laughingstock. Explain why I have the IPCC requesting access to a list of historical cases. Explain how this has happened. I order you to tell me who leaked to the press!'

'Sir I don't know what you are referring to.'

'Sergeant, have you not seen the Television? You must be the only person in this building who has not. Sensitive information broadcast over the airways. All of it from that bloody case you were in charge of.'

'Sir, the case papers I was working on were all handed over this morning as requested. My colleague personally supervised their removal. The letter authorising their removal was signed by your good self, sir. If there is a leak, it has not been through me.'

Siobhan was starting to lose her nerve. McTavish had gone red in the face. His hands shook and, while he was not shouting, his voice had reached an impressive volume. She had no doubt he could be heard in the hallway, probably all the way to the senior officers' mess.

'Young lady, if I find out that you are lying to me, I will see to it that you are drummed out of this force and that you never work again. I will see to it that your husband, if he is party to your behaviour, never defends another case. Believe me I will beggar you. I have worked too hard to have it all destroyed.'

'Is that a threat, sir?' Siobhan felt sick as she said it. She knew it was more than a threat.

'No, you insubordinate bitch, it's a fucking promise. Get out!'

Siobhan stood, half tripping over the castors on the base of the chair as she got out.

'And close the fucking door behind you.'

Siobhan closed the door and pressed the stop button. Walking quickly and looking suitably contrite she made her way back to the Intelligence Unit.

'And how did that go?' Mark raised his head from the pile of logs he was reading.

'Better than expected. Bruce kitted me out well. The old bastard lost it completely. If he tries to bully me out, he has a shock in store.'

'On with the motley then!'

'Anything worth following up.'

'There's a couple of logs about a grow house in downtown St Paul's. It will need a good recce before we act. I thought of asking the team in Avonmouth to help out.'

'Make it so, Mark, make it so.'

'Any idea who is going to replace DI Perry?'

'Not a scooby. We'll find out when they appear. I have a feeling it won't be someone we like. Probably some promotion jockey putting a tick in another box.'

'I'll crack on then, Sarg.'

'You do that, keep Alfie in the loop, he needs some encouragement these days. I'm taking an early finish. It's been a stressful day.'

As she left the building via the front door, Malcolm McTavish was closing the back door and heading for his private vehicle. His temper had cooled. He had spent the last hour reviewing his retirement options. Sooner was seeming a better prospect than later.

CHAPTER 51. QUITE FRANKLY - Tansy

Ray Williams sat at a table in the window of the Jerry Can café. He frequently came here with clients. It was convenient for the police station. It was discreet and it was cheap. Neither he nor his clients looked out of place here. Ray did not trust the private rooms set aside for solicitors and clients in the nick. Today he was meeting Tansy. At 3pm or thereabouts she would be informed that there would be no criminal charges laid against her. She would be freed from her bail. Free to go wherever she chose.

Ray would be there to hear the news. He would be there when she signed the forms, there to hold her hand. He would meet her in the café first. He wanted to meet with her afterwards. There were things he wanted to put to her.

She arrived in a flurry of jeans, trainers, an oversized hoody and a parka coat, hair flying unrestrained around her face. The café door opened inwards, the spring-loaded bell attached to the frame jangled, announcing her entry. It was 2.45pm.

'Sorry I'm late,' she gasped and slid into the seat opposite him. 'You said it was good news.'

'It is, you are being released without charge.'

'Free! Nothing on ma' record?'

'Yes, totally free.'

'Will I get ma laptop and ma phone back? They've had them fer ages.'

'You should do. They have no reason to keep them. Come on let's get in there. There's no time for coffee. Have one after, ay.'

Tansy rounded up her belongings and Ray opened the door for her in gentlemanly fashion. They walked the short distance to the police station in silence.

Tansy handed herself in. The custody officer had the forms ready. Her phone and laptop were there ready to be returned. The whole thing took less than half an hour. As they walked back to the café afterwards, Ray was sure he could detect a bit of an extra spring in her step. She positively exuded life. It was his turn to buy. Donuts and coffee.

'You said you wanted to put something to me. What exactly? I can only just afford your bill as it is,' she joked.

'You mentioned to me that you grew up in the care system, that you were fostered. That you weren't born in Scotland.'

'That's right. I only went there because I thought my sister would be there. She was supposed to have been sent there. She wasn't there, but I stayed.'

'What was your sister's name?'

'She was called Charlotte. I forgot about her for years, well not about her exactly, but I wasn't sure what she was called. They changed all our names, you know.'

'And your name, can you remember what your name was?'

'The first name I really remember was Tracy, Tracy Brown. That was before I ran away the first time, before I went to Scotland. Then I became Tansy and I lived with Marcia.'

Ray took a bite out of his donut. 'My wife is adopted, you know. Her parents died. It was only then she found out. She also found she had a sister.'

'I hope she has better luck finding her family than I have.'

'That's what I want to talk to you about.'

'I can't pay you to find them. I have no job and my savings are running out. I have to accept that it's just me.'

'My wife thinks that you are her sister.'

'Your wife looks like me, then?'

'My wife is blonde, but she has a photograph of both of you as small children. My wife's sister is black. Her own mother is white. Her father was from Jamaica.'

'Was, you mean he is no longer alive.'

'My wife's father is dead. It was his death which led to her and her sister being taken into care.'

'So, what do you want from me? All I remember is running away. My life didn't start until I met Marcia. Until then I was lost. It's had some bad patches since then, but she put me on the right path. I can't help your wife.'

'Take a DNA test. See if you are related. You will both know then, one way or another.'

'The police have my DNA. Can't they use that?'

'They can't, unfortunately. My wife has already considered that. She's a police officer you know. I told her your story. Bits of it rang true with her.'

'What do I do then?'

He reached into his briefcase for the DNA kit. 'You spit in this. My wife's DNA is already on the system. If you are related the website will tell us in a few weeks. If you are her sister, then the other good news is that we've already found your mother. If the test is positive, then I'll tell you the rest of the story.'

'Like why my mother didn't look for me? All I was told was that she was gone. I assumed she was dead. I was told I could never see her again. I was only about four. All I had was my sister. Then she went too.'

'Will you do the test for me, Tansy, not just for me, for you as well?'

'And build up my hopes, only to have it all ripped apart again?'

'Tansy,' he took hold of both her hands and looked her in the eyes. 'You have the same eyes as my wife, you walk like my wife, you are taller than her by six inches, but you walk the same way. And you are just as bloody stubborn. Just spit in the pot for goodness sake.'

'You are that sure.'

'As sure as I can be without the science.'

'OK, give me the bloody test, even if it is just to shut you up. If you are wrong, I won't forgive you.'

She unpacked the kit, filled in the form and signed it then dribbled delicately into the plastic vial.

'You will do the rest?'

'I will do the rest. Are you away back to Glasgow?'

'I have to try and speak to Peter. Is it safe to tell you the truth now?'

'That you are Peter's lover, not an escort girl?'

'That's why I need to speak to him. That's what is under review. He dumped me like a bag of trash, Ray'

'He had to disown you. Tansy. I don't know any of his involvement in anything, but it would make sense for him to disown you. He was looking after you.'

'More like he was looking after himself, always himself and the business first. I'm not sure I can live like that anymore.'

'You look after you, Tansy. I'll ring you when I get a result.'

'You do that, I have a train to catch.'

'You take care of you, Tansy Alexander.'

'Don't worry about me, Ray Williams. Did you say what date your wife's birthday is.'

'21st June 1989'

'Mine too, but in 1990.' Tansy was headed for the door, the jangly bell proclaiming her departure. Ray Williams called after her. 'Irish twins, Siobhan's mum called you Irish twins.' But she did not hear him. Tansy was gone, his words lost in the noise of the rush hour traffic.'

When Ray arrived home, he was surprised to find his kitchen the scene of quite a gathering. Siobhan was sitting around the island unit with her colleague and friend Sarah James and a man he knew by reputation only, a friend a Sarah's with the nickname, "Batman". The tall blonde older man was Bruce Wayne.

The conversation was animated. Siobhan seemed the most animated of the three.

'This cannot be right.' She was staring horrified at the screen of her iPad.

'The science doesn't lie, Shonnie.' Sara was pacifying her.
'But this just cannot be right. My mother was married to Tony.'
'Bruce, explain to her, don't just sit there, say something.'
'What can I say. DNA doesn't lie. You are my daughter Siobhan.'
'But…..'

'Your mother and I were very close before she married. Yes, we did have a bit of a fling before she settled down. It appears you are the result.'

'Well, that's fucking comforting. I am not only the offspring of a bent copper and a murderer, but the alternative is that my father is a thoroughly immoral philandering bastard who shares a name with a fucking superhero.'

Sara started laughing. 'She's got you pretty much sussed.' She addressed the remark to Bruce.

'Hi, honey I'm home!' Ray entered the room, 'Anyone like to pour me a drink, I could use one.'

'Red okay?' Siobhan reached for the half empty bottle on the table and Sarah passed a clean glass from the cupboard. 'Will she do it?'

'She will! I'll send it off tomorrow.'

'Wonderful stuff, DNA, truly groundbreaking. I have just found out that this philandering bastard is my father. Not the drug taking bent bastard who was married to my murdering mother.' Siobhan was very drunk.

Ray read the email which had been printed off and was now lying wine and tear stained in front of his wife. He raised a quizzical eyebrow but said nothing.

'Shonnie darling, it is what it is, it's a 100% match. There is no doubt.' Bruce was conciliatory. 'If it's any consolation, I loved your mother. If things had been different……'

'Don't ever expect me to call you, "Dad". That will never happen. What did my mother have to say on the subject?'

'She came round after we finished the whisky. She had no idea, and I believe her. She was never a good liar, and Tony would have seen right through her. She believed you were his from the start.'

'Sarah, is this man on the level, can I believe a word he says?'

'He's a good guy, Shonnie, very nearly a superhero. He's just not good at people. Give him a chance, it's not as if you need a hands-on father at your age. If your mother won't have him, I'll give him a whirl.'

'Sarah James, I already told you, those days have gone. My life is messy enough as it is. I thought you and Dean were back on.'

'My love life is a bit like the Mumbles lighthouse. On then off then on again… get the drift? Give me a call if you change your mind.' She winked at Bruce who blushed like a ripening tomato, red right to the tips of his ears.

'You lot had better stay over.' Ray suggested. 'I don't suppose anyone of you is up to cooking. I'll phone for an Indian. I hope Tansy is okay.'

Tansy was on the train travelling north. She had tried to call Peter and had gotten no reply. She had left a message and sent him a text.

'Peter Balfour, this is Tansy, I'm home, call me.'

The woman in the bed beside him heard the phone ping. She looked at his sleeping form, saw the message on the screen. She unlocked the phone using the pass code she had worked out for herself. It was 210690, Tansy's birthday. He used it for nearly everything. She deleted both messages. Peter Balfour was hers. This Tansy bitch could do one. Tansy Alexander was the past. Eleanor McVie was the present. She replaced the handset face down on the bedside cabinet. Just as it had been. What the eye never saw the heart wouldn't grieve about, would it.

He had felt her move. 'What's up El. Have you another customer waiting?'

'No Pete, I'm just checking the time. I'm all yours, the rest can go hang.'

She snuggled down the bed nuzzling and nipping the shoulder of the sleeping man beside her. He rolled towards her, returning the affection without opening his eyes. As she lost herself in his embrace, she was sure she heard him whisper, 'Oh god, Tansy I've missed ye.'

'Tansy is the past, Pete, I am the present,' she crooned into his ear, her bright red painted lips making their way down his body.

He froze.

'Fuck, what am I doing?' he thought to himself. 'Fuck you Tansy, where the hell are you?'

His thoughts of Tansy were overridden by the thoughts of what was going on in his groin. He surrendered himself to the attentions of Eleanor's lips and lost himself in the moment.

CHAPTER 52. OPTIONS – Tansy

Tansy returned to Scotland. She didn't really know how to feel. All her emotions seemed to have been put through the washing machine, this time, one of those ones like she remembered in Alice Brown's house, an old-fashioned twin tub with a mangle on the top.

Her life had been boiled in hot soapy water, swirled in the ever increasing layer of grime at the bottom of the drum, then pulled into its component parts with a big set of wooden tongs and beaten into submission with a washing 'podger'. The last remnants of feeling had been wrung out through the rollers of the mangle. She felt numb. She had a feeling that she was only half way through the process. Was there a pause button before the rinse cycle, a chance to take stock before she was immersed in another tub of unseasonably hot water?

Her flat was still as she had left it. She had had a nagging fear that Peter would arrange to have it emptied, but she had pushed it from her mind. He was not vindictive, not towards her.

Joey's flat had been unceremoniously emptied of everything. It had been refurbished, decorated and was now rented out to a young, upwardly mobile couple with a nice, but second hand, Mercedes in the parking garage. Tansy didn't know their names, but he worked in I.T. and she was a manager in a call centre dealing with motor insurance. They were most likely up to their necks in debt, but they would put on a good show until the money ran out.

Tansy took a shower. She let the hot water run over her travel weary skin. She scrubbed herself with her favourite coconut and lime shower gel, washed her hair and wrapped herself in her old fluffy bathrobe which still hung behind the door. Hair encased in a towelling turban, she searched her cupboard for her worn grey joggers and the huge hoody she had liberated from Peacocks, back in the bad old days when she was forced to shoplift to feed her habit. It was big and black with that huge Rolling Stones tongue logo on the front. The inner label declared it 'official merchandise.' Tansy remembered that she had found it under a display, the security tags already removed. She had gone into the changing rooms and put it on, then walked out cool as a cucumber, wearing it. It was so big it had covered the multitude of other sins she hadn't paid for. That was in the days when Joey had run her life. Poor murdered Joey, for Tansy knew his death was no accident.

She put on the playlist of her life, a series of tracks mainly from the nineteen seventies and eighties mixed with Bastille, One Republic and Hozier.

Then there was Peter. She could have loved Peter, but he had made her feel cheap. While he was ruthless and hard-nosed where his businesses were concerned, he did have a softer side, and if what that Bruce guy had said was right, he might even love her. But where was he now? She'd received that text, he said he missed her. She had answered it, but he had not replied. What pride she had left wouldn't let her chase him. He had given her this flat. He had provided her with a lifestyle she enjoyed, but all at a price. The price was her integrity, her self-respect. Was there more than a grain of truth in what he told the police? She was his whore. He had bought her. Now he seemed to have cast her aside like a pair of old socks. She was curious. Should she drive out to his house and have it out with him? She had no right to expect anything from him. 'Get a grip, Tansy,' her mind told her. She curled up in her big sloppy armchair and reacquainted herself with the view from her window while Carly Rae Jepson voiced her inner thoughts, *'Call me maybe.'* Then CeLo Green assaulted her ears. F***you!

Who did she really want to call? Joachim Parral? Perhaps, no not perhaps, definitely. But would he? Or was he too just a passing fling? No one had ever affected her like he did. They seemed to echo each other's thoughts. They were completely on the same page. Would he call her, maybe? Would she go back to Spain? They could live in his house in the mountains, in remote isolation, have a large family of gorgeous looking dark haired perhaps blue-eyed babies. He was far too exotic for Glasgow.

He certainly had the moves, just like Jagger. She was certain that she would worship at the shrine of his life. Oh, yes.

She made herself a mug of instant hot chocolate. "Options" – the name made her smile, what were hers now, she wondered? The police had no evidence against her. She was a free woman. She had taken that DNA test. Ray Williams had rather steamrolled her into doing it. She could not see for the life of her how the police officer wife of a Bristol lawyer could be the sister of a teenage runaway from Glasgow, but stranger things had happened at sea. As the man said, the science would tell the truth. She should download the app. Check for notifications. Who knew? She might be related to royalty! But she seriously doubted that.

She did still occasionally dream of someone called Charlotte. She heard her voice, but she never saw her. Her life had been such a turmoil growing up she was surprised she had survived at all. The music of her life was still playing in the background.

'Don't you worry, don't you worry, child.
Heaven's got a plan for you.'

She turned the music up and began to dance to the Swedish House Mafia. The neighbours could go hang. She didn't make a habit of it.

That night she slept curled up in her chair, snug in joggers and hoodie, her mug of Options going cold on the floor beside her and the strains of Passenger letting her go.

Over a thousand miles away that same tune was re-playing endlessly in another solitary room, a recent addition to an otherwise very Spanish playlist.

Staring at the ceiling in the dark,
Same old empty feeling in your heart,
Cause love comes slow, and it goes so fast
Well, you see her when you fall asleep.
Never to touch, and never to keep.
You loved her too much and you dived too deep.

You only hate the road when you're missing home.
Only know you love her when you let her go,
And you let her go.

Tansy woke with a stiff neck and her left foot had gone to sleep, that sort of pins and needles asleep which makes the affected limb dead to the touch. She massaged her toes and her ankle and winced as the increased flow of blood and lack of bodily pressure improved the circulation. She hopped over to the table and unpacked her laptop from the padded insulated bag the police had wrapped it in.

Ray had given her the log-on details for his account on the genealogy website. He must trust her. Well, he had pretty much convinced himself that she was family, hadn't he.

She logged on. Nothing today. It might take a while to generate a hit. She'd try in a few days' time. Instinctively, she checked her phone. No messages. She knew Joachim wouldn't call. He had too much on his plate. She couldn't help herself. She would tell herself later that her loneliness made her do it. She rang Peter's number. It rang out....... unusual. It usually went straight to voicemail.

'Go away, Tansy, can't you leave him alone.'

'Peter....?' Obviously it wasn't!

'He's mine now... please don't call again.'

Then she heard his angry voice in the background. It was that gruff, low level monotone voice. She hadn't heard it often, but it didn't bode well. Quiet anger from Peter usually resulted in immediate and decisive action. Action to remove the source of the problem.

'Ye din'nae answer ma' phone, have I no' told ye that.'

Tansy sensed that the argument she couldn't see was becoming physical. 'Tansy, hen, is that you......?' She heard him in the background.

'Piss off Tansy, hen, he doesn't need you, he has me now.'

There was a loud **crash,** the sound of breaking glass, the rasp of heavy breathing. Then there was silence.

'No, Peter, no other women,' she thought, wondering why she'd even bothered to think of ringing him. The call disconnected but no one phoned back. She re-dialled the number, but the phone was switched off. The electronic voice announced.

I am sorry but the caller is unable to take your call.

On the other side of Glasgow, Peter was standing with the remains of his phone and the heavy alabaster base of a bedside lamp in his hand.

Eleanor McVie was lying face up on the bed, her red lipstick grinning at him like a really bad joke.

'I didn't much care for her anyway,' was his first thought. The next was, *'Where the f**k am I going to dump the body?'* On top of all the other shit in his life he really could do without this.

Eleanor had come from the docks and back to the docks she would go. Maybe she could keep wee Joey company. Peter made his plans. He had wanted to find Tansy, to explain to her. But that would have to wait.

In the end he decided against the graving dock. In the dead of night, he drove north. The body of Eleanor McVie would not turn up for many years and when it did it would be almost unrecognisable. It was a long way down to the bottom of the loch. The stones were heavy and the rope was stout. She wouldn't smile at the daylight until the rope broke and the gasses that filled her took her back to the surface. He made sure he sent the Audi for valeting and burned his clothes as a precaution. Then he telephoned Bruce Wayne. Bruce in his own inimitable way was straight to the point.

'Buggered it up, have you, Pete? Ever heard the phrase, 'if you want her back you have to let her go first?'.........Well I suggest that's what you do. She's got a lot to cope with without your shit as well. Just be there for her.'

'Where does her mother live….. perhaps…..?'

'I'm not sure that's such a good idea, Pete. Don't ambush her. Remember what I said about surprises.

With a heavy heart, Pete went about his business. The property deal he had set up in Spain had all but fallen through. The vendor seemed to have disappeared. It was a fine property, a fabulous penthouse apartment. He'd never seen anything quite so exquisite. Pete had ideas to keep it as his own, not to develop it as a commercial enterprise. He was tired of Scotland and the hassle which seemed to follow him about. These days business such as he conducted could be done on-line. Meetings could be conducted via Zoom. Face to face was becoming a thing of the past. He imagined himself on the roof, glass in hand, girl on his arm, gazing out over the sea.

He contacted the Spanish realtor. Was the deal still on?

'Si, lo es, el vendedor original está muerto, su hermano ahora está vendiendo la propiedad. ¿Todavía quieres seguir adelante con el trato ? Quiere una venta rápida. Él aceptará una oferta razonable. Fincas como esta no suelen estar disponibles". The excited Spaniard repeated his pitch in English.

'Yes, it is, the original vendor, well he is dead, his brother is now selling the property. Do you still want to go ahead with the deal? He wants a quick sale. He will take a reasonable offer. Apartments like this do not often become available'.

Peter made an offer, a tempting distance short of the asking price.

'I will see what Senor Parral has to say about your offer.'

And so, the deal was done. Peter Balfour only ever spoke to Joachim Parral once, when he'd spent a day in Malaga completing the paperwork and collecting the keys. He found him a personable, well-educated man. They'd hit it off over a coffee that metamorphosed into lunch – seafood with a crisp, white Rioja. It was quite by chance he found out about his relationship with Tansy. Senor Parral mentioned that he was in love with a beautiful woman from Glasgow. A dark skinned young lady with distinctive blue eyes. It was Peter who had grinned and, in jest, asked if her name was by any chance, Tansy. It was a small world after all.

Siobhan made the phone call about a week later. Tansy had not bothered to check the website, what would be, would be. Her mind was still in confusion. She had spent nearly a week without leaving her flat. She had listened to music, ordered every imaginable meal she could have delivered. She was personal friends with the delivery rider. He was a spotty youth of about 19yrs trying to earn a little extra to get himself through college. She played her guitar, and she had written or doodled nonsensical lyrics in a notebook.

She nearly leapt off the chair when the display on her phone lit up. It wasn't Joachim, or Peter. The display read 'Brief', for that was how she had entered Ray's number in her phone.

'Tansy here, who wants her.' She took the call.

'Hi sister! It's Siobhan. I can't believe this, but you really are my sister.'

Tansy was silent.

'I have a letter for you from our mother.'

Tansy's voice was choked with emotion. 'Are you Charlotte?'

'I was, and you were Amy, but that was a lifetime ago. Get on the train, I'll meet you at the other end. We need to read what she's written together. Come and stay for a while, we have loads to catch up on.'

Tansy stood in her apartment, gazed out at the water, took a big breath and packed her bag again.

Ray had been right. The blonde woman who met her at Temple Meads did look like her, around the eyes. There seemed to be an instant bond of recognition.

Siobhan saw the tall figure loping down the platform. 'She always did have attitude,' she thought to herself. Her sister did indeed walk like a cat. Siobhan envied her those extra few inches of leg. What the hell, she was glad they had found each other.

Tansy thought the hug would never end. In fact, it wouldn't. Siobhan was a walking hug. A very efficient and businesslike one, but a hug none the less and Tansy had been short on hugs lately. Ray was behind the wheel, waiting to drive them back to the Williams home. Two teenage boys waited eagerly to meet their auntie. Auntie Tansy was overcome by the welcome.

Later that evening when the boys had gone to bed, Siobhan handed her one of two envelopes. It was addressed to, "My Amy". Tansy opened it and began to read the heartbreaking story of her mother's life, condensed to a few pages of A4.

It took some time for a lot of it to sink in.

'How could they have done that to her? They ripped us apart for their own gain, to cover their tracks!' Tansy started.

'Can we forgive her, do you think?'

'She did nothing that needs forgiving. We need to tell her.'

'And Dad, do you remember him?'

'I remember him, you know. I can smell his aftershave sometimes. He was a big man, wasn't he?'

'Well unless they stood you in a grow bag, he must have been tall.'

They laughed together.

'Shall we go there, then?'

'Down west? I think she's waiting for us. Have you read the last page yet?'

Tansy turned the last page over. It was written in a scrawling hand and with total honesty.

…….and so, girls it is time to turn over the page and start afresh. I will admit I am a little drunk as I write this. Bruce is dozing in my armchair. He is one of my greatest regrets. I treated him very badly. I loved Tony Weaver with a passion, a passion I never quite felt for Bruce. Probably because Bruce is his own man, he needs no-one but himself. I know that now, I love him more for knowing it. One day I hope both of you will find a love as strong. Siobhan, (I think it only right that you remain Siobhan) you have found yours in Ray. Tansy, your father was

headstrong, he was impulsive. Please I beg you consider your decisions better than he did. You are as stubborn as he was.

Now I am rambling, I hope you can forgive your old mother enough to visit me. My door could not be opened for all those years. How could I look after you when I was locked away myself? The door is open now. Believe me when I say, I thought of you every day and never stopped searching.

All my love for the rest of time
Mum.

'Then we must go. With open minds and open hearts, we must go.'

CHAPTER 53. ASHES TO ASHES

Julia Grainger drew in a deep breath. The Court Officer opened the door which led from the dock down the steps to the cells below the courthouse. It was not the door she had come in through. She had expected to get bail. She had been sorely disappointed. Her incredulous and dismayed look to her very expensive lawyer conveyed her feelings exactly.

To be fair, he had tried every tactic available. Ms Grainger would surrender her passport. She would accept conditions which were not far short of house arrest. Would no consideration be given to the fact that her father had been brutally murdered, that her father, had he been alive, would likely have been implicated in the case for which the prosecution was firmly pointing its finger, quite wrongly, at his client?

The prosecution had countered that Ms Grainger was charged with several very serious offences, all of which would undoubtedly lead on conviction to lengthy custodial sentences. She was a person with a penchant for travel and the means at her disposal to easily flee the country with or without the benefit of a passport. She was a woman for whom acquisition of the necessary travel documents would not be a problem.

There was a likelihood that she would try and interfere with prosecution witnesses, those that had not already been terminally interfered with. There was evidence that she was part of a sophisticated international criminal network, which she would undoubtedly employ to her advantage, should she retain her freedom.

The Stipendiary Magistrate had retired to consider the representations. He had not taken more than the time it took to drink his waiting cup of earl grey and eat his rich tea biscuit for him to make his decision.

'Julia Grainger, please stand! Ms Grainger, I have considered the representations made by both the prosecution, and your defence. I find I am in agreement with the prosecution. You will be remanded in custody for three weeks. Your case by its very nature will be committed to the Crown Court for trial. The next hearing will be in three weeks' time. Via video link. Take her down.'

Still on the in-breath, Julia drew herself up to her full height, smiled grimly at Cecil Masterson who was already removing his wig and his gown. Barristers of his calibre did not relish even minor defeats at Magistrates Court.

'I'll see you downstairs,' he mouthed to his client.

Julia was shown into the small windowless interview room below the courtroom. It was painted pale green. The floor was grubby and the atmosphere stank of body odour, disinfectant and an automatic spray of industrial strength air freshener which puffed out of a dispenser screwed to the wall at ceiling level. The table was small and bolted to the floor. The chairs were similarly fixed and were hard and plastic.

A slightly plump, pale faced female jailer equipped with a large set of keys on a long chain stood outside the open door.

'Never mind, luv, time on remand is easier to do. Think of it as time off.'

Julia audibly growled as she slid her expensively clad posterior into the plastic chair and rested her head in her hands. Within five minutes Cecil Masterson joined her. Sitting opposite, he opened his briefcase and pulled out a legal pad.

'I'm doing this for your father, young lady. He was one of the firm's best clients. Now with him gone and you, well, temporarily indisposed, you will need to take stock. Do you have any specific instructions for me, additional to *'Get me out of here, and they can't prove anything'*?

Julia grunted again, like an animal in some form of acute pain.

'As a matter of fact, I do. Pass me a pen.'

Julia Grainger proceeded to write out a specific set of instructions. Cecil read them and raised an eyebrow.

'How on earth did your father come by those?'

'I suggest you ask your senior partner, if he is still living. I believe he conducted most of your firm's business with my father. They are both probably somewhere extremely warm, watching me burn as we speak.'

'And where should I send this item of property, Ms Grainger?'

Julia wrote out the address. She was careful with the spelling, and the post code. 'Make sure it's next day delivery and signed for. Oh, and put a note in with it, the note should say....' She wrote three words on the paper. 'Oh, and send lilies. She loves lilies.' Julia tapped the gold nib of the Parker fountain pen on the paper with increasing firmness. The pen began to leave an expanding blue black blot on the velum. Cecil reached across the table and removed it from her grip. It was one of his most treasured possessions. A gift from Jonny. Placing the engraved gold cap over the nib he slotted it neatly into the inside pocket of his old-fashioned black court coat.

Julia looked up. Her nose and her mascara were starting to run. Her eyeliner was smudged and her lipstick needed attention. Her chemically straightened hair was working its way loose from its severe, 'up do'.

'Just one more thing, Cecil.'

'What might that be, Julia?'

'If it's the last thing you ever do, please get me out of here.'

Cecil clicked shut the lid of his case. He smiled at his client. For the first time in their dealings his smile reached his watery blue eyes. 'I shall do my best, my dear. Now I must go.'

Outside, the jailer was impatiently jangling her keys. A smell of greasy food was emanating from the dimly lit cells passage. Dinner was served.

Cecil smiled to himself as he left. His client was desperate indeed. It was the first time he had ever heard her say, 'please'. He suspected the word was one that was very seldom found in her vocabulary.

When he reached the street, he rummaged in his coat for his phone and made the arrangements.

'Johnathan........ I need you to retrieve an item of property from the Grainger house. Yes, I need you to do it now......... it's in the top of the wardrobe in Grainger's bedroom......yes, that's what you are to do. The keys to the house are in our office safe......yes, it's to be delivered to an address a.s.a.p. with a note. I have the details. I'll message them. Speak later. Thank you, Jonathan. I won't be long, I should be back within the hour, I'm just on my way to order some flowers.'

Cecil scratched his head through his thinning hair. He had no idea what Julia Grainger was up to, but he was certain no good would come of it. Nonetheless, he would follow her instructions, it was after all what he was paid to do, and he knew which side his bread was buttered. He also suspected that he was being followed.

Until this whole sorry matter had been put to bed, he would toe the line as would every other member of Masterson and Finch Barristers at Law. Cecil made his way across the city on foot, stopping at the florists on his way back to Unity Street.

On the other side of the city, Johnathan Finch let himself into Paul Grainger's house. The property was empty, but still showed signs that the last persons to visit had been the local constabulary. He made his way upstairs and found the master bedroom. Mirrored cupboard doors covered two walls. A black ash door led to what he assumed was the en-suite. The huge bed occupied most of the floor space. He slid open one of the mirrored doors. The cupboard was still packed with Paul Grainger's clothing. Johnathon Finch paused briefly to admire the array of brightly coloured shirts and quality tailoring. Standing on the bathroom stool, he found what he was looking for on the top shelf, high up inside the fitted wardrobe. Placing it in a supermarket carrier bag, being careful not to lose any of the contents, he too made his way back to Unity Street. The courier service could take the parcel in the morning. It would need a box at least. Those they had a-plenty, former containers of A4 paper had a multitude of uses. He wrapped the item in bubble wrap and, taking a card from the small silver receptacle on Cecil's desk, reading the text message he wrote the three word message on it and placed it inside the parcel. He taped the box shut and wrapped it in a layer of brown paper. Securing the paper with more tape, he wrote the address on a separate label and stuck it on the side, clearly visible to the delivery agent. He would take it to the post office first thing in the morning. He had just finished applying the last of the tape when Cecil let himself in through the big wooden front door, stopping to give the brass plate alongside it a Dickensian polish with his coat sleeve.

'I'm done here, Sess! Let's get off home, it's been a bloody long day.'

'Suits me, Jonny.' Cecil dumped his briefcase on the desk, hung the bag containing his wig and gown on the hatstand behind the door, covered his Prince Edward style jacket with a canvas suit bag and hung it on the same stand. He shrugged himself into his camel overcoat and picked up his car keys and threw them to Jonny. 'You drive, I have such a headache.'

The slightly battered red Ford Sierra was parked in the next street. Twenty minutes later, Cecil was inserting the keys into the front door of their lovely home at Lock Keepers Lane and he and Jonny were preparing dinner in the huge open plan kitchen with the granite worktops. As the two long term partners embraced each other to mark the end of another busy day turning the wheels of the justice system, neither was aware that their every move was being watched.

'Will she get off, do you think?' Jonny enquired.

'I'd need a magic wand, or a large miracle at least.' Cecil sighed. 'She won't deal, she won't cut her losses. I fear she will be away for a very long time.'

'And the Scot, Peter whatever....?'

'Balfour, they have nothing on him, not even a parking ticket.'

'And the girl.....?'

'Unless it's an offence to travel by train, again, nothing. And Ms Grainger has successfully removed every witness who might have assisted me in defending her case.'

'Bleak outlook, then?'
'Bleaker than a wet day on Dartmoor.'
'And that parcel?'
'Heaven only knows….. but we do as we are instructed.'
'Cecil?'
'Yes, Jonny.'
'I really don't like this house. I have a bad feeling about it.'
'Didn't anyone ever tell you about gift horses?'
'You mean, if it seems to good to be true,'
'Then it probably is.'
'Cecil, I think we are being watched.'

CHAPTER 54. AND NOTHING BUT THE TRUTH

Cassandra was upstairs, tidying away the washing basket full of freshly ironed clothes. She had spent most of the afternoon ironing. Well, these days she had precious little else to do. With the death of Paul Grainger, her little back street employer now had no clients.

After the shock of Bruce's visit and the monumental hangover which had lasted until lunchtime on the second day, she had immersed herself in mundane things, trying not to ask herself the awkward questions which raised their heads above her mental parapets.

'Could she have tried harder to find them?'

One part of her said that she could. But then the realist in her told her that to stir the pot in that direction could have gotten her killed. The oath she had taken as a Police Officer all those years ago came flooding back. It made her laugh – first duty, *'protection of life and property, firstly your own.'* The words of her first training sergeant echoed in her mind. 'Always remember. You are no good to anyone, dead!'

She sat on the bed in her spare bedroom rolling socks into pairs and stuffing them into an already overfilled drawer. She needed to throw some of the older ones out. That was another job she could get done now she had more time on her hands. Picking up the basket, she moved to her own bedroom. The double bed had seemed extremely large compared with the narrow bunk she had slept in for so long, but over the years she had grown used to its size. She toyed with thoughts of having company again, someone to share it with, someone to lie next to in the mornings, to share her life with someone who might laugh at her bad jokes, who might make her a cuppa – tea in bed, in the morning, the way civilised people do - someone else's washing to peg out to dry on the stiff sea breeze.

Cassandra was still deep in laundry and thought when she heard the sound of an engine labouring its way down the track towards the cottage. Not just one, her ears, sensitive to changes in her usually peaceful world detected more than one disturbance. She pulled the bedroom curtain an inch to the left and saw the roof of what looked like an old-fashioned Land Rover and yes, there it was, Bruce's sleek dark sports car, totally unsuitable for the terrain, carefully negotiating its way, one wheel up on the central ridge of the track, avoiding the potholes.

Stand by to repel boarders!' she mused to herself. She sensed who her visitors might be, but was she ready for this?

In the few minutes it had taken her visitors to park, she had descended the narrow stairs, filled the kettle and turned it on, and hidden the strategically placed shotgun behind the curtain which stopped the drafts coming through her front door. There was no way to avoid the invasion now. All avenues of escape were gone, except to run and hide in the Ty Bach at the end of the garden, maybe peer at them defiantly through the heart-shaped hole in the door.

Cassandra's hand shook as she opened the front door and her voice trembled with twenty years of emotion as she spoke. 'You'd all better come in.' No other words emerged.

Bruce ducked under the low door lintel, followed by another tall man, and a fair-haired woman, both smartly dressed, townies she thought. They were followed by a tall, leggy young woman, her mop of unruly black curls restrained under a bandanna and dressed in jeans and converse basketball boots topped with a shapeless grey hoodie. She followed the herd uneasily, like a forest animal entering a clearing, senses on high alert, almost smelling the air for danger. Bruce ushered the others to seats around the kitchen table. The hairs on the back of his neck detected tension. No shit, you could cut the atmosphere with a knife. He heard wooden chair legs scrape on the flagstone floor. He busied himself finding mugs in the cupboard and rearranging the teaspoons on the draining board. Tansy was still standing in the doorway, looking at Cassandra, looking at her mother, her green-blue eyes like lasers. She could have been ready to bolt, but in an instant she took two strides into Cassandra's personal space. Cassandra stepped backwards,

backwards into the corner made by the kitchen worktops. Twenty years of memory flooded her mind, twenty years of guilt, twenty years of remorse, twenty years of living hell. Tears flooded her vision. Instinct made her reach for something, but it wasn't there. There was only grief. The words fell out in an angry growl, words from a time long ago, in a kitchen, across a worktop. 'I will not live like this…..!'

She lifted her eyes and met those of her daughter. More words echoed in her mind, 'Mummy sad again….'

Tansy felt Bruce's hand on her shoulder, quietly guiding her back a step. She took a breath. 'Why?' was the only word which came out.

'I had no choice, Amy, it was me or him. He could have killed us all.'

'There is always a bloody choice, mother. I take it you are my mother. Tell me, are you!?'

'If you want me.'

'Well, I'm here, aren't I. Are you going to stick the knife in me as well.'

The silence rolled around the room. There was no sound of voices, only the hiss of the kettle coming to the boil like the burning of a fuse which had been dormant for years, the dysfunctional Catherine Wheel firework igniting to spread sparks of destruction as it spins itself to a standstill.

'Let me explain, Amy, please.'

'Amy ceased to exist long ago. You lost the right to call me that when you killed my father. I remember him, you know.'

At the table, Siobhan looked helplessly at her husband for guidance and sobbed. 'So do I.'

'So, what happened to him, mother? Does he even have a grave?'

Cassandra was silent. In all the years since, she had never thought about what had happened to Tony Weaver's remains. In her fight to survive it was a question she had never asked. Tansy asked it now.

'Where is my father? What have they done with him?'

Cassandra looked Tansy straight in the eyes and with brutal honesty told her. 'I don't know, and I really don't care! Yes, he was your father, and he was my husband, but he fucked us all up, big time! We've all paid!' It was said with a finality which chilled those listening. 'Tansy, there is a lot you may not want to hear about your father. He is dead. I paid a heavy price for my crime, more than you'll ever know, and you and Siobhan have paid, too. Your father is the past. We are the future. We have to get past it and move on!'

'In a way she's right, Tans. We all came here for answers, but we didn't come to start another war. It's been hard for everyone.' Ray tried to be reasonable.

'But you, and Siobhan have each other, you have family, Siobhan has you and Malcolm and the boys, hell, she even has him!' Tansy pointed at Bruce. 'Who do I have? I have no one, I have a home paid for by a man who bought me from my pimp. Even the clothes I stand up in now, well some of them are stolen. So, tell me, someone, how the fuck am I supposed to feel?'

There was a deep cough and the front door opened without ceremony, and Peter Balfour pushed the curtain aside. He looked exhausted. He was unshaven and his eyes were shadowed with dark rings. He was carrying a box in both hands.

'Din'nae ask me how I got here, the bloody transport in this country is a nightmare, but I met a delivery man in the village, he said he was coming here. Anywa' he dropped me off on the lane. It's addressed to you, hen, I took the liberty of signin' for it.'

He handed the box to Cassandra. She looked at it suspiciously and placed it on the counter. She wasn't expecting a parcel. Her gut said it had something to do with the bouquet of lilies which had arrived earlier. She had thrown them into the compost heap. She hated lilies, a symbol of death. The parcel could wait until later.

At the sight of Peter, Tansy went apeshit. 'You fucking bastard, what the fuck are you doing here, you selfish fucking Glaswegian prick. I heard her, Peter, in the same bed where you stuck it in me. You dump me like a sack of shit, then you get with some whore. Found her on the dock did you, or have you had her cleaned and sanitised like you did me?' The long, manicured nails flashed like the claws of a feral cat. The slap would have been heard several miles away in Fishguard. Blood started to ooze from the three parallel cuts down Peter's left cheek. He dabbed them with his cuff.

'I deserved that, hen, I'll no say otherwise, but I came because I needed tae see ye.' His accent was thick, his voice choking. 'I understand how ye feel, just ken I'll always be her for ye. Bruce left the address on his satnav, that's how I found ma way. Bruce man, yer a bit slow wi the bottle, are ye no, fer fuck's sake, I think we all need a dram!'

Bruce had busied himself rounding up Cassandra's meagre array of glasses, each one liberated from a different pub, no two the same. He had found the bottle of Dufftown in the cupboard under the sink, neatly stashed behind the bleach and the washing powder. The Penderyn Madeira cask was in full view on the sideboard. He did the honours. Neat. There was no ice. There was no choice. 'Water's in the tap,' he added, 'if anyone needs it.'

'Either he needs to fuck off, or I do!' Tansy's rage was re-directed from her mother to Peter. She downed her drink and poured another inch into the chipped Jack Daniel's tumbler, the heaviest glass in her mother's collection. She drained it dry, then with the accuracy of a circus knife thrower launched it at Peter's head. It hit the wall about half an inch to the right of his ear. Shards of glass embedded themselves in the rough plastered cottage wall, and some lodged in his dishevelled hair. He did not move. He just raised an eyebrow.

'Yer aim's a bit off, Tans, but I deserved that as well.' She thought he was laughing at her. Not a good move!

She flew at him again, Bruce grabbing her by the back of her hoodie and the belt of her jeans. This time Peter grasped her by both wrists and swiftly neutralising the attack, wrapped her tightly in his arms. Pinning her close against his chest, anger turned to tears and, as her sobs gradually subsided, attention turned to the parcel.

Ray and Siobhan looked perplexed. This was not exactly what they had been expecting.

CHAPTER 55. DREAM CATCHER - Tansy

'Leave her, Shonnie.' Sandra caught her daughter's arm as Siobhan started to follow her sister out through the door of Sandra's home. 'She'll come back. She needs to do this one thing on her own.'

'But mum, it's going to get dark soon, she won't find the way.' Siobhan was all concern.

'She knows where she's going. If you try to stop her, she may not come back. Leave her be.'

The delivery had been a shock to several people. The fallout had been loud and vocal. There had been accusations made, accusations which were both hurtful and partially true, if Sandra was honest with herself.

The parcel had arrived by commercial courier, a signed for package addressed to Mrs Cassandra Weaver, of all people. The sender was a firm called Masters and Finch. That name meant nothing to Tansy, but Cassandra had seen it before, on the formal headed paper from Grainger's lawyers.

'It's from **her**, Its from Julia.'

The penny dropped. Tansy stood back from the box as though it might explode.

'Why would that bitch send you something in the post? You know who she is, don't you mother?'

Sandra had stared blankly at her daughter.

'That's Grainger's fucking daughter, that's who it is, that arsehole that fucked over my father!' Tansy was shaking with rage. 'What do you suppose this is, then, a fucking bomb or a severed head?'

With that, Tansy had selflessly carried the box outside to where Peter Balfour and Bruce Wayne had stripped off the cellophane wrapping and found a cardboard box. It was not ticking, they had joked, and there was no blood running out of it. What then? They had carried it back inside and placed it on the kitchen table. Tansy had seen the small, engraved plate inlayed in the lid of the item contained in the box.

She had lifted it from its resting place and announced, 'This was my father. One of you killed him. One of you spied on him. One of you has no claim on him at all. This job is mine and mine alone.' Then, she stormed out of the front door carrying in her arms the small pottery urn which the label announced contained the ashes of Anthony Weaver.

Only Sandra had read the note which was hidden amongst the bubble wrap. *'Nothing is forgotten.'* She knew who had sent it and quite frankly she didn't give a damn about it. She slowly ripped it into as many small pieces as she could and threw it to the wind. She was fit for Julia Grainger, whatever the bitch tried to do next.

If Bruce was to be believed, Julia Grainger had been arrested and was currently remanded in custody. Was there anyone else who could bail her out? Her father was dead, he had no more strings to pull, if he even wanted to.

Two hours had passed and there was no sign of Tansy. Sandra was worried.

The red and orange clouds which floated on the horizon seemed to merge with the amber stain which the sun was leaving on the sea. Tansy walked along the narrow path, slowly, one foot after another. The signs on the cliff top were a warning.

'Danger Crumbling Cliffs.'

In the distance she could see the overhangs the wind and the sea had created, their dark hollow voids contrasting with the lighter limestone and grit of the cliffs, nature destroying what nature had created.

DO NOT WALK CLOSE TO THE EDGE proclaimed the notices.

Tansy liked the edge. The closer to it the better, sure footed as a goat, a graceful, elegant, goat. She followed the paths which the sheep had made walking single file to avoid the sheer drop to the sea. The high point of the walk was spectacular. Tansy was enjoying simply standing there, high up on the promontory, feeling the wind on her face and in her hair. She loved to watch the seabirds wheeling on the breeze, launching themselves from their seats in the hollows the elements had made in the ground underneath her. She imagined them like feathered skateboarders all waiting in line, waiting to show off their latest big trick. In the distance she could see the tall white edifice of the lighthouse, a huge white finger pointing a warning to ships in the sea off west Wales. Like the buildings which housed the huge foghorn, nestled at its base, it was no longer fulfilling its original purpose. It was now a house, and a visitors' centre, the light platform an observation point for tourists.

The seagulls dived and screamed one last call before darkness put an end to playtime. Tansy, too, was clean out of tricks, rudderless and without sails. She was drifting, like she had always drifted. There was no safe haven on her horizon, no mooring to cling on to. She seemed to be lost on a choppy sea, waiting for the next gust, the next wave to pick her up and carry her somewhere. But then, wasn't that what she had always done?

She had tried to change, but all she had found was a past which had held only sorrow and anger. She had tried to find a way to forgive. What was she forgiving? Every day on the news she saw mealy mouthed snowflakes of people forgiving the perceived wrongs that others had done them, people who believed that life owed them something, that they should be handed life on a plate. Well, life wasn't like that. Life was what you made of it. Life was taking the chances you found, going forward, not looking back.

She would do this one last thing for him, the father she had barely known, then she would never look back again. It was the least she could do.

Lost in her own thoughts, standing in the increasing darkness, Tansy took one more step. She took the lid off the urn and held her arms aloft like some ancient priestess welcoming the sunset. With a short, 'Rest in Peace', she cast her offering to the west wind.

Earth slid under her feet, marbles of earth like rollers turning under the soles of her expensive trainers, accelerating her downward journey. A terrified seagull flapped and squawked as its nest was demolished by the disintegrating turf which fell from its roof. Tansy screamed, arms flailing as she slid over the edge, darkness the only thing between her and the sea crashing on the Jurassic sandstone rocks below.

Then it stopped, everything stopped. Her hooded sweatshirt was tight under her armpits, she could feel the material stretching, pulling her limbs upwards. Her body resisted the pull by instinct. It would be so much easier to let go. But she would not give in. Had she ever given in? Tansy never gave in, Tansy had never given in. The woman who professed to be her mother had told her that baby Amy was as stubborn as they came.

Her feet tentatively swung inwards looking for some solid ground, something for support. The zip fastener was biting into the skin of her neck, and she was starting to choke. Her feet found only nothingness. Her left shoe had fallen off and she could feel the breeze caressing the toes of her foot. The shoe was gone, now floating with the other flotsam two hundred feet below, where the never-ending sea would chew at it, as it chewed at the cliff. It would end up on some local beach, to be litter picked by the boys on community payback. They would probably joke about finding the body to go with it. Tansy's mind was in overdrive. The soundtrack of her life pressed play and she could hear Blondie, Hanging on the Telephone. What she wouldn't give to be able to phone a friend at this moment in time.

It could have been minutes, or hours later, she really wasn't sure. The voice came from above her.

'Gi us yer hand, ye daft wee thing.'

She couldn't see upwards, and it was dark, but she knew the voice. It probably wasn't God! God didn't talk in Glaswegian and certainly didn't use words like 'daft' and 'wee.'

'Fer fuck's sake Tansy, give me yer hand, any hand will do.' The voice was closer. 'Do it now, hen, please, I can'nae hold on much longer.'

Slowly, so as not to fall downwards and out of the item of clothing which controlled her perilous hold on life, like a child in a classroom asking to leave the room, she raised her right arm.

A strong hand grasped her wrist and pulled. For an instant she thought her arm would fall off, that she would be left like some disjointed cheap plastic doll, the ones you see tied to the front of the council dust cart. Then the pressure on her neck slackened. She felt the brush of rough grass on her back as she was pulled to safety, another hand, this time gripping her left arm, then arms around her body swept her away from danger.

'Peter?' Her voice was questioning and hoarse.

'Yes, it's Peter,' the voice was choking on the thick accent. 'are ye comin' with me or no'?'

'Where to?' she stammered, 'There is nowhere left to go.'

'That's where ye' are wrong, hen. It does'nae matter what ye call yersel' or where ye came from, all that matters is here and now.'

He started to walk her back down the track towards the car park where the lights of a battered Land Rover lit the path to safety.

'All these people love ye, hen. I love ye', we love you because you are you. Not for anything else. No strings attached.'

Without resistance, she submitted to being wrapped in a blanket and sat uncomplaining and slightly sheepish in the middle of the front bench seat. Suddenly everything seemed to make sense.

The heavy old doors shut with a reassuring clunk. Bruce fiddled in the darkness. He finally managed to insert the worn key into the ignition, then pushed the black button on the dashboard beneath it. The ancient engine sprang to life, the exhaust pipe clattering against a loose bracket. Two female voices spoke in unison from the canvas covered rear.

'It's done then. You've done it?'

Tansy sniffed. 'Yes, it's done.'

Now at last, all the Weavers were free. Tansy for one was never taking another backward glance, but she was eternally thankful for gorse bushes and for finally knowing that her family and even Peter Balfour would always be there to catch her. Peter would catch her, Peter was safety. Tansy wasn't sure it was always his version of safety that she wanted.

Two hours later, Peter made his excuses and left them to their family reunion. He felt out of place, his relationship with Tansy clouded by the spectre of Eleanor McVie and the shadow of Joachim Parral. He had indeed buggered things up. Wounds take time to heal.

Looking on the bright side, he had just acquired a substantial bolt hole not far from the Costas where he could hide if anything nasty ever rose to the surface. He had a long drive in front of him. The Land Rover was the easiest to start, and Bruce would never forgive him if he 'borrowed' that Toyota, inviting though it looked.

CHAPTER 56. EVERYTHING COMES TO THOSE WHO WAIT

Joachim Parral picked up his mobile phone. The signal at the Hacienda was poor, so he walked out into the courtyard. He scrolled through his contacts and stared at the number. The option was there, the green or the red. He sighed deeply and closed the leather case around the handset and slid it into the back pocket of his jeans. His flight was booked, he would leave the car at the airport. This place held no real attraction for him now, it was home but it no longer felt like home. It was a place which needed family and now he had none. His father was dead. Murdered by his brother. How Xavier had managed to stage the accident no one had managed to work out. But he had. Or had he?

The body of his brother had been found hanging from one of the Algerian Oak trees out on the far reaches of the ranch. In his pocket had been a suicide note and a full confession. Only Joachim would know his brother's handwriting well enough to know that Xavier had not written it.

He had tried to tell the Guardia Civil of his concerns but as far as they were concerned, there was no proof, they were happy to close the case. A detected murder and a suicide. Everything nicely tied up.

The man with the unintelligible accent had seemed honest and friendly. He had come over to Spain to finalise the deal and he felt he could like him. He had been easy to do business with, though very shrewd in his approach. The Scotsman had negotiated hard and come away with what he wanted, a beautiful penthouse apartment with a pool and a view to die for. He had also offered Joachim a few free lessons in life.

Don't follow your ambitions if it means sacrificing your heart.

Joachim had taken that one on board. His heart lay elsewhere. He would not let her go this easily. His heart had told him she would not live in that apartment, and who could blame her.

The deal was done, and much to his relief, the estate had not been sold, the house at least was still his and some of the surrounding land. He had managed to keep it. Joachim was for once in his life a man of independent means. He had money in his bank account, the world was his.

He turned to face the big front doors of the ancient dwelling that was still his family's home. He turned the big iron key in the lock. He would place it in the secret place under a pantile above the water butt. He would be back for it before too long. Slinging his overnight bag into the rear of the Z3 he lowered himself into the driver's seat. He took a look around, disturbing the dusty gravel with his shoes, noticing that the rose tree clambering around the door was in flower. It would be fine. And now to, where was this place, Wales. He hoped his contact would at least find him transport on the other side. Peter had promised to fix something up.

Tansy, she should be there with him now, dark hair flying in the wind, its curls restrained only by that damned silly bandana of hers. He started the engine and headed off down the dirt and gravel drive. He drove slowly, looking at it all with whimsical affection. The fields were empty. Bulls sold off, horses stabled with neighbours, the estate lay quiet beneath the sun casting short shadows of midday and a gentle breeze through the delicate pink mimosas. Closing the iron gates at the end of the drive, uniting the two halves of the Parral shield to make it whole, he offered up a prayer for his brother and for his father. Hacienda Parral was closed, for a while. For now he was the last surviving member of an ancient family and a new chapter of his life was about to begin.

Several hours later the airbus touched down at Cardiff Wales Airport. A man stood in arrivals with a cardboard sign bearing the name Parral. Of course, it was Peter.

'Joachim, its good tae see ye.' He extended a well-manicured hand to the arriving traveller.

'It is a pleasure to meet you again, Senor Balfour. I hope you enjoy your new apartment, but it seems also that we have something else in common, this young lady, Tansy Alexander, I think?'

'Ah, Tansy? I never meant tae hurt her, but well, in our line o' work things happen.'

'Just tell me you had nothing to do with any of it.'

'None of that had anything tae do with me. The lady concerned will nae be troubling anyone fer quite some time, but it has'nae worked out badly all round, has it.'

'You could say that. How is *she*?'

'Have ye no' spoken tae her? Does she not know yer comin? She does'nae like surprises, ye ken.'

'I've a feeling she'll like this one.'

'Christ, man, I hope yer right. Look, the car's over there. It's not exactly new but it goes OK and it'll get ye there.' He pointed to a beaten up old Land Rover. It's got sat-nav. It's all programmed in fer ye. You take care, and d'ya ken ye have tae drive on the left.'

'You aren't coming with me, then?'

'No, I'm away back tae Glasgow. I can'nae give her what she wants. I'm too old and I'll never be quite legal enough for her. In her heart she knows that, ay and so do I.'

Joachim climbed into the rusting old heap and watched as Peter Balfour stepped through the big revolving doors into the terminal building, the proud owner of a substantial and stylish chunk of Spanish real estate and now flying back to his Scottish home. The Spaniard stashed his bag beside him on the passenger seat and gazed around the dashboard – a speedometer at least and that must be the gear lever.

Ah, yes, the keys were there and there was that black button. Didn't we used to have one of these on the estate? He pushed his bum into the driver's side of the front seat and sniffed. Something a little agricultural to the smell – hay, that was it. He stepped on the clutch, turned the key and pressed the black starter button. The old engine coughed itself to life, rumbling gently. He gazed into the rear view mirror and nudged it into position. The display on the sat-nav illuminated, pinged and rotated to put north at the top. The route was already programmed – in Spanish.

A la salida del aparcamiento, gire a la derecha.

En la siguiente rotonda, toma la tercera salida hacia la A4050

Joachim looked at the signposts and did not recognise the language as anything he spoke. He offered a silent prayer to Peter Balfour for setting the sat-nav to his native tongue.

He followed the directions given by the computerised voice for nearly three hours.

En 200 yardas, tome el siguiente giro a la derecha.

En media milla llegarás a tu destino

He parked the vehicle in the layby at the end of the track and walked the last few yards. The lights were on in the cottage, the front door was open. She was standing in the front garden staring out over the sea. Her back was towards him but there was no mistaking that it was her.

As he approached, he heard her muttering under her breath. 'Damn you, Peter Balfour. Damn you and the horse you rode out on.' He could tell that she was crying. It made him uncertain of his ground.

Silently he crept up behind her and placed his hands on her waist. He whispered in her ear. 'Here's to you, to me and to the future an' 'ow you say 'eet.' *Fuck them all, an' the 'orse...'*

She spun in his arms so fast they both nearly fell to the grass covered floor beneath them.

He kissed her hard on the mouth, it lasted in her estimation several minutes, by the time they heard the voices from the doorway.

She took him by the arm.

'Mum, Siobhan, Ray, Bruce this is Joachim. Joachim meet the family.'

He swept her up off her feet and with his overnight bag slung over his shoulder, he carried her across the threshold.

Suddenly she felt that she had indeed found home, and he had found a place from which he would never be turned away.

In that moment the playlist of her life returned to the beginning. In the words of Bob Marley, 'Everything was gonna be alright.'

GLOSSARY OF ABBREVIATIONS.

CHIS - Covert Human Intelligence Source (an informant)
COPD – Chronic Obstructive Pulmonary Disease
CPS – Crown Prosecution Service
CRU – Case Review Unit

IPCC – Independent Police Complaints Commission

LIO – Local Intelligence Officer

MOT – Ministry of Trasport

NABIS – National Ballistics Intelligence Service
NARK – slang term for an informant
NARPO – National Association of Retired Police Officers

PACE – Police and Criminal Evidence Act
PI – Private Investigator

RADA – Royal Academy of Dramatic Arts

SIO – Senior Investigating Officer
SOCO – Scenes of Crime Officer

UC – Under Cover

ACKNOWLEDGEMENTS

This novel is a work of fiction, none of the characters within it are real. Any similarities between them and real persons either dead or alive is purely coincidental. Any references to the role of the Police Service and the behaviour and conduct of its officers and employees are entirely fictional. All the events described are also fictional.

With reference to the 3D printing of firearms, such weapons are indeed capable of being manufactured. However, the circumstances described within this work are pure fiction.

It is customary to thank all those who have assisted the author in the journey of a novel from its inception to publication. In the case of the independent or Indie Author, these may not run to many.

Firstly, I would like to thank my eldest brother for his input, patience and editing skills. For his suggestions and his sometimes superior knowledge on a subject – such as the flow of trains through the railway station at Bristol Temple Meads!

Inspiration for parts of this novel has been drawn in part from my own experience in the Police Service and from the knowledge and experience of my colleagues.

If you have read and enjoyed my work then I would urge you to add a review on the Amazon site.

COPYRIGHT

The right of Maggie Jenkins to be identified as the author of this work has been asserted by her in accordance with the Copyright, Designs and Patents Act 1988. All characters and events in this publication are fictitious and any resemblance to real persons, living or dead, is purely coincidental

All rights reserved. No part of this publication may be reproduced, stored in a retrieval system or transmitted in any form or by any means without the prior permission in writing of the publisher, nor be otherwise circulated in any form of binding or cover other than that in which it is published without a similar condition, including this condition, being imposed on the subsequent purchaser. A CIP catalogue record for this book is available from the British Library ISBN No 99798325532276

OTHER WORKS BY THE AUTHOR

THE ARROWS TRILOGY

An Arrow Through Time: The Adventure starts on the hillsides of West Wales and in the hilltop town of Llantrisant.

Bullets Through the Mist: The adventure continues through the First World War.

The authors first book

Ginger Like Biscuits – The adventures of a mountain pony: A short book written for my riders in Riding for the Disabled

A series of books of poems inspired by the Outlander Television Series and the work of Diana Gabaldon

Unofficial Droughtlander Relief.

The Droughtlander's Progress.

Totally Obsessed.

Fireside Stories.

Je Suis Prest.

Après Le Déluge

Dragonflies of Summer

Semper in Aeternum

Sia air Ochd

Intervallaqua

Facing the Storm

Reading Between the Lines

The Blue Vase - illustrated by Lyn Fuller

Mille Basia Volume 1

Mille Basia Vol 2

Mille Basia 3 Part 1

■■

All books are available in both paperback and Kindle through Amazon or through the author direct.

The author is currently working on SHELLS ON A DISTANT SHORT The final book of the ARROWS TRILOGY

The author can be contacted by email: authormaggiej@gmail.com

Printed in Great Britain
by Amazon